THE INVISIBLE

The Invisible

Michelle Dunne

Cover and jacket design by 2Faced Design
Published by arrangement with Bad Press Ink

ISBN 978-1-951709-82-2
eISBN: 978-1-957957-18-0
Library of Congress Control Number: available upon request

First published April 2022 by Bad Press Ink
First North American edition published in August 2022
by Polis Books, LLC
62 Ottowa Road S
Marlboro, NJ 07746
www.PolisBooks.com

POLIS BOOKS

For Emily

Prologue

None of them were in a position to laugh. They rarely were when they heard these stories, but that was the whole point of them. They were tension breakers. Or at least they were intended to be. Added to the Syrian sun, which was doing its best to bake them alive under their UN flak jackets and helmets, a bad feeling had settled upon them all. No one mentioned it and no one knew why. There was nothing different about today's patrol, but there it was anyway; surrounding them and weighing them down.

It was at times like this when Lenny Jones really came into himself. He'd retell, in great detail, one of his many one night stand horror stories, and Lindsey Ryan for one loved him for it. The humour he injected into his tone, and the familiarity of it, reminded her that she wasn't alone in whatever situation they happened to be in.

'...Next thing I know, the front door bursts open and this scrawny fucker struts in like he owns the place. She's tearing shreds outta my arse with her finger nails screaming, Bring it home baby, bring it home! Now to be fair to the guy, he was polite enough when he asked me to get the fuck out of his wife. But long story short, that's what actually fixed my nose after it got broken that second time. Turned out he was more wiry than scrawny, if you know what I mean...'

As she half listened to his animated tale, she felt her lips slant into a grin. She couldn't possibly have known that every version of every story would bank itself away in the recesses of her mind, only to be retold as a preamble to the nightmares that would haunt her for the rest of her life.

Lindsey had seen plenty during her thirteen years in the army, good and bad; situations where heavy artillery pummelled the ground around her; she'd called in med-evacs for injured colleagues and friends while they took fire from all directions; she'd been the one to find the body of a comrade hanging from his bedsheets in their UN camp. Poor bastard's home life had gone to shit during his tour – her first tour with the United Nations.

It was all imprinted on her. But none of it tortured her with the relentlessness of Lenny and the girl.

Each time, she would feel the sweat on her body; the weight of the gear she carried that day; the tension in her muscles, and the uneasiness in her gut. She'd see and sense the men around her like she was right there. Every single time.

Adam Street; a natural born leader.

Damien Brady; a scrapper better known as Damo.

Lenny of course; the ginger Northsider whose arse managed to get him in more trouble than the army ever could.

There was the quiet and unassuming Gordon Bennett, and Aidan Wesley, a man who fell deeply in love at least once a week and suffered greatly during overseas missions.

Bringing up the rear of their patrol was Aaron Murphy, aka Murph – the grey man.

They were the brothers she never had and whether she wanted to or not, she knew just about everything about them. Or at least, she had.

It was a routine patrol, but everything about it felt different. Dread weighed heavily in the pit of her stomach as they set off, and that same dread settled back into place each and every time she relived it. She still heard the nagging voice in the back of her mind telling her that something wasn't right. It whispered too quietly back then, but she heard it much more clearly now. Each time her mind took her back to that road in the Golan Heights, she felt the momentary lightness that followed Lenny's monologue, which was exactly what he'd set out to accomplish.

Then came the girl. The most beautiful child she'd ever seen skipping towards her. Night after night she came with her beaming smile. Night after night she made her way far too quickly towards the improvised explosive device that would vaporise her.

In her dreams, like then, Lindsey watched on helplessly as she came closer… ten feet from it… eight feet… six feet… two…

Then came the panic of being physically unable to react. Not being able to run or shout or do anything to stop the carnage that was about to be unleashed upon them all, by which time she welcomed the blow that propelled her through the air and onto the ground like a rag doll.

But the numbness that followed at the time abandoned her on these frequent trips back to Syria. Unlike then, she now felt the blood spatter and the pieces of bone, sinew and brain and as they came to land on her, mixing with her own blood and embedding themselves deep within her. She didn't feel the shrapnel that tore through her skin and burned its way into her flesh then either. But she does now. Every. Single. Time.

Night after night, she had to feel Lenny's calloused hands cupping her face and slapping her cheeks. She had to see his dust covered face, frantic at first and then smiling hesitantly. It was an unnatural kind of a smile that said, Let's pretend you're not completely fucked here, OK?

His eyes though were as genuine as they ever were, and they told her all she needed to know – that she wasn't alone. Night after night she had to see those lights being extinguished by a bullet to the back of his head. Again she must feel the fragments of him become a permanent part of her. Lenny Jones – her brother, her friend… whose head, night after night, exploded all over her.

Chapter 1

Lenny and the girl + 4 years…

It could be better. It could be worse too, Lindsey thought, staring straight ahead with her forearms pressing down on her vibrating knees.

'It looks like shit.' She finally conceded the truth to herself.

She was sitting on a hard wooden chair facing the kitchen door. Frank sat patiently by her side, his wise canine eyes looking straight ahead. She'd asked him to please stop looking at her and as always, he did what he could to make her… happy was the wrong word, but this wasn't Frank's first rodeo. He'd seen Lindsey go postal many times so he knew what he needed to do.

But his intervention wasn't enough to stop her last night as she took a baseball bat to the wall, one of the tables and the porthole in the swinging kitchen door. Amazingly it didn't shatter completely, but it somehow managed to claim the bat and was now doing her the favour of holding it hostage.

The first light of dawn seeped in through the front window of Lindsey's café. It crept along the floor and across the empty tables towards her. She pressed the leg of her pants against the skin on her right calf, letting it soak up the trickle of blood that felt mildly ticklish and annoying. Lindsey was used to blood and this was a subconscious act. Like swatting away a fly.

Below the smashed porthole was where her boot had broken through somewhere close to two in the morning. It was followed of course by her calf and the door didn't want to relinquish that either. Still, she didn't want to do anything about the gash in her leg just yet. She was contented in the company of its pain.

All in all, the demolition of Lindsey's café took less than three minutes. The rest of the night was spent on the only form of therapy that ever worked for her – putting shit back together. Her work was ad hoc and unskilled, but she always took pride in it. When the sun came up, she'd be open for business as usual, but for now she and Frank sat quietly and surveyed the quality of their repairs.

What was left of the once sturdy kitchen door was leaning against the wall and had been replaced with a pair of three-foot slatted saloon type doors. The bat had struck the wall with considerable force at least eight times before tackling the door. That too had been roughly patched up and then covered over with an ugly portrait of dogs who were apparently playing cards. Totally inappropriate as far as café decor went, but her options were limited to the random items she'd picked up at various car boot sales, all bought and put aside for just such an occasion. Lindsey was a frequent flyer at junk sales because she'd bought this almost crumbling three-storey building for a song and fixed it up almost entirely by herself. Just like the last home she'd bought not long after returning from Syria.

Because of how she lived now, it made sense to stockpile items that could be used to replace or cover up just about anything, so that's what she did. Lindsey Ryan had become an expert at hiding damage.

'When the fuck is this going to end?'

Frank nudged her and then rested his muzzle on her lap.

'I can't keep doing this.' She dropped her head until her forehead rested against him, while her finger gently caressed the trigger of a

Black & Decker drill held loosely by her side.

Hot tears ran silently down her face, dampening his coat, but her nine-year-old German shepherd didn't budge. Then she brought the drill to the side of her head. With her eyes jammed shut, she breathed heavily through her nose putting slightly more pressure on the trigger, until finally she roared at the top of her lungs. Frank jumped on her, barking, and she dropped the drill. She cried and tried to shift her focus to the sharp pain shooting up and down her calf. But it wasn't enough.

'I'm losing my fucking mind, Frank.' She wrapped her arms around him. 'I'm sorry buddy. I'm so sorry.'

*

Frank worked like the pro he was to pull her out of yet another nightmare. Without him, she'd quite literally die. But nobody out there would ever know that, because nobody knew her anymore. She sat up and wiped her face roughly.

'Imagine the scone brigade coming in here and seeing this.' She forced a smile for Frank. 'The odd bitch is actually a psycho.'

She laughed now as she imagined what the town gossips would make of all this. It didn't bother her that they called her that. In fact, she liked it. People didn't tend to bother with the town's odd bitch. Of course that was just one cohort. There were other opinions but none of them were in any way accurate and she was happy to keep it that way.

*

Since walking away from her military family, Lindsey had bounced from place to place bringing her own brand of trouble with her. She'd become addicted to depressants, which were prescribed during the one and only counselling session she'd attended.

After what you've seen, it's not surprising you'd want to numb it, the counsellor had said.

When she got clean, she found a new form of therapy. DIY. A new addiction that got fed regularly.

She'd somehow managed to get a degree in social science, and then proceeded to fuck up that new career with gusto. Now she made sure that no one ever had to rely on her for anything more than a cup of tea. For their sake as much as hers.

*

Lindsey had been in the picturesque harbour town of Cobh for nearly a year now and she managed to pass almost eight months without another human being entering her life. Then she met Eileen, and now she owned this café. It both helped her and tortured her in equal measures. Lindsey Ryan was the queen of reinvention, but she still owed a lifetime of penance, and when a payment was due, it was due.

'Shit.' She sat up straight and roughly wiped her eyes.

A key had started its dance with the fidgety lock in the front door. She got to her feet and was through the saloon doors before her anything-but-silent business partner, Eileen Chambers, caught sight of her. In the back kitchen were the narrow stairs to Lindsey's two-bedroom apartment and she took them two at a time. As she moved quickly through her modest home, she could hear Eileen blustering around down stairs and waited for the inevitable…

'Lindsey?' she roared unnecessarily up the stairs.

'Yeah?' Lindsey ran the shower and set the temperature to cold. She stripped down and stepped into the bath, leaving the door open, knowing that if she didn't reply to Eileen from here, then she'd invite herself up and quiz her twice as hard.

'What in the name of sweet baby Jesus happened down here? Were you broken into? Was it That Mad Bastard Two Doors Up?' Her voice went up an octave with the final question.

'I'll be down in a minute.'

Blood had crusted over the gash on her leg, but the force of the water and the viciousness with which she scrubbed her face and body started the flow again. She opened a bottle of TCP which rested on the edge of the bath and poured it on the wound, welcoming the sharp pain it brought. Her stomach was knotted. Her hands were shaking, and exhaustion was a living entity within her. As the last dribble of adrenaline circled the drain, she wanted to curl up in a ball and sleep for a year. More than that, she wanted to eat a fist full of pills and sleep forever.

Frank sat beside the bath and his eyes never left her. He was unfortunate enough to always know what she was thinking but Frank wasn't in the business of judging. To those who didn't know him, he was an overprotective pain in the ass. To those who thought they knew him, he was a lovable rogue. The very few who actually knew Frank, knew he was the kind of service dog that standards were set by. But to Lindsey he was so much more. Frank was the force that got her out of bed each day and stopped her from losing her mind completely. He was more precious to her than anything else the world had to offer and he'd been keeping her alive for some years now. Frank Ryan deserved so much better.

'Well are you alright or not?' Eileen bellowed again.

She took a few shaky breaths and lowered herself into a sitting position in the bath. 'I'll be down in a minute,' she repeated, her voice belying her true feelings, as it was well trained to do.

'Right! Meanwhile I'll find a new tablecloth to cover the big dent in the two-seater, but I'm telling you now, that fucking dog picture is out of here if they don't stop following me around with their beady fucking eyes.'

Eileen was an Irish traveller and this was the first job she'd ever held down. She had a foul mouth and said exactly what was on her mind. She was also one of the most sarcastic people that Lindsey had ever met, and all of the above were just some of the reasons why Lindsey liked her. But Eileen was beginning to notice that Lindsey wasn't what she pretended to be, and as far as Lindsey was concerned, that was a problem.

She curled into a tight ball and wrapped her arms around her head for minute while she clawed her way out of the black hole. Then finally, she reached one hand out over the rim of the bath and placed it on Frank's head, took a few more deep breaths and hauled herself to her feet.

*

The café was busy that day; busier than usual at least. Hers was different from the many other cafés and restaurants that Cobh had to offer, in that it was quite dark inside. Her front window looked out at the narrow main road and a block of flats across the street. They blocked the harbour view that the tourists came for, while inside… well, it had been renovated by Lindsey. The old teak door was painted red, dotted with blisters, and led into a small porch. The place was floored out with dark red mosaic tiles that ran throughout the ground floor and were about as old as the building itself. Like her, this building had a past. It was once The Daunt Bar, a poky little pub mostly frequented by dockers. The old bar remained in place and was possibly holding up the whole building and the one next door. To a trained eye, it certainly looked like her home, and business was held together by spit and chicken wire, but then so was she. Maybe that's why the place suited her well enough. Mismatched tables and chairs were set out in an almost orderly fashion, from the large window, down along the wall passing the bar and around by the display fridge and food prep area. All in all, she could seat about fifteen people comfortably, but rarely did. She had her regulars, but this was the first time she'd seen so many of them here at the same time.

'Christ,' she mumbled to Frank as she glanced out over the new kitchen doors. 'Looks like we have an audience today.'

'What?' asked Eileen, pulling her head out of the oven that she'd been cleaning.

'What are they all doing here?' Lindsey was carrying The Dread with her and would be for the whole day. It always made her feel paranoid, but it couldn't be coincidence that they all showed up hours after she'd trashed the place, surely.

'You mean all those paying customers?' Eileen came and stood alongside her. 'Oh, I'd imagine they came to view these splendid new doors and maybe to see if John fucking Wayne himself dropped them off and stayed for breakfast.'

'You love these doors.' Lindsey nudged her and shoved her way out into the café. Regardless of how she felt, they would all still see whatever their version of her was.

The people of this town were a distraction, and distractions were what kept Lindsey Ryan out of trouble. She may not have wanted to face them just now, but like it or not, she desperately needed them.

The place was noisy with chat and banter passing between tables, up until such time as Patrick Adebayo, or as Eileen and many others referred to him, That Mad Bastard Two Doors Up, arrived through her door at close to lunchtime. Patrick was becoming a regular now too, and just minutes after his arrival her other customers began to leave. That was the effect that Patrick had. The Nigerian man mountain wore a tailored suit and a charming smile everywhere he went, but like Lindsey, he wasn't who he pretended to be either. Unlike Lindsey though, he didn't pretend very well. Nor did he really try.

Cobh, like everywhere else, had its racist element. But Lindsey refused to entertain anyone who felt they could judge another human being based on where they came from, or the colour of their skin. The Patrick effect though, as she'd come to think of it, had nothing to do with any of that. Patrick Adebayo owned the town of Cobh and many of the people in it. He was said to be a lot of things. A loan shark. A drugs king pin. An unmerciful thug. Lindsey didn't like him because she knew that he was a pimp. The comings and goings two doors up told her so. Of course none of any of it could be proven or even challenged given his reputation. No one who crossed Patrick ever came out of it well.

That's why people left when Patrick walked in.

'Lindsey…' he smiled brightly, his voice booming through the enclosed space. 'What is going on with these dogs? I hate them.'

Two people hated her dog picture, Lindsey thought, irritated.

Frank looked up, indignant, and walked away, but he didn't go too far. He didn't trust Patrick any more than Lindsey did. But Patrick wasn't talking about Frank. Or at least he wasn't looking in his direction while he spoke.

He pretended to ignore the fact that he'd cleared the premises, but Patrick loved that people were afraid of him. Lindsey got the impression that he thrived on it.

'The usual?' she asked, returning his smile.

The faking-it-Lindsey was everybody's friend. Even this piece of shit, who made his living off the backs of the women who worked for him. Literally. His building two doors up was a laundrette, which lived up to the cliché beautifully by fronting a large and seemingly prosperous brothel upstairs. As far as she was aware, she'd never met, or even seen, any of the women who worked there, but she pictured them sometimes. She imagined how desperate they must be to find themselves there, working for someone like him and she pitied them. He was said to have many more just like it throughout the county, but he based himself here, in Cobh. A beautiful town that bustled with tourists for at least half the year provided the perfect camouflage for his seedy enterprises. Accompanying him as always were two of his henchmen. One, the Russian, was a permanent fixture and was as notorious as the man himself. The other goon was interchangeable but all were bigger and dumber than the next and they cracked heads for a past time. Like his tailored suit and his charming smile, he never left home without them. But they didn't sit with him. Patrick sat alone at a table for two, while his goons sat by the window.

'My table appears to have some problems.' He laughed when he lifted the wax table cloth that Eileen had used to cover the bat shaped dent. 'No man lives here, and yet this place looks like it has seen considerable violence.'

'It probably has.' She began pouring tea into a pot. 'It was one rotting floorboard away from being condemned when I bought it. I'd safely say it's seen its fair share.' She continued the friendly banter. 'As for your table; I'm afraid most of my furniture has problems. That's what happens when you buy things from the back of a van.' She placed the pot on his table and then looked him in the eye. 'Or maybe it was me. Maybe I'm the violent one.' She held his gaze for a microsecond before bringing back her friendly smile.

He studied her as she walked away.

'You are funny, Lindsey, but you know, I could help you here. I am a businessman. Money is no problem for me. But you,' he pointed at her, his smile broadening, 'you need help here, my friend.'

Lindsey laughed quietly, like a pleasant tea lady would, as he made yet another offer to move in on her business. He'd been doing that a lot lately.

'I have all the help I can handle with that one there.' She thumbed in the direction of the prep area, where Eileen was busy looking busy.

Patrick's mouth turned downwards in disgust. 'No good for you.'

She ignored the comment.

'Here's your tea. Shout if you want anything else. I need to let Frank out the back.'

Frank, for his part, was used to being used as an exit strategy and he turned with Lindsey and headed for the back of the building.

'Did I hear that right?' Eileen followed them through the doors, looking insulted in the most dramatic way possible.

'Yip. He reckons he'd make better scones than you and he's eager to take your place.'

'I can practically smell the cock rot from here. You know he's made people disappear?'

'Patrick's a pimp and a scumbag. Nothing more, nothing less.'

'Don't be so sure, Lindsey. You haven't been here that long, remember? Patrick Abba-whateverthefuck has more people on his payroll than a dirty politician; cops, councillors, judges even! Not to mention your average dog on the street. They keep their eyes peeled and their ears to the ground and in return, that fucker looks after them well.' She rubbed her thumb against her two fingers; the universal sign for money.

'Ears to the ground and eyes peeled for what exactly?'

'Anything. A lot of traffic goes through his door and he keeps tabs on all of it. See Lindsey, Patrick deals in more than just women from what I hear. Whatever sick shit his clients can dream up, Patrick can supply it. And if he supplies something for you, you may be sure, you're well and truly fucked. And not in a good way. He owns you. Photos, recordings, you name it. His black book would be worth our combined weight in gold. He has shit on everyone; therefore Patrick is a very dangerous man. Not to mention, one seriously mad bastard. Don't ever underestimate him.'

'Noted.' Lindsey had heard similar stories from her customers, none of which surprised her. Anyone willing to sell one person, couldn't possibly have a problem selling out another. No, Lindsey didn't need to be advised against underestimating Patrick. But she was quite happy for him to underestimate her.

Chapter 2

Lindsey bolted upright in bed. She swung her feet out onto the floor and reflexively began her muscle relaxation exercises, systematically tightening her neck, shoulders, chest and back muscles, and then slowly releasing the tension. Sometimes they helped. Mostly they didn't. Thirty seconds passed and her breathing was all she heard while she sat on the edge of her bed in the dark. As a trickle of sweat rolled uninterrupted down her neck, she finally realised that this was a different type of wrong. She turned to look at Frank. He should have been on her. His paws should have been on her chest, his damp nose pressed against her cheek, waking her up; pulling her back, but they weren't. She could just about make out his silhouette, but he was dead still with his nose less than an inch from her bedroom door. He was on high alert, which he didn't do lightly. Yip. This was a very different type of wrong.

Her nerves tingled. Whatever woke her, it wasn't an echo from the past but was very much in the here and now. She reached for the bedside lamp and as the room lit up, Frank still didn't move, which told her all she needed to know. Someone was out there.

She shoved her legs into yesterday's black combat pants and picked up the baseball bat that was propped against her wall.

'What is it, Frankie?'

Frank didn't respond.

'OK. Let's have a look, will we?' She opened her bedroom door slowly and quietly. If someone was in her flat then she wanted the element of surprise. It might be her only advantage, aside from Frank. But as in any dangerous situation, Lindsey worried more about him getting hurt than she did about herself. Frank Ryan was no spring chicken, not that she'd ever say that to his face.

But despite any of that, Frank bolted from the room and was half way down the stairs before Lindsey was out the door. Once in the back kitchen, he pressed his nose against the door leading to her small back yard. He was yelping and whining and dancing around until Lindsey was beside him with her hand on the deadbolt.

No one could be out there. The yard was just big enough for the two wheelie bins and two old metal dustbins that were crammed into the space. It was completely enclosed and surrounded on three sides by the high walls of Lindsey's building and the building next door, while the fourth side was an enormously steep bank, covered with overgrown weeds and briars. Nobody could have gotten into that yard without coming through her building.

Frank was trying to burrow through the back door with his muzzle, but she walked to the ugly saloon doors anyway and looked out over them. The café was in darkness. She waited for her eyes to adjust before making her way out to the bar. Silently, she pulled her torch out from under the cash register and shone it ahead towards the front door. The chairs and tables all stood undisturbed and the door was locked. No one was there. Like Frank said. She could feel a hint of last night's adrenaline snaking through her veins again. She wasn't being robbed. Of course if she was, then interrupting them might have gotten her killed but that didn't bother her. Getting robbed would have bothered her though, and a small part of her was disappointed that no one was there. Her mind was in that zone now. The one where she welcomed anyone to challenge her. She worked hard to hide that side of herself and where possible, to ignore it altogether but still, she couldn't help how she felt.

Her breathing was slow and steady as she made her way back towards the kitchen. She pushed through the swing doors just as a loud clatter came from the back yard. The sound of dustbins falling over and Frank let out a volley of loud barks by way of, I told you so, now get over here and LET ME OUT!

It had to have been an animal. But with one hand still wrapped around the bat, she put down the torch and took a firm hold on Frank's collar. Her heart rate slowly increased and her fists clenched and unclenched like they always did when she expected something to happen. She could hear Adam Street's voice in her head. The same tone he'd used as her training NCO all those years ago … Calm, Ryan. Picture the space. Where would you conceal yourself out there?

She slid back the deadbolt and as she pushed open the door, something moved suddenly, causing the wheelie bin to shift forward. Frank strained against her, barking with everything he had. Lindsey dropped the bat and took a firmer grip on the dog. Whoever was there, he was the only weapon she'd need anyway. Frank was a sweetheart who could tear a throat out if he needed to.

The creature hiding behind the bin wasn't her only problem: The cacophony of voices coming from above seemed somehow more menacing. Lindsey guessed there had to be three or four men, young by the sound of them, jeering and hooting like a pack of wild animals. She heard one of them asking, with a hint of panic in his voice, What the fuck we gonna do if she'd dead? Is she dead?'

Once her eyes adjusted again, she could see the outline of four heads leaning over the wall high above them, but it was dark and they were too far away to see their faces.

'Someone's there, they can see us! Can that fucking dog get up here?' The same voice again, and one of the heads disappeared from view.

The other three followed but Lindsey could still hear them. One was laughing and as the voices trailed off, she briefly imagined that they were high fiving each other before her attention returned to her own back yard.

Frank's strength and fitness defied his age and he was pulling hard against her now, towards the bank rather than the bins. She needed both hands to hold onto him as a balled-up figure, like a shadow out the side of her eye, scuttled past and through the door into the kitchen. But Frank's attention was still on the bank; more specifically, on finding a way to claw his way up it. An impossible feat, even for him.

'Frank! Come on.' She pulled on his collar and reluctantly he let her lead him back inside. Her gut was telling her that the people up above were the real threat and not the shadow that was waiting for her inside, so she stayed facing the bank until she was through the door and had it locked behind her. Only then did she let go of Frank. He spent another few seconds barking at the door before Lindsey silenced him. Once he was satisfied that they were safe, that there was no further threat, he turned and trotted towards the tall fridge and started sniffing at the person hiding behind it.

'I know you're there so you might as well come out.'

There was no answer but a bare foot slipped out from behind the fridge and was quickly pulled back in.

'You have until the count of three to come out or my dog is coming in.' Frank didn't seem overly concerned by whoever was hiding in her kitchen, so Lindsey wasn't either. But still; someone was hiding in her kitchen.

'Please…' came a meek woman's voice from behind the fridge.

Lindsey waited silently.

A woman. Four men against one woman.

'Please…' the woman repeated, as she stepped shakily into view. Her face was bloodied, her hair wild and dishevelled. But it was her eyes that jolted Lindsey. They were wide and filled with terror. Lindsey instantly recognised it as a look of pure animal fear.

She was naked too, her body streaked with blood and dirt. She used her arms and hands to cover as much of herself as she could. Her posture was slumped and she couldn't meet Lindsey's eyes, which told her that the woman's physical injuries, and there were many, were not the ones that really hurt. Though her body's cortisol response to what she'd just been through was enough to make her almost vibrate.

'Jesus.'

Lindsey was looking right at her own worst fear. Most days she didn't care if she lived or died. Whatever came her way, she could handle it. Except rape. Women who survived being raped were a hell of a lot stronger than she was and right now she felt both afraid and incredibly sorry for this woman. She also wanted to kill the fuckers who'd done this to her with her bare hands.

She reached for the apron hanging on a wall hook and looped it over the woman's head. It covered some of her at least, but she had no idea how she could possibly help this woman.

'Who are you?' Lindsey asked gently, while she took in as many of her injuries as she could see.

The woman's left eye was swelling and there was a gash above it. Her lip was split. A trickle of blood ran from her hairline, and her right ear and cheek were caked in dried blood, but Lindsey couldn't see any open wounds there. Lindsey's first instinct was to find the pack animals on the street above and let Frank do his worst. Or let Lindsey do hers. But she wasn't that person anymore; a fact that she had to remind herself of on a daily basis.

'Please, lady…' her eyes were pleading with Lindsey, who finally moved to support the woman and hold her upright.

She clutched Lindsey's arm and in doing so, most of her meagre weight fell against her. In this condition, it was hard to put an age on her. She stood several inches shorter than Lindsey and was probably several years younger than her too. Plus, she was extremely skinny, bordering on malnourished.

They looked at each other in silence before the woman broke down. She let go of Lindsey and slid down along the fridge and onto the floor. Lindsey took a small, hesitant step towards her and she curled into herself.

Finally she got on her knees in front of the woman. 'Hey… you'll be alright.'

Before she could think of anything else to say, there was a loud banging on the front door of the café.

'It's them! Please…' she grabbed Lindsey's arm. She was violently shaking. Almost feral with fear.

Frank, who'd been sitting dutifully by Lindsey's side, shoved himself under the swing doors and ran barking towards the front of the café. He took out several chairs along the way and possibly concussed himself on the leg of a table, none of which slowed him down.

'Come on…' Lindsey grabbed her by the arms and got to her feet, pulling the woman up with her. 'Frank!' she kept her voice low and although he was reluctant to walk away, she didn't need to call him a second time. She never did.

Whoever was out there wasn't giving up, so she led the woman upstairs to her flat and into her living room.

It was dark downstairs in the kitchen so Lindsey failed to see the extent of the damage to the woman's face. Her eye was quickly swelling shut; blood ran from her nose and mouth and the gash over her left eyebrow was deeper than she first thought. Now she could see where all the dried blood on her cheek came from too; another gash running from her ear to the corner of her lip, along her jaw line. Blood ran down both of her legs and as Lindsey's eyes came to rest upon her, the woman pulled the apron in every direction in an attempt to disappear behind it.

'You need a hospital.'

'No!' The woman fell to her knees and grabbed Lindsey's leg.

'Please… no.'

'You need a doctor.' She tried to reason with the woman. Lindsey had some first aid skills, but she had no idea how to deal with this.

'No! No doctor… no hospital, please? They'll kill me.'

Her nails were digging into the flesh on last night's wounded calf and it was beginning to protest, but her mind raced past that. The woman's English was much better than she initially thought, but that was neither here nor there right now. Lindsey needed to get her shit together and focus. The next logical step would be to call an ambulance and the police. But the woman was terrified and that terror increased dramatically at the mention of getting help and Lindsey was slow to make another move before finding out what, or who, it was that she was so afraid of.

'Who'll kill you? Those guys?' She pointed upwards.

The woman made a spitting action. 'They are pigs, nothing more.'

'Who then?' Patrick's face appeared in her mind.

She covered her face with her hands, shook her head and cried. There was nothing more she was willing to say, but Lindsey took her fear seriously.

Chances are, whoever she was hiding from now would kill her if she went to the authorities. Or rather, his lackeys would. As far as Patrick Adebayo went, the smoke that filled this town did not occur without fire. Lindsey Oh'd and Ah'd along with the locals as they gave their two cents on the man that most knew only by reputation. But Lindsey knew more about him that she ever let on. She made it her business to. Like for instance, he had an army of people making sure that each of his businesses ran smoothly and wherever his acquisitions came from, they'd never lead back to him.

Aside from coming to Lindsey's a few times a week for nothing more than a cup of black tea, which he could have gotten anywhere, he was rarely seen in the flesh. Patrick as good as owned the town of Cobh and there weren't many who were willing to argue that fact. Chances are, he also owned the woman in Lindsey's care and would very soon come to know if she went to the authorities, several of whom were also said to be on his payroll. The men who attacked her already knew where she was and they'd only just given up banging on Lindsey's door. If her gut was right, then calling help would mean handing her back to Patrick on a plate. Her gut was also telling her that Lindsey's café was now an even bigger target for Patrick Adebayo. But fuck him. Let him come.

'Wait here, OK?'

'No… please don't.' The woman pleaded.

'It's OK. I'm just going to the next room… one minute.' She held up her finger. 'I promise you, I will not call anyone.'

'Fuck, fuck, fuck,' she muttered to herself as she hurried down the hall to the spare room, where she kept a large first aid kit. She pulled it down off the crooked, homemade shelf and hurried back to the woman. She was still kneeling in the centre of the room, where Lindsey had left her.

She stood for a minute with the first aid box in her hands. Where would she start?

Lindsey left her alone again and went to fill a hot bath, which of course was the exact wrong thing to do for a rape victim before she'd been seen by a doctor. But that wasn't going to happen. There was no longer any right or wrong it seemed; just survival and as the bath filled, Lindsey opened a fresh bottle of TCP, a staple in her bathroom cabinet, and poured it into the running water. It wouldn't wash away what had happened to her, but it would go some way towards ensuring that her wounds were cleaned. She left the bath to fill and went back to the living room, where the woman still knelt in the exact position Lindsey had left her in.

'What's your name?'

The woman looked at her finally, but didn't answer. Maybe she didn't understand after all. She was of Middle Eastern descent, but from where exactly, Lindsey had no idea.

'I'm Lindsey.'

'Lena.' The woman's voice was a hoarse croak as she brought her hand to her bony chest.

'Lena, is there someone I can go and get for you? Do you have family here?'

She shook her head.

'OK… it'll be OK.' Lindsey held her hand towards her. 'Come with me.'

Lena took her hand and leaned heavily on it as she stood up. They headed for the bathroom, passing Frank, who was lying across the top of the stairs. No unwelcome guests would be coming up them tonight.

Lena looked at the three-quarters full steaming bath and suddenly, peeling the apron from her body became a matter of extreme urgency. Another second would have been too long to wait. She needed to wash away whoever did this to her and as she stripped, Lindsey closed her eyes as the horror of the woman's life spelled itself out all over her body.

She was peppered with marks and scars, old and new. The most prominent one was what looked like an old scar running across her abdomen, possibly from a rough caesarean or a severe knife wound. There were some small, circular marks that Lindsey strongly suspected were cigarette burns and more recently, her ribs were bruised and her thighs were scratched and torn. So many blotches on her skin that were getting darker by the minute. Blood still trickled out of her and down along her legs as she stepped tentatively into the water and lowered herself down, crying as the TCP made its way into her wounds. Lindsey handed her a washcloth and indicated the two clean towels on the edge of the sink.

'Take your time, OK? I'll find you some clothes.' She scooped up the bloody apron and took it out of the room with her, sure that she never wanted to see it again. Quite frankly, neither did Lindsey. She closed the door gently behind her and moved quietly away from the sound of the woman's sobs.

*

Back in the living room, Lindsey pulled a plastic bag and some rags out of one of the cupboards and began cleaning the blood off the laminate floor where Lena had sat. She ran through some possible scenarios that could see a woman being beaten, raped and what, thrown down a fifty-foot bank?

Maybe Lena had jumped over the bank to get away from her attackers. That's what Lindsey would've done if she had the choice. The animals who attacked her tonight came here looking for her only to cover their own arses, but Lindsey was fairly sure that they wouldn't incriminate themselves by coming back.

Lena belonged to someone. Someone had paid money for her and for sure, they were making a lot more from her and now none of this would be taken lying down.

*

An hour passed while Lindsey sat on her couch, elbows once again bouncing on her knees. She thought of all the ways that Patrick could come for her. And all the ways that she couldn't help Lena. But that wasn't good enough. Lena needed help, not sympathy and right now, Lindsey was her only option.

'Fuck.'

Lena came quietly into the living room, wearing the tracksuit bottoms and hoodie that Lindsey left folded on the floor outside the bathroom.

'Are you alright?' It seemed like the normal thing to ask.

Lena nodded.

'You need some rest.' Lindsey led the way out of the living room and into her spare bedroom.

She wanted to ask if by chance Lena just happened to be in the wrong place at the wrong time and in fact, wasn't one of Patrick's girls at all. But that conversation would have to wait. Lena needed rest and then, hopefully tomorrow, she might feel like talking.

She'd moved all the clutter off the single bed and crammed as much as she could under it. It was almost six in the morning and Lindsey had zero hope of sleeping now. She guessed that Lena probably wouldn't either, but at least she could let her try.

'Is there anything you need?' she asked.

She caught Lindsey by the hand and squeezed it tightly. Then she let go and went to lie down.

Lindsey pulled the door shut behind her and went back to the living room with the little kitchenette in the corner. She stood there for a minute trying to think, but her head was all over the place. Frank seemed to share her feelings as he paced between Lindsey, the stairs, and the closed bedroom door where Lena was hopefully resting and not getting busy killing herself.

She shook her head and left the room again, headed for the bathroom and a cold shower. As she waited for all traces of warmth to leave the gushing water, she went and pressed her ear to Lena's door. There was no sound. Thinking about suicide made a hell of a lot of noise inside the head, she knew that much for a fact. But what did actual suicide sound like?

She sincerely hoped that wasn't what was happening on the other side of this door. The last thing she needed was another corpse on her conscience.

She shook her head again and went back to the bathroom. She waited for Frank to follow her inside before closing the door behind him. He was reluctant to let her out of his sight. Frank always knew when her thoughts were headed somewhere dreary and ensuring she found her way back fell under his remit. Once again, he was hard at work.

As she stood there under the gushing water, she fought the urge to go and find the men who'd done this and she reminded herself, not for the first time, that she didn't do that sort of thing anymore. Her days of going looking for trouble were behind her.

Although something told her that this time, trouble was on its way to find her. But whoever came and whatever they brought with them, she'd be ready.

Chapter 3

'Hey Lindsey! You in there?'

'Yeah.' She wiped her hands on a tea towel and made her way out of the back kitchen, carrying The Dread with her once again.

But today held a very real threat that something dangerous would be coming through her door. Which is why it needed to be business as usual in Lindsey's café. Show no fear. That would be easy enough. Very few people ever knew what Lindsey was thinking, which was fortunate for them.

But the man letting himself in through her closed but unlocked front door was no threat.

'You're late.' She started their usual sequence of friendly banter.

She paused only briefly when she saw the condition of her delivery man's face, before continuing behind the bar to get started on the coffee that he always ordered to take away with him.

Seán Buckley insisted on loudly announcing his arrival from the front door no matter how busy or quiet the café was when he got there. For a man who was so small and thin in stature, he had a voice that boomed through his surroundings. He complained incessantly about the place and yet she saw him almost every day, with or without supplies.

Today though, was not like every other day, for Lindsey or for Seán, and the word fuck repeated itself several times inside her head.

'You need to cheer this place up girl.' He too continued their usual conversation, looking around unimpressed, as he always did. Even though one eye was painfully red and swollen.

He dragged his lightly loaded hand truck through the front door, taking yet another chunk out of its paintwork.

'Look! Look what it says on this box; Lindsey Ryan, the Daunt Bar, Cobh. Sure, this place hasn't been the Daunt Bar since my shoes were in fashion.'

Lindsey glanced down at his black hobnail boots and then back up to meet his eye, the condition of which had yet to be mentioned. Her heart sank but she continued to act as if there was nothing out of the ordinary about the man. He was shaken and clearly needed a distraction.

That she could understand.

His voice quivered slightly as he spoke. There were two boxes on his hand truck when there should be at least six and both of those boxes had been opened. Still, she gave him the grin that she knew he was hoping for, playing along for now.

'Are you done?'

'Where's Frank? I have something for him.' His hand shook as he pulled what looked like someone's finger wrapped in tinfoil out of his pocket.

'What kind of artery clogger are you trying to give my dog today?'

'Ah tis only a sausage from my breakfast this morning. Sure a sausage never killed anyone.'

'You need to stop bringing him your leftovers, Seán. One of these days he'll leave me for you.'

The mention of the word sausage was Frank's cue to appear, seemingly out of nowhere.

Seán had a soft spot for Frank and not one single shit did he give about Lindsey's attempts to keep her dog fit and healthy. As expected, Frank accepted Seán's fatty offering and returned to lick his fingers.

Contented now, he trotted outside for a look around. Despite the communication barrier between dogs and most people, Frank Ryan had a gift for setting up regular deliveries of bacon products for himself. He'd simply target one person with a good heart and a poor diet and the rest just seemed to happen. As she watched him go, she was once again reminded that he was so much more than just a dog.

Seán looked after him and then returned his eyes to Lindsey. He was about to say something, but he stopped himself. Instead he looked at her walls and ceiling and said instead, 'Why? Why'd you do it?'

'Do what now?'

'Why'd you have to do the place yourself? Look at the walls. You could plug the Grand Canyon with the amount of filler you used.'

'But can you see any holes in my walls?'

'And why don't you give the place a flippin' name? Just put Lindsey's over the door. That's what everyone calls it anyway. I'd suggest you get someone who can actually paint to do that though. Maybe even, God forbid… a signwriter.'

'If everyone calls it Lindsey's anyway, why do I need to put a sign up?'

He sat down heavily on one of the chairs. He'd never done that before. Seán was always Too busy to sit down, but could easily spend half an hour standing by the door talking about anything and everyone.

'This place should have been knocked down years ago.'

'Yeah, I know.' She leaned against the old bar opposite where he sat.

She remembered exactly what it was like back then. It was perfect. An almost condemned new home was exactly what she needed at that point in her life. DIY at a whole other level was the only form of therapy that ever worked for Lindsey. This building quite literally saved her life. But the last thing she intended to become was a friendly café owner. Or a friendly anything for that matter. That just sort of happened when she ran out of projects to occupy her otherwise dangerous mind, which was engaged in a constant battle with her. Left to its own devices, it would win. The old Daunt Bar made sure that it didn't and she loved it for that.

Seán on the other hand, seemed to be fighting a losing battle of his own and she wasn't sure how much longer either of them could keep up this chit chat.

He was staring at the floor now and she decided to let him be. He needed a minute, so she went to close the front door again. This day was off to a very bad start. She wasn't ready to welcome the rest of it just yet.

'You were the talk of the town back then, you know that?' Seán didn't raise his eyes as he spoke, quietly for a change. 'A lovely looking girl like ya, tearing the place apart all by herself. We all thought it'd fall down and kill you before you were done. I wish that solving the mystery of the Daunt woman was still all we had to worry about.'

She managed something like a grin for his benefit. 'I should be lurking in a corner dressed in black, pointing mysteriously out to sea with a name like that. Ye couldn't have come up with something better than The Daunt Woman?'

'Some did come up with better names. But I can tell you about them some other time.' He looked around again. 'The place is still standing anyway, I suppose.'

'Because of me.'

'Despite you.'

Again, he looked like he wanted to say something, but wasn't sure how. Finally he said, 'I like you, Lindsey. I just want you to know that.'

He got to his feet and pulled the hand truck past the small bar towards the kitchen, dragging chairs and a table with him. 'But I can't…' he shook his head, 'I can't sit here gabbing all day.'

'So are you gonna tell me what happened or should I go on pretending not to notice your face?'

As the question made its way out, she wondered why she was so incapable of keeping her mouth shut and leaving other people to sort out their own problems.

He took a deep breath. 'I can't bring you any more deliveries, is what happened to my face. I shouldn't be here now, but I'll give you what I have left and then I have to go.'

Lindsey caught him by the arm and made him look at her. 'Who did this?'

'Look, whatever you did, you need to make it right.'

'I didn't do...'

'I don't want to know.' He held up his hand. 'I'm sorry, Lindsey. I really am. Like I said, I like you. But I'm sixty-two years old. I've been around the block enough times to know that you don't ignore warnings from That Mad Bastard Two Doors Up. You shouldn't either. So whatever you did... undo it.'

She went and got an ice-pack out of the freezer and placed it against his swelling eye, her heart breaking for the man, while murderous thoughts filled her head. 'It's OK. I understand, Seán.'

'I better go. I saw them headed towards the old Hardware House when they finished with me. I don't want them to see me coming out of here.'

It seemed buildings in Cobh would always be known as the first businesses ever to occupy them; like Lindsey's was the old Daunt Bar and Patrick's brothel would always be the old Hardware House. She stepped behind the bar and finished making his caramel latte; Seán's usual, only instead of caramel, she topped up his coffee from the whiskey bottle under the counter. The man could do with it.

'I can't, Lindsey.'

'Have a coffee Seán. You need to sit down for a minute.'

'I can't be here...'

'I get it. And thank you for getting what you could to me. Now please, sit down next to my lumpy walls and drink that while it's hot. I'll check the street before you go.'

'Jesus no. That flaky bit on the ceiling might fall down on top of me and finish me off.' He did his best to joke, but he was on the verge of tears. 'I better unload what little I have left on that truck and get home to the missus. She'll have a fit when she sees all this.'

Lindsey walked with him to the door and looked outside to make sure the coast was clear before standing aside to let him out and Frank back in.

Frank was unimpressed with having been shut outside and he passed her with his nose in the air. But he thought better of it and came back to sniff Seán's hand, then glance up at Lindsey. He was reminding her that he'd just had a sausage, despite the great lengths she went to to maintain his health. She smiled at him as he walked away. Frank was a fearless warrior who would die for Lindsey. But he was also the most emotional being she'd ever known and his moods made up just a part of what she loved about him.

Seán hurried from the building towards his truck, which he'd parked several buildings away and Lindsey's gut twisted itself into a knot as she watched him go.

*

Normally her café would be filled with the smell of freshly baked scones and cakes, none of which were her doing. Eileen was a baking enthusiast, which was how she'd convinced Lindsey to turn her disused ground floor into a café in the first place. She might own the place, but Eileen was the real boss. Lindsey was confined to beverages, sandwiches, salads and fry ups. Things that couldn't go too far wrong, because her kitchen skills were seriously lacking by anyone's standards. But so far there was no sign of Eileen, who would have been here by now if she was coming to work today.

Lindsey leaned against the door frame and pulled the zip of her hoodie up to her chin. It was early March and bitter cold, which wasn't unusual for Ireland. She watched Seán's van as it drove off out of sight.

Her café and home was on the slightly more rundown part of town which was only a minute's walk from the better part. It all came down to the view. As soon as the harbour came into sight, everything just seemed to perk up. But it was a view to die for. Spike Island, directly across from them, was formerly a prison island and more recently, a tourist attraction; Ireland's answer to Alcatraz, and just beyond that was the mouth of the second largest natural harbour in the world. The country's naval fleet was housed at its base at Haulbowline, another little island beside Spike. There were only two ships there at present. The rest were on patrol around various parts of the country and the world. Those same vessels patrolled the Med throughout the migrant crisis. They fished dead bodies out of the sea and rescued countless migrants before dropping them off on nearby shores. Lindsey was army to the core. Or at least she had been, but even she had to admit that the puddle pirates were playing a blinder these days. If she was willing to admit it, she might even use the word, heroic. Not that she believed in heroes. No one with the title ever wanted it, but it made her think about Lena and if that was how she'd made her way to this country and to Patrick. Was she smuggled across the Mediterranean Sea, away from one hell and towards another? Lena had a story, that was for sure. But like Lindsey's, it probably wasn't a story that many people really wanted to hear.

Now that her supplies were being held hostage by Patrick, it was only a matter of time before his men showed up to reclaim Lena. As she blinked to break the trance she was in, she realised that the McParland sisters were looking at her, waiting for her to get out of their way and let them in.

The sisters were somewhere in their eighties now, but had been inseparable since birth apparently. Neither was married and had no other family aside from each other. They were serious women who kept themselves to themselves and right now they were looking at Lindsey like she was sent from down below to fuck with their day.

'Ladies…' She forced a smile. Business as usual. 'Have a seat, I'll be right with you.' She stood aside and the women shook their heads in unified disapproval as they made their way to their usual table.

Before going back inside, she looked up and down the street one more time. Still no Eileen. It wasn't that unusual for her not to turn up for work, but she always had a reason. Lindsey could only hope that today's reason had nothing to do with That Mad Bastard Two Doors Up.

*

'Hey Lindsey, I ordered a scone with this!' Martin Powell bellowed unnecessarily, as she set down their pot of tea and walked away. 'And that fucker shouldn't be in here. It's unhygienic.'

She ignored Martin and wondered, not for the first time, if Lena was OK up there. There was no sound from the flat. No footsteps; no chair scraping along the floor; nothing. It was like she wasn't there. Maybe she'd dreamt the whole thing, which wouldn't be that hard to imagine. But she didn't dream Seán Buckley and then she wondered if he was alright.

Eleven o'clock in the morning and it was already one of the longest days of her life.

'Did you hear me?'

'I heard you, Martin.' She pulled herself from her thoughts. 'If you have a problem with my dog then there's no shortage of cafés that you and your friends can take yourselves off to. Don't let us hold you up.'

Martin was one of the first people she'd come to know when she moved here. He was a young loudmouth. But he came recommended, by the sixteen-year supermarket assistant, as a good electrician, which she badly needed at the time. He sorted out the wiring and hung around to help with other bits and pieces, trying slightly too hard to impress her before finally asking her out. Turning him down was like wounding a puppy. But she'd long ago learned her lesson about shitting on her own doorstep. He'd seemed quiet and unassuming back then when he was alone in her house. But as it turned out, he wasn't really that person at all. He was loud and cocky and overly keen to impress his friends. Today he and three other amigos occupied the window seat where local fisherman, Jimmy Duggan, would normally be ensconced, reading his newspaper out loud in an incredulous voice. Like he couldn't quite believe what he was reading.

The cocky individuals in his place all seemed quite pleased with themselves. They smelled like a brewery and were rating some woman's body parts on a scale of one to ten. Frank was standing less than three feet from their table with his eyes fixed hungrily on them all. Frank was a sweetheart of course. But he prided himself on not letting anyone else know that. Martin wasn't the first to complain about him being on the premises. But those who had a problem with Frank could fuck right off. She didn't need or want their custom and today would be the wrong day for anyone to try arguing that point.

Martin eyed the dog uncertainly before asking, 'Well, what about my scone?'

'We're all out. Again though, I'm sure there are plenty of other places serving scones today.'

Martin's smile vanished as he glanced at his friends, two of whom were looking quite amused by her, while one fixed her with a hard stare, which she duly ignored. This little group of wannabe hard men pumped iron and swallowed whatever beefer-uppers were on offer. They had a problem with everyone. First and foremost, women, followed in close second by immigrants. In third place was anyone who didn't have a problem with immigrants. Ironically, they were also errand boys for Patrick. But of course Patrick didn't come here to steal their money, their jobs and their women. Patrick provided these no-hopers with all three, so they were fine with him.

Lindsey walked away towards the bar and as far away from them as she could get. Listening to their misogynistic shit was making her brain bleed and she was about three seconds away from putting at least one of them through the plate glass window and barring them for life.

Three more of her tables were taken up with random groups and the McParland sisters were still there. They sat at a small table right beside the bar, almost hidden from view but watching and listening to everything. Like they always did.

'Give's a sandwich then,' Martin called after her.

'No bread,' she replied, and went to the back of the café and through the swing doors into the kitchen. 'Reign it in, Ryan,' she mumbled to herself. But again, it was Street's voice that she heard. Today of all days… keep your shit together girl.

Martin strutted in, almost taking one of the doors off the hinges that she'd so painstakingly fitted.

She rolled her eyes. 'Martin, whatever it is that you want, it can wait til I come out.'

'Lindsey, you need to be more careful.'

'Do I?' Her blood started to bubble.

'Look, you and me go back a bit, but these guys…'

'What about them?'

'They don't like to be spoken to like that.'

'Oh, I'm sorry. Did I hurt their feelings?'

'You need to cop onto yourself now and stop pretending you don't know what I'm talking about. They're well connected in this town and they demand respect, Lindsey.'

'Martin, you'll be well connected to the toe of my boot if you come in here demanding anything again.' She scolded him, like a parent would a child, and this annoyed him, which made her happy.

'Lindsey…'

'Enough, Martin. If your friends have a problem with me, let them come and tell me themselves.'

'You really don't want that to happen and neither do I. I want to protect you, Lindsey. You don't seem to understand…'

Lindsey tuned out as he prattled on. Like the rest of the town's population, Martin had no idea that she'd ever been anything other than a waitress. They didn't know that people had exploded in her face. Or that she kept a matchbox at the back of her wardrobe containing a tiny tooth that had been pulled out of her forehead. They didn't know that she'd prayed for death a thousand times since she'd gotten her friend killed. She thought about death at least once a day. So they couldn't have known just how little she feared the likes of Martin and his new friends. Or how little she feared for her own safety in general. They knew nothing and that was how she liked it.

'I don't need you to protect me, Martin, but thanks for the offer,' she cut him off finally. She wanted to tear him apart, such was her mood today. But tea ladies didn't do that sort of thing.

He stepped closer and seemed slightly more menacing than the Martin Powell whose voice shook when he asked her out to dinner. 'You haven't heard the way people talk about you, Lindsey. About how you live all alone and act like you're better than everyone. I stick up for you. I let them know that you're off limits.'

'You're my knight in shining armour. Now get out of my kitchen, Martin.'

His nostrils flared and he pointed his finger at her. But he had nothing else to say, so he stormed out of the kitchen. As he pushed through the doors, he was met with Frank's muzzle pressed against his thigh. He froze momentarily, before making his way slowly around the dog who refused to move even an inch, and back to his friends. Ten minutes later, they were gone.

*

'He's a cheeky bugger, that boy Powell,' Grace McParland whispered as she came to the bar to pay for their coffees. 'But I always liked you, Lindsey. You know why?' She shook her bony finger at Lindsey with something bordering on a wicked smile. 'You don't bow down to cheeky buggers like them. You're a different sort I think.'

'How are you, Grace?' Lindsey smiled at her. 'You and Evelyn doing OK?' She worried about the sisters sometimes. There'd been a spate of break-ins in recent months and most of the victims were somewhat elderly. Or just not in a position to fight back.

Grace waved away her concern with a tutt and a shake of the head.

'Good for you.' She reached under the counter and pulled out a covered plate with two blueberry scones left on it. 'Here, take these home for later.'

'I thought you didn't have any.' Her tone was sarcastic. 'You know if that imbecile came in now and saw that you do have scones and I'd hope sandwiches too, given that it's a bloody café, he'd run amuck.'

'Let him. Anyway, they're yesterday's and I'd rather you have them.' She smiled. 'What would he do, beat me up for a scone?'

'It seems life's not worth much more than that these days.' Grace pulled a piece off and held it by her side where Frank could get at it. Which of course he did. This was the down side to owning a café. It meant she had to work twice as hard to keep her dog healthy. 'Don't tell Eileen that I implied people might kill for her scones or anything though. She'll get a big head.'

'Grace…'

'I know, I know. Don't feed him that shit.' She smiled her one-upmanship smile as she wrapped the remainder of the scones in a paper napkin and tucked them into her bag. 'You know it's depressing to see how little anything has changed.'

'In what way?'

'The way he spoke to you; demanding that you grovel to him and his little wolf pack. Men have been dictating to women since the beginning of time it seems. With all the progress the world has made, you'd think they'd have copped on by now. But no. They still think they're above us.'

'I'd like to think idiots like them are a minority now…' Lindsey began.

'Well, you're wrong,' Grace snapped. 'They talk about foreigners hating women and who knows? Maybe they're right. If some of them had their way, we'd all be walking three steps behind a man with a bin bag over our heads,' Grace continued, her voice rising by the second. 'But every country just has their own way of keeping us down. Our own are every bit as bad, only they prefer to keep it all behind closed doors. I'm so damned tired of men persecuting women and it seems it's never going to change. We had more than enough of that in those God forsaken laundries with those... those bloody nuns and why? Because of politicians and priests. Bloody MEN! When will it end?'

Her chin quivered slightly before Evelyn came to her rescue, scolding her for being a silly old woman and pulling her towards the door, leaving Lindsey staring after them, speechless. She liked the sisters. But other than the occasional scowl, she'd never really seen them showing much emotion, or engaging in so much conversation. It seemed that Grace for one had kept it all inside for too long and today was the day when some of it at least, was to come rushing out.

Before they left she heard Evelyn saying, in an overly cheery voice, 'I hope twas Eileen who made those scones and not Lindsey. Sure that poor woman can't boil water.'

Most of her customers liked Eileen. There were others who refused to come in because of her, but Lindsey couldn't care less about them. There were days though when, for reasons outside of her control, Eileen was unable to make it to work. Those reasons were usually her brothers, Danny and Seamus, who pretty much dictated her life. They were also the reasons why she couldn't hold down a steady job before she started working for Lindsey; them and the mere mention of the word traveller. Eileen always said that she would call if only Lindsey would get a phone. To which Lindsey always replied with a change of topic. She didn't do social media or mindless chit chat. There was no one that she needed to be in contact with and she didn't want there to be; therefore she didn't need a phone. If Eileen came to work, great;

her patrons would eat well on those days. Otherwise they'd just have to make do with sandwiches, tea, and coffee from the fancy machine. Either way, she wouldn't normally worry about Eileen. But she worried today because today, everything screamed trouble.

'Any news, Mary?' Jimmy Duggan folded his paper, but didn't look like he was about to go anywhere. Jimmy often had both his breakfast and his tea at Lindsey's and this was the second sitting. He once said that it beat going home and eating alone.

Mary shook her head, her eyes firmly on her grandson. He wouldn't usually be with her and the poor kid looked miserable. Mary was the town gossip. Asking Mary if she had any news meant that you had no immediate plans to leave.

It was the end of the day and Lindsey needed them gone. She had to check on Lena. The fear that she might try to harm herself was growing stronger by the minute.

There was silence for a while before Lindsey finally spoke to the boy. 'Hey, Adrian, head into the back kitchen and look on the bottom shelf right at the back. I think you might find a box with some marshmallows in it. If you do, I'll make you a take-away hot chocolate to go with them.' She smiled at the boy.

His father, Mary's son Brian, had been 'missing' for over a week, which meant that he was probably on a bender. The kid didn't want or need to be in this conversation.

Adrian didn't respond as he slid off his chair and walked towards the kitchen without the usual excitement of a kid on a quest for sugar. But then he was old enough to know his own circumstances.

Mary watched him go and not until he was through the swing doors did she finally speak.

'Somebody did something to him.' She looked from Lindsey to Jimmy, her face pleading with them to agree with her.

Jimmy nodded stoically, but his eyebrows formed a shape of disbelief.

'He was going out to look for a job. That's where he was. He wasn't going anywhere else. But he hasn't come home.' She shook her head angrily. 'The likes of my poor Brian can't get a job in their own country.'

Frank snorted and walked away towards the front door and Lindsey couldn't agree with him more. It was bullshit. From what she knew of Mary's poor Brian, he wouldn't work to warm himself. His diet was mostly liquid and most of his dole went to the bookies. But who was she to shatter anyone's illusions? He was in his mid-forties and still living with his mammy. It seemed poor Mary's illusions were shatterproof. Maybe that's what happened when you became a parent.

'He'd never willingly walk away from his boy; I know that much.' Her eyes were welling up, but her face hardened suddenly as she looked towards the door.

Lindsey and Jimmy looked behind them to see what had rattled Mary's cage and of course it was Patrick Adebayo accompanied by the Russian. In an instant, Lindsey's mind focused. Her breathing steadied and her body tensed in preparation for whatever might come.

'Ah, the woman in charge.' He spoke with a smile, but he carried an air of intimidation with him.

Their arrival was enough to send Mary jumping out of her chair. Without saying another word, she grabbed Adrian by the arm as he came from the kitchen and manhandled him out the door, along with the last of Lindsey's marshmallows.

'Twice in as many days. My tea is that good, eh?' Lindsey replied with a smile of her own as she stepped out from behind her bar. The Dread was back with full force. But they wouldn't see that.

He made an apologetic face and bobbed his head from side to side, as if to politely say, Actually, your tea is shite. His smile, when it returned, was as charming as ever and his voice relatively soft for the giant that he was. 'Let us just say, it's lucky for you that you are so beautiful.'

He laughed at his own comeback.

'What can I get you then, Patrick?'

'We are friends, no?'

'I hope so,' the tea lady smiled graciously. 'Coffee? I know for a fact that that's good.'

Jimmy looked like he'd stopped breathing as he sat shaking his head as subtly as he could. His eyes pleaded with her not to prolong Patrick's visit.

Patrick glanced back at Frank who was emitting a long low growl right behind him. 'Not today, Lindsey. Time is money I'm afraid.' He came further into the café while his partner closed the front door. When he came and stood within a foot of Lindsey, he literally dwarfed her.

She put her hand on Frank's head to calm him as he came to her side, barked once and then went back to his drawn out, aggressive growl.

'Well then, what can I do for you?' she asked, refusing to step back and put some space between them. That's what he expected her to do. But the woman who'd been exploded upon refused to comply. She could only pretend so much. His aftershave was overpowering and heat radiated from his body. She had to hold her neck at an awkward angle just to look him in the eye, but that's what she did.

He smiled in response, just like someone might smile at an ant before squashing it. Finally, he took a step back and studied his nails while he spoke. 'You have something of mine. Give it back and we will remain friends.'

She exhaled loudly. 'Christ, you only needed to ask. I didn't look at it, if that's what you're upset about. Quite frankly, I don't want to know what's on it.' She kept a hint of a smile on her face, as she made her way around the bar and reached underneath it. She touched her baseball bat longingly. But instead of whipping it out and smashing it into Patrick's skull, a move that would surely be her last, she picked up the ancient Nokia phone that also resided on that shelf and handed it to him. 'Here.'

He looked at the phone and then looked at her. He seemed mildly offended, but more likely he was trying to decide if she was being clever or dumb. Lindsey put her money on the latter.

'Not yours?'

He didn't respond.

'Oh.' She put the phone back under the bar. 'I found it under your usual table… so what did you lose?'

'I hope I didn't lose anything. If I did, then I would be very upset.'

'Well, I didn't find anything else.' She sat an empty cup under the coffee machine. 'You sure I can't get you a coffee? Sorry I can't offer much more than that today. My delivery guy didn't show up.'

'That is unfortunate. You know I might be able to help you with that. But first, you must help me. You see, some people came into my house last night; it was a party you understand? But things got a little…' he rolled his hand around, 'out of hand. Boys being boys, you know?'

'Right.'

'Now some of my property is missing and the boys think it might be here.'

'The boys?'

'The boys.'

'Are they friends of yours, these boys? Maybe they have it, whatever it is that you're looking for. Maybe they broke it and are afraid to tell you.'

Patrick smiled knowingly and leaned across the bar. 'Where is she?'

'She? Oh, I thought you said you'd lost something. There was a girl. She fell into my yard last night.' Lindsey's eyes were wide as she told the story, peppered with dramatics. 'I couldn't believe it! I don't know how she wasn't killed coming down that bank! It looked like someone might have thrown her. I went out and tried to help her. I cleaned all the blood off her and gave her new clothes. One of my good tracksuits actually and then she just left without so much as a Thanks. If you see her, tell her I want my hoodie back. That cost me forty quid.'

Patrick pushed himself off the bar and walked towards the back of the café. Lindsey went to follow him, but the Russian stepped into her path and put the palm of his hand against her chest. Frank went nuts and made a go for the man's leg. He jumped back, knocking over a chair before Lindsey could grab a hold of Frank's collar. But there was no quietening him. Even Jimmy looked terrified at the sound of his barking. Frank the loveable rogue, was once again, Frank the warrior.

Jimmy got to his feet looking like it was the last thing he wanted to do. He placed his hand nervously on the goon's shoulder as he righted himself and said, 'Now there's no need to go upsetting the dog like that. Just leave the girl alone. She clearly doesn't know anything else.'

The goon glared at him and Jimmy moved his hand away. But surprisingly, he held his ground.

'Like I said… she left last night. There's nobody here but us.' Lindsey moved between the brick house and Jimmy, straining to hold onto Frank. By now, Patrick was making his way through the swing doors and into the back kitchen.

Lindsey went to move around the giant and again, he stepped into her path.

'What is it you think I'm going to do, beat him up?' Lindsey asked, barely able to make her exasperation sound like tongue in cheek sarcasm. 'Feel free to come with me.' She pushed past him and this time he let her, as Frank snapped at him again. She looked and sounded calm, despite the fact that Patrick wasn't the kind of man who'd wait for an invitation to go up those stairs. Once he did that, the shit would really hit the fan. She could let go of Frank and end this right now, but she had no intentions of doing that. Frank was the biggest threat here, which meant that he'd be the first to be taken out of the picture. If not now, then later and whatever else happened, that couldn't.

Patrick was standing at the end of the stairs looking up, when

Frank went bursting through the doors, almost pulling Lindsey's arm out of its socket. His momentum allowed her to get him close to the back door, which was just behind Patrick, who flinched dramatically as they approached. But Lindsey opened the door and using her knee, she managed to shove Frank outside before he knew what was happening. She quickly closed the door on him. Lindsey wasn't about to sacrifice her dog for anyone. Herself, no problem, but not her dog.

She held up her hands as a show of good will. 'Listen, I'm not sure why you'd think I'd be hiding this girl from you. What's she to me? Go on up; see for yourself,' she bluffed, knowing somewhere in the back of her mind that he'd call it. Of course he would. He was going up there regardless of what she said.

Patrick gestured with his head towards the back door, which sounded like it was being torn apart from the outside. 'You are not afraid of me?' he smiled.

'I thought we were friends?'

He maintained his menacing smile and his eye contact with her as he made his way up the stairs to her flat. And to Lena. Lindsey meanwhile managed to maintain the look of nonchalance. 'There's nobody else here,' she said.

Each of his footsteps on the wooden stairs carried the sound of another nail being hammered into her coffin. Patrick was known for being a ruthless enforcer who liked nothing less than to feel slighted in any way. And if this wasn't a slight, then nothing was.

The Russian was standing close enough that Lindsey could smell sweet tobacco from his breath. She wondered how she'd get past him if she needed to get up those stairs in a hurry. Her back was against the stainless-steel work counter while the pair eyeballed each other in silence, and Patrick made his way through her flat. As she studied the man before her, she came to the conclusion that her best efforts wouldn't be enough to put him down. Not for long enough to get up there and even then, what would she do? Take down Patrick too? No chance.

Frank was barking up a storm and she worried briefly that he might give himself a heart attack. He'd had one already, but she couldn't think about that now because the goon was also moving towards the stairs. He looked up and said something in Pidgin English that she didn't catch.

No reply came. Then what sounded like a door slamming was followed by one loud bang after another. It sounded like everything Lindsey owned was hitting the floor. But there were no screams. Not yet at least. Maybe Lena had found a hiding space, though she couldn't imagine where. Her flat wasn't exactly spacious. Or maybe he'd found her – already dead by her own hand and this was him warming up for when he got his hands on Lindsey?

The noise continued for what felt like an eternity before the footsteps started back down the stairs and only when Patrick reached the kitchen did the goon turn his attention away from her.

He spoke a few words, again in Pidgin English, but Patrick didn't respond. Now it was his turn to fix his cold hard eyes on Lindsey. She maintained eye contact with him. She should at least pretend to be afraid of him. She knew that. But she couldn't bring herself to give him the satisfaction, so they sized each other up in silence for a few seconds. Then he glanced at his goon and walked calmly out the door.

Lindsey was caught off guard when the goon grabbed her by the back of the neck and dragged her through the swing doors. Her shoulder slammed into the doorjamb with force but they kept moving and once they'd reached the bar, he flung her to the ground at Patrick's feet.

'Lindsey!' Jimmy dropped to the floor beside her and tried to help her up before being dragged away.

Lindsey took her time getting to her feet. Her natural instinct was to fight. But she had to think about Lena. She couldn't afford to give herself away, so she took a few seconds to calm her mind. Breathe, Ryan.

'Where is she?'

'I don't know.'

'There was blood on your floor. It was hers, yes?'

'Probably. Like I said, I patched the woman up and then she left. I didn't get her name and I don't know anything about her, other than she was hurt and she left without saying thanks. In fact,' she got slowly to her feet, 'if this is the thanks I get for helping people, I can safely say I won't bother my arse next time.'

Before she was fully up, the goon pushed her to the floor again.

'Leave her alone,' Jimmy tried, but the Russian switched his attention to him with lightning speed.

His hands wrapped tightly around Jimmy's throat as he effortlessly began squeezing the life from him.

'Let him go, and I'll tell you what I know.' Lindsey got to her feet much quicker this time. She looked from the goon to Patrick, her eyes pleading with him to be reasonable. No point in pleading with his puppet. She suspected that he'd enjoy that too much.

Patrick nodded and Jimmy was released. He fell backwards into a chair.

'So, where is she?'

'I found her last night at the back of this building. She was really hurt. You should have a word with The boys about that.'

'Yes, we know.' He placed his hand on Lindsey's shoulder and smiled again. 'Lindsey, I am not a heartless man. There was a party. The boys got carried away. They have been dealt with and it won't happen again. See, I take care of Lena. I put clothes on her back and food in her mouth. I protect her. This was an unfortunate accident. So please, tell me where she is so that I can make sure she's OK.'

Lindsey nodded like she believed him. 'I cleaned her wounds and I gave her clothes. She hardly spoke at all, but I asked her if she needed me to call someone for her; family or whatever. She said that she knew people in the city. That's it. That's all she said. I went to the bathroom and when I came back, she was gone.'

'You are very kind.' He nodded again with the same smile that expressed more danger than humour. 'Where is she?'

'In the city I presume.'

He held her gaze for several long minutes, as the goon began trashing her café. Lindsey fixed her eyes on his, once again refusing to give him the satisfaction that he sought. It took no more than a minute for him to totally destroy the place and once he was satisfied, the goon stood quietly by the door waiting for his master.

Patrick smiled one more time at Lindsey before they both turned and left, leaving her with the distinct feeling that she hadn't seen the last of them.

*

'Jesus Christ,' Jimmy muttered, as Lindsey made her way through the destruction to close and lock the door behind them. Jimmy's voice was hoarse and his face had lost all colour.

She didn't respond. She just stood staring at the door. She could practically hear her blood bubbling towards boiling point.

'Lindsey?'

'Jimmy…' She took a deep breath that did nothing to calm her as she turned towards him. 'You should have left with Mary when you had the chance.'

'Well I couldn't just leave you here, could I? What the hell happened here and who in the name of sweet Jesus are they looking for? You have to tell That Mad Bastard if you know something, girl.'

Lindsey headed for the back door to check on Frank, while Jimmy started picking up furniture.

'Lindsey?'

'You heard me, Jimmy.' She continued to talk to him as she hurried through the kitchen and opened the back door. 'Just some woman who got injured last night. I helped her out and she left. No good deed goes unpunished and all that.' She forced a smile into her voice to try to lighten the situation.

Frank sniffed her feverishly before hurrying through to the café. Once he was satisfied that the threat had passed and Lindsey was alright, he threw her his dirtiest look. Then he walked off towards the swing doors, where he sat waiting for the next time they opened. He wouldn't ask for them to be opened, even though now he could go under them if he deigned to lower himself. But he was making a point. Lindsey needed to be in no doubt about the fact that he was pissed at her. She grinned as she watched him sit with his back to her. God she loved him.

'But clearly she didn't go home.' Jimmy again. 'Or at least, she didn't go back to the cat house.'

'Would you?'

'You're not doing anything stupid, are ya, girl?'

Lindsey caught him by the arm, which was shaking slightly. 'Jimmy, I think it might be best if we don't mention this to anyone else for now?'

'What? Why?'

'Because frankly, it's none of my business what goes on in any of Patrick's establishments. I don't need to be on his radar.'

'It might be too late for that, girl.'

She blew out a long breath. 'Well, having people talking certainly won't help. So we'll keep this to ourselves, yeah?' She knew she was asking too much.

'Sure. It's just a shame you didn't think to mention that to Mary Kelly before she went tearing out the door. She'll be looking for her bullhorn as we speak.'

He was right. But there was nothing she could do about that either. 'Hey thanks, Jimmy… for trying to… you know. But that was incredibly stupid.' She gave him a quick hug, despite her aversion to hugging. It's what a normal person would do. And she did admire his efforts.

Jimmy was not someone who would do well in conflict and no doubt he knew it. And yet he stayed.

'I know, girl.' He rubbed her back briskly. 'I nearly shit in my second-best pair of Levis.'

*

Jimmy stayed until the place was back in order and Lindsey made them both a coffee and a less than fresh ham sandwich before letting him go home. Aside from the fact that she owed him that much at least, she also wanted to make sure that he was alright before letting him go back to his empty house. For her part, Lindsey was putting off going upstairs and finding whatever awaited her there. There was nowhere for Lena to have hidden up there, so her thoughts about what might have just happened were getting darker by the second.

As she stood at the bottom of the stairs, she wondered briefly if she was about to find the body of this woman in one of her rooms. But then she thought better of it.

'They'd hardly still be asking where she was if she was already dead surely?' She directed her question to Frank, who was by her side once more. 'Unless of course they're setting me up.' She looked sharply at him as the thought occurred to her.

She took the stairs two at a time and headed for her small sitting room, with Frank right behind her. Not too close, but close enough. She stood in the doorway for a few seconds, dumbfounded.

The room was almost exactly as she'd left it that morning. She took a step inside and looked around. Frank trotted towards his mat, circled it and lay down, again with his back to her. That was reassuring. The room was as clean and tidy as the little kitchenette.

'Where did all that noise come from?' she mumbled.

She walked down the hall and pushed open the door to the spare bedroom. It too was spotlessly clean and tidy and there, sitting on the spare bed, was Lena. She was still wearing Lindsey's clothes and was perched on the edge of the bed, looking like she'd been nervously waiting for some time.

The bruising on her face had darkened significantly and her cuts looked even more vicious than they had last night, but Lena looked younger than she had. Maybe the tracksuit that she was wearing, borrowed from Lindsey, and the ponytail in her hair helped with that? Lindsey guessed that she was in her early twenties.

'Lena?' Lindsey looked nervously around the room and behind the door. How could he not have found her? 'Are you alright?'

'Lindsey...' she got to her feet. 'I am so very sorry.'

Her English was good and she sounded nothing like the broken woman that Lindsey expected to find. She sounded strong, considering what she'd been through.

'He didn't find you?'

She shook her head.

'You knew who he was?'

'Everyone knows who he is. I presume Hector was downstairs too? Where there is one, you'll find the other. Did they hurt you?'

Lindsey shook her head, confused. 'Hector... the Russian?'

'Yes, the Russian. They caused a lot of damage, yes?'

'Nothing that can't be fixed. They know what happened to you.'

'Of course they know.' She smiled bitterly. 'They would have profited handsomely from it.'

Lindsey let out a long breath.

'If I go back there my choices will be to wait for someone to finally kill me, or go by my own hand and beat them to it.'

'You're not going back there.'

A look of hopelessness passed over Lena's face. 'I have nowhere else to go.'

'Well for now at least, you'll stay here.'

She smiled again. 'I cannot. You've shown me great kindness, but I've endangered you enough.'

'How did he not find you? Where did you hide?'

She looked to the ceiling and pointed upwards.

Lindsey looked up but had no idea what she meant. There was nowhere to hide in the attic. It was a shell of a space. She had a heavy bag hanging from a chain at which she vented her frustrations almost on a nightly basis. Aside from the bag, there were some free weights and a scattering of ropes, resistance bands and a pull up bar. Her car-boot haul was crammed into the other end, but that was it. There was nowhere to hide.

Lena gave her a curious glance. She caught Lindsey by the hand and led her back to the kitchenette. On the ceiling above the fridge was a small square panel. Lindsey remembered stuffing herself in there with rolls of prickly insulation wool during her renovations. She'd coughed, choked and even got stuck when she rolled onto her side. In the end she decided to rip up the floorboards upstairs and go at it from another angle. She closed up that little square and never planned to look in there again. Until now. It was a tiny, suffocating space between the two floors and she admired the woman immensely for having no complaints about being in there.

'It's not exactly a palace up there, is it?'

'I wouldn't know a palace.' Lena smiled.

'What will you do?'

She shook her head.

'Do you have any family?'

She shook her head again.

Lindsey thought about the scar across her belly, but didn't ask if she had children. It was none of her business. 'Friends?'

'Those still alive are in Syria or Europe. I don't know.' She shrugged. 'Not here.'

'OK, well… you have one friend here now.'

A tear rolled uninterrupted down Lena's cheek and off the end of her chin.

'Stay as long as you like,' Lindsey looked around. 'And thank you for tidying up.'

'Some things I could not fix.' She gestured towards a sizable pile of broken glass and crockery, resting in the dustpan.

'You'll find there's nothing of value here.' Lindsey smiled. 'I don't think they'll be back tonight, Lena but I need to go out for a bit. Will you be OK here by yourself?'

'Please, don't worry about me. But you need to be careful. It's not safe out there for you now either. Not with Patrick watching you. And he will be watching.'

'I'll be fine.'

Leaving Lena alone in the kitchen, Lindsey went to her bedroom and closed the door. She leaned heavily against it for a minute, then pulled her hair loose and ran her hands through it before tying it up in another messy ponytail. Instinctively, she smoothed down her side fringe which covered the lumpy scar that burst angrily out of her hairline and snaked its way towards her temple.

She blew out a long breath and headed for her wardrobe. She shoved on an oversized hoodie and zipped it right up to her chin. Then she went back to Lena in the sitting room. 'I'm going to leave Frank here with you.'

'Lindsey, I've never gotten along very well with dogs.' She looked uncomfortably at Frank, who was still pretending to ignore Lindsey. But his ears pricked at the sound of his name. 'He sounded so vicious downstairs.'

'I promise you, Lena, Frank will never hurt you.' Frank got up and walked over to her. 'It's his job to protect people. That's all he was trying to do.'

'Then you should take him with you.'

Lindsey shook her head and lowered herself to Frank's level. She pointed her finger at him, like a parent would to a child, and told him to stay. He wasn't happy of course, but he did as he was told. Still, he whined in protest as she left.

All was forgiven. Again.

As she stepped outside the café, she breathed in the smell of the sea. There was a strong smell of seaweed around the town tonight and fish too. Flocks of seagulls floated overhead, waiting for their chance to feed. The town was the personification of peacefulness to those who didn't know what went on behind closed doors, here and all over the world. She let each scent fill her nostrils and clear her head. Then she pulled up her hood, put her head down and started walking.

It was about a mile to where she was headed. Through the town, passed the Old Hardware House, the square and the promenade was a little area near Whitepoint Strand, which was usually reserved for holidaymakers to park up their campervans. It was now occupied by two older model mobile homes and a Hiace van, whose owners were about to get a visit, whether they wanted one or not. It was the beginning of the tourist season so lots of strangers were milling around, admiring the serene beauty of the harbour town and Lindsey blended with them as best she could. Anonymity was always a good thing, but even more so this evening. She kept her head down with her fists clenching and unclenching the whole time. She never used to do that before Syria, the thought just occurred to her. But of course there were a lot of things she didn't do before Syria.

Once she passed the promenade, things quietened down. There were fewer people around and when she got to the deep-water quay, there was a large fishing trawler berthed there.

During the summer months, some of the largest cruise liners in the world came to visit Cobh. Usually they were greeted by pipe bands, and those same bands would play as they pulled off after spending a day or two marvelling at the town's beauty and hospitality. It didn't feel as hospitable these days. Not to Lindsey at least, but she tended to have that effect on places.

'Eh! Eh, lady!' A man with a distinctly French accent called to her from the trawler's deck.

She turned to look at him, but kept walking.

He walked with her along the length of the boat. 'Lady, you want looking for me, eh?'

She ignored him and kept walking.

'Maybe you want good Frenchman, no?'

She picked up the pace, headed along the area known locally as the five-foot way because that was roughly the width of the walkway. It had railings on one side separating it from the sea and on the other side was a car park, then the train tracks at the end of the line between Cobh and Cork city. Further along the car park gave way to campers and the Chambers' family caravans.

There were locations all over Ireland where the travelling community set up temporary homes. The law, as well as the locals, preferred these to be out of sight and certainly not slap bang in the middle of their town's tourist area. Regular attempts were made to move them on, but so far they'd all been unsuccessful. Or at least, they didn't succeed in moving them very far. They'd been in this spot for two days having been moved from the green area of a nearby housing estate.

The Chambers came to Cobh after one of their caravans was burned out. Eileen was supposed to have been inside at the time. This was an attempt to punish her for having the balls to walk away from an abusive partner. Danny, Eileen's brother, was up on the roof of one of their remaining caravans. He sat with his legs crossed and a crowbar resting on his lap. Clearly he was expecting trouble.

Their need to protect their home so aggressively was down to a feud between the Chambers and the family of Eileen's ex, which was actually how she'd come to know Eileen in the first place. Back when owning a café couldn't be further from Lindsey's mind.

She'd been patching up the walls on the ground floor when she was interrupted by a loud thump and her front door shook. When she opened it, a scrawny, tattooed and dirty looking individual fell in on top of her. He smelled like sweat and cheap beer. Before Lindsey could marvel at his mullet or straighten him up in any way, an even scrawnier teenage girl came barrelling towards him, pummelling him with everything she had.

Seeing Eileen's bloody nose, Lindsey chose to let the dropkick fall to the floor and give the skinny girl a minute to do her worst. Then she hauled Eileen inside and dropped her friend face first onto the footpath. By the time the police came, Eileen was upstairs and Lindsey indicated the power tools on the floor when she told them that she hadn't heard a thing outside. Their families were at war ever since and knowing how travelling family feuds worked, this would last for generations.

'Here comes trouble,' Danny grumbled, as he banged on the roof of the van.

Seconds later, Seamus was at the door, his hand resting on something by his side but out of sight. A weapon of sorts no doubt.

'You'd better come in,' Seamus grinned, stepping aside.

Lindsey never liked Seamus. He always looked at her like she was a buffet and he was half starved. 'Is Eileen in there?' She pointed at the door before stepping inside.

'Ah, are ya not here to see me?'

'Seamus, shut the fuck up and get outta the way.' Eileen shoved past him and headed for the next caravan. She nudged Lindsey to follow her and ignore the litany of abuse that Seamus hurled at them.

Eileen acted tough and she was most of the time. But Lindsey suspected that she was slightly afraid of her brothers. They were the law in Eileen's life. They determined what she could and couldn't do. When she could go to work and when she couldn't, which is why Lindsey never rode her for not turning up. It wasn't up to her. That was the life of an Irish travelling woman; the men were in charge. Lindsey couldn't imagine such a fate, but there you go.

'Lindsey, I'm really fucking sorry. You know anyone else would fucking fire me. Or is that why you're here?'

'You're OK then?'

'Why wouldn't I be OK? You know Danny has some nice phones at the moment. Get one and I'd be able to save you the trouble of coming looking for me.'

'If I had a phone, people might be able to contact me for stuff.' Lindsey smiled. 'Anyway we didn't have a lot for you to work with today.'

'How come?'

'Seán was robbed.'

'Dirty, scummy bastards.' Eileen thumped the table and shook her head. 'Listen…' she hushed her voice and looked out the door before closing it. 'The boys are transporting a bit these days and I had to make a few runs to the city. That's why I couldn't come in.'

The boys were of course her brothers and she strongly suspected that what they were transporting was either drugs or stolen merchandise. Or maybe both. But that wasn't her concern.

'Trips like that sound like they might be bad for your health, Eileen.'

She made a no shit face and rolled her eyes. 'Yeah but you know yourself; you can't send a boy to do a woman's job.' Then she smiled and nudged Lindsey again. 'Tell Jimmy Duggan I'll be back to rescue him from your baking tomorrow.'

'Jimmy would never endure my baking. But I'm sure he'll be glad to hear it.' Lindsey grinned and turned to go.

She worried about Eileen. But like everyone else, she did what she had to do. She just hoped it didn't come back to bite her. 'I need to talk to your brother for a minute. See you tomorrow.' She wanted to know that Eileen was OK. That Patrick hadn't gotten to her too, but Danny Chambers was who she had really come to see.

'If he tries anything, don't be afraid to break his fucking face.'

'I meant your other brother.'

She closed the door to keep in what little heat Eileen had and then she made her way around to the ladder on the back of the other van. She climbed to the top and was greeted with the tip of the crowbar.

'You mind?' She gently shoved it away from her face.

'You shouldn't sneak up on a fella, Lindsey.' He shuffled along the roof of the caravan to make room for her to sit alongside him.

'Did you manage to get what I asked for?'

'That was weeks ago. What makes you think I didn't sell them on?'

'Because you're not as big a bollocks as they say you are.' She grinned.

He laughed quietly, slid forward and jumped to the ground. Danny disappeared inside for a minute, while Lindsey made her way back down the ladder. She waited patiently for his return.

After a minute, he stuck his head out the door and motioned her inside where she was greeted once again by Seamus. He was sprawled on the couch this time, scratching his balls with a grin on his face and his eyes on Lindsey. She also took note of the sawn-off shotgun leaning casually against the same couch.

Danny shook a small box to get her attention and then he placed it on the table. He gestured for her to take a look, which she did gladly, to distract herself from Seamus. She picked a brown leather belt from the box and Danny took it from her. He held it out to demonstrate that it was in fact a simple belt and then he smiled as he pulled on the buckle, which easily came away from the leather to reveal the smooth, sharp three inch blade attached to it. Yes, that would do nicely. She'd asked for easily concealable weapons and it seemed Danny had come up trumps.

Lindsey was physically very fit and had enough hand-to-hand skills to defend herself one-on-one if needed. When she asked Danny for these, it was more just to have them to hand, maybe in her wardrobe for a rainy day.

Now though, she wanted to be armed because she was protecting more than just herself. Now she felt the need to protect the woman in her care who she guessed had been through more than enough in her lifetime. Plus she was certain that Patrick, or at least one of his henchmen, would be back and she needed to be ready whenever that happened.

Danny also supplied her with a tactical stun gun and an expandable baton, all of which she could carry on her person at all times. She examined each item closely. The blade slid in and out of the belt buckle with little resistance and was perfectly concealed. The stun gun worked and the baton was security grade.

'Perfect,' she mumbled. Now this was when things usually got interesting with travellers. 'How much?'

He thought for a second and then waved her away. 'You looked after our Eileen when it mattered. And sure you've no man to look after ya. This one's on the house.'

'What the fuck?' Seamus protested, but both Danny and Lindsey ignored him.

She smiled, hiding her surprise. 'See? I knew you weren't a total bollocks.'

She put the belt on and tucked the baton into her sock. She covered it with the leg of her pants. The stun gun went in her pocket and as she stepped outside, Danny followed her.

'Danny before I go...' she moved closer to him and lowered her voice so that Seamus wouldn't hear her. 'How often do you make a run to the city?'

He stared at her for a few seconds and she could tell that he was both suspicious and annoyed that Eileen had told Lindsey their business, but she had to ask.

'Why do you wanna know?'

She shrugged. 'If I wanted to transport something... how often do you go?'

He shrugged back. There wasn't enough trust between the two to have a proper conversation about this, but she needed as much information as she could get.

'Depends. What do you need to transport?' Then he grinned, 'Cakes and shit I presume?'

'Exactly. Cakes and shit.' She looked around and her eyes came to rest on the old transit van parked across the front of the two caravans. 'Is that what you use?'

'Again, it depends.'

She needed to think before she said anymore. 'Thanks for the stuff, Danny.' She turned to go but Danny caught her by the arm.

'You know, I hear things.'

Lindsey looked pointedly at his hand until he removed it. 'Do you?'

'Hmm. Some things that're true, some that're bullshit. I heard one story today that I'm sure has to be bullshit.'

'Yeah?'

'Yeah. See no woman would be stupid enough to fuck with Paddy Abba-Whatsisfuck. That much I know. And yet, the story I heard is about a woman who did.'

'Is that right?'

'It couldn't be, but yeah. That's what I heard. But I reckon anyone with a bit of cop on would know that slippery bastard has a longer payroll than a dirty politician. So if anyone was fool enough to fuck with him, they'd want to know exactly what they were doing.'

She could see where Eileen got her vocabulary from. 'I didn't hear that one, Danny. But then I don't get out much.'

'That's good.' He nodded. But his face of course said that he didn't believe her. 'Because Paddy has his guys parked up at Belvelly Bridge and they plan on being there around the clock as of now. Apparently they're looking for one of his brassers. But word is, that's not all they're on the lookout for. I mean, there's a market for just about anything, isn't there? Men, women … whatever. Cakes and shit too I'd say. Anything that won't be missed, you know yourself. Would you be missed would you say, Lindsey?'

Without waiting for a response, Danny stepped back inside and closed the door.

Fuck.

Belvelly Bridge was the only road onto and off the Island of Cobh, which meant that as of now, she was well and truly screwed.

*

As Lindsey headed back towards town, she was no longer thinking about the trouble that she might encounter on her way home. She was considering her next move. She had to get Lena out of town and so far, Danny's tricked out van seemed like her only option. But now she had to come up with a way of getting past Patrick's men as well.

As her mind wrapped itself around a new mission, her gut was slowly twisting itself into a knot. So slowly that she didn't even feel it at first. If Frank were with her, he'd have felt it. He'd have let her know before she got anywhere near the three French fishermen, who were unloading fish boxes from the trawler onto the quay. But as it was, she hardly noticed them. Their boisterous voices weren't enough to penetrate her thoughts. Neither was the sound of their laughter but as they threw a pile of empty fish boxes onto the trawler's deck, the sound set off a loud explosion in her head. Add to that the horn from another passing trawler and the tension in her gut spread throughout her body, elevating rapidly. Her shoulders squared and her heart started to pound.

The fishermen; still a hundred yards away, looked busy, but one of them was watching her while pretending not to be. She was sure of it. The other two had their backs to her but all three had bulges under their top layer of clothing. They were carrying.

But they couldn't be. She had to be imagining it. She slowed her pace as she glanced up at the High Road. The town of Cobh began at the sea and worked its way upwards. It was known as much for its gargantuan hills as its scenic beauty. Every road and every building was overlooked by another high above it. Right now, she had the worst possible vantage point. She could be seen from everywhere, but Lindsey could only see what was right in front of her and she was certain now that she felt more eyes on her. Her guard came fully up and she half wished that Frank was with her given how outnumbered she was. Or wasn't. Was she?

The three men were no longer pretending to work. One of them was walking towards her; the one who'd been looking at her. His hands were raised and he was speaking calmly to her in French. But he didn't fool her for a second. He looked back at his buddies, who were turned to face her now too.

One of them glanced up to the High Road, confirming her suspicions that they had someone up there. Or maybe he was just looking.

She moved towards the quay wall anyway, to be out of sight from above but the Frenchman was still coming towards her. She needed to be obscured but she couldn't have her back to the wall with this guy either and he was getting closer, moving slowly and still glancing back at the other two. They were moving in her direction now as well. Who the fuck were these guys?

She couldn't stand around and wait for them to surround her. Win or lose, she had to make a move. She steadied her breathing and waited until he was within range and then she dropped him with a perfect heel kick to the kidney. He went down like a sack of rocks and Lindsey jumped over him as she and the other two so-called fishermen, ran towards each other. They collided with force and this time it was Lindsey who landed like a sack on the ground, put there by and with the two men. Her back and hips exploded with pain and the wind violently left her body. Maybe she hit her head, but for a minute everything went black.

When she came to, another face was leaning over her. 'Lenny?'

'It's me, Lindsey... Jimmy.'

The Frenchmen were shouting in their native tongue, pointing between Lindsey and their friend, who was sitting on an upturned fish box, his face and body contorted in pain.

'You shut the fuck up, Frenchie!' Jimmy roared at them, and this jarred Lindsey. She pushed against him and got to her feet.

She looked at Jimmy, confused for a second. What the hell was going on? What was Jimmy doing with them?

She looked more closely at the three Frenchmen. They were looking at her like she was a crazy person or a vicious animal that might pounce any second. They were wary. Why were they wary? They had the numbers. They had the upper hand.

'What happened, girl? Those lads want to call the cops.'

They wanted to call the cops? The knot in her stomach made its presence felt as embarrassment warmed her face. She was certain that they'd been coming at her. Almost as certain as she was that she couldn't trust what her mind told her anymore. She was a crazy person.

'Lindsey?'

She shook her head and pushed past Jimmy. She had to get away from all of them, Jimmy included. But before she did, she approached the fishermen with much more hesitation that she had the first time.

The two who were still standing glared angrily at her, while the one on the fish box glanced up mournfully, pain etched on his face. A part of her wanted to explain herself. But where would she start? Plus, she still didn't know for sure if what went through her mind was real or if it was the bitch that lived inside her head. She had no idea anymore.

'Je suis désolée,' she mumbled to the men, using what little French she had and she walked away while she still had the chance.

'Lindsey!' Jimmy shouted after her.

The fishermen shouted something else, but she didn't turn around. Instead she broke into a run and didn't stop until she reached home.

Chapter 4

Naturally, Jimmy was first through her door the next morning. He'd been standing on the doorstep, impatiently waiting for her to open up. She almost didn't. It took a full forty minutes just to turn the lock to the open position and Jimmy was the reason for that. Lindsey was used to losing her shit. She did it all the time, but she liked to do it alone, which was why she actively avoided people for as long as she could after arriving in Cobh.

'Jimmy.' She wedged open the door and walked back inside.

She'd been lying on the couch staring at the ceiling all night, kept sane only by Frank whose muzzle rested on her belly. He stayed there, hardly moving for as many hours as it took for her heart to slow down and for her mind to quieten once more. During those hours she vividly pictured just about everything, from that road in Syria to the kid who pulled the trigger on Lenny. She pictured a blade gliding gracefully across the veins on her wrists. The swollen tide, just across the road, with currents capable of making sure that no one would ever have to find her. She thought, too about the oblivion that certain drugs could bring her. Eventually she shut those ideas down, like she nearly always did. But it took time.

'That's all you're gonna say? Jimmy.'

'What can I get you?'

'They said that you came at them with a knife!'

'Is that right?' She feigned disinterest, wishing that he'd just fuck off. As much an' all as she liked him.

'You left this behind.' He held up the blade from the belt that Danny had given her.

She looked at it for a second and then took it from him.

'Did they do something to you? I'll believe your side quicker than theirs. I mean, surely there's no way in the world you're just gonna rush a shower of Frenchmen, wielding a knife for no reason, is there? Because that's what they're saying; that you were acting all weird, talking to yourself even. They said they just wanted to see were you alright and you gave one of them an awful kick altogether, before rushing the other two with that yolk.' He indicated the blade in her hand, prompting her to put it away under the bar.

Lindsey was still silent and for the first time in her life, she was glad to see Martin Powell coming barrelling through the door.

'Lindsey, are you alright?' He looked more like a hooligan than ever before.

Despite the cold, Martin was wearing an off-white vest, presumably to show off his physique and he looked like he was bulling for a fight. He was accompanied by two other men. Lindsey had seen them both with Martin at different times over the past few weeks and while she didn't know either of their names, she had seen one of them in a police uniform on other occasions. He wasn't wearing that uniform now and aside from them, there was no one else in the café.

'Lindsey?' Jimmy asked again.

'Why wouldn't I be alright, Martin?' Lindsey half smiled at him, as she began pouring a coffee for Jimmy in the hope that he'd take her lack of response as his cue to drop it.

She doubted he would. But it'd buy her time at least; time to come up with a plausible explanation that didn't include telling him what PTSD looked like.

Martin followed her behind the bar, also ignoring Jimmy and he placed his hands on Lindsey's shoulders like she was a lifelong friend whose battles he suddenly needed to fight. 'Lindsey, I can protect you.' His voice was low. Conspiratorial.

Frank nudged his way roughly between her and Martin, forcing Martin to step back. He'd been glued to her side all morning and would remain there until Lindsey's self-destruct sequence hopefully stopped short. As of now, it was still counting down.

'Should he be in here, what with the food an' all?'

She shoved passed him, around the bar again and handed Jimmy his coffee with what she hoped was a reassuring smile.

'Throw on a pot of tea, Lindsey, and bring down a cup for yourself too. We need to have a talk.' Martin again. It seemed no one in this town could take a hint.

'I'll get your tea but I can't join you.'

'Why not?'

'Because I'm busy.'

He looked around the café, empty aside from him, his two friends and Jimmy, and he grinned. 'Yeah, I can see that. Now sit down and have a cup of tea girl, will ya.'

Lindsey hid her annoyance well as she gave in and decided to join them. If for no other reason, she needed the distraction. And for now at least, she needed to play the game as far as Patrick and his lapdogs were concerned.

Jimmy meanwhile took a seat at another table. He sat watching her, letting her know that he wasn't leaving without satisfying his curiosity.

Clearly today was going to be a right old bitch.

She made tea for the threesome and brought a strong coffee, containing a good glug of whiskey, for herself. At first Martin and one of his companions sat inside the window. But the off-duty Garda sat quietly by himself near the bar, until such time as the other two dutifully joined him. It was clear who was really in charge of this little group. Or maybe he just didn't want to be seen by any of his on-duty colleagues as he hung out, drinking tea with two young thugs. Though according to the grapevine, he ran an outreach programme and was a mentor to these and other wayward youths. It sounded like a nice story.

Lindsey joined them under the watchful eye of Eileen, who was working hard to make something edible out of the meagre ingredients she had to work with. Frank curled up at her feet when she sat down. His was the only company she actually wanted today.

Rather than asking what they felt the need to talk to her about, Lindsey sat and quietly sipped her coffee. She generally spent more time listening than talking anyway. Sometimes it paid off; sometimes it gave her a headache and she already had one of those.

'So Lindsey, you got a visit last night from…' Martin started.

'Garda Halpin isn't it?' She held her hand towards the Garda, ignoring Martin completely. 'We haven't actually met. I'm Lindsey.'

'Ben.' He nodded and shook her hand. He was studying her too. 'You know who I am?'

Lindsey shrugged. 'I've heard about your outreach programme. Sounds great.'

'I'm Charlie.' The other guy piped up. 'You know me. I've been in here loads.' He grabbed Lindsey's hand and shook it roughly as soon as Ben let it go.

Charlie was no more than sixteen years old. Maybe even younger, with a whiskery beard that probably took six months to grow. He also looked like his mammy still picked out his T-shirts for him. She wondered what a man like Ben, who was well into his thirties, was really doing with a kid Charlie's age. She trusted him even less suddenly. Lindsey was all for outreach. But this wasn't that.

'Sure, yeah.' She smiled at Charlie, with no idea who he was. Then she sat back and let them take the conversation wherever it was they wanted to take it. Once again, it was Martin who spoke first.

'OK, you need to listen to me, Lindsey, because people are saying shit. And you should know that things are gone to the fucking dogs out there.'

Lindsey couldn't help it; she grinned. Martin was such a plank.

'Like I was telling Ben this morning…' he continued, 'three of my friends got the shit kicked out of them the other night. And I mean a real beating, just because someone said that they might have done something. You catching my drift? Now Christy and the lads are well able to fight their corner. But even they didn't stand a chance against these guys and you wanna know why? Because these fuckers were specially trained.'

'Yeah?'

'Yeah! There's these ex Special Forces lunatics up in Cork. Treacherous cunts they are and they're training rag heads on how to maim and kill fellas going about their business. They've become so good at maiming and killing that some of them now do it for a living. You catching my drift, Lindsey?'

'I think so.' She did a good enough job of feigning interest, but she was more interested in Ben and the way he was completely ignoring Martin. He was staring right at her.

'From what I hear, the main guy who trains them is like a world champion cage fighter or something,' Charlie added, shyly. 'He owns a gym and apparently if you try to walk in there, you get the shit kicked out of you by these commando fellas. You have to be invited. Old Dogs Boxing Gym it's called.' He chuckled childishly, then glanced at Ben. 'What a stupid name for a gym.'

Lindsey's hand froze with her cup half way to her mouth.

'Now these are serious fuckin' lads. They know what they're doing and it's only a matter of time before they turn these Muslim fuckers into an even bigger threat than they already are.'

Lindsey despised narrow-minded little shits like Martin. They didn't know one single thing about any culture other than their own.

Yet they still spewed hatred whenever their mouths would open wide enough.

Choose your battles, Ryan.

'Calm down, Martin,' Ben cut him off. 'Lindsey hasn't said that she wants our help yet.'

Ben's eyes hardly left Lindsey's as he spoke to Martin. There was something quite menacing about him.

'Your help with what? I'm sorry lads, but I'm not sure what we're talking about anymore. Is it Patrick, or specially trained Muslims that I should be worried about?'

'They're one and the same, Lindsey,' Martin replied dramatically. 'Like I said, who do you think works for Patrick?'

'Everybody,' Charlie replied, quietly.

'Oh. Well, I do appreciate you coming here lads, I mean it. Thanks. But there was nothing to it. Apparently one of Patrick's girls took off or something. He came in here looking for her and that's it.' She sat back and sipped her coffee again.

She always managed to look relaxed, regardless of how she felt on the inside. And at this moment in time, she felt like a volcano ready to erupt. On the inside. 'Now I don't know about the lads that beat up Christy what's-his-name, but they've nothing to do with me.'

'We heard a different version of what happened here.'

At well over six feet tall and built like a barge, Ben dwarfed the man-child on his left and Martin on his right. Everything about him was designed to intimidate and she wondered if that was why he went for a career in law enforcement.

'Ah. Well there'll always be versions won't there?'

He nodded. 'I heard the one where Patrick accused three young lads of helping that same girl to disappear. In that version he kicked seven colours of shit out those boys. Or rather, his specially trained friends did.' He grinned. 'And then for some reason, those boys pointed him in your direction. I saw the damage he did to them. That's why

I'm wondering why you're so relaxed.'

'You don't seem like the kind of man who'd listen to rumours and the like.'

'I find that when it comes to Patrick Adebayo, there's rarely smoke without fire.'

'Fair enough.'

'So, are you gonna tell us what happened yesterday?'

'How are the three young lads… your friends?'

Ben didn't answer. He just continued to look at Lindsey with a grin that was barely visible to the naked eye.

'Anyway…' she got to her feet. 'I need to get back to work.'

'Where is she now?'

'Who?'

'The girl, Lindsey!' Martin exclaimed, like she really didn't know who they were talking about.

'Oh. How would I know?'

'The lads said she landed in your yard and that they saw you taking her inside.'

'You have some nice friends.'

'They're alright lads. Though now they have a bunch of broken bones and Christy has a face like a dog's dinner. Totally uncalled for.'

'Is that right? Well they might have seen her coming in, but did they ever consider the fact that she might have made her way back out?' She thumbed in the direction of the front door. 'Feel free to follow her.'

'Don't be like that, Lindsey.' Martin again.

'Hey, none of my business what you boys get up to in your spare time. But frankly I'm getting tired of being dragged into other people's shit. So one more time for the cheap seats at the back; I'm not harbouring any hookers and if anyone else says that I am, I'm gonna set Eileen on them.'

Martin got to his feet. 'Hey, you need to…'

'Shut the fuck up, Martin.' Ben was still looking at Lindsey and his tone never changed.

'Call out if you want more tea, yeah?' She turned and walked away. Conversation over.

She walked behind the counter and seconds later, Ben got up and left with the other two trailing behind him.

'Watch him, Lindsey,' Eileen muttered after they'd left.

Lindsey nodded. There was no question which one she was referring to.

'I'm serious. He's clashed more than his fair share of heads over the years. Halpin, I think his name is.'

'Any joy in there?' Lindsey nodded towards the kitchen.

Eileen shrugged. 'I just don't believe in all these flourless fucking cakes that all the hippies are eating these days. But that's what we're left with.' She walked through the swing doors, leaving Lindsey alone to wonder about the men who just left.

'Lindsey?' Jimmy asked once more, sounding more impatient.

Lindsey rolled her eyes and exhaled loudly. 'Jimmy. I was walking by myself and they scared me. That's all. Maybe in hindsight they didn't mean me any harm, but as a woman alone, you can't be too careful. I over-reacted. I'm mortified about it. Now can we please let it go?'

He looked sympathetically at her and finally nodded. 'I just want to make sure you're alright, that's all. I can see how they might have scared you. I thought there might have been something up too. I tooted at you, but you never waved. I came alongside, but by the time I got there, everyone was on the ground and they were shouting at me to call the cops. You poor girl. You must have got an awful fright.'

Lindsey nodded and smiled, hoping that that was the end of it. But of course it couldn't be.

'Who's Lenny?'

Lindsey tensed.

'I'm sure that's what you called me.'

She forced herself to look pleasantly confused. 'You know Specsavers check ears now too, Jimmy.'

He nodded, with a look of sheer pity in his eyes. Finally he got up, squeezed her shoulder and left.

'What's he on about? Who gave you An awful fright?' Eileen asked with a curled lip and a raised eyebrow.

'No one. I just had a run in with some Frenchmen on my way home last night.'

'Them fuckers on the trawler?'

'The very ones.'

'Sleazy bastards they are. They've been serenading me in French every day since they got here. The sooner they push off again, the better.'

'Mmm,' Lindsey replied. 'Fancy deep cleaning the kitchen seeing as it's quiet?'

Eileen rolled her eyes and turned towards the back kitchen once more. And that was the end of the day's questions, aside from the many that hurtled around inside Lindsey's head. The loudest of which: When will this nightmare fucking end?

*

That night, after she'd taken it all out on the heavy bag and followed it up with a punishing body strength routine, Lindsey sat sweating and panting on the attic's bare floorboards. She let her mind wander back to a Sunday night, over a year ago. It was during a particularly self-destructive time for her, which was always when Adam Street would reappear in her life. Street was one of the people Lindsey spent the majority of her thirteen years in the army with. But their careers, along with five others, all began to end around the same time.

But that wasn't what she was thinking about. She was thinking about a particular conversation with Street. He'd stayed the night on her couch and they talked until dawn about old times. They laughed about the highs and lows of both of their love lives back in the day. Street justified his womanising ways with the fact that he was a young pup with a six pack, which he had to take full advantage of. Lindsey slapped him on the stomach, which still held its shape at nearly forty, and she asked what was so different now? He shook his head and said, 'I'm just an old dog now, girl.'

Martin's information was skewed of course, like all good stories were. Street wasn't a world champion cage fighter. But he was an all army champion boxer several years running. He'd also trained a couple of Olympic boxers in his shitty looking, but very functional gym, that didn't have a name last time she was there. Nor was he Special Forces, but he was good enough to be. As for working for a man like Patrick; never. Not knowingly at least. But training people who might need to defend themselves; now that had Adam Street written all over it.

*

Over the coming days, Ben, Martin and Charlie were daily visitors to Lindsey's. Never all together, but one of them would come by every day and stay for a couple of hours at least. Martin ordered tea and brought as much drama with him as he could. He warned Lindsey constantly about how much safer she'd be with him around. Ben would order black coffee and sit in near silence at the bar. He, more than any of the others, was getting on her nerves.

She needed to play the game, and play it smart now that she had Lena to think about. That meant keeping everyone on side. Lena was still living upstairs like a prisoner, which was no fun for either of them. She couldn't leave the flat for fear of being seen and Patrick's reach was long, so it wasn't as simple as putting her on a train to Cork. Lindsey had to figure out a way to get her as far away from here as possible. Then maybe she could pack up and do the same.

For now though, the only fresh air Lena got was to sit on a chair in Lindsey's tiny back yard for short periods of time at night. Her days were spent sneaking around the flat as soundlessly as she could, while the evenings saw her awkwardly trying to stay out of Lindsey's way. Truth be told, Lindsey actively tried to avoid her too. She found that they had nothing much to say to each other. Just small talk and regular assurances that everything would be alright. Which of course was bullshit. It wouldn't be alright. But whoever was coming for Lena would have to go through Lindsey first and it did give her some pleasure to picture Patrick's face when she was going all out in the attic night after night. Sometimes, when she dared to admit it, that pleasure bordered on excitement.

She'd also started leaving Frank behind whenever she left the flat. She did this for Lena, so that she'd always have someone there to protect her. Being without him allowed Lindsey's more self-destructive side to rear its head far more often, but that was a sacrifice she was willing to make.

When he could, Frank prevented Lindsey from doing stupid things. Like attacking French fishermen and throwing herself in the tide. She'd also been feeling a strong urge to go in search of the pieces of shit who attacked Lena, and then had the neck to show their faces in her café.

'Apparently,' Mary Kelly was overheard saying to a group of golfers wearing blazers, who clearly couldn't get a table anywhere else in town, 'Jacinta Caldwell's poor young fella was put in hospital. His whole face broken. And three of his friends aren't much better.' She looked around and lowered her voice, but could still be overheard by the McParland sisters seated at the opposite end of the bar. 'They were specially trained Muslims, I heard.' She glanced around again. 'Sent by You Know Who.'

'They must have forgot to pay on their way out.' The loudest of the group cackled. She'd referred to herself as the lady captain three times since she'd begrudgingly taken her seat in Lindsey's.

Lindsey found herself wanting to hurt the golfers as much as Jacinta Caldwell's son and his friends.

She slid to the floor after locking up early that day. Frank came to her immediately and rested his muzzle in her lap.

'What is wrong with people, Frank? When did it become OK to treat another human being like a toilet?'

Frank whined.

'And make jokes about it?'

Silence.

'The human race is completely fucked, isn't it?' She got to her feet and headed for the attic.

Her feelings towards the golfers bothered her. In general, Lindsey took people with a grain of salt. Their opinions might annoy her at times, but everyone was entitled to those. Lindsey believed in living and letting live. But the urge to hurt people seemed ever present these days:

The men who'd thought nothing of gang raping a woman.

The ones who claimed her and others like her, as their property.

The ones who gossiped about it all.

The ones who spoke with practised grandeur and laughed about the exploitation of less fortunate human beings.

Pretty much every fucker in this town.

'Where are all my nice customers gone?' She asked Frank one last question, before letting fly at the heavy bag. It wasn't what she needed to blow off steam tonight. But she couldn't trust herself to leave the flat.

*

Lena, unaware of the private battle that Lindsey fought within her own mind, passed her time by cleaning the flat. When Lindsey walked in the room, she expressed her gratitude again and retreated to the spare bedroom. Once there, she made no sound at all for the rest of the night. It was torture and something had to give.

Lindsey needed to get her out of there safely and so far she could only think of one impossible way to do that. She'd been thinking about it a lot and each time she came to the same conclusion: We're fucked if we get caught.

She also knew that she probably couldn't do it without the help of Danny Chambers. That could be a massive problem in itself.

*

'Here, Lindsey?' Eileen locked the door behind her as she arrived the next morning.

'Morning sunshine.'

'We need to have a chat.' Eileen literally dragged Lindsey out from behind the bar and shoved her into a seat.

'OK, this is dramatic, even for you.'

'No; serious shit is what this is. That bollocks, Ben? He's on That Mad Bastard's payroll.'

'I guessed that much.'

'I never asked you about the rumours because quite frankly, I don't want to fucking know. But if you're doing anything stupid, you need to be careful girl. That's why Ben is making this place his home. He's watching you, not watching out for you.'

'I know that.'

'And you're not worried?'

Lindsey looked at her and gave a half smile. That's about all she was capable of.

'Nah…' Eileen grinned back. 'I didn't think so.'

After a quiet minute, Eileen slapped the table and got to her feet. Her job was done. 'Let's let in the day with all its lunatics then, will we?'

*

Today was Charlie's day to visit her. He sat alone at the table by the window drinking a can of Sprite through a straw. Lindsey watched him for a while before deciding to join him. She couldn't help but worry slightly for the boy. Martin was old enough and stupid enough to take care of himself, but something about Charlie screamed vulnerability.

'You mind?' She gestured towards the empty seat opposite him, holding a coffee in her hand.

Charlie startled and sat up straight. 'Yeah… sit down.'

'I could do with a break. It's been mental here all day.' She smiled.

Mental of course meaning that she had two other customers to deal with that morning.

'You know it took me a while, but I do remember you now. You used to pass by my window all the time. I don't remember you coming in much though.' Up close he looked even younger than sixteen. 'Do you live near here?'

'I used to, kind of.'

'With your parents?'

His face darkened. 'Just me and Mam.' He looked out the window.

'So, do you want to tell me what's really going on here, Charlie?' She suspected that the kid had no idea. Not really. 'Or should we just keep pretending that you're here because you love how I brown the toast just right?'

'I don't know what you mean.'

'Sure you do.'

He shrugged. 'It's time for me to step up now that my dad is gone.'

There was a long pause, which Lindsey didn't interrupt.

'He's probably up in Dublin for work or somewhere. Or maybe England. He has a sister over there.'

'How long have you been looking for him?'

'I've always been looking for him.'

Poor kid. 'So you're looking after your mam in the meantime?'

He nodded.

'Why are you involved with these guys then?' She knew the answer of course, because she'd known a lot of kids like Charlie. He was desperate for someone to look up to; a father figure as they say, and Ben was filling that gap for now.

She also knew that Ben didn't have Charlie's best interests at heart.

He looked out the window again.

She didn't push him. Instead she sat watching him in silence until he finally spoke again.

'Ben looks after us.'

'Who?'

'All of us.'

'In return for what?'

He shrugged again. 'Not much.'

'Did he tell you to come here?'

He nodded.

'Well I'm glad you do. Is he paying you?'

He looked at her surprised, then nodded.

She smiled at him. 'You know you can come here without him having to tell you to, yeah?'

'OK,' he mumbled, then seemed slightly terrified as he looked towards the door.

Lindsey turned around to see Patrick standing just inside. This time he was alone and looked as charming as ever in his tailored grey suit. It was just a tad too shiny for the real world, just like his smile.

She got to her feet and turned to face him. 'Welcome back.' She smiled politely.

'Shukran.'

'Have a seat, let's have a cuppa?'

'I'd rather not, Lindsey. You know it's time that I come clean; I can't abide what passes for tea in this country.'

If he wasn't such an unimaginable bastard, Lindsey might have liked Patrick. Or at least the way he tried to act so much better than he was. 'How about some shai then?' Again she smiled like she was talking to an old friend.

'My associates are under the impression that you lie.'

'I'm sorry to hear that. Please…' she gestured towards a table, 'have a seat? Let me make you that shai and we can talk properly.'

The last thing she wanted was to prolong his visit, but there was a game she needed to play. And she needed to play it smart.

He raised his eyebrows and nodded as he took a seat. The only other person in the café was Charlie, who was doing a terrible job at playing the part of an innocent customer. Even though that's exactly what he was, whether he realised it or not. Chances are, Patrick had no idea who Charlie was. Ben worked for him. Charlie did what Ben told him to do, for pocket money.

But then who knows? Patrick made it his business to know people.

Eileen was in the back kitchen cleaning when Lindsey barged through the swing doors to find Frank eating a slice of frozen bread off the floor. She immediately wrestled it from his jaws.

'Eileen, please don't leave this shit out where he can get at it. You know he'll eat anything and I need him healthy.'

Frank grudgingly gave up and walked off, but he'd look for another slice as soon as Lindsey left.

'What's up your arse?'

'Nothing.'

Lindsey filled a pot with water and placed it on the stove. She rooted out some cardamom pods and began crushing them.

'I just happen to respect my dog's digestive health more than he does.'

'Yeah, whatever. So what the fuck is that?'

'Cardamom.'

'Carda-who?'

'It's for tea.'

Eileen picked up the giant box of Barry's tea bags. 'These are for tea? Girl are you that bad around a fucking kitchen that you can't make a pot of tea?'

'It's not that kind of tea,' Lindsey mumbled.

She dropped the crushed pods into the water and waited for it to boil. She pulled a large jar of loose tea from the back of the cupboard and scooped two spoons into a tea pot and then added the spiced water. Lindsey had developed a taste for Arabic tea during her first tour overseas, in Lebanon. Lebanese people were renowned for their hospitality. No matter how much artillery had fallen in their vicinity the night before, you would always be offered a glass of shai when you entered their shop. Or in some cases, their homes. A local woman there even taught her how to make it and because of her, Lindsey knew that it needed ten minutes to brew during which time she went upstairs in search of some of the small glasses that it was traditionally served in. She'd brought fifteen of these glasses home with her but had only ever used one.

Until now that is. As she entered her sitting room cum kitchen, Lena, who had been standing over the sink eating some bread, immediately walked to the corner of the room and proceeded to look uncomfortable.

'Lena, are you OK?'

'Of course. Thank you, Lindsey.'

'You know you don't have to stay out of my way whenever I come in and please eat something more substantial than bread. And now I'm actually begging you; please stop saying thank you.'

'This is your home and I am a stranger to you. I don't want to disrupt your life any more than I have already.'

Lindsey half smiled. 'I was born disrupted, Lena. You, on the other hand… please, just make yourself at home for as long as you're here. We'll figure it all out soon, OK?'

She didn't want to tell her that Patrick was downstairs. First she wanted to hear what he had to say. She found the glasses and turned to leave.

'I have some books in a box under my bed if you get bored.' She smiled as reassuringly as she could at the woman before leaving her in peace.

Downstairs Lindsey placed thirteen of the glasses in a spare cupboard and then took two of Eileen's flourless buns off the cooling tray. She placed one on a plate and wrapped one in tinfoil. She checked her watch.

Three minutes left for the tea.

'The tea will be just a few minutes more.' She smiled at Patrick, who was busy examining his phone.

She brought the wrapped cake to Charlie, who looked extremely uncomfortable. 'Here you go, Charlie. You ordered that to go, yeah?' She looked pointedly at him.

He glanced nervously from her to Patrick. He nodded, but he didn't make a move to leave. Instead he took the cake and looked out the window, ignoring Lindsey's glare. In the end she had no choice but to walk away and leave him there. She didn't want to draw attention to Charlie, nor did she want details of the man's visit to get back to Ben and that imbecile, Martin. Though Ben at least would probably know all about it, depending on how close he actually was to Patrick.

Back in the kitchen she filled two of the little glasses with shai and loaded them onto a tray, along with some sugar cubes. Then she went to sit with Patrick, a man she loathed.

Still, she smiled as she placed a glass in front of him and sat down opposite.

He dropped three lumps of sugar into his glass. Lindsey took two and then they both stirred in silence for what felt like an age, before he finally took a sip. 'You surprise me with your shai.'

She smiled again as hatred bubbled inside her.

'Irish tea is not tea. It is piss.'

Yet he ordered and drank it every time he came here.

'It all comes down to what we're used to, I suppose.'

'Yet you make and drink shai?'

'Sometimes. But I'm in the tea business.' She gestured to her surroundings. 'And I try to give my patrons what they like.'

He bowed his head in acknowledgement. 'It seems I have found this Irish hospitality that so far I have only heard about.'

He was putting on a great show. In fact, he was playing the part of an upper-class gentleman so well that Lindsey was just about ready to give him a standing ovation. Followed by a baseball bat to the side of the head. But she continued to smile at him.

'Where is she, I wonder? My Lena. You say she left. But if so then it would stand to reason that we would have found her by now, no?'

Lindsey shrugged. 'Depends. If she went to the city, then…'

'You don't understand.' He leaned forward, his hands clasped together on the table. 'I have a vast family. Lena is a part of that. So the rest of my family would make sure that she was returned safely no matter where she went. There is nowhere my family could not find her. Do you understand?'

'I do.' She nodded, like she hadn't noticed the threat. 'I really hope you find her.'

'Indeed. You live alone, no? You have no husband. But then women have no need of husbands anymore, am I right?' He was smiling now. 'Not when you can have a lifetime of fun, no?' He wagged his finger at her then, 'Little respect… but lots of fun. Have you encountered death before?'

She could almost hear Charlie's heart pounding behind her and she measured her words before speaking. 'I'd safely say, we all have. The world is a changed place, isn't it?' She didn't care to point out that the pot was talking to the wrong kettle about lifestyle choices.

'Your family?'

Lindsey shook her head. 'None to speak of.'

'That is sad, no?'

She shrugged.

'I am not an unreasonable man, Lindsey. That is why I am here alone this time. I want to give you the opportunity to be truthful. Hector is such a sceptical fellow.'

'And you don't think I have been truthful?'

'I think you are hiding something. I think you know where my Lena is. But what you need to know is that you don't interfere with family matters. You will not help yourself and you will not help Lena.'

'I'll remember that. But I own a café, Patrick. I bake cakes and make sandwiches. I mind my own business and I do my best to stay out of everyone else's. What I can say is that I did my best for that girl. Maybe if those protecting her had done the same then we wouldn't be having this conversation.'

A loaded silence followed. When it came to people giving a little in return, it seemed Patrick was out of practise. He didn't have an immediate response.

She filled the void before he had too much time to think about it. 'Anyway, I haven't seen her since. The next day I went back to making tea and baking cakes. Flourless for now, I'm afraid. My delivery man seems to have done a bunk.' She gestured towards his untouched plate. 'But I'm sure if she needed somewhere to stay, she'd go to someone she knows. And trusts.'

Patrick got to his feet. He stood over her, looking down for a moment.

'It is foolish to invite trouble into your home.'

'I don't.'

He smiled and left. She watched him go and only when he was out of sight did she mutter Fuck, under her breath.

Chapter 5

'You alright, Charlie?' Once she'd regained her composure, Lindsey placed another can of lemonade in front of the boy and sat down opposite him.

He nodded silently.

'Good.'

'Why weren't you afraid?'

'Of what?'

'Of that fucking nutter. He's coming back for you, you know that?'

'Nah he's not.' She smiled, as if such an idea was preposterous.

Charlie didn't reply.

'So is that what you're gonna tell Ben when he asks about your day; that you think Patrick's coming for me? I promise you, he's not,' she lied.

He shrugged. 'Ben wants to protect you.'

'Why would he want to do that? He doesn't know me.'

'He just does. Women can't defend themselves against the likes of him.'

She sat forward and looked him in the eye, hiding the pity that she felt for him. 'You know I admire you. You're switched on, Charlie.' She tapped the side of her head. 'So let me ask you this; your friend, Ben… you really think he cares about me? Or might there be another reason why he sends you here?'

Charlie was looking at her now and she could see that he was mulling over her words. 'I care about you.'

'I care about you too.' And she did. The boy was so vulnerable, she couldn't help it.

'No, I mean… when you first opened here, you used to give my mother food at the end of the day.' His face flushed red. 'But don't tell anyone that. She used to come in here. I always waited outside.'

Lindsey sat back and looked a little harder at him. 'Your mother is Fiona?'

Fiona James was the homeless woman who came into the café on the first day it opened. She asked for a drink of water. With no other customers at the time, Lindsey chatted to her for a while and then brought her some tea and a sandwich. She took one bite and wrapped the rest to take away with her. For her son.

From that day up until about a month ago, she came by every evening at closing time, as instructed by Lindsey. She took away whatever leftovers were there. This meant that Charlie was in fact only fifteen years old. Lindsey had heard all about him from Fiona, who had him when she was only that age herself.

He nodded.

'I haven't seen her in a while. How is she?'

He shrugged again.

'Where's she staying?'

'She got a spot in a place for women and children in Cork.'

'And you?'

'I stay with Ben sometimes. I'm no child.'

'I can see that. Is he related to you?'

'No, but he's a cop.' He said this like it meant something. 'It's an outreach thing.'

Before he could say anymore, the McParland sisters shuffled through the door. They stopped briefly to look at Lindsey and Charlie before deciding that there was nothing of interest there. They continued to their usual spot at the back of the café, near the prep area. Eileen would look after them. But that left Lindsey with Mary Kelly who scuttled in behind the sisters. She looked like she might burst if she didn't vent whatever gossip was fresh on her mind.

Lindsey got to her feet. 'Hey Charlie, you know you can come here anytime you need to, yeah? Day or night.'

'Eh… OK.'

'And Charlie? Know what you're getting into and exactly whose battles you're fighting, OK? Some things just aren't worth the money, cop or no cop.' She smiled, like she was scolding him playfully, but she hoped that her words would reach home.

'Lindsey?' Mary's forced and dramatic whisper halted Lindsey on her way back to the counter.

'What can I get you, Mary?'

'Eileen?… Eileen!'

'Keep your hair on woman, I'm coming,' Eileen called, just as loudly from behind the counter.

'Yeah and so is Christmas,' Mary retorted. 'Bring me tea and a chicken sandwich. Today if possible!' Then she lowered her voice dramatically and returned her attention to Lindsey. 'I'm after hearing something now that I can't unhear.'

More drama. Outstanding.

'Yeah?' Lindsey continued behind the bar, busying herself with making the tea.

'My Brian came home last night…'

'Finally.'

'Yeah, but wait. He says that he was walking along town a couple of days ago, dead late; like three in the morning and he happened to be passing the old Hardware House.'

'Uh huh.' Mary really was clueless about her son.

She lowered her voice. 'He said that he saw a van pull up onto the footpath, right outside the door.' She looked around again. 'There was a small child carried... carried inside. I mean you hear about all sorts going on in there. But grown women are one thing. They can make up their own minds. But children, Lindsey. Children!'

Lindsey stomach turned, but she didn't give Mary the reaction that she was hoping for. After all, Brian wasn't a reliable witness to anything. 'And did you go to the cops, Mary?'

Mary looked at her, aghast. 'Are you mad? And blab about That Mad Bastard? Sure I'd be as good as dead myself. Or worse, he'd take it out on my Brian for telling. Anyway there'd be no point. They were foreigners that were carrying the child, not Cobh lads. Our own lads wouldn't get involved with the likes of that.'

Of course not. Lindsey remained silent and sceptical.

'Now I'm not racist or anything, but there needs to be a system for tracking these foreigners. They can't be left to wander all over the country, doing whatever they like and then disappearing afterwards. They all hide each other, see. That's why the cops can never do anything about any of them.'

Lindsey could have smacked Mary. But she didn't.

'He was a foreign child too by all accounts.'

By all accounts was really just one account. That of her drunken son who needed a story to distract his mother from the fact that he'd fucked off on a bender and forgot about his own son. Again.

Still, it was a harrowing thought, and Lindsey didn't like that it had been put in her head. She had enough problems of her own without worrying about what was probably a bullshit story, conjured up by an idiot.

'Hey, Lindsey?' Mary leaned across the bar and grabbed a hold of her arm. 'They didn't hurt you, did they? Those dirty bastards? I would have stayed only I had Adrian, and...'

'They didn't hurt me, Mary. It was a mix up, that's all. Best not to say any more about it, yeah?'

'Of course. I know how to keep myself to myself,' she fibbed in that conspiratorial tone that screamed, I know how to do no such a thing.

'I'll go check on your lunch.'

'Tell her to make sure the chicken is cooked this time. She nearly bloody killed me the last time,' Mary called after her.

Lindsey said nothing, knowing that Eileen would have a comeback.

She didn't have long to wait.

'Tell her the deli meat version of chicken is perfect for her delicate fucking palate. And tell her as well, not to worry if she gets a slight taste of rat poison in today's delightful concoction. It's just a new butter I'm trying.'

'Tinker,' Mary called out.

'Battleaxe,' Eileen responded.

Eileen and Mary had a bit of a love/hate relationship. They drove each other nuts and the majority of their conversations were loaded with insults. But when Eileen missed work, Mary was the first to ask where she was. Likewise, Eileen looked just as relieved to see Mary today, her first day back since Patrick and his henchman scared them out Lindsey's door. Not that either of them would ever admit that they slightly cared for each other. A bigoted gossip hound and a foul-mouthed traveller were the last form of entertainment in Lindsey's café.

Minutes later the place filled up with teenagers; three boys and a girl, all of whom Lindsey knew. They were her regulars and it was good to see them. They never wanted anything by way of conversation from her. She liked them for that alone. They were as boisterous as ever, sure in their naivety that nothing in the world would never really harm them. It bothered her slightly though that, aside from the odd glance and some hushed conversation, they never even acknowledged poor Charlie. He was the same age as them and suddenly looked like the loneliest kid in the world. By the time Lindsey brought the two cans of Coke to the table of four, Charlie was gone.

*

'Lena, you really don't have to clean my house,' Lindsey spoke as she tried to placate Frank, who was slobbering all over her. She'd hardly seen him all day and she missed him as much as he missed her.

'It is the least that I can do,' Lena replied, still cleaning. 'You really need to take him with you downstairs. He just cries all day when you're not here. He's a very upset dog.'

Lindsey smiled and scratched his ears. 'Yeah, I know.'

The two women still knew nothing about each other, but it was clear that Lena had paid her dues. And probably those of others as well. Now she tended to stay in the spare room until Lindsey left in the morning, then retreated back there when she came back up in the evenings. The only time she talked was to reply politely to whatever Lindsey said to her. Like now.

'I'll give you your privacy.' She nodded and once again headed for the door.

'You don't have to.' Lindsey called after her. But Lena was gone.

Lindsey rolled her eyes and went to get a beer from the fridge. She didn't have any. She slammed the fridge door shut and paced the small room in frustration. Frank mirrored her feelings as he paced alongside her. She thought about the heavy bag upstairs and the gloves on the floor beneath it, but that wasn't what she needed tonight. She wasn't quite sure what she needed, but she found herself thinking about Street suddenly and what he might be working on.

It had been over a year since she'd seen or spoken to him. Not that that would make any difference when they saw each other again. With army friends, it didn't matter how much time passed between conversations; they always picked up exactly where they left off. That's just the way it was. She also thought about Damo, Murph, Gordon, and

Wesley. And of course, Lenny. She always thought about them at times like this. They'd come and gone from each other's lives over the past few years, but were always there or thereabouts in the background. Except for Lenny. Lenny never really moved to the background. He was with her every single day and would be for the rest of her life. It wasn't as bad as it had been, but she still saw him every now and then. Or at least, she imagined she did; walking in the street, driving past in a car, or she'd hear him laughing out loud, but when she'd turn to see him, of course he wasn't there. Lenny was dead and the image of his head being ripped apart was one that would never leave her. It was of course the main reason why Lindsey didn't sleep. But all that was a long time ago now, and she continued to pay her penance. It seemed a further payment was due tonight.

Street was still paying too, but somehow he always did it better than her. He did it without ever losing his shit. A talent that she simply didn't possess. If he were here now, he'd know exactly what her next move should be.

'I need air,' she mumbled to Frank.

She went to her room to change. Lindsey was half way between thirty and forty, and as she stood in her underwear and glanced at the mirror, she didn't notice the physique that any twenty-year-old MMA fighter would be proud of. All she saw were the angry scars running across her chest and left shoulder and down along her arm. Scars that once sent her into a black hole whenever she looked at them. Nowadays she pretended to embrace them. They're a symbol of all you've survived, was the lecture she gave herself when she felt like she did tonight. She'd stand there and make herself look at them while she remembered all of the things that failed to kill her:

The Middle East.

The ambush.

The loss of her friend.

The damage that had been done to some of the best people she'd ever known. Because of her.

The PTSD.

She'd come within an inch of ending her own life once before. And she'd often put herself in situations that dared other people to end it for her. She still did that sometimes, despite her efforts to stop. But she'd survived. She'd done damn well to make it this far, so anything else was a bonus really.

Tonight she shrouded her lean, muscular frame in a man-sized black hoodie and tracksuit pants. On her head, a black skip cap held in her bundled hair. She needed air, not attention but just in case, she wrapped her new leather belt around her waist, under her hoodie. She tucked her baton into her sock, covering it with her pants before leaving the flat with an eternally grateful Frank, who needed this as much as she did.

Rather than going right and through the town, Lindsey opted to go left, along Harbour Row in a slightly quieter direction. She broke into a run and seconds later, she was sprinting past the long row of buildings similar to her own. Each was painted a bright but different garish colour and it was these colours that made Cobh as picturesque from the water as it was from land. Most had shop fronts on the ground floor with flats upstairs, except for the McParland sisters who lived five doors up from Lindsey and apparently they'd always occupied their entire house. At the end of the row was East Hill. A mammoth running task, and just what she needed. She tore into it and before long her muscles and lungs burned and she could feel at least some frustration leaving her body. There was a Y-junction half way up the hill where she sometimes stopped for a minute to take in the breathtaking view. But not tonight. Frank wouldn't let her. He was working her hard and as they kept going, up, up, and up, until the road finally levelled out, she wondered if another human being could ever know exactly what she needed, when she needed it, like he did.

They ran for over an hour and only during that time did she begin to feel like her old self again. Once away from the town, she stuck to the quieter country roads, enjoying the isolation more whenever she felt the baton rub against her bare leg. Frank would defend her until his dying breath of course. But she'd never let him. Either way, she wouldn't be caught off guard again.

*

As it turned out, it wouldn't be a member of Patrick's fan club who'd catch Lindsey off guard, but Grace McParland. Dressed in an ancient black dress and looking like something from a gothic horror film, she walked through Lindsey's door at three minutes past eight the following morning. She was as pale as a sheet, but eerily calm as she walked towards the bar. She hugged an ancient laptop close to her chest.

'Morning, Grace.' Lindsey smiled, but immediately sensed that something was wrong. 'Where's Evelyn?'

Grace placed the laptop on the bar and the bundled-up charger on top of it.

'What's that?'

'What does it look like?' She turned to leave. 'The answer is Raymond… my Raymond.'

'Grace…?'

'I'm going to be with my sister.' She walked towards the door as straight backed as she'd arrived.

Before she left she turned and offered a few more words to Lindsey. 'I know you, Lindsey. I have for quite a while. We both have. So I know you'll understand this better than anyone.'

When she did leave, she pulled the door closed so that Lindsey had to go find the keys again to open it. Her bad feeling intensified with each second that passed.

Eileen was about to slip her key in the lock as Lindsey swung open the door again.

'Did you see which way Grace went?'

'That way,' she thumbed in the direction of town. 'Why? What did the old biddy do now?' Eileen shoved past her and went inside.

Lindsey stepped out onto the street and sure enough, there was Grace, walking with purpose towards town.

'Grace?'

She didn't turn around.

'Are you sure you're alright?' Lindsey asked anyway. Her gut was telling her that something was up; that she should go after her.

But Grace waved her off without turning around. Lindsey shook her head and went back inside.

As she got behind the prep area, she thought she heard Grace's voice, shouting in the street. But that couldn't be right. Grace McParland did not shout in the street.

'Tell everyone...' the voice said, loudly, 'Patrick Adebayo sells children. He was seen kidnapping one...' she roared. 'Tell everyone, he sells children. He sells...' the voice stopped as abruptly as it started.

Lindsey hurried through the café and out onto the street. By the time she got there, Grace was being manhandled outside Patrick's front door. One of the interchangeable goons had a hand across her mouth and was pulling her around like a rag doll.

Without thinking, Lindsey charged him. Her two feet left the ground as she drove her shoulder into his ribcage. He let go of Grace who stumbled and eventually fell over on the footpath. The goon crashed to the ground with Lindsey on top of him. There was an umph as the wind temporarily left his body.

Before he had a chance to recover himself, Lindsey jumped to her feet and took a fighting stance, ready for whatever he came with.

'Lindsey, no. Stop it...' Grace pleaded with her.

The man, who she hadn't seen before looked up at her, shocked momentarily. Then his face hardened again and he got quickly to his feet. He was about her age and strong looking. She'd taken him by surprise, but from here on he'd have the upper hand physically. He was about to come at her when Hector stepped out and came between them. He balled his fists around his friend's T-shirt and without uttering a word, he ordered the man back inside, just as Ben showed up in uniform.

'What's going on here?' he asked, his tone official. There was a female cop with him.

Lindsey didn't answer. Partly because she had no fucking idea what was going on here.

'Nothing, officer,' Hector answered with a smile. 'The old lady had a fall. Lindsey and James were trying to help her up, but she's having difficulties.'

Grace, for her part, looked frailer and more miserable than ever. Lindsey stooped to help her, but she was unable to stand. 'Why did you have to butt in?'

Her voice was low and Lindsey wasn't sure she heard her correctly. So she asked, 'What?'

'Why couldn't you just mind your business?' Her words were barely audible, but were unmistakable this time.

'There's an ambulance on the way.' Ben's partner knelt beside Lindsey as she spoke kindly to Grace. 'You'll be alright, Ms McParland. I'm so sorry about your sister.'

Lindsey looked sharply at the woman beside her. Evelyn? What the hell was going on?

'You wanna tell me what happened here?' She turned to Lindsey.

'I'll take it from here,' Ben said, offering Lindsey a hand up.

'I'll wait with Grace until the ambulance comes.' Lindsey didn't know Ben's partner and so she didn't trust her enough to leave Grace on Patrick's doorstep. Not after she'd just accused him of selling children.

'You don't seem to understand, Ms Ryan. You just assaulted a man.'

Hector laughed. 'Officer, please. That was a misunderstanding.

There was no assault. James won't be pressing charges.'

Ben smiled back. 'Never the less, Lindsey…' he held his hand towards her again. 'You need to come to the station.'

'That's alright, Halpin,' his partner replied, her tone slightly clipped. 'I'll bring her back with me.'

Lindsey looked at the woman beside her again. It didn't take long for her to realise that she didn't like Ben. Perhaps Lindsey could trust her after all.

Before he had a chance to answer, sirens were heard making their way towards them. Minutes later, Grace was in the hands of two kind and capable paramedics. She was crying and looked utterly defeated. Like being saved was the last thing she wanted.

As the ambulance pulled away, Ben opened the back door of the squad car and motioned Lindsey inside. Frank followed her without waiting for an invitation.

'The dog can't come,' Ben said.

'Then I don't come.' Lindsey replied. 'Unless I'm under arrest for something. Am I under arrest?'

'Of course not,' he replied with a smile. 'We just need to have a chat. Frank can come.'

At the station, Lindsey was led to a small but airy interview room. It had a window looking right out at the harbour. The Chambers' caravans were also clearly visible. She could see Seamus sitting on the roof of one. She couldn't see a weapon. But that didn't mean there wasn't one.

'So, what happened this morning, Lindsey?' Ben asked, as he gestured for her to take a seat.

He and his partner sat across from her. Frank sat straight backed by her side as always.

'What happened to Evelyn McParland?'

Ben grinned. 'Right then. Why don't you ask the questions?'

Lindsey stayed quiet, waiting. It was his partner who answered.

'I'm Garda Helen McCall, Lindsey. We appreciate you coming in. The McParland's were broken into last night. The house was ransacked and like a lot of elderly people, they didn't believe in banks. The sisters were inside at the time and both women were tied to chairs in the front room. Evelyn suffered a suspected heart attack. She was dead before they left the house.'

Lindsey's heart sank. Whatever opinions people held on the sisters, they were a pair of frail old ladies, who wanted nothing more than to be left alone. She of all people could relate to that and she was filled with the urge to find out who'd done it and go return the favour.

'Who was it?'

'We don't know.' Ben answered before his partner had a chance to. He threw her a glance that said she was talking too much.

Frank growled quietly, and Lindsey scratched his ear to quieten him.

'There's a gang who've been targeting the elderly between Midleton, Cobh, Glanmire, and Cork city,' Helen replied and Lindsey could tell that she was doing so partly just to annoy him. She was growing to like Helen McCall.

'You know who they are?'

'It's a joint effort, but we're closing in on them.'

'Now would you mind telling us what happened this morning?' Ben interjected, sounding mildly irritated by the two women in the room.

'Grace came in this morning looking shook. She said something about going to be with her sister, and then a few minutes later I heard her shouting in the street that Patrick was selling children. So what are you going to do about that allegation? And why am I here while that piece of shit and his minions sit back and count their money?'

'Patrick Adebayo does not deal in children. We can't prove that he's anything other than a legitimate business man.'

'So all three floors of the old Hardware House are taken up with dry-cleaning?'

'Mr Adebayo owns several businesses, Lindsey. The laundrette is just one. He also owns a cleaning service; you know, for homes, offices etcetera. He has a computer repair shop and a phone shop, both in Cork city. He provides accommodation for his staff, some of which is over the laundrette. That's what we know.'

Lindsey was looking at him like he'd lost the plot.

'We have no proof of anything else,' his partner added.

She sounded almost as annoyed about that as Lindsey was. But Patrick didn't get to where he was by being stupid. He got there by buying off the right people and at least one of them happened to be sitting right in front of her.

'And to answer your other question, you're here because a call came in to say you launched a seemingly unprovoked attack on a man in the street. Obviously the caller failed to see Grace McParland lying on the ground. I'll be making it my business to pay a visit to the man who put her there.' Garda McCall made a point of not looking at Ben. 'In the meantime, Lindsey, you're free to go. And if there's anything you need, give me a call.'

The conversation was over. Or at least, Lindsey's involvement in it was. But she imagined Garda McCall getting an absolute earful once she'd left because Ben was fuming.

Chapter 6

It was Helen who walked her out of the station and Lindsey took the opportunity to suss her out.

'You really believe Patrick is accommodating his staff above the dry cleaners?'

'Course not.' Helen blew out a long breath, as if she'd wanted to get out of that room as badly as Lindsey did. 'We're fighting a losing battle here, Lindsey. Every time we get something on him, the kybosh gets put on it. Evidence goes missing, witnesses can't be located, warrants don't get issued on time, you name it.'

'And what about the possibility that he's dealing in kids?'

'That's not new either. But again, anytime we've managed to get into one of his places, it's been clean. And why wouldn't it be? He gets enough notice that we're coming, for fuck sake.'

Helen was frustrated and Lindsey couldn't blame her.

'How'd you get that?' She gestured towards the yellowing bruise across Helen's cheek.

'Oh, it's all fun and games around here, girl.'

'I can image. Mind yourself, yeah?'

'You too.' Helen turned and as she jogged up the steps to go back inside, she said, 'I like your dog by the way. He seems like a good judge of character.'

Lindsey nodded in response, and then she and Frank headed

home. There was nothing else they could do.

*

'Did you hear?' Eileen was leaning against the bar crying when Lindsey walked in.

She closed the door behind her. There were no customers in, and it was a day to keep it that way.

'Evelyn McParland is dead.'

'I heard.'

'Where's Grace? Is she alright?'

'They took her to the hospital.'

'What was she up to, drawing That Mad Bastard out like that?'

'I think she figured it was the fastest way to get herself killed.'

Eileen raised her eyebrows, 'Can't fault her planning then.'

'Didn't work though, did it?'

'Will she top herself do you think? I mean like, do we need to start checking up on her at home or something? I'll tell ya now, I don't think I have that in me. I could do without finding someone like that.'

'Suicide isn't as easy as it looks, Eileen. Why else would she want someone as brutal as Patrick Adebayo or Hector to do it for her?'

Eileen choked on her tears for a minute before pulling herself together and muttering, 'Good then,' with a solemn nod of the head.

'Go on home.' Lindsey pulled a bottle of Powers whiskey out from under the bar. She half-filled a mug and took a body shuddering gulp.

'I can stay.'

Lindsey shook her head. 'Go. You have protection?'

'Why are you worried about me all of a sudden?'

After Seán Buckley, Lindsey worried about anyone associated with her.

When her sarcastic question went unanswered, Eileen pulled up her T-shirt and tugged on her brown leather belt. Just like Lindsey's. Of course she had protection.

'I'll see you in the morning?'

Lindsey nodded and walked Eileen to the door, then closed and locked it behind her. She stood with her forehead pressed to the wood for a few minutes before making her way back to the bar.

'One for the road,' she said to no one, as she topped up her mug again.

As she took a sip, her eyes drifted towards the decrepit laptop sitting on the shelf beside the coffee machine. She picked it up, along with the bottle of Powers, and brought them both to the nearest table. When she opened the machine it was of course, dead. She plugged it in and then waited an eternity for it to boot up. Enough time to top up once more.

'What's so important on here, Frankie?' she mumbled. 'Why was this the last thing she thought about before throwing herself to the wolves, eh?'

When it finally came to life, Lindsey was greeted with a sepia toned image of a toothless, grinning baby wearing a baggy white dress with a frilly collar. And a password request.

The answer is Raymond… my Raymond. Lindsey could only assume that the baby smiling back at her was Raymond. Grace's son before he was probably removed from her care by the nuns at the Magdalene Laundry.

Lindsey typed the word Raymond, and seconds later, Grace's desktop appeared before her. There wasn't much on it, bar shortcuts to some out-of-date software and several folders. One was titled Pictures, while the others were titled with people's names. She recognised some, but there were more that she didn't. Naturally enough, her attention was drawn to the folder entitled, Lindsey Ryan. This was the only one she clicked on.

Inside were three documents. The first was a newspaper article from the Irish Independent with a bold headline Irish Soldier Killed and Another Injured in Golan Heights Ambush.

'Grace, you dark horse.'

Lindsey glanced over the four-year-old article outlining the day that changed her life. The reporter explained in vivid and dramatic detail how Section One, under the leadership of Sergeant Adam Street from Cork, was ambushed as they patrolled a section of road close to the Syrian border. He colourfully depicted the children who were playing on the road and even the little girl who accidently triggered the IED '...which almost killed Cork woman, Lindsey Ryan, leaving her severely scarred, while Private Leonard Jones, also from Cork, was caught off guard by a sniper as he administered first aid to Corporal Ryan...'

She closed the article and clicked open the next document, also from the Irish Independent. This time the story, pretty much a repeat of the previous one, was accompanied by a photograph of Lindsey, Adam, Damo, Wesley, Gordon, Murph, and Lenny's mother, Carol, all looking suitably miserable. Lindsey also looked particularly wasted, as did Murph. They were popping pills like smarties back then.

This time the headline read, Distinguished Service Medal finally awarded posthumously to the family of Private Leonard Jones from Cork, following a petition by fellow members of the defence forces.

Lindsey declined to read on and instead clicked into the third and final document in the Lindsey Ryan folder. Thankfully there were no more newspaper articles. Instead, there was a letter from Grace McParland to Lindsey and it was time stamped at seven sixteen that morning.

Lindsey,

It might surprise you to learn that since you moved in here (without ever really explaining yourself – good for you) you've managed to become someone that my sister and I could almost admire. But as you've probably seen, we know quite a bit about you. Actually, we know a bit about everyone. That's the benefit of having people think you're old and decrepit. They tend not to acknowledge your presence while they spill their guts. But we had to actively search to find anything on you. So I feel I should at least come clean about that and let you know something about us in return. It might help you understand what I've done and what I'm asking of you. Not that there's much to know about us. We lived very boring lives really. But we grew up in an Ireland that was very different to the Ireland that you grew up in. When we were young girls, our lives were dictated by the church. They decided who got to be happy and who didn't. Who was human and who wasn't. In a way, it wasn't much different to the way things still are today in other parts of the world. All these wars in the name of religion. Except back then, most of the violence and misery happened behind closed doors and just about everyone had a blind eye.

When I was seventeen years old, I fell in love with a man called Declan Kelly. He was eleven years older than me and being the stupid girl that I was, I thought that he might love me too. Well, he did; for about seven painful minutes and those few minutes took me from being a hairdresser's apprentice with her whole life ahead of her, to a pregnant slave in a laundry.

My prison was run by the same church who said that Declan's life should continue as normal, but I needed to be locked away like an animal; a disgrace to my family. By the time Raymond was born, Evelyn was the only person in this world still speaking to me. She stood by my side back then and has been there ever since. As far as I know, my son went to live with a family in America, for a good price I'd imagine. His name isn't Raymond Kelly anymore either. It never was I suppose. It was a lifetime ago true, but you might be able to understand how my sister and I lost interest in the human race right around the time that one of us ceased to be seen as human.

Now look around you. The whole world is at each other's

throats; all killing each other in the name of one God or another. A person's worth is defined by what they believe, what they look like or even who they love. You saw it all for yourself, first-hand, Lindsey. You put your life on the line, standing up for things that the likes of me and Evelyn could only dream about. If only women had had courage like that when we were young. I can only imagine the life we might have had!

You've led everyone to believe that you're no more than a tea lady. You let no one see your true colours. Except of course for the down and out – the homeless, the hungry, the wayward teens and the lonely and contrary old women. We saw it. Why do you think we looked you up?

I'm rambling a bit now, but my point is that nothing has changed. Except that now, all the violence and misery is out in the open. People only have to look at their phones and there it is. Not only that, but it's happening right in our faces. Seven doors up from my house, two doors up from yours. Women being enslaved, and it seems everyone still has at least one blind eye. Convincing themselves that everyone inside that building actually chooses to be there. The do-gooders go on about how terrible it all is, people having to flee their homes only to find themselves in a different level of hell. People take to the streets, or to their keyboards and protest about life being cheap and about people being bought and sold like cattle. But at the end of the day, no one does a good God damn thing about any of it and I've had enough. Enough of all this hatred. My sister was killed for a measly one thousand, two hundred and twenty-seven Euro. That's what life is worth these days. So I've decided to check out. I'm done.

But before I go, I'm going to take one small leaf out of your book. I'm going to stand up, just like Evelyn and I always talked about. My blind eye is seeing more clearly than it ever has. That man exists for no reason other than to prey upon vulnerable girls, like I once was. I'm going to say out loud what everyone else whispers and in return, he'll give me exactly what I want.

I've written so much more than I planned to, but this wasn't meant to be a sob story. This was meant to be a request. If I fail and there really are children in there now too, please Lindsey; help them. I don't know anyone more capable than you.

Goodbye Lindsey.

Grace & Evelyn McParland

P.S. Look after Frank. He's a good dog.

P.P.S. Tell Eileen, don't ever settle down and most importantly, don't ever settle! That's always a worry with traveller women. Some of them don't know their worth. (And tell her to put more cinnamon in her apple tarts. They're nice. But they could be nicer and you can tell her I said that.)

*

Lindsey's stomach was bunched in a knot as she reread the words that surprised her even more the second time.

Dark fucking horses indeed.

It had been at the back of her mind since she'd heard it… what if it was true? What if there was a child in there?

Now it seemed that Grace had called her out on it.

Lindsey dropped her head onto the table and tapped her forehead on it repeatedly until Frank finally shoved himself awkwardly across her lap to stop her. She pulled back and used both hands to scratch his ears, letting him know that he didn't have to worry just now. But she did ask, 'What the hell am I supposed to do with this, Frankie?'

Chapter 7

'Lindsey...' Lena got to her feet as Lindsey entered her sitting room. 'I'll give you your privacy.'

'We need to talk,' Lindsey put her hand up to stop her.

'OK.'

'How long have you been with Patrick?'

Her face dropped.

'Lena, I know this is the last thing you want to talk about and I'm sorry that I'm asking you to. But it's important.'

'About four years.' She sat back down and lowered her eyes to the floor. 'But not all here. Most in Cork city, some in Midleton, and about a year in Cobh.'

Lindsey fought to keep the emotion out of her voice, but her heart broke again for Lena. 'Have you ever seen children in there?'

Lena looked up at her now, but didn't answer.

'Lena, have you ever seen children?'

'No.'

'But?'

'But... I heard some talk.'

'What kind of talk?'

'Hector telling Patrick about some fresh meat up for grabs.'

'Fresh meat? But not necessarily children?'

'I bit a man's penis so hard that it bled.'

Lindsey didn't respond to the abrupt change of topic. But the phrase, fresh meat took on a whole new and disturbing meaning.

'He hadn't washed in a very long time. Minutes later, I was unconscious.'

Lindsey still didn't respond. She just waited while Lena gathered herself.

'I was coming to, but I kept my eyes closed. Sometimes, it was nice to lose consciousness. No one tended to bother you then. Hector and Patrick were in the room. Hector said that a boy had become available from direct provision. He said that his mother had just died and the boy had no father. No one would be looking for him because he wasn't documented, he said. He'd gotten word that he was ripe for the picking.' She looked up at Lindsey finally, disgust etched on her face, 'Those were the words that he used. Ripe for the picking.'

Lindsey sat beside her for a minute, not speaking. She needed to think. Lena, for her part, let her. She sat there quietly, knowing that Lindsey would have more questions. Finally she thought of one.

'Where would they take him?'

'I don't know. But if it was here, in Cobh, then they'd put him in the attic… but not before…' she stopped speaking and lowered her head again.

'Not before what?'

'I pray maybe not in his case,' her voice was barely a whisper now. 'With us… women were broken first.'

Lindsey lowered her head into her hands.

'But I think maybe he would be more valuable untainted.' Lena turned in her seat to face her and caught Lindsey's hand in both of hers. She was making sure she had her attention. 'Lindsey, Hector is not human. Whatever you are thinking, you need to know that first.'

Lindsey nodded and then quietly left the room. She stood on the landing for a few seconds, before turning towards the stairs to the third floor. Frank was already waiting for her near the bottom step. She took her time going up and once there, she stood in the middle of the space, trying to imagine the same room, two doors up.

'There is a door, like a cage, right here.'

Lena's voice was so soft she hardly heard it. She didn't hear her footsteps either, but now she was standing at the top of the stairs.

'There are mattresses scattered on the floor. At that end…' she pointed to Lindsey's car boot haul, 'a toilet. No walls, no door, just a toilet. At the other end…' she pointed to the far wall, 'a trunk. The old kind that stands up. Almost as tall as I am but not quite. That's where you spend your first night after they…' she heaved in a breath. 'You stand, hunched in there and they lock it. There's no room to sit or lie down. No room to stretch out your arms or bend your knees. If what they've already done to you didn't kill you, you feel sure that this will. Then they let you out and you're not you anymore.'

Lindsey had a dozen questions, but she couldn't bring herself to ask any more of the woman.

'What are you thinking?'

'That I'd like to kill them,' Lindsey answered honestly.

'Me too.'

'How many people sleep in that room?'

'Only those lucky enough to get a break to sleep. Never for more than a few hours and never more than two or three at a time, depending on how busy it is.'

'If there was a child?'

'He would be up there. Patrick isn't stupid. He argued with Hector about it. If any of the more traditional customers saw a child on offer, they might cause trouble. Hector argued that they wouldn't know. Only the select few he said and they would pay dearly for the pleasure. A child would be in the attic. Anywhere else is open to everyone.'

Lindsey felt sick. The conversation between two men about selling a child was enough that she couldn't pretend anymore. She couldn't unhear any of what she'd heard. Now she was left imagining what kind of suffering might be taking place two doors away from where she stood.

*

Lindsey spent the whole night sitting cross legged on the floor in her attic, staring at the wall. On the other side of that wall was an unused, almost derelict building and through just one more wall was possibly a little boy, orphaned and stuffed in a trunk.

Or maybe there wasn't.

Somewhere close to five in the morning, she got to her feet and went to examine the wall. It was solid.

Frank was still curled up near where she'd been sitting, but was looking at her through hooded eyes.

'I know,' she said, glancing at him. 'I can't go busting down walls. Although, I'm sure I could get through two buildings without anyone noticing,' she mumbled with half a grin.

But it wasn't funny. That had actually been her plan. She stood there, looking around the room for five more minutes before addressing Frank again. 'Right, come on.'

She gathered her baton, blade, and stun gun before heading down to the ground floor and through the café. Frank was waiting at the front door by the time she got there. He was trying not to be, but she suspected that he was a little bit excited. Like her, Frank got a little bored with suburban life and the prospect of something happening was all but getting the better of him. It would have excited her too, if it didn't involve the kidnap of a child and the possibility of getting someone, other than herself, killed.

Outside, the streets were quiet. No one was around, but she still decided not to pass Patrick's front door. His was, after all a 24/7 establishment, and she didn't want to be seen. So she turned towards the McParland's house and jogged until she came to the end of Harbour Row. She rounded the hair pin bend and up Harbour View, another steep climb which Cobh had in abundance. She kept going until she was roughly above her house. There was a row of houses, whose back gardens overlooked her and she moved quietly now around to the back of the first house and down through their sloping garden. She studied the buildings below and discovered that she was directly above the old Hardware House. She studied the bank. It was troublesome no doubt. But it was doable with some planning and the right gear, which she had.

At the bottom of the bank, right of the back yard, was a small flat roof – possibly a bathroom, above which was the attic. There was a small and ancient looking skylight in the roof through which no light shone.

In theory, she could get down there, onto the flat roof. It'd be easy enough to get from there, up onto the apex, and somehow get through the skylight without alerting anyone. Then she just had to hope that the attic wasn't a busy space. Better yet, that it was completely empty and no child was being held captive in there.

Frank was whining beside her.

'I know,' she looked apologetically at him. 'I promised you that there'd be no more of this shit. Not after last time. But you know we can't sit back on this one.'

He lowered his head, resigning himself to whatever was coming.

'This'll be the last time though. I mean it. We'll go somewhere nice after this and I'll stay the fuck out of everyone's way.' Assuming of course that she managed to pull this off without getting herself, Lena, and possibly a boy, killed in the process. That was a far more likely scenario.

Still, she had to try.

*

The sun was up by the time she got back and Eileen had already arrived for work.

'Have you been out all night, you saucy bitch,' she bellowed.

'I'm gonna head up and...' Lindsey pointed towards the ceiling.

'Scrub your fanny?' Eileen laughed because she couldn't help herself. 'So go on; who was he?'

Frank wasn't in the mood for early morning banter and was already under the swing doors and half way up the stairs. Maybe she'd mistaken his need for fresh air for excitement, because he wasn't like her. Frank was always five steps ahead of Lindsey. He could see the fall well before it came. He was probably thinking that she was about to get a bunch of people killed and then he'd be left to pick up the pieces again. And Frank Ryan was almost always right.

'Ah Christ, I was only joking.' Eileen was slightly indignant now that Lindsey had walked past her without a retort.

Lindsey picked up a tea towel and threw it at her with a forced grin, before making her way upstairs. She didn't want to drag Eileen into any of this, so she had to keep her nervous energy under wraps and do her best to appear as normal as possible.

But Eileen Chambers wasn't an easy woman to fool.

*

'Lindsey?'

Lindsey was outside Lena's door, waiting like a creepy landlord when she emerged.

'You have more questions?'

'The skylight in the attic?'

'Jammed shut. Or maybe just too old. Either way, it cannot open.'

'What's under it?'

'Under it?'

'Yeah; a mattress? Someone sleeping?'

'The mattresses move. They could be anywhere, but the window is covered with a black drape lest we should see the stars and get any ideas.'

Lindsey nodded and walked away, back up to her attic. She had to step over Frank who lay across the bottom step and refused to get out of her way. 'Cry baby,' she muttered as she passed.

He snorted in reply.

Once upstairs, she stood under her own skylight for a minute. She'd never tried to open it, but she imagined it'd shatter with her first touch. She turned her back on it and went to pull out one of the black storage boxes jammed against the wall. They were the biggest ones she could find at the time when she was packing up the tools from her old barna shed. She'd amassed a sizeable collection, each tool bought for a specific job, and some hadn't been used since. This box was filled with her larger tools; a strimmer, her jigsaw, a human powered lawnmower. She shoved the box aside and pulled out the next one, filled with smaller tools. Stuffed down the side was a small cardboard box which once contained a Black & Decker drill. Now it held, among other things, a knife whose sole purpose was to cut through hardened putty. She'd used it to replace a broken pane of glass in the old sash window at her last house. She'd used a rubber mallet with it and not that it mattered at that time, but it was too noisy for this job. Still, she sat them down side by side until she'd considered them fully. The drill box also contained a glass cutter, roughly the size and shape of a pencil with a little wheel at the end. This was the first tool she'd bought for that same window replacement. She'd cut the glass before realising that the putty too would need to go if she were to replace the glass properly. A rock would have been as effective and a lot faster, but she prided herself on doing exactly what it said on YouTube. She lay the cutter down beside the mallet and the knife.

If Lena was right about there being a drape covering the skylight window then it would have to be secured top and bottom, or else, given the angle of the roof, it would just flop down and leave the window exposed. In theory, she could cut the glass, pop it through and the drape would catch it. Then she could take down the drape and shimmy on in.

In theory.

Of course, anything could go wrong. She should have far more up to the minute information about that room. If Patrick was worried about having a child on the premises, then maybe he put a guard up there with him? Maybe there was no drape and the glass would shatter to the floor and alert one of the goons. Maybe there was no one there who needed her help. Maybe, maybe, maybe. There were a lot of maybes but the one certainty was that she couldn't wait. Another day for Lindsey to plan could mean another day of pain for someone who'd already had too much.

'What's the quietest time in the attic?' she asked, without turning around.

Once again, Lena had approached soundlessly but Lindsey could sense her watching.

'Busiest time is early morning. The clients have gone home to their wives and some of the girls get to sleep. From around mid-day, everyone is busy again and the attic is deserted. Except if someone is in the trunk.'

Lindsey resisted the urge to go and raid Danny Chambers' weapons arsenal and let herself in through Patrick's front door.

'What about night time?'

'The attic will be empty. Everyone will be working.'

Lindsey nodded.

'Lindsey? Everyone will be working.'

Lindsey closed her eyes and was glad she hadn't turned to look at Lena.

'You know what will happen if they catch you?'

Lindsey didn't reply. She just sat studying her tools, wondering if there was a better way. Of course there was. There was always a better way, but one wouldn't come to her until it was much too late.

'Lindsey?'

'I'll protect you,' she mumbled her reply. She sounded more confident than she felt, but that didn't make it a lie.

Lena guffawed, which surprised Lindsey enough to finally look at her.

'You think I care about what would happen to me? Tell me, what more can they do?'

Lindsey turned back to her tools.

'I worry for you, my friend.'

'Please don't.'

'Someone should. Aside from that poor beast who is pining at the bottom of the stairs.'

Lindsey half smiled. 'He's not pining. He's sulking, there's a difference. It's not that long since I promised Frank a quiet life.'

'And what will he do if you don't come back?'

'He'll finally get the retirement he deserves.'

There was silence for a minute, while Lindsey returned her concentration to the matter at hand and away from the fact that she needed to shut up.

'You care for strangers, but not for yourself. Why?'

No reply.

'I care little for myself too. But I have many, many reasons.'

No reply and she didn't turn around.

'What are your reasons, Lindsey?'

'Tell me about the trunk. What's used to lock it?'

'A small padlock. It didn't need to be very big because we had no space to move inside. We couldn't break through even if we still had the will. And even if we did break through; where would we go?'

She rooted through the black box again and pulled out a hacksaw.

'You're planning to go in there? Women spend their days wishing they could get out, while you go to great lengths to get in.'

'If I have any more questions, I'll find you.'

Lena nodded with a sad look on her face, neither of which Lindsey saw. She was just relieved to hear her footsteps as she made her way down the stairs.

Chapter 8

Lindsey decided on six pm and why not? It was as bad a time as any. According to Lena, everyone would be working from lunchtime onwards, but Lindsey figured the real freaks wouldn't come out until after dark. But while she sat cross legged on the old floorboards, surrounded by all the tools she imagined she might need, one questioned nagged at her; 'How can you plan for something that's already a cluster fuck, Frankie?' she mumbled.

'What are you up to?' Either Eileen had also come soundlessly up the attic stairs or Lindsey was in another world entirely.

'I'm taking a day off.'

'Yeah, OK. You'll find a lot of people use their days off for gardening and horse riding and what not. But I suppose looking at ropes and getting splinters in your arse is fun too. So whose neck are you planning on wrapping those around?'

'Yours if you don't get back to work.'

'It's like that, is it?'

'Did you want something?'

'I want a lot of things. But for now I just want to tell you that Patrick's downstairs. He's wondering where you are and giving me the stink eye.'

'Shit.' She got to her feet.

'Still taking a day off?'

Lindsey followed her down. It wouldn't be a good idea to go missing right before Patrick was about to lose another of his assets. As she passed through the back kitchen on her way to the café, she acknowledged that this was an optimistic thought, but she sprinkled some flour on her hands anyway and went to cover her bases.

Eileen guffawed. 'You seriously think anyone's gonna believe that?'

Lindsey wondered briefly where Eileen had conjured up the flour from, but instead of asking she just hurried through, like any busy woman would. She went behind the bar and got started on a coffee, giving Patrick no more and no less attention than usual as he sat looking into a full cup of black tea.

'Still no Lena,' he said to the cup.

Lindsey looked up at him, but didn't reply.

He went to drink from the cup but then pulled back, like his senses had been assaulted. He placed it back on the table, paused for dramatics and then got up and left.

As he went, Lindsey felt her body harden. Suddenly she no longer cared about the risks. One way or another, she was going into his house today and whoever she found in that attic was coming out with her. If Patrick or any of his goons tried to stop her, she'd burn his fucking house down.

She placed a full cup of coffee in front of a woman she'd never seen before.

'Ma'am, I didn't order that.'

An American tourist, clearly lost.

'It's on the house,' she called back, as she headed once more towards the kitchen and the two flights of stairs to the attic.

She took her time to study the tools of her trade. Whatever that was these days. She'd need enough abseiling gear to get herself in, but also to get the boy out, taking into account that he could be injured.

Badly. She might have to carry him. She examined her ropes in detail, knowing that they were in perfect condition or they'd never have been packed away after their last use. She pulled out harnesses and carabiners and then she stopped. She looked up at her own skylight and dropped what she was doing.

One of her first problems would be getting through someone's back garden, climbing over their little picket fence and abseiling off their ledge without being seen. An even bigger problem would be humping it back up to that garden lugging a child, in whatever condition he might be in, again without being seen. Thinking of it in exactly those terms, she realised that it was the most moronic idea she'd ever heard of. Let alone come up with herself.

She walked over, stood under the skylight and shook her head. She wondered if she was even capable of tactical thinking anymore.

Ryan, you idiot.

*

As six o'clock galloped towards her, she was very much aware that her whole plan was reckless. It had also changed entirely in a very short space of time, but there was no room for self-doubt now. She took a minute to close her eyes and breathe. To see what she was about to do in her mind's eye and how she would do it, successfully. She mumbled some words to Street and to Lenny. Though neither of them were there with her, she could hear their responses as clearly as if they were. She even pictured Damo. Like a greyhound out of the traps, he was already half way to the building two doors up. As always, they had more faith in Lindsey Ryan than she did.

'This could still be nothing more than a bloody rumour,' she spoke to her most loyal companion as he paced the floor around her. 'But what if it's not?'

She pulled a table over to the skylight. It was too tall for the café, but was perfect for this. If she returned with a child, his legs might not be long enough to reach something lower. She climbed up and pushed open the window. It needed force. Then using the strength in her upper body, she pulled herself up through it.

The pitch on the roof wasn't very steep, but if she got any of this wrong, she'd have a long time to think about it on the way down. The rope attached to her harness had a grappling hook at the end of it. She threw the hook, which caught first time on the ridge. She tugged on it a couple of times and when she was relatively happy that it would hold, she pulled her legs out through the skylight and climbed quickly up.

It was getting dark now and the street was mercifully quiet. She'd be silhouetted at the top of the building, but it was three stories up and no one really had a reason to look up there. That didn't mean they wouldn't. But her plan had so many other faults, she chose not to dwell on that one. Once she got up to the ridge, she straddled it, facing her own chimney. She studied the long terraced row of old buildings and as expected, she saw nothing but moss covered back yards and darkened sash windows. Patrick's building was behind her. All was quiet as she looked over her shoulder, but she knew that his wasn't as innocuous as it appeared. She needed to cover a distance of about thirty metres, from where she sat, across the building next door, and to a spot that would put her directly above his skylight. She removed the hook from the rope and tucked it into the side pocket of her small backpack. Using a clove hitch, she secured the rope to the chimney, with the other end tied in a figure eight to a carabiner attached to her harness. If she fell, there was every chance that the ancient chimney would follow her down. But she couldn't dwell on that either. She checked it and double checked it before bringing her legs around and changing direction.

'Right. Let's get on with it, I suppose.'

She blew out a long breath. Still straddling the pitch, she lowered her torso so that her chest was touching the ancient and rough ridge capping, minimising her silhouette as much as possible. Slowly she began moving along in the direction of Patrick's building. The slates were as old as the buildings themselves, but to send one shattering onto the footpath below would just be careless.

The skin on her thighs soon began to chafe under their firm grip on the ridge, but she kept moving. Her only focus now was on the skylight up ahead. She thought about nothing else. Not getting caught. Not what would happen to Lena, not even the boy whom she was going to pluck through the roof. Just the skylight, and when she finally reached it, she stopped still where she was for a few minutes, studying it. She could see the black drape on the inside. It looked like a black sheet might have been stuck to the four corners of the window, drooping in the middle like a small hammock.

She attached a second rope to a second carabiner, tying the grappling hook onto the other end of it. She hooked it onto the ridge and carefully began making her way down. Once she came near the skylight, she used her foot to test the slates surrounding it. They seemed steady enough, so she moved to just below the window. Taking a broad stance, she planted her feet on the roof and let the rope take her weight. She pulled her glass cutter and a tiny jar of kerosene out of her pack. An overly enthusiastic set of YouTube twins once told her that this would make a smoother cut. It didn't the first time. But she hoped for the best this time round.

'This is the most stupid shit you've ever pulled,' she whispered to the glass cutter.

Still she dipped the cutter's wheel into the kerosene and as she placed the wheel against the edge of the glass and started cutting, she briefly acknowledged the fact that she was probably about to send a giant pile of shit hurtling towards a fan. Again. The last time she'd done this, the glass had shattered. The same thing happened this time and as the pane smashed inwards, she closed her eyes and hunched her shoulders. Then she adjusted her grip on the glass cutter and waited like a moron to see what would happen.

The little hammock caught some of the glass, while the rest crashed onto the floor. She held perfectly still, waiting to hear someone coming thumping up the stairs and over to the window. She would douse them in kerosene and slash them with her glass cutter before subsequently being shoved off the roof.

But no sound came. There were a few sharp edges left around the outside of the glass, but before breaking them too, she decided to stick her head in and see if in fact there was a reason to make another stupid move. She gently tugged on the top corner, which was held in place by what felt like a thumb tack. She pulled it lose and the corner dropped. She waited for another minute. Patrick and his entire army could be waiting for her behind this make-shift curtain, all smiling at each other as they watched her slowly breaking in. But still, there was no sound. So she popped the tack on the opposite corner and the shade fell down fully, along with the glass that it had managed to catch. She was in.

A couple of deep breaths and she lowered herself onto her knees, hoping that the slates held out under her. She poked her head in through the window, careful of the sharp edges.

The first thing to hit her was the smell coming from the overflowing toilet in the corner of the room. She pulled her head back out and before poking it in again, she filled her lungs with fresh sea air.

Inside was bleak by anyone's standards. Mattresses were strewn around in no particular order, each one grubbier than the next. Otherwise the room was empty. Just the stench of human waste and desperation. And an almost Lena sized trunk stood against the back wall.

'Shit.'

The presence of the trunk meant that she had to go in.

She used the handle of the cutter to shatter the last remaining shards of glass and as they fell to the floor, she lowered herself in feet first. She was done waiting. The first thing she did was gather up the glass and place it in a zip lock bag. The smell in the room was foul.

She hurried towards the trunk and quickly examined the lock. It was a cheap padlock. It wouldn't be a problem to cut through and as she pulled out her hacksaw, she heard something behind her.

She froze.

When nothing hit her over the head, she turned slowly but didn't see anyone. There had been a sound though, and something had made it.

She stood up and walked slowly back through the space. She paid close attention to the stairs, which were behind a cage door. That was also padlocked from the other side. Out the side of her eye she saw a pile of blankets move in the corner farthest away from the trunk. As she walked towards the bundle, her fists clenched and unclenched by her sides. She paused for a breath, then pulled on the blankets to reveal a ball of bony knees and elbows, wrapped around a shock of jet-black hair.

'Shit,' she muttered, more forcibly this time.

She didn't touch him, nor did she say anymore. After a few seconds, a pair of brown eyes like saucers looked up at her. She stared back at a face of pure innocence. It was the same face that came to her night after night with the beaming smile. A part of that smile was in a box in the back of her wardrobe and her fingers automatically went to the scar near her hair line.

Of course this wasn't that face. But it was the same age and possibly the same origin. Her body turned cold.

He whimpered softly.

Get a fucking grip, Ryan.

'It's OK,' she whispered. 'I'm not going to hurt you.'

She had no idea if he understood her or not, but he radiated fear. She could only hope that her own discomfort wasn't as obvious.

She held her hand towards him. 'I'm here to help you. Please, come with me.'

He didn't budge. She closed her eyes and tried to think of the basic Arabic she'd picked up while deployed overseas. 'Ana huna limusaeadatik.' I'm here to help you.

He wasn't moving and she was running out of time. Someone could come up here any second. 'Please… ana huna limusaeadatik. We have to go now, before they come.' She pointed towards the stairs.

His eyes drifted towards the stairs and then back to Lindsey and finally he made a move to stand. But his legs could hardly hold him. Lindsey slowly reached her arm around him and he recoiled dramatically at her touch.

She closed her eyes as an invisible rope tightened around her heart and she imagined pouring petrol all over this building and everyone in it before striking a match.

She took her hands off him, but offered her shoulder for him to lean on. After a few long seconds, he did and she hurried him towards the window. She'd need to tie a rope around him and attach him to her harness. She wondered how she'd manage that without touching him. But as it turned out, that was the least of her worries.

The boy pulled against her as she tried to get him to the window.

She showed him her harness and rope and quickly acted out what she needed him to do. But he shook his head and then pointed towards the trunk.

'What?' Her eyes followed his outstretched arm. 'We need to go now.'

He shook his head and moved haltingly towards the trunk. The boy seemed to be in considerable pain.

'Fuck, fuck, fuck.'

She hurried towards the trunk, pulling out her hacksaw as she moved. It took no more than a couple of minutes to cut through the cheap lock and when the trunk opened, she was once again hit with the smell of human waste.

This time it came from the boy crouched inside the claustrophobic space. He looked to be about twelve or thirteen years old, also Middle Eastern. His eyes hurt from the sudden invasion of light in his tomb.

He didn't dwell on it for long however, as he burst from the trunk and swung his fists wildly at Lindsey. He managed to knock her on her ass, and land a solid punch to her jaw before she could stop him.

'Calm down.' She grabbed his wrists.

But her quiet words were lost in the almost animalistic sound coming from him.

'Shhh!' she begged him, as she shoved her hand across his mouth. 'Shut the fuck up or we're all dead.'

Her words seemed to reach him finally and he dropped to the floor. Seconds later he was sobbing. Lindsey ran her hand through her hair. Two of them. How the fuck was she supposed to get two of them out?

'OK… we need to move. Do you speak English?' she asked the older boy.

He nodded, but didn't look at her. He was still crying, but now he was slapping himself in the head as well.

'Do you?' she asked the younger child. He looked to be about six, maybe seven.

He just continued to look at her, which answered her question.

'I'm going to take him out.' She spoke to the older boy again, as she pointed towards the window.

He grabbed her by the wrist, his eyes suddenly pleading with her. 'No, please! Don't leave me here.'

She cupped his face and promised him, 'I'll be back. I'll be right back, just stay quiet and stay out of sight.' She hurried over to the trunk again and closed it up. She pulled a small padlock from her pack and snapped it into place. She took the old one with her. They weren't an exact match, but they were both small and both cheap, so maybe it wouldn't be noticed until someone went to open it. Now she really had to move.

As much as she wanted to, she couldn't wait for the boy to comply. So she pulled out a rope and wrapped it around his waist. Then she tied a bowline and attached it to her harness. It all happened in a matter of seconds and by the time she was moving towards the window, the older boy had said something which seemed to reassure the younger one. He stopped pulling against her and began moving with her, finally.

Given the size of the window, she struggled to get both herself and the boy outside and once she did, she felt certain that the slates would give under them. Once again, she took a broad stance out on the roof, this time with the boy pressed against her front. Before moving off, she pulled the bag of shattered glass out of the pocket half way down her leg. She sprinkled the glass into the guttering below. She wanted to make it look like the window was broken from the inside. It might give the impression that somehow, the boys had gotten themselves out. Of course that wouldn't explain the lock on the trunk, but hey, confusion was the most she could hope for.

She pulled a few times on the hook. It was secure, so she pointed upwards. She couldn't afford the time to make him understand or to take away some of his fear, like she desperately wished she could. Not if she stood any chance of getting back for the other boy. Now that she knew he existed, failing to get him out would just about kill her and she knew that. So she started walking.

He was tiny and frail, but his weight against her as she pulled them both up along the roof was a hindrance. Once she got him there, he took one look over the ridge and panicked, pushing back against her.

A slate gave way. It slid down along the roof, slapped against the guttering and then there was a brief silence as it fell three storeys. The noise as it crashed against some bins in Patrick's back yard set off a string of obscenities in Lindsey's mind, some of which slid gracelessly from her lips.

She anchored herself to the roof as best she could, while using her free hand to try to calm the boy. 'Shhh,' she said in his ear. 'Hadi… quiet.'

He stopped struggling finally, but his breathing was loud and erratic.

She listened for sounds from the yard, but didn't hear any. Maybe they hadn't heard it. Either way, she couldn't hang around. She held tight to the boy as she pulled her leg over the ridge, hoping that it would reassure him that he was safe.

Or as safe as one can be on a roof with a waitress while trying to escape from ruthless human traffickers.

She hauled him up and pulled his leg over. She was leaning forward, so he was too. Her chest was pressed against his tiny back. She pointed ahead and held out two fingers. 'Just two buildings.' She tucked the hook away again and started moving forward, pushing him along. She didn't have time to wait for a level of comfort that would never come. Not now that she had to go back a second time. As reckless as it was to go in once, it was damn near suicidal to try it twice.

Chapter 9

Lena's deep thoughts were broken by their arrival through the skylight. She was standing in the middle of the attic looking like she was trying to solve a puzzle. Four legs coming through the tiny opening weren't what she expected and she jumped with fright.

Frank however, looked like he'd been impatiently waiting for exactly that. He ran back and forth a couple of times, then he jumped up and landed his front paws on the table.

Lindsey unclipped the boy from her harness and lowered him to the ground. She got down right behind him. Frank for his part backed off a little when he saw the boy, whose bony fingers buried themselves into the flesh on Lindsey's hand. He disappeared behind her, using her body to shield himself from whatever danger he was expecting.

Lena was frozen to the spot, staring at them both. It took some repositioning, but Lindsey finally managed to bring the boy into sight. She desperately wanted him to feel safe. Though she was now convinced that they were anything but.

Their fear and vulnerability seemed to have taken on a life of their own and the looks on both their faces made it clear that all their hopes were now resting with her. And it was about to get worse.

'Who is this?' Lena asked, swallowing hard as she knelt down on one knee to look at the boy with a quivery smile on her face.

'I don't know yet.'

The boy was glued to Lindsey, but his eyes were on Frank. He made his way slowly and unthreateningly towards them. Ever the professional.

Lena looked at Lindsey and smiled a more genuine smile now. Her eyes filled with emotion.

'You did it,' she whispered.

Then she returned her attention to the boy and held her hand towards him. 'Ma aismak?'

What little Arabic Lindsey knew, she guessed that Lena had just asked the boy his name, to which he responded by trying to climb under Lindsey's skin.

'Ma hu aismuk ya sadiqi? What is your name, my friend?' She smiled affectionately at him with her hand still held out towards him.

He pulled his face out of Lindsey's hip, just enough that he could make eye contact with Lena.

'Reem,' he mumbled.

'Hello, Reem. My name is Lena and this is our friend, Lindsey. Do you understand me when I speak in English?'

Reem nodded, and Lindsey was eternally grateful to Lena for taking some of the pressure away. They had a name. They all understood the same language. That was as good a start as they could hope for.

'I need to go back to the neighbour's house. Will you two be OK here for a minute?'

Lena looked alarmed and rightly so.

'There's another one.' Lindsey climbed back up on the table, ignoring Frank's protests as he all but knocked her back to the ground.

'Lindsey you can't…'

'Go back downstairs. If you hear someone up here that isn't me, find somewhere to hide.'

Lena nodded nervously. 'OK, Lindsey.'

Finally, she took Reem by the hand and led him towards the stairs.

His eyes never left Lindsey.

She pulled herself through the skylight again and retraced her route back to Patrick's place. Her thighs burned now as skin parted with flesh under the rough caress of the ridge tiles. Again, she lowered herself down and poked her head in through the skylight. She was met with the second boy's face, just inches from hers. His hopeful eyes watching out for her return. So much for staying out of sight.

'Did anyone come up? Do they know that Reem is gone?'

He shook his head and began climbing frantically and noisily.

'Wait!' She held out her hand to stop him. 'I have to come in to tie you on.'

She hurried through the window again and wrapped the second rope around the boy. Because he was bigger than Reem, she went out the window ahead of him to get a firm stance before pulling him up. Before going any further, she explained a little bit about the height and the ridge at top in the hope of avoiding another panic scene. He was almost as tall as she was. It would be a lot more difficult to stay upright if he pushed against her.

But all he was interested in was getting out of there and Lindsey couldn't blame him for that. She felt the same way herself and a large part of her expected at least a henchman or two to come barrelling through the cage door any second.

When they managed to reach the ridge before that happened, she almost allowed herself a second of relief. Almost.

Again, she pointed ahead holding up two fingers. 'Two buildings over.'

As they shuffled along, she tried to ignore the voices of at least three men directly below them on the street. She glanced down but couldn't see them. She did however, see a red Ford Fiesta as it slowed down dramatically on the road below.

Was the driver looking up?

Knowing her luck, he absolutely was. This was one more thing that she couldn't dwell on. What good would it do her? If she was caught, then stopping now wouldn't change it so she continued to slightly shove the boy, who to be fair, was moving along pretty well. She imagined he'd do whatever he had to do to get as far away from that trunk as possible.

'We're going through that window.' She pointed to her skylight just up ahead. 'There's a dog in there, he's not going to hurt you. You're going in first.'

It was an awkward manoeuvre and Lindsey nearly lost her footing twice. But eventually they both made it through and once again, Lena was there to meet them.

'Lena, I thought I told you to stay downstairs. Where's Reem?'

'He is safe,' she said, looking at the second boy. Her eyes filled with sadness this time. 'And who is this?'

Lindsey looked to the boy, waiting to see if he'd answer. He eyed Lena warily for a few minutes.

'This is it? Are there men here?' he asked instead.

'Nope; just us,' Lindsey replied.

He looked somewhere between relieved and panic stricken.

Then Lena smiled and said, 'Don't worry my friend. This Lindsey, she is more than any five men of your choosing.'

Lindsey busied herself removing her harness and untying the boy. She ignored the doubtful curiosity in his expression as he scrutinised her.

Finally he said, 'I am Amir.'

Once Lindsey was untied, Frank launched himself at her, and Amir stumbled to the floor in his haste to get out of the way. The look on his face said that he expected the dog to devour Lindsey. When she smiled, scratched his ears and covered him in kisses, he looked at Lindsey with the same expression. But Lindsey was busy savouring the moment of elation that came with winning a small battle. She might not get another chance when the actual war caught up with her.

'Like I said, he won't hurt you,' she said, to calm Amir. Though quite frankly, she was tired of people looking at Frank like he was some kind of animal.

'Lena, can you take Amir downstairs? I'll just tidy up here,' she asked, pulling herself back to their situation.

Lena nodded and gestured to the boy, who was understandably hesitant. He had after all, just gotten out of a trunk.

As soon as they were gone, Lindsey let out a long breath and lay flat on the floor with Frank draped across her. Her right hand rubbed the stiffness out of her damaged left shoulder with more aggression than was needed, but she hardly noticed.

'Now what, Frank?' She glanced down at him as she spoke. 'What the hell am I supposed to do with all these people?'

He strung together a whine, a snuffle and half a bark.

'I know. I'm so much more fucked up than either of us ever realised.'

Getting to her feet, she felt old all of a sudden. She closed and locked the skylight and then pulled the table to the side. She made a point of returning it to the back of the pile of car boot shite.

The heavy bag called to her, but she shook her head. Instead she slapped herself hard across the face and headed for the stairs.

*

When she pushed open the sitting room door, she was greeted by three hopeful faces. They all stood around waiting to find out how their lives were about to change.

Fuck.

'Anyone hungry? I'll make some…' she gestured towards the door and promptly left. She had no idea what to say to them. They'd want to know what her plan was; how she was going to save them, and Lindsey had no fucking idea how to answer their questions.

Frank trotted inside and curled himself at Reem's feet. Lindsey didn't stop him. He naturally gravitated towards the weakest person when Lindsey wasn't busy falling apart. His protective nature was what made him who he was, and because she had yet to see the boy looking anything other than terrified, she imagined that he needed Frank's skillset more than she did now.

Her hands worked on autopilot as they removed some bread from the freezer and defrosted it in the toaster. They were all out of deli meat, so she sliced some cheese and arranged some plates. She couldn't possibly think about eating. In fact, she wasn't thinking about the food at all. Instead her mind was running through options, until she finally realised that she didn't really have any. She was hiding three refugees in her flat and all three belonged to one of the most dangerous men in the county. If they were found out, there was every chance they'd all be killed. Or maybe just Lindsey and Lena. The boys would possibly be returned to the hell of forced prostitution.

All three of them had probably felt a world of pain before they reached Irish shores at all. But once they became so-called human traffic, they were bound for a whole other level of hell. They became the people that no one gave one single shit about. At least not in any way that mattered. To most people, they were completely invisible.

So what in the name of God was she supposed to do with them?

*

That night, Lindsey divvied out her beds, leaving herself without one. Given that Lena was far more maternal than she was, she gladly gave her double bed to her guests. She had intended on taking the spare room, but Amir begged her to let him sleep alone. He didn't care where, just not the attic. Given what she imagined he'd been through, she couldn't blame him, so she gave him the spare room.

Sleep brought nothing but chaos to Lindsey's mind anyway, so she was happy enough to avoid it. Her lumpy second-hand couch would no doubt help her with that. But first she changed into shorts and a vest and went to the attic, where she exerted herself for another two hours. In truth, she could have gone for two more, but as she went round after round with her heavy bag, a thought occurred to her.

When Patrick and his goon had come looking for Lena, she got lucky. She managed to hide herself, but barely. There were three of them now and Lindsey needed to be prepared for anyone who might follow. Until such time as she could get them as far away from Patrick as possible.

Sweat rolled off her skin as she stood looking around the space. There was literally nowhere to hide up here. The stairs led to one room with low rafters and bare walls and floorboards. There wasn't so much as a wardrobe to hide in. Just a heap of plastic storage boxes filled with her old stuff. But even they were mostly transparent.

She went back down to her flat and into the kitchenette where she studied the ceiling. She grabbed a torch from the drawer and pulled a chair up to the tiny hatch. She climbed up and shone the light in. She couldn't see anything but dust in the air and piles of glass fibre insulation. She pulled herself up, but immediately got back down again.

'Shit.' Her bare arms stung from the glass wool.

She moved quietly to the spare room. She listened at the door for a second and then knocked gently. She waited for Amir to answer. When he didn't, she said, 'Amir? It's Lindsey. I just need to get something from under the bed. Can I come in?'

The door opened slowly and she could tell that he'd been standing on the other side of it, waiting for the other shoe to drop. But he pulled himself together when he saw that she was alone.

He let her in and went and stood at the end of the bed.

His face said that he was feeling a lot of things and safe wasn't one of them. She wanted to reassure him, but she couldn't right now. His fear was justified and there was nothing she could do about it. Bar getting him and the others as far away from here as possible. In order to do that, she had to focus on the matter at hand.

She pulled out one of the many boxes that were stored under the bed. This one was filled with clothes that didn't really have a place in her tiny wardrobe. She carried the box back to the sitting room, pulled out a pair of overalls and put them on. She tucked the sleeves into a pair a yellow rubber gloves that she'd found under the sink and pulled herself up through the hatch again.

With no room to even crawl on hands and knees, she belly crawled along, unable to see more than two feet ahead. The going was rough, with no floor to speak of. Just rafters with insulation in between and when she finally reached the end, she rolled onto her back and shone the torch around, trying to get her bearings.

'OK… up there is the back wall of the attic,' she whispered to herself. But in her mind, the lads nodded in agreement. 'And my bed should be right under me.'

She pushed up against the boards overhead. They weren't in the best nick, but they wouldn't give way that easily either. She turned onto her belly again and crawled backwards until she could feel the opening. She lowered herself down into the kitchenette, making as little noise as possible. She went back up to the attic and sat on her tool box where she proceeded to stare at the wall.

To a normal onlooker, Lindsey may have looked like someone in the midst of a mental crisis; dressed as she was, staring vacantly ahead one minute and pulling sheets of chipped plasterboard out of her shit pile the next. But how she looked wasn't something that she spent much time thinking about. She laid the sheets out side by side on the floor and then paused to examine the back wall.

'I'm gonna be short by about three inches.'

She looked at her shit pile again.

'Fuck it. We'll just have to make it work.'

She checked her watch. She tapped the face, shook it, listened to hear the ticks and then checked it again. It still said that it was half six in the morning. The vacant staring obviously took more time than she realised and Eileen could arrive at any time. This would have to wait until later.

*

'Eileen, will you be OK by yourself down here today?' She asked, as soon as Eileen walked through the kitchen door.

'What the f…?' she eyed Lindsey from head to toe. 'What in the name of sweet Jesus Christ are you wearing?'

'Spring cleaning clothes. Will you be alright by yourself for a while? I have a few things I need to do.'

'It's lucky for you that I have no aversion to people telling me bare faced lies. But you'll tell me anything I might need to know, right?'

Lindsey considered her request. Telling her what she might be up against would give her a chance to be prepared. But not telling her would give her plausible deniability, which Lindsey thought was the lesser of two evils. The last thing she wanted was to involve Eileen in her hare-brained situation, but it was getting a bit late for that now, too.

'I'll take that as a yes.' Eileen rolled her eyes and sighed dramatically. 'I wish you would have told me that you were planning a meltdown today. Now I'll have to spend the day listening to Mary fucking Kelly harping on about My Brian while Jimmy pretends not to be head over heels in love with Declan from Spar. Like yeah, Jimmy. No one notices that you just happen to come in at the exact same time as Declan's elevenses every single day. And no one notices the disappointment on your face when he gets his coffee to take away – just like he always does.' She threw her hands in the air and raised her voice another notch, 'Ask him out for fucksake, Jimmy! It's the twenty-first century. No one gives a shit!'

Lindsey raised her eyebrows. Eileen wasn't herself today. Not that she'd ever admit to feeling anything less than Herculean. 'You done?'

'But why does Declan come all the way over here for a take-away coffee when they actually have nicer take-away coffee in Spar?'

'Did you always want to be a salesperson or…?'

'He probably fancies you. Or me? Or fucking Jimmy!'

They both just looked at each other, possibly wondering the same thing. What are we talking about?

'What are you doing, anyway?' Eileen started busying herself moving a small mess around. 'Let me guess; based on the outfit, I'd say you'll be spending the next little while rolling a dead body in plastic and trying not to leave your DNA lying around. Am I getting warm?'

'You're good.' Lindsey's response was just as droll. 'I'll be upstairs doing bookwork and the likes.'

'Bookwork my arse. That's my job too, remember?'

'Look, can you manage or not?'

'Oh I can manage.' She pointed a cup measure accusingly at Lindsey. 'You know I can sniff out trouble a mile off though, don't ya? And right now, you reek of it. What're you doing, Lindsey?'

'You know, Grace McParland said that you should put more cinnamon in your apple tarts.' That'd change the subject.

Eileen froze. Lindsey peeled off her marigolds and waited for the silence to pass.

'Notice how she had to wait until she attempted death by fucking nutcase before passing on those pearls of wisdom?'

Lindsey half smiled as her pastry chef, book-keeper, and friend reached for the tub of cinnamon, which she stared sadly at for several more seconds. She put it back on the shelf. Lindsey took her turn to break the silence.

'If anyone else comes in today reeking of trouble, drop a few pots and pans in the kitchen to let me know, yeah? Use your instincts. Or your sense of smell; anyone you're not sure about, OK?'

'What about Morse code? Or maybe a few smoke signals?'

Lindsey couldn't help a small, genuine smile. Eileen was the most sarcastic person she'd ever met. But somehow it suited her.

'Open up when you're ready. Business as usual, yeah?' She slapped Eileen on the shoulder as she passed her, headed for the stairs.

'Go. But whatever you're up to…' she pointed the cup measure again, but didn't finish whatever warning she was about to give.

*

When she reached the flat, Lena, Amir, and Reem were eating breakfast. It was the first time she'd seen Lena eating comfortably. No matter how many times Lindsey instructed her otherwise, the woman would not go through her cupboards. It seemed that having the boys to look after was helping her as much as she was helping them. Reem at least. Amir looked like he hated the world and everyone in it. Pretty much how Lindsey felt these days.

She went and sat beside Reem for a minute. Frank was already there and she felt the usual warmth he instilled in her when she saw Reem's hand resting on Frank's head. His fingers moved slowly back and forth over his coat. Frank for his part was holding perfectly still, so as not to startle him or make him move away from him. Frank the therapist.

'Reem?'

He looked tentatively up at her and moved his hand away from Frank.

'Lena and Amir will be here with you today, and so will Frank. I can tell that he really likes you.' She smiled at Frank. 'I'll be working just upstairs. You can go in any room you like and you can use, or play with, or read anything you like. But you must be quiet, OK?' She was speaking to all three of them. Of course Lena didn't need the instruction and she guessed that Amir wouldn't take it well directly. So she spoke as if it were for Reem's benefit only. She just hoped that Amir would get the message. The last thing she wanted was anyone downstairs hearing sounds coming from her flat. Especially sounds of children.

Reem glanced at Lena and then returned his attention to his toast. He lowered his free hand back towards Frank's head.

'He hasn't said a word since telling me his name yesterday,' Lena said.

Lindsey nodded. 'If you hear pots and pans falling downstairs, take the boys and hide, OK?'

*

Minutes later she was sitting on her attic storage boxes, staring at the back wall again. She needed some kind of access point. She got to her feet and went to examine the floorboards near the wall. She estimated the spot where she'd ended up in the crawl space and hunched down to get a closer look. Taking a pencil from behind her ear, she marked out a rectangle approximately thirty inches long by twenty inches wide using the nails for guidance. They attached the floorboards to the joists. It stood to reason that if she cut alongside them, she could make a hatch which could rest back on those same joists. Thing is, she'd need her circular saw to do it and that wasn't a quiet piece of kit. So that job would have to wait.

Next she needed a false wall of sorts and that's where the plasterboard came in. This whole thing needed to happen fast because her house guests might need it at any time. She had to work with what she had, so she stood the first sheet of plasterboard against the ceiling beam running from left to right across the room. It stood no more than three feet from the back wall, but it was the only one she could use without having to cut and shape the board. She didn't have the time or the tools for that.

The sheet just about touched the floor, so she nailed it into place and followed with the remaining sheets. To say that it looked rough was an understatement and in contrast to the ancient timber floors, walls and ceiling all around her, the old white, chipped plasterboard stood out like a sore thumb. But she had an idea for that too. Eight rolls of wallpaper lay unopened in the pile, along with enough paste to make it stick. The guy who'd sold her the tables and chairs for the café insisted that he couldn't do any better on the price. But he threw in some of the ugliest floral wallpaper she'd ever seen. She didn't argue and it seemed now that that was a good thing. They'd go some way towards making her new wall look a little less conspicuous.

*

One hour rolled into the next as she wallpapered, making sure the pattern matched well enough to fool someone into thinking that she did it for aesthetic reasons, but still the wall was like a sore thumb.

'Why would someone wallpaper one wall in an otherwise shitty looking, woodlice infested room?' she muttered.

She went to the back yard, behind the bins where several paint tins were stacked. Various colours dribbled down their sides. At least three of them were magnolia and they were enough to, albeit roughly, cover the walls and ceiling beams in the attic.

'You'll do.'

'Is it your nerves? Are they shot?' Eileen asked without a hint of a smile. Without waiting for a comeback, she added, 'I suppose if you're determined to have a breakdown, you may as well have this while you can still appreciate it.'

She held out a cupcake decorated far more elaborately than any cupcake needed to be. 'I found a small bag of flour in the cupboard.'

'Are you bored or something?' Lindsey looked at the frosty creation.

Eileen responded by taking a bite so big that most of the decor ended up on her face. Lindsey put down one of the tins of paint, reached out and took the remains. She fit it all in her mouth, picked up the paint again and departed with a stuffed and slightly deranged smile. If she was thinking clearly, she would have acknowledged the fact that it was one of the nicest things she'd ever tasted and that Eileen was wasted in her café. But for now she had other things on her mind.

*

It was always her intention to do something with the attic space and as she looked around hours later, she was disappointed with the rushed end result. She'd painted everything bar the floorboards and the newly wallpapered wall. It was messy, but she supposed it looked plausible. Like a woman with no clue what she was doing had attempted to brighten the place up.

She briefly imagined what she could have done, if she were less restricted for time and tool usage. But as it stood, anyone who came to inspect might actually feel sorry for her. Given her current situation, that wasn't altogether a bad thing.

'Jeeeesus!' Eileen stood at the top of the stairs with some toast on a plate. She looked around at the room she'd only been in a handful of times. 'It looks like Laura Ashley threw up in here. What the fuck has gotten into you?'

'Just felt like doing something other than making tea today. Is that for me?'

She handed over the plate and went and sat on the storage boxes. 'Pretend we still have cheese, and that's a toasted sandwich.'

Lindsey took as big a bite as she could from the sandwich, not realising how hungry she was until the food was in her hand. 'We're just about out of everything now, aren't we?' she shoved the words out through her full mouth.

'We still have bread in the freezer. I did try to get some supplies from the shop today.'

'And?'

That aul bitch with the scarecrow hair refused to sell me more than one pack of anything. I asked her what good ten easy fucking singles were gonna do us and you know what she said?'

'What?' Lindsey tried not to react to the fact that Patrick seemed to be using the whole town to strengthen his message to Lindsey.

Eileen shrugged. 'Tough shit, she said. She also said… hang on, I want to get this right…' she sat up straight and grinned, 'she said, Tell that stuck up bitch to get her priorities straightened out and to stop pissing off her boyfriends.'

Lindsey shook her head and took another chunk of toast.

'So I threw the easy singles at her head. Sorry.'

Lindsey laughed with her mouth full.

'So to answer your question, yes, we are just about out of everything. Our situation is as dismal as fuck. So you wanna tell me what you're up to or will I keep guessing?'

'Nothing.'

'Oh OK. So the folks playing house down in your sitting room are your long-lost cousins, yeah?'

'You weren't supposed to be in there.'

'And they are?'

'Technically, they're not.'

'Well, you wanna tell me what they're not doing here then? I knew you were up to something. First That Mad Bastard takes our supplies hostage and makes you his new favourite person. Then you come see our Danny to get tooled up and now this. You're not exactly subtle, Lindsey so you must know that people are talking now.'

'Yeah, well when it comes to me, people are always talking.' Lindsey took a seat on a box beside Eileen and continued to look around at her handiwork while she finished her imaginary toasted sandwich.

'Yeah, that's kinda what I like about you. But these are dangerous rumours. These are people saying that you're fucking with Patrick Ada-whatsit. Well actually, I heard one where you were hiding a jihadist. But what can I say? It's a small town and that's how it rolls.'

'Do they look like jihadists to you?'

'How the fuck do I know who's a jihadist? Anyway, the most popular story seems to be the one where one of Paddy's hookers robbed him blind and now you're hiding her. Now that shit could easily get you killed.'

'I love it.' Lindsey got to her feet and went to the back wall to inspect the floorboards again.

'What?'

'Patrick buys and sells women. Yet the women are still the villains of the story.'

'I didn't say that. You ask me, they'd be perfectly right to scoop the man's eyes out of their sockets using a rusty spoon before they rob everything he has. But I'm just telling you what I heard. Now they might not look like jihadists, but she did look like someone who's seen her fair share of cock rotted fuckwits and she's as cagey as hell. So I know she's hiding from someone. As for the two boyos; I don't know what the story with them is, but...'

'And what should I do, Eileen? Hand her over?'

'I'm not saying that either. I just want you to know what it is that you have here, Lindsey. Once you know what you have, then at least you can plan accordingly.'

'What do I have?' Lindsey mumbled, suddenly realising that she'd have to loosen one section of the wall so that she could get behind it to cut the access hatch.

'What you have is ten pounds of shit. And you have it in a five-pound bag girl. You should look more worried.'

'Would that help?

Eileen didn't answer. But Lindsey sensed that she was making a face behind her back, and she grinned despite herself.

'I presume you're not going to add truth to any of those rumours?'

'Woman, please. What can I do to help?'

'You can carry on as normal. Take care of yourself and continue to know nothing about any of this. Now go home and thanks for the sandwich.'

As Lindsey walked Eileen downstairs and locked the café door behind her, she thought seriously about what she'd said. Eileen was warning her that she needed to be more careful and she was right. It was unfortunate that Mary and Jimmy happened to be there when Patrick came. Their version of events were being Chinese whispered all over town. However Patrick Adebayo didn't need anyone's version but his own. He was coming regardless of the town gossips; it was just a matter of when. Hence the new hiding space in the attic. She needed to get that finished and until such time as she could figure out what to do with her new house guests, things had to at least appear to be business as usual.

Chapter 10

It was early the next morning when Lindsey finally finished up in the attic. The walls, ceiling and beams got a second coat of paint. A rough hatch had been cut into the floorboards, which was easily lifted and replaced onto the joists and the false wall was fixed back into place. One panel was slightly looser so that she could access the hatch from both sides for the time being. There was a three-inch gap between that panel and the wall, covered only with wallpaper. She couldn't move it too many times or it would become an obvious flaw, but all in all, it didn't look too bad considering. It wasn't until she clambered down through the ceiling hatch into the kitchenette that she found her first problem.

Still in her overalls and looking like she'd had a fight with a DIY superstore, her skin and eyes burned from the insulation wool. The looks on the faces of her guests as she lowered herself out of the ceiling was enough to tell her that she was not a pleasant sight.

'It's OK.' She tried a smile.

Water poured from her eyes as she searched for her first aid box. She had some eyewash in there and she desperately needed it. She also needed to do something about the wool up there. She was sure that if the situation arose, which it surely would, Lena and Amir would battle through it. But Reem was a child. She couldn't add this kind of pain to what had already been inflicted upon him. Inflicted upon all of them.

Lena jumped to her feet and hurried from the room. She returned seconds later with the supplies that Lindsey needed.

'Sit down, Lindsey.'

Lindsey did as she was told, taking the box from Lena. She pulled out tubes of eyewash and handed them to Lena. She tilted her head back.

'Pour those in my eyes.'

Lena obliged. They stung like hell, but there was no time to sit there and wait for perfection. It was a new day and before long the foot traffic would begin downstairs and they had no idea what kind of trouble that would bring.

Lindsey got up again and went to the hot press in the bathroom. She pulled out as many sheets as she could find and then stuck her head back in the sitting room door.

'Come with me.'

Lena put her arm around Reem's shoulders, while Reem looped his fingers through Frank's collar. They all followed Lindsey up to the attic.

She was interested first to see if they noticed how fucked up the decor was. If they immediately noticed that it had a false wall that might be used to hide people? Or did it just look like a badly renovated room?

'What do you think?'

They stood at the top of the stairs, looking around. Lena and Reem looked unsure about life in general, while Amir still looked like he wanted to kill someone.

Reem walked over to Lindsey's heavy bag and started feeling the soft leather. Lindsey watched Frank and how he stayed by Reem's side. She could feel anxiety rising within her. She needed her dog like she needed air and seeing him with all his attention focused on someone else made her feel like a meltdown might be coming. It was all totally irrational of course, and Frank proved that by raising his head and trotting over to her, leaving poor Reem alone at the punch bag.

He pressed his muzzle against her, and she lowered herself to one knee. She hugged him gratefully. This too would pass and then he could go back to making Reem feel like he wasn't totally alone in the world.

You selfish bitch, Ryan.

'It's very nice,' Lena replied politely, pulling Lindsey back out of her own head.

'What does this room look like to you?' she finally asked.

Lena walked around looking thoughtfully at everything. She took some minutes to respond, but when she did, it was exactly what Lindsey wanted to hear.

'It looks like maybe a man lived here once.' She also stroked the heavy bag. 'A husband perhaps. Maybe not a nice one. He is gone now and the woman is making the place her own again. Pretty.' She smoothed down the wallpaper. 'A nice room where she can have some peace from her guests.' Lena grinned and once again showed herself to be stronger than some might give her credit for.

Lindsey smiled through her still burning eyes. 'That's exactly what I want it to look like.'

She walked to the wall and pulled gently on the loosened panel. She gestured for Lena, Amir, and Reem to squeeze through ahead of her. It was a tight enough space, maybe three feet wide, but about eight feet long with the hatch in the middle. Lindsey lifted it and let them take a look inside.

'This leads to the hatch in the kitchen.'

Reem looked horrified as he craned his neck to see into the pitch-dark hole in the floor. But horrified was a signature looked for him. Lindsey wondered briefly what he would have looked like before his life took such an unnatural turn.

Amir's face said that it was the dumbest plan he'd ever heard. Justifiably so.

'It's OK.' She smiled reassuringly at Reem. She picked up a small torch. 'I've left one of these just inside the hatch in the kitchen, so it won't be so dark in there.'

None of them spoke. But the looks on their faces said that they didn't want to know what this was for.

'I'm going to think of a way to get you out of here, OK? This is just temporary; in case anyone comes. You'll climb up through the kitchen and come out here. Then you just have to wait for me.' She sounded every bit as calm as she was trained to.

Lena appeared to relax a bit, making it easier for Reem to believe that they'd be alright. Amir was another story. But he had yet to verbalise his complaint.

'Now we're going to practise. You three go back downstairs. I'll crawl through and put these sheets in place so that the nasty wool won't make you itch.'

Her hand moved to reassuringly rub Reem's shoulder. It was an instinctive move, but she caught herself before making contact with him. He surprised her then by reaching up and placing his hands gently across her eyes. They were red and watering, but his soft, cool hands felt like a soothing balm. Then he pulled back just as gently and followed the others back around the wall. Her breath caught in her chest as she watched him shuffle through.

Lindsey would fix that into place now that they'd seen it. All other access to this point would be through the hatch from now on.

*

Over the next hour they practised. Lena would push Reem up through the hatch and follow him up. Amir was last to climb in. He needed to pull the small step ladder up there with him and replace the hatch. By then Reem should almost be at the back wall, ready to push up through the new hatch and into the attic. It was slow and stunted. But the more times they did it, the quicker and quieter they became. Reem in particular got the hang of it quickly. But this probably wasn't the first time in his young life that he had to hide in fear for his life.

'You shouldn't have to be so good at this,' she spoke softly to him as he clambered back down for the last time.

Either he didn't hear her, didn't understand her, or he simply didn't answer.

*

It was almost nine am when the first sounds travelled up from downstairs. Despite the fact that she'd been up for more than twenty-four hours, Lindsey needed to get back to work today. Or at least appear to and still, it took everything she had to drag herself downstairs.

'Your friends are here,' Eileen announced, as she pushed passed Lindsey carrying what looked like one strange giant scone.

Lindsey had no idea where she was getting ingredients to make anything at all. But she decided to take the piss anyway rather than ask. Eileen would prefer it.

'Clearly you wasted all your talent on that one cupcake yesterday.'

'Kiss it, Lindsey.' She shoved through the doors like she was picking a fight with them.

Lindsey tried to shake off The Dread that accompanied her yet again. Then she followed Eileen out to the busier than ever Lindsey's café. Word had spread.

Fucking Mary Kelly.

'Hey!' Ben looked up from his coffee with what bordered on a smile, which soon turned to concern. Or something like it. 'What happened?'

Lindsey took a second to remember what she looked like. She'd had a shower and cleaned herself up, but her eyes were bloodshot and still stung.

'Nothing, I just...'

Ben stood and came towards her, looking overly concerned for her welfare.

She didn't buy it for a second.

'You've been crying.'

OK, that'd do.

She shrugged and shook her head dramatically.

'You can tell me.' He gave her shoulder a reassuring squeeze.

She wanted to break his hand. She liked this version of him even less than the brutish thug that she knew him to be. But she didn't tell him that. Instead she told him exactly what he wanted to hear.

'Patrick thinks that I'm interfering with his business, Ben. I know what happens to people when Patrick thinks they've crossed him.'

Ben was quiet for a second before asking, with an ominous tone in his voice, 'But you didn't, right?'

'What, cross him? How stupid do you think I am?'

Ben took it upon himself to hug her, like he thought he had the right.

Lindsey bristled, but he didn't seem to notice. She looked over his shoulder at Charlie, who was sitting at Ben's table with his head down. He looked different; frightened.

'Thanks, Ben.' She pulled back, tapped him on the chest and forced herself to smile.

She turned away from him and went behind the bar. She busied herself making a coffee that she desperately needed, while subtly eyeing Charlie. Something about him made Lindsey want to get him as far away from Ben as possible.

She shook her head. What was she gonna do, add him to the fucked-up situation upstairs? Stay out of it, Lindsey.

'Hey, Lindsey?' Eileen stuck her head around the swing door and gestured like she was having a serious neck spasm. 'A little help in here?'

'When did he arrive?' Lindsey whispered when the doors swung shut behind her.

'About a minute after I opened up.'

'Did you want something?'

'No. You looked like you were ready to pounce, so I thought I'd better get you out of there before he noticed. Never mind him though. Did you see the gang up the road?'

'What gang?'

'All the do-gooders outside the McParland house. They're all, flowers, candles and alleluias. The same fuckers never gave the time of day to Evelyn when she was alive. Or to Grace for that matter. Where is she anyway?'

'Who, Grace?' Lindsey shrugged. 'Still in hospital I'd imagine.'

'What'll she do when she gets out? Live in that house with her sister's ghost for company? Poor old biddy.'

'Speak of the devil…' Lindsey glanced over the top of the saloon doors as the prayer group shoved their way in off the street.

She recognised Seán Buckley along with Mary and Adrian Kelly. Some of the others she knew only to see. Lindsey wished that they'd taken themselves off to another café to give their post mortem on the events that took place in the McParland's house. But that didn't look like it was about to happen. People were moving tables around to make room for them. Some were even sharing their seats.

'Fucking hell.'

Ben got to his feet as Lindsey begrudgingly went back out. He was finishing up a phone call as he shrugged on his jacket.

'You off?' she asked, with what she hoped was a teary smile.

'I'll be back in a while.' He rubbed her shoulders again.

She was starting to think that Ben had an ulterior motive of his own, as far as she was concerned. Right now though, she was more interested in Charlie and the fact that he still hadn't looked at her.

'You're quiet today,' she said, when Ben was gone. 'Mind if I have a seat?'

She reached behind the bar for her rapidly cooling coffee. She thought about Irishing it up a bit, just to settle her mind. But she thought better of it. It usually helped her for a while, but in the end, it only ever succeeded in strengthening her demons.

Charlie didn't answer, so she sat down anyway.

'So, are you gonna tell me what's wrong, or will I start guessing?'

He looked up sharply, panic in his eyes. 'Wh… nothing. Nothing's wrong, Lindsey. I swear. Please don't say anything to Ben.'

'About what?'

'About nothing. There's nothing to tell. I'm fine.'

Christ.

'Did someone hurt you?'

He shook his head.

She glanced towards the door to make sure that Ben was actually gone. She was conscious of the crowds around them, but the noise of their chatter was enough to drown out what she wanted to say to the boy. He looked more childlike than ever.

'OK, how about I do the talking?' She kept her voice low. 'Whatever's going on, you know you always have options, Charlie, yeah?'

Charlie shook his head and brought his hands to his face. 'You don't get it.'

'Fine, I don't get it. So help me out.'

He squeezed his eyes shut.

'OK. So, your options; the first thing you need to do is consider all of them.'

He raised his eyes to meet hers.

'What are they?'

'I don't have any.'

'You always have options, Charlie. Even if they're not obvious at the time. Right now, without knowing anything about your situation, I can tell you that you have two options.' She glanced towards the door again before continuing.

'One: say nothing and go along with whatever it is. But only a fool would do that without knowing exactly what the consequences would be. And I'm not just talking about legal consequences. I'm talking about what'll go on in here afterwards.' She tapped the side of her head. 'Don't take anyone's word for what will go on inside your head when all is said and done because that's what'll cause you more problems than anything else. Trust me on that.'

'And option two?'

'Me.'

He looked up at her again, confused.

'Come to me, Charlie.'

'What can you do? You can't help me, Lindsey. Besides, they already think you're up to something. Why do you think they're here all the time?'

'Don't worry about me. Just listen, OK? If my front door is closed, you bang on it, any time, day or night. You don't have to tell me why you're here. I won't ask and Ben will never know. But if the time comes when you don't know what else to do, come here. I'll help you.'

Ben was back and as he came through the door he looked suspiciously at Charlie. 'Hope he wasn't making a nuisance of himself?'

'Nah.' Lindsey smiled her perfectly genuine fake smile. 'He was giving me a list of required ingredients for the perfect pizza. I'm thinking of getting an oven in here and this guy reckons it needs a fried egg on top.'

Charlie's smile could just as easily have been a grimace, as Lindsey got to her feet and left them to it.

*

The prayer group stayed for most of the morning and so did Ben and Charlie. Eileen doled out slices of her giant scone to everyone. But Lindsey's mind was on Charlie. She didn't know what was going on with him, but whatever it was, it made the blood drain from his boyish face and his hands shake.

She had to remind herself again, that for Lena, Amir, and Reem's sake, she needed to keep her nose out of everyone else's shit. But of course that wasn't about to happen.

*

Four o'clock the following morning, the witching hour, brought with it a frantic knocking on her door. Instinctively she knew that it was Charlie. She was out of bed and half way down the stairs before he'd finished knocking and as she swung open the door, he practically fell into the porch.

'Hey, it's OK.' She caught him by the shoulders to keep him upright.

He was shaking from head to toe and despite her current situation, she'd never seen such terror on a person's face.

'Charlie, what is it? What happened?'

Charlie jumped dramatically when Frank came sniffing furiously around them.

'It's alright; it's just Frank.' She used one hand to hold Charlie steady and the other to get Frank to back up. Which of course he did.

'You said you'd help me. You told me to come here.' He was panicking.

'I did. I'm glad you came.' Lindsey's calm and rational tone came so naturally to her, she didn't even have to try. But the last thing she felt was calm or rational right now. Was she about to add another person to her fucked-up situation?

'Look, you just need to get me out of here, OK? I know you've been doing it, Lindsey. Everyone knows it. Please…?'

He was becoming hysterical and Frank was getting wound up too. Lindsey looked at Charlie in silence, as she wrapped her hand around the top of Frank's head and scratched at his ear. She was trying to think. Of course she had to help the kid. But first she needed to know what was going on.

'You're safe, Charlie.' She nodded finally, with as much reassurance as she could muster. 'Just tell me what happened?'

'You said you wouldn't ask. I just need you to get me out of here, like, tonight.'

'What makes you think I can get anyone out of anywhere?'

'He would have killed that woman for running. But you got her out of here. Everyone knows it and apparently she wasn't the first or the last.'

She muttered under her breath.

'So why is everyone saying it, if it's not true?'

'Because they're idiots. Now tell me what the hell is going on here.'

'I can't.' Charlie started to cry. Then he dug his knuckles into his eyes in an attempt to either blind himself or plug the tears.

'I said I'd help you and I will.' She put her hands on his shoulders and with a little bit of force, she lowered him into a chair. 'But I need to know what I'm up against or I won't know what I need to do.'

Silence again, expect for Charlie's choked sobs.

'Whatever you tell me now stays with me. You have to trust someone eventually, Charlie so I'm asking you to trust me now. I need to know what my options are.'

More silence. This time she let it settle, sure that Charlie would feel the need to break it sooner or later. She sat there, quietly watching him.

It took a while for him to straighten the details out in his head. At least well enough to be able to explain them.

'Ben got me a job in there.' His voice was no more than a whisper. His head was in his hands as he spoke.

'In Patrick's place?'

He nodded.

Lindsey cursed Ben and the horse he rode in on.

'OK. And?'

'I hate it in there. Everyone looks sick or something.'

More silence.

'My job is just to do this and that; tidy up the place, bring drinks to people and that kinda thing. Tonight when I went to work, everyone was like, panicking or something. I asked Derek what was going on and he said to keep my mouth shut and stay out of the way.'

'Derek?'

'One of the security guys. But he's alright.'

'OK…?'

'I was taking empty glasses out of one of the rooms when Derek came through the door. Literally, Lindsey! He was thrown through the door, by Hector. He kept shouting, Where are they, tell me where they are… but he was hammering him at the same time. Derek couldn't have answered if he wanted to. Then Hector started kicking him in the head, like a football. Over and over and over again until there was nothing left to kick.' His shoulders started to shake and he seemed to almost convulse as the tears started to flow.

Lindsey couldn't blame him. Charlie was gonna carry this with him for the rest of his life. But she couldn't help him with that.

'Did he kill him?'

'I don't know. He wasn't moving when Patrick came in. Then the two of them dragged him out.'

'Who were they looking for?' She wanted to know how much Charlie knew. She suspected, very little.

He shook his head. 'I heard one of the women say that the boys were gone.'

Lindsey didn't respond.

'There weren't any other boys there though. Only me. There aren't any other jobs there for men, only security.'

She marvelled at his naivety. Her heart would have broken for him if she could think that way for a minute. But she couldn't afford a minute. She needed every second now to think of a way out of here for these people. Now she needed to know if that included Charlie.

'Are they after you? Did they know that you were watching?'

He shook his head. 'I shoved myself in beside the wardrobe. They didn't see me.'

She waited.

'But Patrick told Hector to get Ben on it. Ben will make me help him. I don't want to, Lindsey.'

'OK. It'll be alright. Wait here a minute?' She got up and headed for the back kitchen.

She went through the kitchen doors and leaned against the wall. She let the back of her head knock against the cold concrete for a minute. It seemed her five-pound bag was now holding fifty pounds of shit against a giant fan.

Chapter 11

Lindsey carried herself from the kitchen like a person who was in complete control, but by the time she got back to where Charlie was sitting, he looked like he was about to fall asleep. Handing some responsibility to someone else was a weight off his narrow shoulders. A decision she hoped he wouldn't live to regret.

He straightened himself up as she came and sat down opposite him. He looked painfully hopeful. It was that look of hope that she'd been seeing far too much of lately.

'What time did your shift end?'

'Six am.'

'So you left early? Did you tell anyone you were leaving or where you were going?'

He shook his head. 'I just legged it as soon as they dragged Derek out of there.'

'So no one saw you leave?'

'One of the women did, but she looked kind of out of it.'

Lindsey nodded. 'And where are you staying tonight?'

His panic returned. 'What do you mean where am I staying? I'm staying here! Or wherever the fuck you've been taking people; that's where I'm staying tonight!'

'Calm down, Charlie. Where have you been staying? Where are you supposed to go when you finish work at six?'

'Ben's place.'

'OK. Well then, you need to go to Ben's house. Tell him you're sick, that's why you left work early.'

He jumped to his feet. 'What?!'

'Listen to me…'

'Get me out of here, Lindsey! You did it for them, just…'

'Charlie, sit down and listen.' She pulled him gently back into his seat. 'First of all, I haven't gotten anyone out of anywhere. But that doesn't mean that I can't get you out of here. I just need time to plan. If you disappear, then sooner or later they're gonna come here looking for you too, aren't they?' Because somehow I've become fucking Houdini.

He didn't reply, but his eyes filled with tears again. She fought with herself about sending him away, but it was the only way.

'Just listen; they're getting Ben to look for whoever is missing, yeah?'

He shrugged. 'I think so. It sounded like it.'

'OK…'

'You should have seen what they did to Derek. Just because he was on duty when they went missing. Why were there boys there?' He looked like he'd just realised the answer to his own question.

'Same reason there are women there.'

Charlie heaved a couple of times and then threw up on her floor. Frank moved just in time to avoid the splatter.

Lindsey handed him a napkin, but didn't offer any words of consolation because there weren't any.

'Oh Jesus…' he cried, as he dried his mouth.

'But they got out, right?'

'But what will they make me do to find them? You have to get me away…'

'And I will, Charlie. But for now, you need to go back to Ben. Look, he's more subtle than the others. He has to be. He's still pretending to be a cop, remember? He'll use intimidation first and before it goes any further than that, you'll be gone. I promise.'

The word promise almost choked her. But rather than dwelling on it, she went behind the bar to find a pen. She scribbled her phone number on another napkin and handed it to Charlie. The number was linked to the ancient Nokia that she kept under the bar. It hadn't been switched on in a very long time, but it was time to resurrect it.

'This is the first place he's gonna look, you know that? They know, Lindsey.'

'What do they know?'

'They don't know how. But they know that you know more about her than you're letting on. Ben has a serious thing for you. His whole face changes whenever they talk about you. I don't like it.'

'You don't need to worry about me, Charlie.'

'This'll be the first place he looks for sure.'

'Let him look. In the meantime, this is my number. If I'm wrong, or you feel like things are moving too fast, call me. I'll get you away.'

'Lindsey, I can't…'

'You can. A day or two at the most and I'll have something in place for you. Until then, be sick. You don't know anything about anything, is that clear?'

She stood and encouraged him to do the same. The longer he wasn't at Patrick's or Ben's, the more questions he'd have to answer. That is, assuming someone would actually notice his absence.

She opened the front door and encouraged Frank to go outside. As he sniffed the lamp post and raised a leg, she checked the street. There was no one around. She turned again to Charlie.

'You have my number; use it any time day or night, OK? I have your back, Charlie. Please trust me on that.'

He nodded, wiping his face with his hands. He was paler than she'd ever seen him and his skin was clammy. He looked genuinely sick, but that was good. It might actually help him.

Now all she had to do was bring her old phone back to life so that Charlie could contact her and then somehow figure out a plan to smuggle four people out of town. And she needed to do it in a hurry.

*

Frank trotted upstairs while Lindsey locked up again after Charlie left. Surprisingly, her hands weren't shaking. Her heart wasn't hammering in her chest either and her breathing was steady, so Frank was happy enough to leave her alone for a bit. For now her mind was busying itself with three scared boys and a woman who'd endured enough. She was resigning herself to the fact that one way or another she was going to help them, consequences be damned. That in itself was enough to bring a certain peace to her restless mind.

When she finally went up, all of her house guests were in her living room. They looked as uncomfortable as always, but none more than Reem. The child was completely withdrawn and Lindsey worried that he'd simply seen too much in his young life.

Frank, the professional lifeline, pressed himself against Reem's leg.

'Is everyone OK?' She asked, by way of enquiring why they were all up.

'We heard the banging.'

She wanted to ask why they didn't immediately go to their hiding place, but she didn't. Instead she told them the truth.

'That was Charlie. He'll be joining us when we leave here.'

'How will you take another person when you cannot even take us?' Amir asked in his usual angry tone.

'She has gotten us this far, my friend.' Lena countered.

'He's right, Lena. It won't be easy. But then, it was never going to be easy. Amir, I won't leave Charlie behind, any more than I'd leave you behind. The same people want all of you.'

'And she is what stands between them and us.' Lena again.

'Then we are dead.'

She wasn't going to placate Amir, partly because he might be right. But mostly because she knew it wouldn't help and blowing smoke up holes was never one of Lindsey Ryan's strong points.

Instead she said, 'Why don't you all get some rest?'

'And will you rest, Lindsey?' Lena asked with a kind and sympathetic smile, as she caught Lindsey's hand in hers.

'I will if you all get off my bed.' She grinned, indicating the couch that they were sitting on.

Lindsey had no expectations of sleep though. She had too much to think about and sleep would bring nothing but more chaos.

*

For what was left of that night, Lindsey sat on her couch staring at the hatch in the ceiling. But rather than thinking about the logistics of getting three people up there on very short notice, she was thinking about Charlie. She wondered if he was OK. If anything happened to him, it would be one more thing to weigh on Lindsey's conscience until the day she died. She'd sent him back to Ben, alone and terrified.

'You sleep sitting up now?' Lena was standing in the doorway. 'Not like Frank.'

Frank was curled at her feet half asleep. He lifted his head at the sound of his name, sighed at being disturbed and lowered it again.

'I worry about you, Lindsey.' She came and sat on the arm of the couch. 'You try to do too much. It will be bad for you.'

'This is short term, Lena. Don't worry, everything will be fine.'

'This is what I mean. Somehow, we have all become your problem. It is being left to you to come up with a solution and it's not fair.'

Lindsey couldn't help half smiling at the madness of her situation.

'What I say is funny?'

'No. It's just not as unusual as you might think for me to find myself on the wrong end of a bad situation. I have a knack for it.'

'For me, it is always the wrong place at the wrong time. Is that what they say? But this time…' she shook her head. 'I was in exactly the right place at the right time.'

She was quiet for a minute and Lindsey let her gather her thoughts.

'I made three attempts to escape through different gardens up there.'

'How did you get out?'

'I was not at Patrick's that night. I was taken to a house instead. He charges extra for that of course. There was supposed to be one man and I was to be there for one hour before Hector came to get me. There were seven other men inside the house. They all took their turn but it seemed that wasn't enough. They had more plans for me. One of them went outside for a cigarette; the door was open so I ran.'

Lindsey's gut twisted. She'd survived many things in her lifetime but vulnerability was her biggest fear.

'So you jumped?'

Lena nodded. 'Finally, yes. When I realised that there would be no other way. But what if I had succeeded the first time, or the second? I would have found myself in someone else's yard. Someone ordinary. Someone as frightened as I was perhaps. Or someone who wouldn't dare to go up against a man like Patrick. Lindsey, I would surely be dead. Right time, right place you see? And I thank Allah for bringing me to you. But I worry for you.'

'You don't need to worry about me. I'm so sorry for what you went through here, Lena.' She meant it with all her heart.

Lena smiled through her tears. 'I've spent many years without a home now, Lindsey. That was not the first time. But I swear it will be the last. I will take my own life before anyone touches me again.'

Lindsey could think of nothing to say. Then Lena spoke again in a slightly brighter tone.

'You know, I wasn't always such a pathetic creature. Once upon a time I was studying English and Economics at Al-Baath University in Homs. The first woman in my family to go to college. I even managed to get there against my father's wishes, but that's another story altogether. Unfortunately, I ran out of time before I could get my degree.'

'Wow.'

She was responding to Lena's university achievement, but was still unable to respond to the fact that this wasn't her first gang rape. Whether it was naivety or just plain ignorance, she just never imagined what life must be like for the millions of displaced people all over the world. But then how could anyone imagine such a life?

'I had hoped to also be the first woman in my family to marry for love. But then another so-called holy war put me on the wrong boat and turned me into this.' She gestured to herself in disgust.

'You're a survivor, Lena. It's not too late to have everything you want.'

'Maybe not. But now that I bear the scars of many men, there will be no love for me.'

'Your scars are nothing to be ashamed of. If anything, you should be proud when you look at them.'

'Proud?'

'Yes, proud. Proud of the fact that you were strong enough to survive. Scars remind us of what we've come through. When life starts dragging you down, you look at them and know that things will never be that bad again. Whatever happens from here, you're strong enough to get through it.'

'You can't know this.'

Lindsey lowered the zip on her hoodie and let it slip down along her arm exposing the gnarled skin above her left breast, across her shoulder and down her arm.

'I can.'

Lena reached out and traced her fingers across Lindsey's scarring before asking, almost in a whisper, 'How?'

'Syria. IED.'

Lena pulled her hand back as if she'd been electrocuted.

'It seems like a lifetime ago,' Lindsey assured her. 'These scars brought me to my knees for a time. But now when a man walks into my café and tries to intimidate me, I remind myself that I've already had the worst day of my life. If that didn't break me then nothing will.' You're so full of shit, Ryan.

More often than not, she would welcome death with open arms. She imagined it'd be more peaceful than living as she did, but she wasn't about to tell the woman that.

'I knew you were not just a woman.' Lena half smiled.

'There's no such a thing as just a woman, Lena.'

Chapter 12

'Hey Lindsey, you up there?'

Lindsey hadn't closed her eyes for a minute, but time had gotten away from her. Now her little sitting room was filling with people and Eileen's voice bellowed up the stairs towards her.

'Yeah!' she shouted back, getting to her feet.

'Ben is here and he's being an impatient fucker,' she shouted.

Lena and Amir froze.

Lindsey shoved them towards ceiling hatch. 'Grab Reem and get up there. Don't come down until you're sure he's gone.'

Within a minute they were up there, but she could hear them shuffling around overhead. Ben wasn't here on a social call; not at this hour and it seemed he wasn't about to wait for her to come down either. When Lindsey reached the top of the stairs, he was already half way up to meet her.

'Ben. What's up?' She asked, blocking his way as she continued downwards.

'Just checking up.' He gave her a smile that was as fake as her own, only less convincing. 'Making sure you're alright. Any more unwanted visitors?'

'Nah. I don't expect any either. Sorry about yesterday. I was a bit… emotional.' She shook her head. 'I was just heading down. Coffee?'

'That's OK.' He blocked her path. 'Patrick isn't the type to forgive and forget, Lindsey, so I'd say emotional is an appropriate response to your current situation.'

'My current situation? There's nothing current about my involvement, Ben. Listen, if anything, I tried to help. Not that anyone seems interested in that little detail.' She nudged passed him as gently as she could, ignoring the urge to shove him down the stairs.

'I'm interested.' He put his hand on her shoulder. 'Hey, can we have a word in private?'

'I'm late. We'll talk downstairs.' She kept walking, giving him little choice but to either follow her down or force his way up.

Frank's glare greeted him on the landing so he eventually conceded and turned to follow her. She suspected that Ben wasn't ready to show his true colours yet. But as sure as day turned to night, he would eventually. Men like him always did. And now that the hunt was on for Amir and Reem, it was only a matter of time.

'Actually, I was hoping you'd pop in today.' She smiled brightly, pretending not to notice the threat between man and dog.

Eileen was standing at the end of the stairs when they got there. She looked like she was ready to take the stairs five at a time if Lindsey needed help.

'Why don't you find us a table where we can chat and I'll make some coffee?'

Ben was slow to leave the back kitchen, but eventually he did.

'You OK?' Eileen mouthed.

Lindsey nodded. She followed Ben out to the café and slipped in behind the bar to brew two coffees. Then she joined him at the window seat. She leaned back in the chair opposite him and took a sip, looking far more relaxed than she felt.

'So you actually wanted to see me today?' He grinned and picked up his cup.

The way he looked at her made it clear that he wanted her. Not because of her winning personality, or even that he particularly liked her. He wanted her because she wasn't easily had.

Ben was a good-looking bloke and he knew it too. Under normal circumstances she might have found herself trying him out for a night or two. When it came to sex, Lindsey Ryan didn't question her partner's morals any more than they questioned hers. But she did prefer them to be strong, silent and most importantly, anonymous.

'Why sound so surprised?'

'I got the impression that you don't like me very much.'

'Oh haven't you heard? I'm an odd-ball. And that's just according to those who are too polite to say what they really think.'

'Why is that?'

She shrugged. 'I suppose I've always struggled a bit with…well, making friends. And let's face it, you're a little bit intimidating.' She grinned, telling him exactly what he wanted to hear.

She could tell by the smile playing on his lips, that she'd hit the spot.

'Intimidating?'

'Look at you!'

He laughed quietly, his head inflating like a balloon.

'I'm sorry, Lindsey. I'd never mean to intimidate you. I want the opposite actually. I want you to feel safe and to know that I'm here for you.'

She gave him a, Bless your cotton socks kind of look and sipped her coffee, wishing that it contained a dash of something stronger.

'So, was there a particular reason you were hoping to see me today or…?'

His demeanour had changed completely. The aggression that emanated from him as he invited himself up to her flat had all but disappeared. Or maybe he was just as good a fake as she was. When he wanted to be.

'I have a bit of a problem and you're the first person I thought of as it happens. But you can say no if you want to, I mean…'

'Lindsey,' he reached over and took her hand. 'Just ask.'

She blew out a long, dramatic breath. 'I've worked so hard to get this place up and running, Ben. You have no idea. But I'm on the verge of having to shut it down. I haven't had a delivery in ages. No matter what I order, or who I order from, it just never arrives. My suppliers are playing dumb, and I'm worried.'

'I don't think this is down to your suppliers, Lindsey. This has Patrick written all over it.'

You don't say?

'You need me to get you supplies?'

She shook her head. 'I have to go myself, there's too much that I need. But from what I hear, there are some guys parked up at Belvelly Bridge deciding who gets to pass and who doesn't. I've somehow landed on Patrick's shit list and I just don't want any grief from them. I thought maybe you might have some influence?'

According to Danny Chambers, they were looking for Lena. But you may be sure that Amir and Reem had sped to the top of the priorities list by now. The real money was to be made from them.

'I know who they are. Not the most pleasant lads you'll ever meet.'

'I need to feel protected, Ben. To be able to make a living and feel safe. Is that asking too much?' She played to his knight in shining armour ambitions, as fake as they might be.

They were both trying to gauge each other's true motives and she was dying to ask about Charlie. But she didn't want to raise any flags in his mind, so she kept her mouth shut and Ben wasn't volunteering anything.

He shrugged, looking doubtful. 'I suppose I could come with you? I can make sure they don't bother you.'

'Thanks Ben, but I need Eileen with me. She knows more than I do about what we need.' Lindsey did her best to sound utterly let down. She reached across, squeezed his hand and got to her feet. 'I'm sorry for asking. I probably overestimated the kind of power that you guys have these days. I'll figure something out.'

She gave one last sad smile.

He caught her by the wrist and stood with her. 'Hey, leave it with me, OK?'

She smiled and nodded. 'I better get to work. Thanks Ben and hey, I know you're doing the best you can and I'm asking too much.'

And there it was. The look of I'm the man on his face.

'I'll sort it,' he called after her, as she walked away.

*

She waited another ten minutes after he left before going back upstairs and when she got there, the place was in silence. As it should be. The only problem was the stepladder. It was still under the hatch in the ceiling. A dangerous mistake had she been someone else.

'You can come out.'

There was shuffling overhead as Lena, Reem and Amir made their way across the ceiling above her and finally came out through the hatch. When they were all back in the kitchen she asked the question.

'Can anyone see the mistake we made?'

Lena picked up the stepladder, clearly annoyed with herself.

'If I were someone else, that would have pointed me right to you. Look I know this situation isn't great and we're all new to this. But it needs to happen more smoothly and much more quietly. Are we in agreement on that?'

Lena nodded.

'Mistakes like this can't happen.'

'It was me.' Amir shook his head. 'I was the last one up. I should have pulled it up with me.'

'Like I said, we're all new to this. We're learning as we go. I'm going back downstairs now as normal. I'd like it if you all spent time practising getting into position. I also think that someone should sit near the top of the stairs, but not in sight of the back kitchen. You're listening for anything out of the ordinary downstairs. You can take turns with that.'

No one responded for a second, but then Amir pulled the step ladder into place. He caught Reem by the hand and directed him up first. He was taking the lead and Lindsey was happy to let him. Amir needed to feel in control of something. A feeling Lindsey fully understood.

'Good. I'll leave you to it.'

She glanced at Reem as she left the room. He was at the top of the ladder looking down at Amir waiting to be pushed upwards. As far as Lindsey was aware, Reem hadn't spoken a word since getting here; at least not in her presence. Apart from telling them his name. She wondered if maybe he was afraid of her. If maybe he talked to Lena when they were alone together. She hoped so. But as much as she hated to admit it, the sight of Reem unsettled her. The sheer innocence on his face, his age and his beautiful Syrian complexion reminded her of the little girl she'd met on the worst day of her life. The same little girl whose bone fragments were still lodged in various parts of Lindsey's body.

So she left Reem for Lena to care for. Maybe he could sense her discomfort around him. Maybe that was why he didn't speak. Either way, there was nothing she could do about it. He was a beautiful, innocent child and his mere presence was like a dagger in her heart.

As she closed the door behind her and headed for the stairs, something completely unexpected happened. Her mobile phone rang. It hadn't rung in over six months, but then she hadn't charged it in as long. Now she kept it with her for Charlie's sake.

'Hello?' She answered hopefully.

'Linds… list… hea…d…'

'Hello?' The line was severely broken and the voice she heard wasn't Charlie's. It was Adam Street's. 'Street? Is that you? I can't hear you…'

The line went dead.

'Fuck!'

She checked the display, but it just showed unknown. She scrolled quickly through her contacts until she found his number and hit dial. But the signal was gone.

'Fuck!' she muttered again, clutching the ancient phone to her chest.

Adam Street was one of the few people in this world who could honestly say that he knew the good, the bad, and the ugly sides of Lindsey Ryan. They'd worked together for over thirteen years in the army and served four tours overseas with the same unit. Street was there with her when she was an army recruit, green as grass. He was there when she became one of the first female instructors in the Irish infantry. He was there through all the laughs and most of the tortuous exercises and he featured heavily in most of her stories. And she in his. He was also there with her when PTSD took its hold on her and refused to let go. He saw her through the best, the worst, and the most self-destructive times of her life. She trusted him more than any other human being on Earth. She also hadn't seen or heard from him in almost a year.

She hit redial five more times with the same result; no signal. She talked softly to her phone, willing it to ring again. But of course it didn't.

'Did you just see a good ghost or a bad ghost?' Eileen was standing at the end of the stairs again.

Lindsey looked up from her phone. 'It rang.'

'Seriously? You've had a phone all this time?'

She pulled the ancient piece from Lindsey's hands. It was incapable of connecting to the internet, which was why it suited her as well as any phone could.

'What the fuck is this?' She held the phone up to her ear and shook it. 'Do you need to slot coins into it?'

Lindsey smiled because she couldn't help it and snatched the phone back.

'So who was it, Alexander Graham Bell looking for his prototype back?'

'It was Street.' She laughed quietly. Sometimes she forgot how much of a tonic Eileen could be.

'Who?'

'A friend from before.'

'Well maybe you can ask him to come help you out here, girl, 'cause if you ask me, you're getting in way too deep with that lot.' She nodded towards the stairs. 'Look, you might as well save me the trouble of snooping and just level with me. Tell me what you're planning to do so that at least I won't put my foot in it.'

Lindsey looked out over the kitchen doors. Jimmy Duggan was out there, reading his paper. Mary Kelly's grandson, Adrian, was at another table drinking a can of 7-Up, with Martin Powell of all people.

'What's Martin doing with Adrian?' Lindsey mumbled, though she had a good idea. Ben had spotted another vulnerable kid.

'You can crack their heads together later. But for now you need to focus on me please. You were about to fill me in.'

'Yeah. I'm not sure yet.'

'Wouldn't you want to start getting sure?'

'Yeah, I would.'

'Because maybe you haven't noticed, but it's not a fucking mansion you have up there. How exactly are you supposed to explain them away if someone goes up? It's becoming a popular tourist destination these days.'

'I've sorted that part out for now. But I need to get them out of here and I think I need your brother's help to do it.'

She looked at her phone again, hoping for a much better option. One that was unlikely to come soon enough.

'Lindsey, my brothers are fucking idiots. Yes, they're running all sorts of shit in and out of town. Things though Lindsey. Not people.'

'I know. Look, I haven't worked out the details yet so don't say anything, yeah?'

'Don't worry; I can keep my mouth shut. But you need to be careful. You're playing with fire, girl.'

She couldn't argue with that. But at least now an idea was forming in her mind. Street was back. Not that he'd ever left. Not really. If anything, Street was always watching from a distance. He'd lost one member of his team and not wanting to lose another, he kept tabs on all of them. The fact that he was getting in touch now meant that something was up. She needed to find him. Plus, if anyone could help these people it was him.

'What was all that about?' Lindsey pulled up a chair beside Martin, just as Adrian got up and left quite abruptly.

'Just chatting to a buddy of mine.'

'He's a bit young for you, isn't he?'

'Well, I'm not planning on dating him like,' he scoffed. 'You have nothing to bloody eat in this place.'

'Tell me about it. So Martin, you're pretty clued in to what's what yeah? What do you know about the guys on the bridge?'

As Martin shuffled enthusiastically closer to her, she marvelled at how easy it was to play an egotistical male.

'Patrick's keeping it manned 24/7. He still thinks you know where she is. Or so I hear, plus...' he leaned in closer again and lowered his voice, 'two more brassers are missing now.'

He didn't know.

'Did you hear me? He thinks you know something.'

'That why you're here?'

Martin shrugged. 'I won't lie, Lindsey. We were told to keep an eye on you.'

'Right, and what exactly do you think I might have done with her? I suppose I'm responsible for the other two as well, huh?'

He guffawed. 'Don't be stupid. Even I know you couldn't hold out for this long if you actually knew something. A grown man would cave the second Hector's name was mentioned. This is a waste of time. But hey, if they wanna give me the cushy job, I'll take it.' He smiled brightly. Like a man who had it all figured out. Idiot.

'Pity they're not all as switched on as you, eh?' She smiled. 'Anyway, back to the guys on the bridge; they weren't the lads you were talking about the other day, were they?'

'Who?'

'You said they were trained by some Special Forces guys in Cork?'

'They could be, Lindsey. You have no idea how many people Patrick has working for him. You know, I wouldn't be surprised if he was paying those guys to train his men.'

'So have you been to the Old Dogs Gym then?'

Martin sat up straight. 'I don't need a bunch of wannabes to train me up. I compete, Lindsey. I'd kick seven shades of shit out of any one of them assholes.'

Lindsey almost laughed. Poor Martin really didn't have a clue. 'And what makes you think they work for Patrick?'

'Maybe they don't work for him directly. Patrick is very picky about who gets to work for him. And from what I hear, they train all the foreigners mostly. They're a bunch of GI Joe mercenary type lunatics so they'll work for the highest bidder. They run training camps in some derelict buildings in Cork, where apparently even the cops are afraid to go.'

'And how do you know all this?'

He tapped his right ear. 'I hear things, Lindsey. You'd be surprised how much I hear.'

She nodded stoically.

'You need to be very, very careful.'

She shook her head as she got to her feet. 'Leave Adrian Kelly alone, OK?'

Martin held his arms out wide and painted on the surprised expression of a highly offended man.

'What? I was only chatting to him!'

Chapter 13

The noise inside Lindsey's head amplified as the day wore on. There were many possible consequences if it all went tits up, which was highly likely. They ranged from a solid beating, to being wiped off the face of the Earth. For Lena and the boys, it would probably be an awful lot worse. Rumours were rampant and the ones that bordered on being comical were just as dangerous as those that hovered closer to home. They were out of time, and she was eager to get her plan in place.

Jimmy Duggan had been hovering over a cup of cold tea for over an hour. He glanced at her from time to time before finally bringing himself to openly pry.

'Hey, Lindsey?' It was an aggressive whisper, despite the fact that the café was otherwise empty. He jerked his head several times, which she took as an invitation to join him at his table.

'What can I do for you, Jimmy?'

'People are saying things,' he whispered.

'Aren't they always?'

'This is different. They're saying that you're hiding women from two doors up.'

'Right. Because I have a warren of caves running under this building. We're slowly digging our way to China.'

She didn't want Jimmy to be in her line of fire, but Lindsey was on her last nerves.

Jimmy, for his part, didn't seem to notice. He looked thoughtfully at the floor as if to consider the possibility, before speaking again.

'You know Julia Mulcahy? Well she was at the memorial for Evelyn and when we came over here for tea afterwards, you came up in conversation. As usual. It started with Julia saying that you flirted with her husband, Trevor...'

Lindsey raised her eyebrows. 'Who the fuck is Trevor?'

'Mulcahy. He works in the accountant's office along the road.'

'Oh right... yeah.'

Trevor the accountant was in his late fifties and roughly twenty stone in weight. He was balding at an alarming rate and sweated profusely, regardless of the weather. Julia Mulcahy's marriage was probably the safest in town by a long shot.

'Anyway, as they do, the women got into a bit of a bitching session...'

'They must have been really cut up about Evelyn.'

'Girl, there's always time to be bitchy. Anyway, Julia says that Trevor was headed to the office the other evening and he overheard a couple of Patrick's boys talking about you. How you flattened one of their security men. Big fella by all accounts. They reckon you're an undercover or something.'

'That's right, Jimmy. I was specially trained by some lunatics up in Cork. I came here to singlehandedly take down a criminal enterprise and save the town of Cobh.'

Jimmy laughed. 'Yeah, I told them it was a bit farfetched alright.'

Lindsey grinned and got to her feet again. This conversation was making her queasy. She busied herself cleaning until such time as Jimmy finally got up to leave.

'Hey before I go; anymore, eh... episodes?'

'Episodes?'

'You know; like with the French lads?'

'That wasn't an episode, Jimmy,' she lied, feeling another episode stirring inside her.

'Good.' He nodded and after a few more false starts, he finally left.

After that no one else came in and by four o'clock the place was a ghost town. She'd sent Eileen home and was about to close up early. But as she shoved the front door closed, it burst back at her. It brought with it a white-hot flash of pain as it bulldozed her face. She fell backwards onto the floor, bringing two chairs crashing down with her.

Blood ran from her nose, down her throat. She was momentarily blinded and unable to react. The front door slammed shut. Two men grabbed her under the arms and dragged her backwards. They lifted her off her feet and slammed her down on top of a table, pinning her there. Her vision returned as her legs were pulled apart. She was yanked forward so that the man leaning over her was pressed hard against her.

She'd never seen him before. He was roughly the same size, shape and dumb-fuckness as Hector, whose enormous hands were on her shoulders, pinning her to the table.

They both towered over her, but the interchangeable goon roughly pulled her up against him to demonstrate his strength. Hector grabbed her face in his hand and squeezed so hard she thought her teeth might break. They weren't going to be talked around this time. That much was clear as Lindsey struggled to catch up with her situation.

Frank was going berserk upstairs. The fact that he wasn't tearing down meant that he was behind a closed door.

What was going on up there? Even if they were in the crawl space by now, would these two find them anyway, after they were done doing whatever they planned to do with her?

'I'm going to tear this place apart if you don't tell me what you've done with our property.' Hector's breath on her face smelled of cigarettes and garlic as he spoke through gritted teeth. 'And while I do that,

Malik will tear you apart. Is my meaning clear?'

He squeezed her face even tighter. This added to the pain from where the door struck her and she thought her head might explode, but she had to push past it. She was about to be left alone with the animal between her legs. If he got the better of her, she would not survive it. She'd make sure of it.

She forced herself to focus on Malik, who seemed to be looking forward to his time alone with her. She lowered her eyes until they came to rest on his Adam's apple. There it was; bobbing as he swallowed his excitement. The clearest thing in her mind now was that she was only going to get one shot at him. If she missed, she was dead. This meant she couldn't use her fist. Her knuckles might glance off and leave her wide open.

No, she'd go open-handed, using the webbed bit between her thumb and forefinger. Despite the pain of her face being crushed, she could almost feel his cartilage crunching as she imagined taking the breath from his body.

His hands roughly travelled to her breasts and squeezed. She wished for her time alone with him to come now, so that she could take her chance and be done with it, one way or another.

The two men exchanged a look before Hector went behind the bar and found her baseball bat. For a second Lindsey imagined what it would feel like if and when she was struck with it. But she shut it down.

Focus on Malik.

'Where are they?' Hector asked, in a calm and rational manner.

Malik removed his hands from Lindsey's breasts and hooked his fingers into the waistband of her jeans, pressing himself against her again.

Hector slammed the bat into the display fridge, shattering it completely.

'I don't know,' Lindsey replied, refusing to let either of them see her fear.

'Where are they?' he shouted. He battered his way through the swing door and into the back kitchen.

'I don't know,' she replied in the same tone, still watching Malik and his Adam's apple.

He punched her in the face as soon as Hector disappeared, but she was expecting it this time. Yes, her head felt like it had exploded all over her plastic tablecloth. The pain was excruciating, but she didn't give him the satisfaction of hearing her express it. Instead she absorbed it and focused again on his throat as he began unbuckling his belt.

Hector's footsteps started on the stairs. It was now or never, so Lindsey bolted up towards him and slammed her hand into the cartilage in his throat. As she'd imagined, she felt it crunch under the force of her blow. Years of army training and years more of working her frustrations out on the heavy bag meant that she wasn't going to stop now. She needed to gain and secure the upper hand.

While Malik stumbled back, clutching his throat, Lindsey brought her knees to her chest and kicked him full force in the stomach. If he wasn't winded before, he was now. He fell backwards against a table, sending it crashing to the floor and him with it.

Upstairs was hosting a riot of its own. She could only hope that it was a one man show; that the others were safely hidden and that he had the good sense not to go through the door that separated him from Frank. But for the minute, she couldn't do anything about any of that. She could however, make sure that whatever or whoever he found up there, he wouldn't be leaving with them.

She dragged Malik into a chair before he had a chance to recover himself and she moved behind him. While he gasped for breath, she wrapped her arm around his throat, locked at the elbow. She applied enough pressure to keep him in a state of distressed embarrassment.

She pressed her blade against his carotid. He couldn't breathe and was starting to panic. She didn't care. All she cared about was being the first thing Hector saw when he re-emerged through the kitchen door with whatever prizes he was planning on leaving with.

'Bi… bitch…' Malik slapped her arm like a wrestler tapping out.

She didn't ease her grip. Frankly, she didn't care if he died. What she did care about was the fact that it had now gone quiet upstairs, aside from Frank's barking. He was becoming increasingly frantic. She worried that he'd give himself another heart attack if she didn't get to him soon.

Footsteps started down the stairs and she tightened her grip even more on Malik's neck. He'd stopped slapping her arm and she almost smiled for a second at how much strength an unexpected and well-placed blow could steal from a body. No matter how big that body was.

Hector came through the door and froze. They stared at each other for several long seconds before he slowly raised his hands in a gesture of surrender.

She didn't buy it for a second.

'It's my turn to talk now.' Lindsey found her voice, having not been sure that she would. 'Are you satisfied that there's nothing here belonging to you?'

Hector gestured towards his colleague. 'Please… my friend; he can't breathe. You must let him go.'

'I will slice this fucker from ear to ear if you don't answer me. Are you satisfied that she's not here?'

'I am.'

'If I let him live…' she looked at Malik for a second who appeared to be losing consciousness, 'assuming that he's not already dead, will I see you back here again?'

'No.'

'I'd like to believe you. Know this though; I am who you think I am. If you think I'm alone here or that I'm the only one being watched then you're even dumber than you look. I have a whole fucking army behind me just waiting for you to fuck up. Like you're in the process of doing right now.'

Hector looked hesitant now.

'I want you to come back. I fucking dare you to.'

'Please, look at him.'

She could feel the body going limp against her. 'I care about him as much as you cared for me when you came through my door. Now open it.' She gestured with her head towards the front door.

Hector walked slowly towards the door and Lindsey never took her eyes off him. She moved the blade around to the back of Malik's neck and loosened her grip slightly.

'Take this piece of shit and get out of my home.'

Hector moved just as slowly towards his friend and balled his fists around Malik's T-shirt. He pulled him to his feet, but as suspected, he was unconscious. Hector had no choice but to heft him up onto his shoulder, which he did without breaking a sweat. Then, finally, he left.

The second he stepped outside, Lindsey slammed the door shut behind them. She leaned her back against it and slid to the floor, where she cried tears of pain and anger.

*

Five minutes was about as much as she allowed for self-pity. Tears flowed, limbs trembled and breathing came in sharp ragged gulps. Finally she held her breath for fifteen seconds and then exhaled until her lungs were completely empty. Then she held for ten seconds before exhaling, then five. Then she pulled herself to her feet. She checked that the front door was locked, straightened her clothes and walked with purpose through the café to the bottom of the stairs.

There she took a series of breaths and walked slowly up. She followed the sound of Frank's barking but was worried about what else she might find. When she finally opened the door, he almost floored her. He barked, jumped and sniffed her frantically. He ran forward and back on the landing, down and back up the stairs and then hefted his front paws back up onto Lindsey's shoulders. To say that he was emotional was an understatement. She was just glad to know that he was OK, and the feeling was mutual.

He'd been alone in Lindsey's room and the big tough Russian hadn't dared go in there. She walked to the sitting room and as expected, it was destroyed. The couch was upturned and everything breakable was broken. But there were no people. Broken or otherwise. That was good. She headed for the bedroom next. Boxes were kicked open on the floor and her crooked shelves were ripped down from the wall which annoyed her more than it should have.

'You can come out now,' she said towards the ceiling.

Following a few seconds of silence, she heard them shuffling around overhead at which time Lindsey closed her bedroom door. She pulled an oversized hoodie from her wardrobe and put it on. With the hood up, she pulled the zip up as high as it would go. The time for thinking had passed. Now she had to actually do something to put an end to this, before Hector came back and did it for her.

She was met by all three of her house guests as soon as she stepped outside her bedroom door. Lena's tear-streaked face fell even further and she dropped to the floor.

Lindsey remembered what she must look like. She could still taste blood in her mouth. Her nose felt like it was swelling and her eyes with it. The sight of her clearly frightened Lena, and did nothing for the others either.

Reem turned his back to her and pressed his forehead against the nearest wall, while the rage building inside Amir was like a mirror of her own. She wasn't in the mood to explain herself or what had happened. But the blood running down Lena's arms forced her into a conversation that she would have much preferred to skip altogether. She needed to get out of there. But first she had to find out just what had happened up in that attic.

'Lena, what happened to your arms?' Her voice sounded flat. Just like it always did when a storm was brewing inside her.

Lindsey found her eyes drifting towards Amir.

Lena glanced at her arms and then looked at Lindsey like she was missing the bigger picture.

'Look what they've done to you.' Her voice was no more than a whisper.

Before Lindsey had a chance to answer, Amir spoke up. He sounded much stronger than a kid his age should in such circumstances.

'She tried to come down when she heard what was happening. I had to stop her.' He looked at his hands and then at Lena's scratched arms. 'I apologise if I hurt you.'

Lena shook her head and then covered her face with her hands.

'Good, Amir. You did what you had to do.'

If he hadn't, they'd all be in trouble.

'They shouldn't be back tonight. But keep your guard up, I have to go out. Reem, I need you to take care of Frank.'

She took the boy's hand and placed it on Frank's collar. Frank objected of course, but she left him there anyway. She didn't know exactly what she was about to do. But whatever it was, she didn't want to be stopped.

Chapter 14

No one bothered her as she walked through the town, hidden beneath her baggy hoodie. But a part of her wished that they would. Tonight was just like old times. She was headed for trouble with more enthusiasm than she'd normally allow herself to feel. But knowing that anything could happen and just how little she cared was what spurred her on. Frustration oozed from her pores along with its close friend, fury. Both would explode out of her before the night was through. Just like old times.

Still, she couldn't bring herself to laugh when she saw Seamus Chambers' stupid face looking down on her from the roof of their caravan. He was the very picture of a slack jawed yokel, as he stared at her battered face. It was the first time she'd ever seen him speechless. Mind you, it was the first time she'd seen him looking at her face rather than her ass, too.

'What in the name of Sweet Holy Jesus…'

'Where's Danny.'

Seamus thumped the roof of the caravan with the crowbar.

Danny emerged, only half trying to hide a machete behind the door. He too froze when he saw her, but he recovered himself a lot quicker than his brother did. He shook his head and opened the door for her to come inside.

'So it's true then?'

She didn't respond. She had no interest in hearing his take on things.

'I thought that poor fucker Charlie was having me on.'

She looked sharply at him. 'What do you know about Charlie?'

'I know that he's a fucking liability. He was standing on top of the railway bridge last night threatening to jump. I gave him a couple of slaps to calm the fucker down and then he starts mouthing on about you.'

She continued to stare at him, fighting the urge to beat the rest out of him.

'I thought he was full of shit. I mean you couldn't possibly be that fucking stupid, surely? But now that I see you've gotten the royal treatment, maybe he wasn't so full of shit after all.'

'Where is he?'

'He's fine. So, little boys, eh? I knew that poncy fucker was low. But not that low.'

'I need your van.'

'Oh, you need my van?' He smiled. 'No explanations, but you need my van. What do I look like, Avis?'

'Since when do you need explanations?'

'Since you involved my sister in whatever brain fart you're currently having.'

'Eileen's not involved in anything.'

'But she knows about it?'

'She knows.'

'Then she's involved.'

'Not what I wanted. But there's nothing I can do about that now.'

'How many are there? Charlie reckons three.'

'Again, where's Charlie?'

She was sure that tomorrow, she'd want to know exactly how Charlie knew there were three. But now, she couldn't give one single shit who knew what.

'I'm here.' Charlie stepped out of one of the tiny bedrooms.

He looked like he'd lost weight that he could ill afford to lose. He also looked like he hadn't slept in a very long time. The sight of Lindsey had even more of a negative effect on his appearance.

'Why's he here?'

'What dozy prick is gonna come here looking for him?' Danny stroked his machete.

'And you're giving me shit?'

'You're a scrawny bird with a Micky Mouse blade stuffed down her skinny jeans. We're tinkers. See the difference?'

She looked down at the black cargo pants, a variation of which she almost always wore.

'As much as I'd love to stand around and talk about my skinny jeans and the Micky Mouse blade that you gave me, I need you to tell me about your van, Danny. Now that you know what I need it for let's cut the crap will we?'

Danny finally separated himself from his weapon and sat down. He patted the seat beside him.

Lindsey didn't want to sit. Adrenaline was moving at speed through her body and if she didn't keep moving, she'd either explode or crash. Neither would be pretty. That's when she looked at Charlie to see that he was crying quietly. She wished for the words to console him. But she was useless to other people at this moment in time.

'The van's not here now.'

'Where is it?'

'Tied up with other business. You're playing with fire, woman. But this one last time, I'm gonna help you. And I mean it when I say it's the last time. You put my sister in harm's way, I no longer owe you. You owe me.'

'When will it be back? I need it sharpish.'

'It'll be back tomorrow. But it needs some modifications.'

'Like what?'

'You have a target the size of a Range Rover on your arse and you live on an island. One way on, one way off. What was your plan? Pile all those fuckers into the back of a van and off you go?'

'You hide shit in there all the time, Danny.'

'Small shit, Lindsey. You're talking about much bigger shit. You're talking about the kinda shit that walks and talks and you know… breathes.'

'Fuck.'

'It'll work. It just needs some adjustments. I'll make those adjustments tomorrow night and you can have it the day after. On one condition.'

'Go on.'

'Take that fucker with you.' He gestured towards Charlie. 'This place is cramped enough as it is.'

Charlie didn't respond as he was treated like a spare teapot.

Lindsey nodded. The last thing she needed was another person. But she needed the van. And she had to at least try to help Charlie. If and when her rational mind returned, it'd eat her alive if she didn't.

'One more thing…'

'You just don't know when to quit, do ya?'

'Eileen needs to come with me.'

'Fuck that. She's needed here.'

'It's the only way I'll get out. It has to be the two of us. Two skinny girls in skinny jeans shopping for cakes and shit, remember?'

Danny got to his feet. 'I like you, Lindsey and I'm willing to help you. But if anything happens to my sister, I will fucking kill you. You know that, right?'

'I do.'

There was silence, except for the sound of Danny's nasal breathing. He was thinking out the pros and the cons before committing to anything. Eventually he conceded.

'She'll pick you up in the van the day after tomorrow. If there's any hold ups, I'll get word to you. Remember what I said though, Lindsey. Any harm comes to my sister…'

He left the words hanging in the air, as he pointed his thick finger in her face.

She nodded and held out her hand, which eventually he shook firmly. She was in no doubt that he meant every word. But if anything happened to Eileen, she'd gladly present herself to Danny on a plate.

Before leaving she turned to Charlie. 'Where's Ben now?'

Charlie looked even more panicked suddenly.

'Don't worry, I didn't see you. I just need to find him.'

'Probably at home, but…'

'Where's that?'

'Lindsey, don't go there.'

'Just tell me where it is, Charlie.'

'The big white house on the High Road. He lives in the basement flat. Please, Lindsey…'

She let herself out, not wanting to hear his pleas. The transport was sorted. Now she needed to sort the lads at the bridge.

'At least you're still walking,' Seamus called down to her. 'They must have liked you.'

She ignored him as always and headed towards the next caravan. The door was answered on the first knock.

'Eileen…'

'What the fuck happened to you?'

'I'm not opening tomorrow but I still need you to come in. I'll put a note in the window saying that we're waiting on supplies. We're getting these people out of here.'

'Lindsey, I…'

'I need to know now; are you OK to do this with me?'

'Of course I'll go with you, you idiot. Are you OK though?'

'I'm fine. I'll see you tomorrow.'

Eileen nodded as Lindsey turned to leave.

Once outside, she headed further away from town towards Whitepoint strand. There she took a right up the hill and onto the High Road. She knew the house that Charlie had talked about. She remembered thinking how much she'd loved it when she first arrived in Cobh; a tall, grand old building with bay windows, towering above the deep-water quay. It looked straight out at the mouth of the harbour. It was old, but she imagined it'd be a beautiful fixer upper. Like most other lovely buildings, it had been divided into as many rentable spaces as possible. But still, it was a stunner.

Her head pounded and her face throbbed as she walked up the steep driveway. She headed for the narrow steps leading down to the basement flat.

'Lindsey?' The door opened before she had a chance to knock. Ben had obviously seen her coming.

'Ben...' she struggled to change her demeanour. She felt like a walking time bomb. But she needed to be something very different if she hoped to get what she needed from him. Her bruises would help, but she needed to calm herself down and remember why she was here.

'Jesus, what happened?' He grabbed her by the shoulders and examined her face.

She let him lead her inside.

'Who did this to you?'

'Who do you think? They were looking for her again. What do I have to do to make them believe me? I don't know where she is, Ben!' She added a hint of hysteria to her voice.

'Did they...?'

She shook her head.

'I was closing up early, I'm completely out of everything. I tried to stop them, I just... I couldn't.' She turned away from him, closed her eyes and let the tears flow. Frustration always brought tears with Lindsey, which usually frustrated her more. But right now, they could only help.

'Lindsey, this was a warning. If you know anything, you need to tell them. Or tell me; I'll sort it from there. You won't have to see them again.'

Ben the hero. 'Don't you think I would have told them if I knew anything? They beat the shit out of me. They searched my flat twice. If she was there, they would have found her.'

Ben ran his hands through his hair. He was frustrated, but trying to hide it. He was so sure she'd break down and tell him everything about Lena. But even he was starting to doubt the logic now. Surely she, an emotional woman, couldn't withstand this kind of treatment if she really did know something?

He took her hand and led her towards his small, messy kitchen. He helped her to sit down and she let him. Then she watched as he moved around the kitchen, presumably looking for first aid supplies. Or maybe a knife to finish her off.

His jeans hugged him in all the right places, while the muscle in his back and shoulders flexed and moved, scarcely covered by the black vest that he wore. Ben was an imbecile with a very nasty streak. She also suspected that his moral compass was as misguided as Patrick's and Hector's. But if she couldn't punch him repeatedly in the face, maybe there was another way to vent her frustrations. And who knows; it might get her exactly what she needed from him. It could even be referred to as a two birds, one stone scenario.

He pulled a chair up in front of her and sat with his knees almost touching hers. He then commenced mixing Dettol antiseptic liquid with water in a cereal bowl.

Before he had a chance to start dabbing her face, she got up and straddled him in his chair. Without waiting for him to respond, she pulled his vest over his head and forced her tongue into his mouth.

Ben was used to being the aggressor; the leading man in his own sex life. He was slow to respond when taken by surprise. But when she pulled on his belt buckle, he shot to life, picking her up and sitting her down hard on the kitchen table. She pulled open his jeans while he worked quickly on hers and as soon as her legs were free of them, he tried to enter her.

But she shoved him back into his chair, lest he forget that she was the one driving this. He hit the chair with such force that he slipped right off and onto the floor. She was down, straddling him again before he had a chance to do anything about it.

What happened from there couldn't be described as love making by even the most hopeless of romantics. It was fast and hard enough that it bordered on being painful. There was certainly no love and zero respect. Just semi-violent, emotionless sex, made better by the knowledge that, before long, she could cut him from her life completely.

When she'd finished and he'd cried out loudly with his release, she wasted no time getting her pants back on and sitting back on the kitchen chair, like nothing had happened.

Ben stayed lying on the floor, breathing hard and staring at the ceiling with his jeans around his ankles. She wished he'd get over it and get dressed so that she could get to why she was really here. But she couldn't rush him. She'd already blown her cover and now she had to try to get him to believe that she was still the damsel in search of her white knight; whose flaccid penis currently lay like a dead slug against his left thigh.

'I… I'm sorry, Ben.'

He sat up and reached for his jeans. He paused before pulling them back up. 'I can't say I expected that.'

'I've never done that before. I don't know what I was thinking.'

He was looking at her now as he struggled into his pants. He was suspicious but she could tell that he wanted more. She hadn't given him the chance to savour any of it. That was good.

'You must think I'm a crazy person.' She smiled a quivery smile.

'I don't think I've ever had a woman come at me like that before.'

'I just… I feel like I've lost control. The business I've worked so hard for will fail if I can't get supplies, and then this happens.' She gestured to her face. 'And all because I tried to help someone. Ben, you were the first person I thought of. I'm not asking you to go up against Patrick or anything… I don't want you to get hurt.' She smiled shyly and his face now told her that she had him back. 'I've been thinking about you a lot actually. And then I come here and scare you half to death.'

He sat down in the chair opposite her again. He reached out and put his hand on her knee.

'It takes more than a beautiful woman having sex with me on my kitchen floor to scare me.' He leaned in and kissed her.

It was long and slow and as his tongue mingled with hers, she felt nothing. She'd managed to vent a morsel of her frustration and now it was time to move on. She sincerely wished that he'd do the same. But this was her game and she had to continue to play it for now.

She pulled back slowly and caught his face in her hands. 'I'm sorry; I'm just really scared. I can't concentrate.'

He ran his hands up along her arms and smiled, like he expected her to fall in love with him.

'Lindsey, what happened here?' One of his hands came to rest above her left breast, outside her clothes.

Shit. Despite the hurried nature of their encounter, his hands still managed to find their way inside her top. She wasn't thinking about what he might be feeling, so the brief time that he got to spend actually touching her, was enough for him to find the mottled skin that she went to such lengths to hide.

'Oh… that's old. Car accident when I was younger.'

'Wow. You really are accident prone, aren't you?' He was still smiling that stupid smile. 'Can I see? It felt kinda nasty.'

'Next time, OK?'

'So there'll be a next time?'

'Well, assuming that the lads on the bridge don't decide to finish the job.' She gestured to her throbbing face again. 'I'm going for supplies with Eileen the day after tomorrow.'

'I'll see to it.'

She looked him in the eye now to see if she could trust him. Of course she didn't. But she had no choice but to believe that, for the sake of his curiosity, he might do this one thing. She could worry about his next move later.

'I believe that you're telling the truth.'

She leaned forward and kissed him. She made sure it was a kiss that would leave him hungry for more. Then she rested her forehead against his.

'Thank you, Ben. I knew you'd take care of it.'

As she stood up, he remained seated and wrapped his arms around her waist. He pulled her top up slightly so that he could press his lips to her bare stomach.

'Stay here tonight.'

She rolled her eyes while she stroked his hair tenderly.

'My head is all over the place tonight. I think I just need to be alone…'

He stood up. 'You're seriously gonna leave after doing what you just did to me?'

She laughed quietly. 'Yes. But on the promise that I'll come back and do it properly next time.' She pulled away slowly and headed towards the door.

'I like the sound of that.' He grinned. 'But why don't I come over tomorrow? I'm presuming you'll be closed if you have no supplies?'

'I wish you could. But Eileen will be there all day. Thanks to Hector, we have a lot of cleaning to do.'

'OK, so…'

'The day after tomorrow. It'll be Eileen and me driving a white van.'

'OK. And I'll see you when you get back.'

She reached in and kissed him on the cheek. 'Thanks, Ben.'

And then she left.

As she walked down his driveway, she smiled to herself at how easy he was. She could feel him watching her. His eyes bored holes through her back and she sincerely wished that she could be done with him now. But she had to get through the next two days before she could drop the pretence with Ben. Just two more days.

Chapter 15

Lindsey sat in the darkened café that night, staring blankly out the window and chewing on her thumb nail. The damp street basked in the orange glow of the street light, but she was blind to it. She saw only the images in her mind. The various steps of her plan coming together. Some fitting. Others, not quite.

Frank whined at her feet. He looked relaxed, but he was on alert. Like her.

'I know.'

She said nothing for a few more seconds. 'It was nice not knowing that these people existed, wasn't it? Blissful fucking ignorance.'

Frank jumped up on the small couch beside her.

'Am I about to get them all killed?' She glanced briefly at him. 'I have a fucked-up plan that depends on too many people who can't be trusted.'

She thought for a few more minutes.

'But if Ben keeps thinking with his dick and if Danny comes through… we might just get away with it.' She turned to face Frank now. 'I know. That's a hell of a lot of ifs.'

*

Danny Chambers was an expert at getting away with shit. He'd been doing it all his life. Eileen was brought up with the same propensity for keeping her business private at all costs, so if they were stopped along the way, Lindsey wasn't worried about Eileen bottling it. Of course she'd rather keep her out of it and do this by herself, but because she didn't trust Danny, Eileen was an insurance policy of sorts. An Irish travelling man will look for opportunities in any situation, but she was fairly sure that he wouldn't fuck over his own sister. Plus, Eileen made her cover story seem more plausible so the plan depended as much on her as it did on Danny.

Her encounter with Ben was already forgotten. It pretty much summed up Lindsey's sex life post Syria. The only difference between him and the men she normally sought out was that Ben wasn't anonymous. That might pose a problem down the line. But for now, she didn't care. Her biggest problem was that she'd revealed herself and a fictional cover story to Hector and in doing so, had painted an even bigger target on her back. She just hoped that she piqued Ben's curiosity enough for him to want to keep her in one piece for at least another thirty-six hours.

She looked to the ceiling as Amir's raised voice reverberated through it. He'd been arguing for the past twenty minutes at least. It was possibly a one-sided argument as his was the only voice that could be heard, but his frustration and anger were crystal clear.

That was another worry for Lindsey now. Of course she couldn't blame him for any of it. She'd probably let loose too in his position. But his emotions, if left unchecked, could blow their cover before they were safely away. She ignored him for now as she continued to run down her plan, if it could be called that. Adam Street was the final piece.

A part of her wished that Street might have found someone to settle down with. That he might be living a quiet life somewhere new. But deep down she knew that her wanting it for him didn't mean that he'd ever allow himself to be happy. Like her, Street blamed himself for

Lenny and for the fucked-up lives that the rest of them now lead. Her included. Therefore, knowing him like she did, it was safe to say that he'd spend the rest of his life punishing himself.

Adam lived in what was once an old bag factory until he converted the ground floor into a boxing gym. He made the upstairs liveable for himself. On either side of him were similar buildings which for years were occupied by the homeless and the addicts of Cork city. Lindsey had been a frequent out of hours visitor to Street's gym at one time. But it didn't have a name then that she knew of.

Her gut told her that the gym Martin talked about was Street's. She also knew that she couldn't just rock up on his doorstep with a van load of people. If she was wrong and Street was no longer there, then she and everyone with her would be fucked. She didn't know Street's current situation either. The name change on the gym could be a result of new management, who knows? Maybe he'd finally shacked up with someone. Or more likely, he'd found his own puddle of shit to jump into because that seemed to be how they were both wired.

She had to find him by herself first. That meant that she needed to find somewhere to stash her guests in the meantime. Somewhere where even Patrick Adebayo and his countless lackeys couldn't find them and only one place came to mind. It wasn't ideal, but nothing was these days.

*

'What's going on?'

Lindsey went back upstairs to interrupt what looked like a long running rant from Amir. Her own voice sounded flat. She wasn't really interested in what was going on. Just that it would stop for long enough to get them all out in one piece.

Amir stopped for a minute while he turned to face her. But he started up again almost immediately, in Arabic first, before remembering his audience and switching to English.

'We cannot live like this anymore!' He pointed dramatically to Lena. 'These people are contented to live like prisoners in someone's attic, but I refuse. We are not animals. We are people, whose only crime was to be born wrong. I cannot stay here any longer.' His voice went up just enough to crack at the end.

Reem hid behind Lena who looked as patient as ever.

Frank looked up at Lindsey and she gave his ear a brief scratch to let him know that she agreed with him. He should make his way to Reem, which he dutifully did.

'We're leaving here the day after tomorrow. Can you keep it together for one more day?'

There was silence as they all looked at her.

'Where are we going?'

'I need to straighten out the details first and then tomorrow, I promise I'll fill you in on everything, OK? One more day.'

She respected Amir enough to speak to him like a man, rather than the boy that he was. After all, the world now demanded that he grow up before his time and he was doing his best.

No one answered and Lindsey headed back downstairs, before someone decided to start another argument. She was also fully aware that she might be about to land them all back at Patrick's mercy, so the less time she spent chatting and getting to know any more about them, the better.

As if detachment was still a possibility. If they didn't get through the next few days, then neither could she. Though that wasn't something she worried about as she sat once again inside the café window, sorting through the details in her mind. Sometimes she mumbled them out loud as she pictured Street, Damo, Gordon, Murph, Wesley, and even Lenny, sitting around the table with her, pouring tea from an industrial sized pot. Her old team. Lads who would turn a situation like this into an all-night piss-taking and banter session. There'd be just enough pearls of wisdom, sense and experience thrown in that by the time the group broke up, everyone would be as sure, confident and as ready as they could ever be. She never missed them more than she did tonight. She got to her feet, breaking the trance just before their images became warped. It'd all catch up with her again soon enough.

It was almost two in the morning. She headed back up to the sitting room, which was where she slept these days; on the floor, having discovered just how uncomfortable her lumpy old couch was. Even more so since it had been kicked around the room by both Patrick and Hector. But when she got there she realised that not quite everyone was asleep.

Reem was sitting on the floor holding what looked like a bunch of photographs, one of which he was staring at. Frank lay quietly by his side. She stood still at the door for a second, unsure whether or not to continue inside. Reem didn't seem comfortable around anyone but Lena and Frank and even then, he still hadn't spoken as far as she was aware. She didn't want to scare him. Though he was looking at her now.

She walked slowly towards the couch and picked up the pillow that sat there.

'I'll go sleep downstairs, Reem.' She spoke softly.

'I very much like this dog.'

His voice was so soft and childlike. He could speak. And he could speak English.

Lindsey smiled her first genuine smile in days.

'So do I.'

He looked at the photo in his hand again as she went and sat on the floor near him. 'But you know, Frank isn't just a dog. Frank is magic,' she whispered dramatically.

Frank glanced up at her and she was certain that if he could have rolled his eyes, he would have.

Reem's eyes widened though and he shuffled closer to Frank. Clearly he wanted to hear more about Lindsey's magic dog.

'Magic?'

'Yes! Didn't you ever meet a magic dog?' she asked, sounding surprised.

'Dog's aren't magic,' Reem replied, but she knew that he wanted to be proven wrong.

'Oh well that's true of most dogs. But some dogs are very, very special. And Frank is one of those.'

'Why is he magic?'

'Well…' How to explain this to a child? 'You know how there's a lot of war and… other bad things that happen in the world?'

Reem nodded and lowered his eyes to the floor.

'And you know when something horrible happens; something really, really scary?'

He nodded again, but barely.

'And you still see it in your head all the time? Or you still feel it, even after it's all over?'

Another nod.

'Well sometimes if you're lucky, a magic dog will come along to take care of you. When you have a bad dream, he'll wake you up with a kiss.' She smiled, as she leaned in and gently brushed his cheek with her fingers. 'When you feel sad and lonely, he'll make you feel better. They know when something bad is inside your head and they'll take it away. Like magic.'

'Where do they come from?'

Lindsey shrugged. Frank came from one of her retired army colleagues whose life by then was dedicated to training and breeding service dogs. But that answer wasn't magical enough for Reem tonight.

'No one knows,' she said instead. 'But everyone knows there are only a few really special ones. They get sent to the people who need them the most.'

'And you need him?'

She nodded. 'I do.'

'If I had money, could I buy a magic dog?'

Lindsey stroked his hair, suddenly wanting nothing more than to take away some of his horrors.

'You can't buy them. These dogs don't care if you have money or not. You just need to be on the lookout. But you should know that they don't always look like Frank.'

'What do they look like?' he asked, wide eyed.

She shrugged again. 'They can look like any kind of dog. Usually though, they look lost and lonely. Like they have no family. That means they're looking for you.'

Reem looked at the photo again.

'What's that you have there?'

He handed it to her.

It was a picture of her and the lads in their UN uniforms. This one was taken in Lebanon, not Syria. They were all tanned and smiling and looked like they knew something that the rest of the world was still trying to figure out.

'You are a soldier?'

'I was,' she mumbled, lowering the photo.

Reem leaned in and pointed to the UN blue peaked cap on her head.

'This blue; this means you were the good soldiers?'

She nodded. 'You should get some sleep. We have a big adventure coming up and I'm gonna need your help.' She did her best to smile reassuringly.

He smiled again and then he surprised her with a hug, before running from the room and into the room that he shared with Lena.

Lindsey remained seated on the floor, feeling utterly broken hearted. She picked up the photo again and glanced briefly at it. Maybe this was a sign; that maybe they actually were there with her. She dropped it onto the table and shook her head at her own stupidity. She and she alone was attempting to pull this off and when it all went to pot, she'd have no one to blame but herself.

She hauled herself to her feet, wiped herself down and slapped herself a few times in the face for added focus. Then she crept along the landing to her spare bedroom, now occupied by Amir. She opened the door as quietly as she could, but wasn't surprised when Amir's head shot up off his pillow.

She gestured for him to follow her out of the room. She needed to keep Amir under control and the only way to do that was to make him feel like he had some control over something in his life. Which to be fair, really wasn't too much to ask for.

She went back to the sitting room and waited the thirty seconds or so for him to get dressed and follow her.

'Close the door.'

He did as she asked without speaking. He looked like he expected another argument.

'We're about to do something very dangerous and I'm going to need your help to pull it off. But I need to know that you're ready.'

He stood still staring at her for a few seconds. Finally his face softened slightly and he came and sat down beside her on the couch.

'What are we about to do?'

'The day after tomorrow, Eileen, the lady who works with me downstairs, is going to arrive here in a van. That van will have a hidden compartment…' I hope '…which is where you and the others will need to hide.'

She could see his anger bubbling towards the surface again.

'The others are going to be scared. You're the man of this little group, Amir. I need you to show them the way. Let them know that everything is going to be OK. I'm going to tell you exactly what my plan is, so that you yourself will know that everything will be OK. You'll be away from here soon and you'll have your lives back.'

'And what lives will they be when we are being hunted like animals. What life will we have when people come to know what we are?'

'Well right now you're not the only one who's being hunted. Everyone is, including me. And what do you mean, What you are?'

He slammed his two fists down on the couch and turned his back to her.

She got his meaning. There was a good chance that Amir had been sexually abused. Reem too.

'Amir...' She put her hand on his shoulder but he refused to turn around. She continued anyway, cursing this conversation. 'What you are, is a young person with his whole life ahead of him. Everyone has a past, kid, and some happen to be ugly. But your future depends on you.'

Jesus Christ, she sounded just like the kind of do-gooder she hated. Chances are, Amir's past meant that his future was fucked, just like hers. But what was she gonna do, tell him?

'You make tea. How are you supposed to take us away from here? Will you stop ten men from doing whatever they want, like we're nothing? Will you stop them...?'

Lindsey reached forwards and flipped the photograph on the table so that he was looking now at Lindsey the soldier. The woman that she went to such great lengths to hide in her new life, but had no choice but to introduce now.

Amir picked up the photo and stared at it. Then he turned to face her again.

'This is you?'

'Yes.'

'A soldier?'

'When you look at me you see a woman who makes tea. What do people see when they look at you?'

'They see nothing.'

'Oh they see something. But it depends who's looking. When I first saw you, I saw a refugee from another country. But what else are you?'

'Nothing.'

'That's called self-pity and it needs to stop. Did you go to school before all this?'

'Of course.'

'What did you want to be when you grow up?'

He was becoming upset now, so it took him some time to gather his words. 'I wanted to design great big buildings.'

'So, you're a student; a friend, a son, a grandson, an architect in the making.' She smiled. 'A footballer maybe?'

He grinned and nodded.

'And that's just the tip of the iceberg I'll bet. Everyone is more than what they appear to be through the eyes of strangers. People see no more than a tea lady when they look at me, because that's exactly what I want them to see. I want them to underestimate me. Just like they'll underestimate you. That might just be what gets us all out of here in one piece.'

'You've been to my country?'

'Yes.'

He was quiet for a while as he studied the photograph.

'You never say anything.'

'Sometimes it's better to talk less, while you watch and listen more. Besides, it's in the past.'

'Not for me.'

Not for me either, she thought.

'These men look at me and they see weakness.' She gestured to her own face, with the gash across the bridge of her nose, which thankfully wasn't broken, and her bruised and swollen eye. 'You see Amir, when people expect little from you, they leave you with the advantage, and that's why the man who did this to me had to be carried out of here, unconscious. They might look at you and see weakness too because they don't know how strong you are up here.' She tapped the side of her head. 'They might think that they broke you. But I know that they didn't. You have a fire in your belly that they know nothing about, and that gives you the advantage. I might not be a match for ten men like you said. But I'll fight like hell to keep you all safe. I'm not afraid, and I need you not to be either.'

'I'm not afraid,' he huffed. 'But a woman and a boy can't fight them all.'

'If we use our heads, then hopefully we won't have to fight anyone.'

Amir didn't respond. He just looked absentmindedly at the photograph again.

'Get some sleep. Tomorrow, we'll go through everything in more detail.' She got to her feet.

'I've heard you, fighting in your sleep.'

She stopped half way to the door, but didn't turn around and didn't respond. She didn't know how to.

'Do you see the face of someone you loved?'

'In a way, yes.'

'So you're not just a blundering tea woman?'

'Only by day.' She forced a smile and left before the conversation could continue.

This is exactly why Lindsey needed to be alone in life. She needed to be able to live out her nightmares in peace, without anyone else having to wonder what the hell was wrong with her.

*

That night she slept on the small couch inside the café window. Or at least that's where she spent the night. Sleep wasn't on the agenda. Instead, most of the night was spent running through what would happen from the time Eileen arrived with the van, up until she found Street. If she could manage that much and find out Street's situation, then she could decide where to go from there and she'd hopefully have Adam's help in doing that.

But the night was long. Every now and then she heard movement, first in the back kitchen but there was no one there. Then behind the bar; no one there either. She found herself hunching down behind chairs, sweating, and frantically searching for people who weren't there. Her heart hammered in her chest, her limbs trembled as her tortured mind spread its misery throughout her body until finally, the adrenaline vanished and exhaustion floored her. Literally.

Three loud thumps on the front door and Lindsey shot up off the couch.

'Lindsey, you in there?'

It was Eileen. And it was morning.

She roughly wiped her eyes and stretched her facial muscles to make herself look human, before opening the door and letting her in.

'Christ, you look rough.'

'Thanks.'

'Look at the face they gave you! You're black and fucking blue.' She looked past Lindsey then. 'Jesus Christ, look at this place!'

'Nice, isn't it? Coffee?'

'Yeah, but I need a decent one, so I'll make it myself.' She gave up on finding her keys and went behind the bar, where she began expertly interfering with the coffee machine. Before long she placed two cups on the table and took a seat opposite Lindsey. 'Right, what's the plan?' she asked, taking a sip.

Lindsey breathed in the strong aroma and willed her mind to focus.

'I need to bring Amir down for this, so just give me a minute,' she brought the cup to her lips and sipped.

'The small lad?'

'The bigger small lad. Things are getting the better of him and I'm afraid if I don't make him a part of the plan then he'll become another obstacle. We have enough of those already.'

Eileen raised her eyebrows and went back to drinking in silence. She wasn't letting on, but Lindsey could tell she was worried. With good reason too.

Once both cups had been drained, Lindsey exhaled loudly and got to her feet.

'Hey seriously though, are you OK? You don't look so hot.'

'I think we've established that.'

'I'm not talking about the fucked-up state of your face. I'm talking about the state of you in general. You look like you could slice a fella's willy off and use it as a bow to play an imaginary violin.'

Lindsey shook her head. 'Where do you come up with these scenarios?'

Eileen shrugged. 'It's just what you look like.'

'Wait here.'

Lindsey went upstairs, leaving Eileen's question unanswered. When she got there, the sitting room was deserted. But she could hear movement coming from Amir's room. She knocked once and waited for him to answer.

'Come downstairs when you're ready.'

*

'Well, is he coming?' Eileen was brimming with nervous excitement suddenly and Lindsey knew that, as far as she was concerned, Amir might as well be from another planet.

She nodded.

'And you look like the world is ending, because…?'

'Be nice to the kid, alright?'

'I'm always nice.' She wasn't being sarcastic that time, which should have been funny.

But Lindsey was about to explain her plan to people who had no reason to trust her. Whatever confidence she had was replaced with The Dread and a near certainty that the whole thing was about to go catastrophically wrong. And it all started with saying it out loud.

Chapter 16

'Sit down, both of you.'

She adopted her old military instructor's tone; detached, assertive, and oozing confidence that she didn't necessarily feel.

'I'm gonna talk for a while and I need you both to listen very carefully. If you have questions, please save them for the end, OK?'

They both nodded and took their seats opposite each other. Amir eyed Eileen warily and Eileen returned the gesture. But within seconds Lindsey had their full attention. It was amazing how a change in demeanour could make two naturally argumentative people instantly agree to do as they've been told.

'Eileen, I'm assuming that Danny will come through with the van. So tomorrow you're gonna come here no later five forty-five in the morning.'

Eileen's mouth dropped open but Lindsey continued before she had a chance to speak.

'We need to get everyone into the van before the rest of the town wakes up. We'll leave here around seven. There're lads on the bridge and they're looking specifically for these three people. I've done what I can to sort that, but we might still have some trouble with them. If we do, Eileen and I will be armed.'

She glanced at Eileen who raised her eyebrows dramatically. But her hand automatically went to her belt.

Amir, for his part, looked infinitely more worried.

As she went on to explain the rest of her plan, her small audience sat in silent captivation. When she finished, she was surprised to find that neither of them had anything to say. She expected to have a fight on her hands. Neither one of them were a stranger to roughing it, but she expected that Eileen at least would argue just for the sake of argument.

But no. Lindsey had somehow managed to make her plan sound like a good one. Like, what could possibly go wrong?

'Anything?' she asked.

Amir shrugged. 'It sounds better than a lifetime spent in an attic.'

'Eileen?'

'Five forty-five in the fucking morning?'

Lindsey allowed herself a smile. But like anything worth smiling about these days, it was short lived as there was a bang on the door.

All three of them froze. Lindsey put her finger to her lips.

'Lindsey?'

Ben.

'Amir, go up and hide the others. I'll get rid of him but it won't be easy, so be quiet. Go.'

Her voice barely made any sound at all, but he understood and moved quickly.

'Eileen, we're cleaning and doing an inventory for tomorrow.'

Thanks to Hector, the place was a wreck. So that much at least seemed plausible.

They both sat there in silence for another few minutes, giving everyone upstairs a chance to hide. She hoped that Ben would go away, but of course he didn't. His pounding just got more persistent.

Finally, she looked to the heavens and got up to open the door, while Eileen went about sweeping the shattered glass from the display fridge into a pile.

'Ben? Hey… what are you doing here?'

'Just checking in. What took you so long to answer?'

Even though she was half blocking the door, he moved around her and invited himself inside, squeezing her shoulder as he passed.

'Any chance of a cuppa?' He smiled, taking the seat that Amir had just vacated.

'Sure. I only have time for a quick one though. Eileen is here.'

'So? Why didn't you answer?'

'I did. I assumed you were someone looking for breakfast so I took my time. We spoke last night; I wasn't expecting you to show up.'

'I know. I was worried about you, that's all. Plus…' He got up and caught her by the hand with a grin on his face, 'I couldn't stop thinking about last night.'

'Yeah, me neither,' she lied with a smile. 'Did you want tea? We're just about out of coffee I think.'

'Sure, why not?' He sat back down. 'Actually, why don't we have it upstairs?' He got to his feet again. He was acting like a scalded cat.

She gave him a knowing smile and wrapped her arms around his waist.

'I hope you're not getting any ideas?'

'Oh I have lots of ideas.' He pressed her against the bar. His hands took in as much of her as they could, while his tongue invaded her mouth.

She returned his enthusiasm for the shortest possible length of time. Then she freed up her mouth and pressed her forehead to his.

'Eileen is here,' she whispered, as if the disappointment was killing her.

'So what? Let's go upstairs.'

'Lindsey, I could really do with your help in here?' Eileen burst through the kitchen door sounding like she wanted to kill Lindsey, just like she normally did and Lindsey loved her for it. 'I mean, I'm sorry to interrupt you two lovebirds, but we're not gonna get this done today if you can't tear yourself away from him and come help me.'

Ben pulled back. He looked like he wanted to launch Eileen face first through the window.

Lindsey gave him her most apologetic look. 'Sorry,' she mouthed with a shrug, and a soft smile. Then she spoke to Eileen, keeping her loving eyes on Ben's. 'You know it's thanks to Ben that we can even go tomorrow, Eileen.'

'Since when do the cops have that kind of power anymore?' Eileen snorted.

'Not the cops. This cop.' She kissed him, briefly this time and then extricated herself from where she was wedged between the bar and Ben's bulging groin. 'Give us a minute will you, Eileen?'

Eileen, to her credit, huffed and puffed a bit longer before disappearing through the swing doors.

She ran her hands down his bare arms. 'Ben, I'm nervous about tomorrow. Obviously Patrick doesn't want me to have supplies. Just let me get this over and done with, and then…' She leaned in and gave him what would be the last kiss he'd ever get from her. 'My concentration can be all on you. Assuming we get over the bridge that is.'

'Fine.'

He was annoyed, but she didn't care. Instead she directed him towards the door, but before he left, he turned to face her again.

'Hey, how long have you had this place? Less than a year, right?'

'That's right.' Hector. Of course.

'So where were you before that? What did you work at?'

'Why do you ask?'

'Curious.'

'I worked with the homeless in Cork.' Her actual line of work in the juvenile system gave her enough insight to be able to bluff about the homeless scene in the city. But her bullshit lies weren't going to cover her for very long. She needed to get the hell out of here.

He didn't answer for a while, then, 'My offer to come with you still stands.'

'I know. But we'll manage.' She opened the door.

'Lindsey, come on!' Eileen's voice bellowed from the kitchen.

'I better go. See you soon, yeah?'

He put his hand up to stop the door from closing in his face. 'As soon as you get back.'

'As soon as I get back.'

Finally the door was closed and locked and Ben was gone. But Lindsey was left with the feeling that his so-called protection was fleeting at best.

*

'What the fuck was that?'

Eileen looked like she didn't know whether to laugh or slap Lindsey in the face. Either would have been justified. Lindsey shook her head and walked past her and around the bar. She reached under and pulled out the whiskey. She quarter filled a coffee mug and drank before replying.

'Don't ask.'

'Did you take one for the team, you saucy bitch?' Eileen laughed finally. 'I think that fucking ape might be in love or something. Did you see the chunk of wood in his pants? He barely fit out the door.'

Lindsey laughed. She couldn't help it. Eileen was the perfect tonic to ease some of the tension she was feeling. If she was here with her army buddies, this is exactly the kind of conversation they'd be having. Except it would probably be about one of their sexual escapades. Unlike Lindsey, they liked to let everyone know exactly what they got up to.

'So, was he any good?'

Lindsey topped up her drink and took a smaller sip this time. She shook her head. 'I might have taken him by surprise. Then again…' she grinned, 'it did exactly what it said on the tin.'

Eileen laughed the laugh of an eighty-year-old smoker, despite the fact that she didn't smoke. She was still laughing when she headed for the kitchen again.

'Where are you going?'

'Have you seen the fucking state of this place? I'll sort this shit out while you sit down there. Relax, clear your head and then concentrate on not getting us all fucking dead tomorrow.' She turned around with a broad smile on her face and disappeared backwards through the door. 'No pressure!' She called from inside.

Lindsey knocked back what was left in the mug. 'Yeah. No pressure.'

*

That night she sat on her coffee table surrounded by her house guests and explained to them what the next few days would entail.

Lena did her best not to look terrified, while Reem looked withdrawn, like he always did. He was clutching Frank for dear life. If they had specific concerns, they didn't voice them and Lindsey didn't ask. Instead she got to her feet determined to call an end to this day.

'OK. I need to get some stuff from my room and then I need you all to get some sleep. We have an early start tomorrow and it's gonna be a very long day.'

She felt sick as she rooted under her bed and pulled out the three boxes that she needed. She dragged them to the sitting room and then told everyone to go to bed. When they'd gone, she went to the attic where the rest of her stuff was stored.

When she had everything laid out on the attic floor, she wondered about Danny's van. A lot of this would depend on his modifications and on there being enough space to fit everything they'd need, along with four people. Everything had to be concealed. If anyone insisted on taking a look inside the van and saw the gear that she needed to bring, it wouldn't exactly tie in with their shopping story.

'Lindsey?' Lena arrived at the top of the stairs with a plate holding two slices of buttered toast. 'You haven't eaten.'

Lindsey didn't have it in her to smile at the kind gesture. She just took the plate, suddenly realising that she actually was hungry.

'You are a soldier alright; prepared for any war.'

Lindsey didn't answer. She was concentrating and wished that Lena would leave her to it.

'Do you have all this so you can hide yourself away when life becomes unbearable?'

'Something like that.'

'And this…' she swept her hand across Lindsey's bruised face, 'being beaten and threatened; having to take care of a house full of strangers. This is not unbearable enough for you yet?'

'We're women, Lena.' Lindsey smiled. 'We can bear a hell of a lot.'

'You know, Lindsey; I'm starting to see that you are right. How can I help here?'

'You're already helping. You've been great with Reem. I just… I don't think he's very comfortable with me. Having you take care of him has made all this a little bit easier. For him and for me.'

'Reem is not comfortable with anything. His life is what no child's life should be. But here's a thing; Reem spoke no words to me before last night. Then he woke me up in the middle of the night to tell me the most wonderful story about a magic dog. I thought I would never see a light in his eyes like that. But there it was; light in the darkness. All thanks to you the soldier, and your beautiful soldier dog.'

Lena stroked Lindsey's face affectionately and it was nearly enough to finish Lindsey.

'I'm glad to hear that,' she finally brought herself to say. 'You should get some sleep. I'm better by myself here.'

'And we are better with you.'

With a slight bow of the head, Lena left Lindsey alone and once she'd gone, all Lindsey could think about was the heavy bag hanging from the ceiling not twenty feet from her. The tension that she felt was unbearable and she needed to release it somehow.

For a second she wished that Ben was there. Not Ben specifically of course. In fact, preferably someone else. But someone all the same. She needed a release before she imploded and as the idea of making her way to his house flitted briefly through her mind, she stripped down to her vest and underwear, sure that no one else would come up here, and launched herself at the bag instead. Its chain rattled loudly when she threw the first kick and she couldn't bring herself to stop for over two hours; until her skin was slick with sweat, her muscles and lungs burned, and her mind was finally clear. At least clear enough to sort out what she needed to take tomorrow, how exactly each piece of kit would prove useful and the best way to compensate for what they would not have.

As the last item was strapped to the outside of one of the two backpacks, she checked her watch and it was almost time. She needed to shower and get dressed. Then she needed to get, what was possibly her most reckless idea to date, under way.

Chapter 17

It was exactly five-forty-five when Eileen let herself in that morning.

'Christ!' She said with a start, before closing and locking the door behind her. 'Have you been here all night?'

Lindsey was sitting on a chair with her elbows resting on her vibrating knees. She sprang to her feet. 'Show me the van.'

'Well, good morning to you too, sunshine.'

She opened the door again and gestured for Lindsey to lead the way. Eileen followed her and opened the back door of the fairly new Ford Transit van. The inside was empty and looked just like the inside of any other van. Eileen smiled as she hauled herself up into it. She walked to the front where she reached down to the floor.

'Move back just a tad there if you will.'

Lindsey moved back and Eileen slid the whole aluminium floor covering towards Lindsey. It came about six feet out of the van, then she gestured for her to step inside.

Lindsey jumped in and walked to where Eileen was standing over an impressively subtle hatch in the floor, which would be concealed even more when the aluminium floor slid back into place. She pulled it open and Lindsey got on her belly to look inside. It was cramped alright. She wouldn't fancy spending any time at all enclosed in that space, but aside from the obvious discomfort it would bring, it was perfect. Danny had air holes drilled into the floor, top and bottom and somehow it didn't seem overly stifling in there. She hadn't noticed the holes when she looked inside in the first place. That was good. He even had bottles of water stashed in there.

'How long are they going to be in there d'you reckon?'

'Best case scenario, an hour or so after we leave here.'

'Worst case scenario?'

'Worst case scenario, no time at all because we'll be caught.'

'Right. Well, that answers that. Shall we go round up our passengers before our audience arrives?'

Lindsey was surprised at how well Eileen was taking all this in her stride and it made her wonder again about the real day to day life of a traveller. Their culture was known to be secretive and yet settled people seemed to think they had them all figured out. Uneducated travellers, gypsies, liars, thieves. Good for nothing. Clearly they didn't know the half of it. Or maybe they did, who knows?

'One more thing…'

Lindsey was still examining the van, but she was listening.

'You and I both know what'll happen if That Mad Bastard gets a hold of this gang. But what d'you reckon he'll do with us?'

Lindsey shrugged. She'd been thinking about that and the only conclusion she'd come to was that she'd do whatever it took to make sure Eileen got away.

'Hi Lindsey.'

Lindsey froze for a second as she was about to stand up. She lowered herself back onto her belly and looked inside the hatch again. It was pitch black in there.

'I suppose it's probably a good thing that you can't see me.'

'Charlie, is that you?' Christ, she'd almost forgotten about Charlie.

'Yeah.'

'Are you alright in there?'

'Well, it won't be much fun with three more people stuck in here with me. But yeah, I'm grand.'

'OK good. Stay there. We're gonna load up the others so find a comfy spot if you can, Charlie, and expect to be there for a couple of hours, yeah?'

'A couple of hours? I expected longer, I think. That'll be alright.'

Lindsey smiled sympathetically. The poor kid. 'Good stuff buddy.'

She got to her feet and moved quickly out of the van. 'Close it up for a minute and stay here. I'm gonna go get the others before the sun comes up.'

'Righto.' Eileen shoved the floor back into place and closed the back doors as Lindsey jogged inside and up the stairs.

The streets were quiet so it was now or never. When she got to her sitting room, she was glad to see all three of her house guests standing around the coffee table, waiting beside the two heavy but manageable backpacks.

'Is everyone ready?'

They all nodded except for Reem.

'I told you about Charlie, he's already in the van. You'll be there for a couple of hours and there's a good chance we'll be stopped and searched. So it's silence all the way. Let's go.'

She held the door open for them and they made their way down the stairs and into the kitchen. There they gathered in a nervous group waiting for her to lead the way, which she did. She stepped outside and checked the street as Eileen opened up the van and moved the floor again. Only when that was done did Lindsey beckon the others to come outside. They moved quickly leaving a ripple of terror in their wake. Once they'd climbed in one by one, Eileen directed them down the hatch. Lena was the last one out the door and she paused as she passed Lindsey.

'You must listen to me now, Lindsey...' she had a quiet urgency in her voice. 'If it comes to a choice between your life and mine; I wouldn't have made it this far without you. We'd all be in there still, wishing we were dead.'

'It'll be fine, Lena. Now go.' She smiled and gently nudged Lena out of the door to where Eileen was impatiently waiting.

There was a lot of bumping around as they tried to settle themselves into the uncomfortable space. Lindsey scanned the streets and windows of nearby buildings. The place was deserted. It was a good start, but she wasn't about to count her chickens just yet.

'OK, close it up,' she said to Eileen, who had already started sliding the floor back into place.

Lindsey jogged inside and back upstairs while Eileen pottered around downstairs. Leaving at six am would alert suspicion. They had to wait at least an hour. Lindsey used this time to go through her stuff, starting in her bedroom. She pulled a day sack out from under the bed and began filling it with what she deemed to be essentials; some outdoor gear and a couple of changes of clothes. The small pile of photos that Reem found also made their way into one of the side pockets. As she closed the zip with a slight struggle, she paused for a second to look around. She had no idea if or when she'd be back here. It wouldn't be the first time she'd walked away from a life she'd built. She knew this could happen, so she didn't feel any real sentimental attachment to the place. Still, she was proud of the little business that she'd built and the home that she'd restored with what little DIY skill she had. So yes, she felt a pang of regret; regret that she couldn't build and live a normal life, like a normal person. But that regret was short lived because of course normal was just a word. It meant fuck all and would never really apply to her anyway.

When she got outside, Eileen was leaning casually against the back doors of the van smoking a cigarette.

'What are you doing?' Lindsey asked with half a laugh.

Eileen gave shit to every smoker who ever asked her to bring their coffee outside.

'According to everyone, these things settle your nerves. Besides, it could be my last one.'

'And your first.'

Eileen grinned. She took the backpack off Lindsey, crushed the cigarette under her sneakered foot and jumped in the back of the van. She quickly lodged the pack in with the people under the floor. 'Everyone alright?' She asked.

'We're OK,' Lena's voice was quiet and calm.

Lindsey tapped the floor and Frank trotted in. She went in after him with a travel box. True, if he was loose in there, he'd be a serious deterrent to anyone who opened the back door. But his safety was her priority. It was up to her to deal with anyone on the bridge who didn't feel like listening to Ben. Assuming of course, that he'd actually done what he said he would, and warned them off, though she was having her doubts about that.

'OK, let's go.'

*

The watery sun was already up and the town was blissfully quiet as they drove through with Lindsey at the wheel. The early morning mist clearing beyond the mouth of the harbour was a beautiful sight and she drank it in, not sure when she might see it again. The town of Cobh was situated on a little island aptly named The Great Island. There was one road on and that same one road off. She knew exactly where Patrick's men would be and that there would be no avoiding them. So they passed the five or so miles to Belvelly in silence and as expected, the quaint little hump back bridge leading to the Fota Road and the mainland was in the process of being blocked by a rusty old Land Rover and a Honda Civic. Both vehicles had been parked up opposite the bridge. They pulled themselves into position as the van approached. The manoeuvre was quick and efficient. Almost like they'd been expecting them.

'If this goes tits up, Eileen, don't hang around, OK? I can take care of myself, so I'll catch up with you.'

'If this goes tits up it'll be for them, not us,' she replied with a grin.

Lindsey smiled in admiration at the scrawny but fierce girl by her side. 'Well then, let's do this.'

They approached slowly with their eyes on a man child who was no doubt armed, and first to let his face be seen. He looked like he might be a blade man. A nervous one, until such time as the Range Rover's doors opened and two more men got out to join him. All three stood in a line across the bridge. They were expecting them alright.

'You prick, Ben,' she muttered.

'Christ.'

Lindsey brought the van to a halt fifteen feet from them, as two more sleepy looking characters got out of the Civic. None of them looked older than nineteen.

'Here we go.' Lindsey lowered her window.

'Step out of the van please,' the oldest of the five demanded of her.

Lindsey did as he asked.

'Where are you off to at this hour?'

'What's this about?'

'Lindsey, right?'

'Right.'

'And she is?'

'My chef, Eileen. We're in a bit of a hurry lads. We need to be back before the lunch rush. But call in if you're around. Lunch is on me.'

'I'd have lunch on you any day.'

Lindsey slapped him playfully on the arm and laughed as she pushed off the van and went to get back in the driver's side.

'I'm still gonna have to take a look in the back. There's a lot of talk about you. You understand, yeah?'

'You don't think Hector could have persuaded me?' She gestured to her face. 'I don't know who you guys think I am, but hey, knock yourself out. What's a small town without gossip, eh?'

'Open'er up.'

Lindsey went around the back and opened both doors.

'There.' She stood back and smiled. 'Packed full of bombs and them rocket launcher things. Oh and there's a hooker hiding behind my dog. Wouldn't go in there if I were you though. He hasn't had breakfast yet.' Her smile broadened.

He smiled back at her now like she was the bimbo that he wanted her to be. 'Plenty of room in there, isn't there?'

Lindsey looked inside and nodded. 'I suppose there is.'

He stepped closer to her, leaned in and whispered in her ear; 'You could have a lot of fun in there.'

He didn't mean for it to sound playful. His voice held more than a hint of a threat and his hand was on her ass clutching hard.

'I suppose you could.' Lindsey looked inside again and then she lowered her voice to match his. 'You do know Ben though, don't you?'

'Yeah, I know Ben.'

'So you know that he doesn't have a sense of humour about these things, yeah? Not like you do.'

'So you're saying I can't tap that ass because that ass belongs to him?' He stepped back with a cheeky grin on his face now. He was goading her. 'You gonna tell on me, are ya?'

'Nothing to tell is there?' She closed the doors and made her way past him towards the front of the van again. She wasn't stupid enough to rise to his bate. 'So lunchtime then, lads? I know you'll be hungry having been here all night.' She was smiling at them all like they were her best friends as she climbed into the driver's seat. 'Hope it wasn't on my account.'

'Thanks, Lindsey,' said the youngest looking lad.

She didn't know him, but he seemed to know her. But that's what happens when you've managed to become a small town's own oddity. Whoever he was, she was just happy to see him sitting in the driver's seat of the Civic and starting its engine. He moved the car enough to clear her way over the bridge and she wasted no time in starting the van up again.

As she pulled away she beeped the horn, and gave a friendly wave to the imbeciles. They were off. As they drove passed Fota Wildlife Park, they both breathed a sigh of relief, but it wasn't until Eileen made known her plans to, 'Knife the fucker if he put his mouldy hands on my arse,' that they both laughed. It was a nervous laugh, but a much needed one. The alternative was that one of them might explode.

*

The distance from Cobh to Cork city was about twenty-five kilometres on a relatively good main road. But that's not where they were headed. At least not yet. So they took the flyover at Tivoli, just a few miles from the city centre. Where they were headed couldn't be further from the bustle and mayhem of the city streets.

Spanning a distance of over twenty kilometres through the Counties of Cork, Limerick, and Tipperary, the Galtee Mountains were one of the few places on Earth where Lindsey felt truly at home. It was also one of the few places where she felt confident that she could hide these people and keep them relatively safe. She just had to get them there in one piece. And it was starting to look like that might actually happen.

'Eileen!'

Her happy thoughts were interrupted by the sound of radio static coming from beneath the passenger seat, followed by Danny Chambers' voice sounding less than calm.

'Eileen, pick the fuck up, woman!'

Eileen looked around bewildered, before finally pulling a Motorola handset out from under her seat. She looked at it puzzled for a second. Then Danny roared her name again.

'What you want?' she barked back.

'They know.'

'What? Who knows… how?'

I just got back to find Seamus in a fucking heap. That lump of shit, Hector, and at least five other fuckers were here. They were looking for the van. They fucking knew, I'm sure of it. They're gone after ye and they left not long after ye did. They'll be right behind you.'

'Why the fuck didn't Seamus stop them? What's that shotgun under his bed for, decoration?'

'Seamus' nose is coming out the back of his head and he has fewer teeth now than the day he was born. He couldn't stop shit. Get out of that van now, Eileen.'

Eileen looked worriedly at Lindsey, who was busy checking the wing mirror. There were two cars racing up behind them; a black BMW and a grey Audi.

'Shite,' she muttered.

'Eileen, get the fuck out! Lindsey, stop the van and let my sister out or I swear to fuck I'll come for you.'

'Yip, she's pulling over now, Dan. I'm getting out.'

Eileen twisted the knob on the top of the handset and switched it off as the two cars raced past them. They were just approaching the junction at Blackpool.

To their right was the Blackpool shopping centre. To the left was the road to Fairhill and straight ahead was the N20 road to Mallow. That was where they needed to go but between them and the N20, right at the traffic lights, the Audi and the BMW pulled across to block the road.

Eight men that Lindsey could count jumped out and lined up in front of the cars. Each of them held a weapon; baseball bats, crowbars; all more than capable of doing damage.

Lindsey slowed the van. They were about two hundred yards from Hector's men with nowhere to go but forward or back. And there was no way they were going back. Not now.

'Oh, fuck me.' Eileen's hand went to her belt buckle.

'Lock your door, we're not stopping.'

Eileen pressed a button and all doors locked as Lindsey sped up again. She didn't want to kill anyone, so she didn't give it too much boot. Just enough to keep them moving.

When the men realised that she wasn't stopping, two of them rushed the van and somehow jumped on, like they'd just finished watching the whole Die Hard series. As they began battering it with whatever weapons they had, Lindsey was quick to admit that she'd been an idiot for slowing down.

It was a large wrench that smashed through the driver's side window. It passed Lindsey's face, before slamming into Eileen's temple. What followed the wrench was a man's hand which wrapped itself around Lindsey's throat. He was standing on the running board and if she had time to think, she would have cursed Danny for his ridiculous taste in van accessories. But she wasn't thinking about that because a second guy was hanging on Eileen's side. He was banging on her window with a crowbar until that too gave way and smashed inwards. Eileen was fighting her own fight, while Lindsey struggled to breathe and keep the van moving, sure that if they stopped even for a second, they were dead.

With one hand on the wheel, her brain finally kicked into gear. She'd instinctively tried to prise open his grip, which was crushing. This was a waste of precious time and energy. She began fumbling for her blade and as she did, she could feel the van slowing down. They were in fourth gear. If she didn't get him off her and change down soon, they'd stall and then they were fucked.

It probably took three seconds for her to free the blade from her belt, but it felt like an hour. By then it was too late. They were stalling. Their transit van with a floor full of easy targets shuddered to a stop and Lindsey clocked the other six men strolling in their direction, confident that they were going no further. A second hand, also attached to the beast who was attached to the van, came through the window and began grappling with her face.

Eileen was struggling beside her and Lindsey couldn't tell what was happening to her. She jammed her blade into the cartilage of the hand around her throat. Blood started to pour from it and the other hand tightened momentarily on her face. Finally it fell away, but not before Lindsey managed to pull her blade out. She wasn't about to lose her most valuable weapon and as she dropped it into her lap, she started the engine again. It was broad daylight in a city suburb. Sirens would be heard soon, but not soon enough. This time she didn't care about killing people. Not when they were quite happy to kill her, so she gunned the engine.

Out the side of her eye she could see that Eileen was viciously punching someone whose head and shoulders were inside the van. As they took off, he lost his grip and fell back onto the road.

Lindsey floored it, crashing through the two parked cars. At least one man was thrown across the bonnet of the Audi. She sped towards the N20 and as she glanced in the wing mirror, she could see three men lying in the road. One was pulling himself up, writhing in pain. They'd live.

'Are you alright?' she asked Eileen, looking at her for the first time as she put a hand to her own throat. It felt like it had been crushed.

'I'm fucking perfect,' Eileen growled.

Her face was bloody, most of which was pouring from her nose. She also had a split lip. In her lap was her blood-soaked blade.

She opened the glove box and pulled out a small first aid box. She rummaged through it until she found a wad of gauze, which she pressed to her nose.

'Are you?' she mumbled through the bandage.

'Fine.'

'Fucking tinkers.' She kicked the dash.

Then she glanced at Lindsey and they both did that thing that lies between hysterical laughing and hysterical crying with a few painful snorts thrown in on Eileen's end. Their hands were shaking, and Lindsey felt like puking, but she kept the boot down. She didn't know if she'd damaged the cars enough to stop them. Or if she'd damaged the men enough to deter them. She had to continue as if neither were the case and assume that they were behind her.

But if they found out where she was headed then they'd need a hell of a head start to get out of sight on that mountain and with the company she was presently keeping, that would be a damn tall order.

Chapter 18

The rest of the journey passed in silence as they sped along a road that Lindsey knew well. She pressed down harder on the accelerator every time the road opened up enough, so while the journey normally took about an hour, they reached the tiny village of Kilbeheny in just over forty minutes. She didn't need signposts to tell her where to turn off and before long they were driving up the kind of road that would rip apart the underside of your car if you attempted it at any speed greater than ten miles per hour.

'How the fuck do you find places like this?' Eileen was looking ahead at the mountain now which towered over them.

At the foot of the mountain, in a little place called The King's Yard, was a farm house. Lindsey half expected to see the man who lived there out front. He gave advice or directions to hikers, or just seemed to enjoy a chat with the more seasoned visitors. He made space for a tiny car park on his land, with a little honesty box strapped to a pole. You could drop in a few quid to leave your car for the day. But today, both the house and the car park seemed deserted. This was good. It meant that she could hide her people here with some degree of confidence that they wouldn't be found.

'We're here.' She pulled the van to a halt in the car park and immediately got out. She hurried round the back, sure that the others would be in dire need of some fresh air. She quickly let Frank out of his box and then had to wrestle him off her in order to get the others out. He was emotional. Again. Of course he'd been aware that Lindsey was in danger and that he was locked in. Again. This had become yet another habit she needed to break.

'It's alright, Frankie,' she whispered, and gave his ears a quick scratch.

She grabbed the floor with Eileen and they pulled it back. The smell of vomit hit them immediately and Eileen wasted no time removing herself from the vicinity. Lindsey helped them out one by one, starting with Reem. It was Lena who'd been sick on herself. It was no wonder with the rough ride they'd had.

Once outside, they gulped down the cleanest, freshest air the country had to offer. Then they took a minute to actually look at where they were. A part of Lindsey expected to see beaming smiles on their faces as they took in the majesty of their surroundings. But clearly that was just how she felt about the place. These people just looked worried, as always, so she didn't bother pointing out the sights. Instead she decided that it was time to get them settled and give them something to concentrate on other than how they felt.

'OK.' She shoved one of the large backpacks out of the van and hauled the other onto her own back. 'Grab the gear and follow me.'

With Eileen's help, Charlie managed to get the pack onto his back. He struggled under its weight, but it wouldn't be for long. They weren't headed up the mountain, as tempted as Lindsey was. Instead they were headed for the small wooded area at the foot of the Galtees. They walked for about ten minutes, first around the woods using a trail that was popular with walkers, then heading deeper into the woods. She found a spot close to the centre point, which provided good shelter and great cover from all directions. It was as good a hiding spot as they could hope for tonight.

Lindsey dropped her pack and then helped Charlie with his.

'This is it for now.'

They all stood looking around for a minute. Reem looked frightened and Charlie looked lost. But the other two started to look surprisingly OK with their current situation and she was tempted to ask, It could be a hell of a lot worse, am I right? But she didn't. She wished the whole world could see what she saw around the mountains of Ireland. The calm that magical places like this could bring to the mind and body was nothing short of miraculous. But she didn't have time to wake anybody up to that warm fuzzy feeling just now. She had more urgent things to think about, like finding Street and getting them all out of this shit storm in one piece.

It was still early, but already it felt like a long day and she needed to get a move on. If Street wasn't where she hoped he'd be then she'd have to rethink everything. But rather than dwelling too much on that, she busied herself with one of the packs. She pulled its contents out onto the soft forest floor. She'd brought enough groundsheets to also make some overhead cover using short bungee cords and the surrounding trees, essentially making three small camps for them to shelter under, hopefully just for one night. The other pack was filled with non-perishable foods and the tools needed to heat and eat it. There was enough there for a week if they rationed it. Though she sincerely hoped that they wouldn't need to. Still, she explained this to them just in case. Hope for the best, but always prepare for the worst; a motto that had always served her well.

She'd packed more than enough warm and waterproof clothing, too. Just about everything she owned. It was quite cold here now, but it would be freezing by nightfall. She provided them with waterproof matches and torches and before getting ready to leave, she showed Amir how to safely light a fire in a wooded area. Once that was done, she pulled out her cooking gear and went about heating some beans. She needed to leave, but she wasn't inclined to do so until she knew that they were warm, fed, and relatively settled. She also wanted to be sure that they'd know how to take care of themselves after she left. Of course, they'd been taking care of themselves in conditions far worse than this for some time now. But still; at this moment in time they were her responsibility and that knowledge weighed heavily on her.

As she filled three mess tins with beans and began heating them one at a time over the fire, Lena came and sat alongside her. She slapped Lindsey's hand away from the task and she took it over. Once she'd given them a good stir, she turned and smiled fondly at Lindsey.

'No one will bother us here.'

Lindsey returned her smile with a nod, hoping that she was right. 'We need to get going.'

Lena stopped her as she went to stand. 'You eat first.'

'Well I'm starving.' Eileen sat down heavily.

She still wasn't done wrestling with her nose. It wouldn't stop bleeding for more than a few minutes at a time.

'Will you please let me look at that?' Lindsey pulled the nearest pack towards her and took a first aid kit from the side pocket.

'They might need that, I'm fine.' She held up another wad of gauze that she'd pulled from her pocket and held it tightly against her face. She was a mess, with dried blood smeared across her cheeks and chin.

'You look like you've been butchered.'

'Wasn't I?'

'We heard a lot of commotion,' said Lena. 'The van shook so much. We didn't know what was happening to you both.'

Eileen removed the gauze for long enough to give a frightening smile. 'No need to worry about us. We're tough old birds.'

'Says the old nineteen-year-old,' Lindsey laughed.

'Yeah well, it would have been rude to just call you old.'

Even Amir was smiling now, as Lena handed out spoons and placed one mess tin on the floor before placing another on the fire. 'Eat,' she said.

They both did as they were told and in all honesty, a gourmet feast wouldn't have tasted as good.

*

As they headed back to the van, Lindsey veered off towards the farmhouse.

'Where are you going now?'

'Give me a second.' She climbed over the small surrounding wall and knocked on the door.

There was no answer, but she could hear movement inside.

'Hello?' She called out and knocked again.

Finally the door opened a fraction.

'Hi.'

He opened the door a little wider, looking more than surprised to see her. 'I know you…'

'Lindsey.' She smiled. 'We've met before but I don't think we ever exchanged names.'

'John. Is everything OK? Do you need something?'

'No. It's just the first time I've ever come here and not seen you outside, greeting people.'

'Not many people to greet this time of year. Usually just the few diehards like yourself who don't need my help.' He smiled slightly.

'Well I just wanted to let you know that there are a few people camping just inside the wood. They won't bother you.'

He looked beyond her towards the wood. 'What are they doing there?'

'An outdoor survival course. This is the part where they have to fend for themselves.' She smiled, knowing that the story would be plausible. Courses like that did happen here, quite regularly in fact. 'I hope to be back to pick them up tomorrow at the latest.'

She didn't know this man very well. But the last thing she needed was him getting spooked in the middle of the night and calling the cops.

'I just didn't want you to worry if you see smoke coming from the camp fire or whatever.'

He nodded. 'Well, living in the middle of nowhere at the foot of a mountain, I don't spook easily. But when you start hearing noises, it's nice to know for sure that there actually is someone there.' He smiled. 'Thanks for letting me know.'

'No problem. Take care.' She turned and walked away, happy that he wouldn't be calling the cops any time soon.

'You too, Lindsey.'

At this moment in time, Lindsey envied the man his life of solitude.

'Who was that dude?' Eileen asked, finally wiping her face relatively clean using a spit-soaked tissue.

'The Galtee Mountain man. You ready to face the road again, old bird?'

'Oh I'm ready.' She pulled the blade from her belt and nestled it in her closed fist. The business end protruded threateningly through her knuckles. 'They won't be fucking up this masterpiece again.'

Lindsey smiled as she started the van and took off at a slow crawl back down the mountain road until they came to the main road again. Then she took off at speed. She had no idea where Patrick's guys were now. But wherever they were, they'd be a hell of a lot more pissed than they had been before she rammed their cars and injured at least three of them.

As they sped down the Mallow road approaching Blackpool, Lindsey pulled the blade from her belt and rested it in her lap.

'Do not slow down,' Eileen muttered.

She had no intention of it. But as they approached the crossroads, it was clear, as was the rest of their journey to Parnell Place in the city centre. That too gave her an uneasy feeling. It just meant that the other shoe had yet to drop.

The city streets were teeming with people, all going about their daily business. But according to talk, Patrick's people were everywhere, so Lindsey wasn't ready to relax just yet. She pulled the van to a halt behind the bus station, which was also busy. They both sat, looking up and down the street for a few minutes before getting out. They both expected trouble that didn't look like it was coming. But Lindsey kept her guard up and her blade out, concealed under her long sleeve.

'Don't tell me we're getting on a bus?'

Lindsey shook her head. 'This way.'

Even though both windows were smashed, she locked the van anyway. Then they walked back out onto Parnell Place at the side of the bus station, and turned left. Less than a minute later they took another left down a laneway that she knew like the back of her hand. Lindsey almost lost her life here once. It was also where Street lived; half way down on the right-hand side. On either side of his place were abandoned buildings. He pretty much had the lane to himself; usually.

Today though there was a very large man dressed in black, loitering between Street's front door and the neighbouring building. He looked like he meant business, but Lindsey didn't acknowledge or address him. She was fairly certain though that he was military. Or at least he had been. Most soldiers were easy to spot; the male ones more so.

She pulled a small bunch of keys from her pocket. When she found the one she was looking for she slipped it into Street's front door. Before she could turn the key, a large arm made its way across her chest, blocking her way.

'Can I help you?' she asked, turning to face the man who was about the same height as her but twice as wide. Not bad looking otherwise.

'That's my line,' he replied, in a throaty voice with half a smile.

'Well, if you could move that trunk of an arm, that'd be great.' She returned his smile, while her free hand adjusted its grip on the blade.

'Not before you tell me what business you have here and why the hell you have a key to this building? Then we might talk about the knife that you have aimed at my balls.'

Her instincts were telling her that this guy was a friend of Street's. But she wasn't ready to trust anyone she didn't know just yet.

'I'm here to see Street and where my knife ends up, depends on you.'

'And how do you know Street?'

'Does it matter?'

'Kind of. Some nasty people around here these days.'

It seemed she was right; Street had found a puddle of shit to play in.

'Well, I'm presuming he doesn't hand out his house key to just anyone. Unless he's changed dramatically since I last saw him.'

He stood back, taking his balls out of range and looked at her for a minute. Then he wagged his finger with a knowing grin on his face. 'What's your name?' He asked, like he might already know it.

'Lindsey.'

'Ryan? You're Lindsey Ryan?'

Eileen glanced at Lindsey now before returning her hard stare to the giant in front of them.

'Listen, there's no need for blades. Why don't you put that away? And tell scrapper there to put hers away too, unless she plans to use it.'

Lindsey turned to look at Eileen who was ready to pounce on someone at least a foot and a half taller, and three stone heavier than she was.

'But I admire her spirit.' He smiled at Eileen, who looked like she wanted to hurt him even more now.

'We haven't met.' He held his hand towards Lindsey. 'I'm Levi.'

She shook his hand with some hesitation.

'I've heard a lot about you.'

'From Street?'

He nodded.

'So, where is he?'

With that, Street's front door opened and Lindsey was momentarily stunned to see Damien Brady standing there.

'Damo?'

'Jesus Christ!' Damo laughed, and manhandled her into a bear hug. 'Look what the fucking cat dragged in.'

Damo was one of her oldest friends. She'd served four tours overseas with him, two in Lebanon, one in Chad and one, the last one for all of them, in Syria. He looked exactly as he should, considering how he lived; scraggly, dirty brown hair with a hint of ginger. Chipped teeth and a nose that had been broken several times. He was wiry and restless, like he always had been. Damo was a brawler with the social skills of a hob nailed boot. But she loved him dearly.

'You're breaking me, Damo,' she laughed, and finally he put her down.

'Are you giving her shit, you big fucking ape?' He directed his abuse through a fucked-up smile at Levi.

'Just testing her,' Levi replied. 'Now her friend…' he grinned at Eileen. 'I wouldn't mind testing her a bit more.'

'You'd be a brave boy,' Lindsey offered, but she couldn't help smiling at the girlish grin on Eileen's face, as she fiddled with the blade between her fingers.

'What the fuck?' Street appeared behind Damo, shoving him out of the way.

He looked at her for a few seconds. Then he caught her face in his hands, smiled broadly and also hugged her, though less painfully. In that moment Lindsey found herself thanking God that she was finally home. Street had fresh bruises on his face and was limping pretty noticeably. But he was here.

After a minute he stood back and looked at her. 'Will there ever be a day when you turn up on my doorstep not looking like you went ten rounds with Katie Taylor?'

'Yeah, but you should see the other guy,' Eileen offered from behind her.

'I thought you might be the other guy,' Damo replied, eyeing Eileen, whose face still had a coating of dried blood smeared across it.

'Nah. But you should see that other guy.' She smiled awkwardly.

Eileen was more than able to hold her own. But she had two men scrutinising her now, and she didn't seem to know how to handle it.

'Damo, leave my chef alone. We need to talk.'

'You'd better come in then.' Street stood aside.

Inside was just how Lindsey remembered it. The ground floor was a boxing gym, as basic as they come as far as gyms went. But it kept more kids off the street and out of trouble than anyone could count. Or at least it had. Today there were just two men working out. One on the heavy bag and one skipping. Both looked military fit.

'Chef?' Damo asked Eileen.

'Believe it or not, that one owns a café. And she couldn't boil a fucking egg,' Eileen responded, and Damo fell in love instantly.

Street was quiet as he made his way up the stairs to the second floor, and Lindsey noticed that his limp was worse than it seemed at first. She could tell that he was in pain. Not that he'd ever admit it.

'What happened to you?' she asked anyway.

'You first. And where's Frank?'

'He's otherwise engaged.'

The first floor was another shell of a concrete room. Street had put up partitions to give the impression that he had a separate living and sleeping space. It was basic, but meticulously clean and tidy. It did the job and suited his needs perfectly. Lindsey felt at home here and as she sunk into the leather recliner that no longer reclined, knowing that it was Street's chair, she breathed out a sigh of relief just for being there. Now she just had to hope that by bringing her problems to Street's front door, she wouldn't be bringing more trouble to her friends. Clearly they had enough of their own; the details of which she had yet to find out.

Chapter 19

'OK, I'll go first, shall I?' Lindsey conceded, knowing that it would go better that way. 'You know the Galtee Mountains?' she asked, with half a smile.

'Oh this'll be good.' Damo got to his feet, snorting out a laugh on his way to the fridge. There he collected four beers and handed one to each of them. When Eileen declined, he placed hers on the coffee table beside his own.

'I think I've heard of them,' replied Street who, like Lindsey, knew the Galtees like the back of his hand.

'Well I've ensconced a few people there who need to go somewhere else at the earliest opportunity.'

Damo and Street were silent; waiting.

'Why don't I try explaining this?' Eileen sat forward. 'You two seem to be of the same variety of fucking lunatic as she is, so I'm sure you'll catch on quick. She's been hiding a load of Anne-fucking-Frankes in her attic; behind walls, under floorboards; you name it. Meanwhile she's drinking spicy tea and getting beat up by the local pimp and his goons. She's bribing bent coppers...' She turned to eye Lindsey now; letting her know that she knew exactly how she was bribing said copper, '...sweet talking fellas at checkpoints, almost turning the pair of us into road kill and now we're expected to return with a van load of eggs and shit and they're hiding in a fucking hedge somewhere.' She paused for breath. 'Are ye with me so far?'

She had Damo and Street's full attention. Only when they were sure she'd finished did they turn their stare on Lindsey. Street jabbed his thumb in Eileen's direction and raised an eyebrow in silent question.

Lindsey shrugged. 'Something like that.'

'Exactly like that,' Eileen mumbled, flopping back on the couch, like she'd just unloaded a heavy burden.

Street sat back too, his eyes still on Lindsey.

Damo smiled broadly. 'You haven't changed a bit, Ryan. So…' he went and sat alongside Eileen on the same couch as Street, making it a tight and uncomfortable squeeze for everyone. 'Tell me more about you.'

Eileen rolled her eyes, got up and moved to the lone armchair that Damo had vacated.

'Your turn.' Lindsey directed her question to Street. 'What've you two been up to?'

Street was only half listening. He was thinking now. That was him through and through. He was the thinker; the born leader. Damo was the one who answered, looking slightly wounded by Eileen's sudden departure.

'Well our boy Adam there was stabbed in the leg last night.' Damo smiled broadly again. He really did look like the lunatic Eileen thought he was. 'No good deed goes unpunished and all that.'

'That's why you'd never find me doing one of those so-called good deeds,' Eileen huffed.

'Yeah well, we showed a few moves to a poor little fucker who was getting the shit kicked out of him, by his dad of all people. Dad wasn't impressed.'

Eileen however, was impressed, despite herself.

'You're getting a bit of a name for yourselves.' Lindsey grinned. 'The Old Dogs?'

'You heard of us?' Damo beamed.

She'd never seen him so smiley. It was unsettling.

'Yeah; apparently some of your lads had a run in with some innocent boys in Cobh. Gave them a bit of a going over that wasn't viewed as particularly fair given that they were trained by...' she looked to Eileen, 'What was it they called them? Treacherous cunts, was it?'

Eileen nodded. 'Something to that effect.'

'Oh, OK.' Street nodded. 'And did they give any mention to the fact that same chap and four of his friends punctured Ali's lung a couple of months ago? He was threatening round two, only Ali was ready for him this time.'

'These fellas always leave out the important bits.' Damo shook his head.

'Different lad, I think. This was a retribution thing.'

Damo grunted and sat forward in his chair. 'A bunch of kids from outside the city get ferried up to us a couple of times a week by the cops in their youth outreach bus. They're vulnerable as fuck, the lot of them. We do what we can to point them in the right direction but we can't promise them riches like others can.' He shrugged and sat back. His face as he swigged from the bottle told Lindsey that he was venomous towards the people who took advantage of them.

Youth outreach. So that's how Ben knew about them.

'I knew it was you.' Lindsey smiled, trying to bring Damo back. 'The name describes you both perfectly.'

Eileen looked from Damo to Street, where her eyes lingered a little longer. Then she glanced at Lindsey, letting her know that she didn't quite agree with her on that one. Adam Street was very easy on the eye, to most women at least.

'Seems the bigger the shit hole a kid comes out of, the bigger target he is. You know... coming over here to steal our women and our jobs etcetera, etcetera.' Damo was still stewing, but he'd pull himself out of it soon. He always did.

'You remember An Tús Núa?' Street asked, not for a second alluding to the fact that Lindsey worked there for almost two years.

Sometime after leaving the army, when she finally kicked her pill addiction and got her life back on track; or as on track as it was likely to get, she qualified in Social Science and went to work with the troubled youth of Cork city. Turned out, she was more fucked up than all of them put together, so she moved on. But while she was there, she'd roped Adam into training some of their kids. He gave them an outlet for their frustrations and a focus for their energy, and he did it like no one else could.

Lindsey just nodded her reply.

'They have an outreach programme for migrant kids and teens nowadays too. We're just an extension of that.'

That made sense. It made even more sense that Street would get involved with that too. He was a sucker for an underdog. Always was.

'Come on, I'll show you.'

'I might wait here.' Eileen piped up as they all got to their feet. 'I've seen more than enough for one day.'

Lindsey nodded and followed Damo downstairs. Street followed haltingly behind them.

'And what's his job?' She asked Damo when they got outside, nodding in Levi's direction.

'The gym's been getting a bit of unwanted attention lately. Levi is there to tickle anyone who isn't here to work out. Isn't he a beefcake?'

Lindsey laughed. 'Not my type.'

'Why, because he knows who you are?'

'That's one reason.'

'Damn girl, I'm sorry,' Levi responded with a smile. They didn't even try to conceal their conversation from him. 'I can call you Denise if you like and you can call me whatever the fuck you want.'

'Too late. And it could have been beautiful.'

She tapped him on the chest with a grin, and followed Damo into the building next door they'd converted into an extension of the original gym, but they hadn't broken through the wall. Possibly because it might bring down both buildings if they did.

'Of course it would,' Levi continued with a broad smile. 'You're Lindsey-fucking-Ryan.'

'What've you been telling him?'

'Just what a pain in the arse you are,' Street replied.

Everything about it mirrored next door, from its concrete floor painted red and the whitewashed cinder block walls. It too smelled of stale sweat and was as basic as you like. Just a large boxing ring, heavy bags and speed bags, and a whole heap of body strength equipment. There were also at least fifteen teenagers, mostly boys but two girls that she could see. They were all nationalities including Irish, working out with various trainers, who all looked military. Martin's Intel wasn't too far off. Except for the actual big picture that is.

'Boxing and self-defence,' Street said, as he looked around. He'd never allow himself to be proud of something like this.

'You did good, Street.'

He ignored the comment, naturally.

'You wanna tog off and go a few rounds?' he asked instead.

'I think I've gone enough rounds for one day.'

'Throw them a few pointers at least?' Levi asked from where he stood, just inside the door.

'Nah, I'll leave that to the experts.'

'Come on!' he chuckled. 'You can't show up here looking like you went bat shit crazy on some poor bastard and not share a few pearls of wisdom. You're Lindsey-fucking-Ryan.'

'Call me Lindsey-fucking-Ryan again and I might just go bat shit crazy on you.'

'See? I knew I could charm my way into your life.'

'Be careful what you wish for buddy,' Damo added.

'If you're all finished feeling each other up, I could do with a beer.' Street wasn't up for the banter and Lindsey guessed that he was in pain. His limp was getting worse.

'Me too.' Lindsey followed him next door and as they got upstairs, Eileen was there, waiting impatiently for them to come back.

'So, about my people on the Galtees?'

'I heard a rumour that you were hiding a wanted woman and were about to get fucked up for your efforts.'

'How'd you hear that?'

He shrugged. 'I hear things. I've been trying to call you but your damn phone is out of service. Word is, her pimp is fairly hard core and has significant reach.'

'Yeah, I heard that too,' Lindsey mumbled.

'Mmm. I heard some bent cop was sniffing around too. Presumably the same one that Eileen there mentioned earlier, and from what I gather, he's just as bad as the fuckers who rearranged your face that way. Assuming it wasn't him?'

'It wasn't him.'

'We have two guys down there as we speak, tasked with getting you and the girl out of there tonight.'

'You what?'

Damo nodded. 'But considering the fact that you're smuggling four people and not one, it's probably just as well you beat us to it.'

'As nice as it is to hear that Patrick and his friends are keeping us in their thoughts, we have another problem to consider today.'

They all looked to Eileen.

'We're expected back in Cobh later with a load of supplies for the café. We go back there empty handed and we'll have some explaining to do.'

'She's right.'

Lindsey had no intentions of going back to Cobh. Not any time soon at least, but she knew that Eileen would and she needed to provide her with cover.

'What'ya need?' asked Damo.

Eileen shrugged. 'Stuff. Coffee, tea, flour, eggs, milk… That Mad Bastard put the kibosh on us, so you name it, we need it.'

'We can sort that out.' Damo put his beer down and headed for the stairs. 'Well you comin', or what?'

Eileen shot a look in Lindsey's direction. Lindsey responded by throwing the keys of the van at her. There was no one in the world she trusted more than Damo and Street. Eileen would be perfectly safe with him.

'If he says he can sort it out, then he can sort it out.' She smiled at her friend. 'You can trust him.'

Eileen arched her eyebrows and got to her feet. 'Fine. Well he might as well know that I have a blade in my pants and I'm not afraid to use it.'

Damo fell even deeper in love.

*

After they left, Street got to his feet, hobbled to the fridge and returned with two more beers.

'Show me your leg,' Lindsey demanded after he sat down.

'If you want me to take my pants off, just say so.' He grinned and took a long swig. He sat back with no intention of showing her his wound. 'So about Frank…?'

'He's on the Galtees looking after the kid, Reem. Street, you can hardly walk. How bad is it?'

'He should be with you, looking after you. The blade hit the bone, but it's well stitched up. Levi's a medic, believe it or not. What about you… just facial injuries?'

She nodded. 'And trust me, I'm looking forward to getting my dog back.'

'Who was he?'

'A friend of Lena's pimp.'

'How's he now?'

'Embarrassed.'

He grinned again and took another drink. 'Tell me about this copper.'

'You seem to know more about him than I do. Why don't you tell me?'

'Nice guy; almost crippled a fifteen-year-old a few weeks back, I believe. All in the line of duty of course.'

'That sounds like him. How's he on your radar?'

'I have the chatter with the cops in the outreach programme. They're onto him. They just can't nail the fucker. How deep are you in with him?'

'I'm not. He's on Patrick's payroll but as far as I'm concerned, I'm done with him now.'

'And as far as he's concerned?'

She shrugged. Ben had no love for Lindsey, she was perfectly clear on that. But he was a man who liked to be in control; to say when things started and when they finished. He'd want her now just because he couldn't have her, and he wasn't likely to take that lying down.

'Doesn't matter. I won't be going back any time soon. But your guys in Cobh, I need you to contact them.'

'What'ya need?'

'I need them go see a guy by the name of Danny Chambers. They'll find him sitting on the roof of his caravan out near Whitepoint. He'll be holding a crow bar and has a sawn-off shotgun inside the caravan. He should be easy enough to spot.'

Street laughed. 'Another friend of yours?'

'Something like that. He's Eileen's brother. I need him to know that Eileen will be coming back by herself, and that he needs to keep an eye on Ben the copper. Eileen is well protected, but they need to know what they have to protect her from. If they don't already.'

'I thought she might be a pikey alright.'

'Don't call her that.'

'Hey, it's no bad thing. Besides; I like her.'

'Yeah, so does Damo by the looks of it.'

'A match made in heaven I'd say.' He laughed and then they drifted into silence for a few minutes before Street finally spoke again.

'You took a hell of a risk, Lindsey.'

'It seems I don't know how to avoid this shit anymore.'

'Are you OK? I mean is that all that was done to you?' He waved a hand across her face.

'I'm OK.'

He nodded and after a few more minutes of silence he finally smiled again. 'It's fucking good to see you, Ryan.'

Chapter 20

Street spent a while on the phone to various people before finally coming to sit alongside her. He had what amounted to a decent plan. In short, one of his contacts had a shelter for vulnerable people in the city – at risk women and children mostly. They only had space for two so it was decided that Amir and Reem would occupy those spots. The woman who ran the shelter managed to find a bed in another refuge for Charlie. Lindsey would look after Lena for another night.

'So, this Ben bollix; what does he know about you?'

'That I make tea and sandwiches.'

'Right. So try to imagine what things might look like inside a peanut sized mind like his. Patrick's guys get their hands on you, the helpless waitress, would open the door for him a bit, wouldn't it? He'd get to be the big swinging dick, saving the day and all that.'

She let this settle on her for a minute.

'Hector searched my flat while I was pinned to a table downstairs,' she mumbled. 'Ben fucking sent them.'

Of course he did. He'd been watching her every move and reporting back to Hector.

Lindsey was playing Ben and of course, he was playing her too. That was the name of the game. But her late realisation of something so obvious annoyed her no end. How the fuck had she missed that?

'It was dumb luck that Hector didn't find them.'

'Not just them.'

She didn't acknowledge his concerns.

'We'll get the boys to the shelter and I'll camp out with Lena until then. They won't find us on the Galtees.'

Street shook his head.

'It's the best option and you know it. Besides, I could do with the peace and quiet.'

She flopped back in the chair, suddenly looking forward to a day or two on one of her favourite mountains. Granted, the circumstances weren't ideal but it beat hiding out in her flat.

She couldn't think about her beloved Galtees right now though as Ben invaded her mind. Her dislike for him began to turn to hatred. It didn't occur to her to be bothered by the fact that she'd slept with such a low life. Sex was merely a tool that she used when her mind filled with things she couldn't control; nightmares from her past, nightmares from her present. Problems that she needed to solve and situations that felt out of control. When she felt on the verge of exploding, sex was one of her releases, nothing more. Boxing and running were the others, but there were times when they just wouldn't do. So no; her fling with Ben wasn't on her mind. Instead she was thinking of all the ways she'd like to hurt him.

As always, it was as if Street could read her mind.

'Forget about him.'

'Who?'

'The prick that you're plotting your revenge against. He'll get his, don't worry. You can only play both sides for so long.'

'I'm not worried about him.'

'Right.'

'He is a cheeky fucker though.'

'And you shagged him.'

'What's that got to do with anything?'

Street laughed quietly. 'When are you gonna settle down with a real man, eh?'

'As soon as a deaf mute with a six pack becomes available.' She grinned and picked up her beer. 'You know I can picture us years from now, sitting in a nursing home having this very same conversation. You'll have been slapped on the wrist for feeling up nurses, and I'll be on extra medication so that I don't make the porters feel uncomfortable.'

They both laughed out loud and for Lindsey at least, it felt like a lifetime since she'd found something genuinely funny. And it was funny because it was true.

*

The next few hours were spent talking about everything except their current situation. They talked about old times, old friends, old flings and old stories. It was a tonic to Lindsey. So much so that by the time Damo and Eileen returned, she felt almost like her old self; calm and unflappable.

'How'd you two get on?' she asked, as they arrived at the top of the stairs.

'Well we went to get the van and there was some guy's hairy arse hanging out the driver's side window. He was in the process of trying to rob the fucking thing until this fella…' Eileen thumbed in Damo's direction, 'literally picked him up by the elastic in his underpants and flung him at the number three bus.'

Eileen was impressed, though she did her best to sound like she wasn't.

'I mean, did you get what we need?'

'And then some. We have enough supplies to last us months.' She turned to look at Damo with half a smile. 'You know for a ginger snap, he's not the worst.'

Damo ran his hand through his unruly hair, which to be fair, only had the slightest hint of ginger to it. He smiled like a halfwit. Eileen had yet to learn that it was impossible to offend Damo. In this case, he heard exactly what he wanted to hear; that he wasn't the worst. Or in Damo's mind; that she liked him.

'Glad you think so,' Street replied with a smile. 'Because Damo there is going to be escorting you back to Cobh.'

Eileen shot Lindsey a look.

'I can't go back just yet, Eileen. I need to get Lena and the others away from Cork altogether. Plus, I need to keep a low profile for a bit.'

'You mean you need to avoid Ben.'

Lindsey shrugged. 'Until everyone's safe at least. No matter what happens, do not trust him, yeah?'

'I'm a traveller, Lindsey. I trust no one.'

'I'm sorry, I just have to say it…' Damo piped up, 'I might be in love with this woman.'

Eileen rolled her eyes, growled something and walked away.

Lindsey and Street stifled their smiles. When she didn't come back, Lindsey followed her behind one of the partitions to what was effectively Street's bedroom, in that it had a bed and a chest of drawers in it.

'You OK?'

'I'm fine. You could have told me before we started this that you'd be leaving me stranded though.'

'I'm not leaving you stranded. Street's guys are gone to see Danny. They'll tell him everything, so he'll be keeping an eye on Ben if he wasn't already. Or, you can come with us? We can get you away too.'

Eileen mulled it over for a second before replying. 'Nah. My moron brothers would literally starve to death if I left.'

'Well then, Damo will be going back with you.'

'Yeah, about him…'

'Eileen, Damo speaks before he thinks and he's a bit rough round the edges…'

Eileen snorted.

'But you won't find a more trustworthy person anywhere in the world. I promise you, no matter how much he jokes around or acts the idiot, he will do whatever it takes to keep you safe.'

'He's not gonna try to get into my pants or anything is he?'

'I mean he might try.' Lindsey laughed. 'Nah, not unless you want him to. He's a good guy.'

'And what do I say when Ben, or anyone else for that matter, comes looking for you? You're supposed to be home today with me. That's what you told him.'

'I know. Say that I just disappeared while you were picking up supplies. You waited around but I never came back and you're pissed as hell about it.'

'And what about the café?'

Lindsey pulled the keys out of her pocket and handed them to Eileen. 'Whether I'm gone for a week, a month or a year, you're in charge. You run that place better than I do anyway.'

She looked at the keys in her hand. 'You're actually handing your business over to me?'

'Until I get back.' If I go back, she thought.

'No one's ever trusted me with keys before.'

'You've always had a key.'

'Yeah but it's your business; your home.' She pointed to the other keys on the bunch. 'And you're handing them both over to a traveller. Mary Kelly would say you were a trusting eejit.' She sounded genuinely touched, which was a little unnatural for Eileen.

'Mary Kelly says a lot of things. It's your home if you want it while I'm gone. There's no one I trust more to look after it and if something happens and you have to leave,' she shrugged, 'just lock the place up as best you can.'

Eileen looked at her for a second and then reached over and

hugged her tightly, surprising Lindsey. Eileen Chambers was most definitely not the hugging kind. Neither was Lindsey.

'Whenever you do decide to come back, you'd better be in one piece,' she mumbled into Lindsey's neck.

She pulled back and got a grip on herself, then walked out of the room, back to where the lads were sitting side by side on the couch.

Eileen sat on an armchair facing Street, but she spoke to Damo. 'I always knew there was something about her.' She thumbed towards Lindsey. 'But I always assumed she was on the run from some asshole of a husband. Or, given how cagey she is, maybe that she'd accidentally killed that asshole of a husband or something. I never guessed she was a soldier girl though.'

Damo raised his bottle and drank most of its contents in one go while Lindsey wondered how much he'd told her. Not that it mattered now.

*

It was mid-afternoon by the time they left Street's place with their plan set out. Damo would hide in the floor of the van, with Eileen alone up front. Damo had Old Dog written all over him. Putting him in full view in Lindsey's place would be asking for trouble. Eileen would spit venom about Lindsey to whoever asked, and hopefully, with Danny Chambers on the case, she'd have no problems from Ben. Like Patrick, an Irish travelling man also has a long reach. Still, if it weren't for Damo, she'd worry more about Eileen. Ben was a coward who sent thugs after women to make himself look good. She'd like to crush him, but she had more important things to think about now.

As soon as the van left, Lindsey, Street, and Levi loaded themselves into a very old flatbed truck, also parked behind the bus station. Another guy she hadn't met before was riding in the back. Without wasting any more time, they were headed for Kilbehenny and the Galtee Mountains.

On the drive there, Lindsey gave as much information on each of her people as she could; Lena, Reem, Amir, and Charlie; how each of them had come to find themselves hiding at the foot of a mountain. More importantly, why she was fucking over one of Ireland's most dangerous men for them.

As the old truck bounced and rattled its way up the mountain road to the King's Yard, they passed a dirty and half-starved Jack Russell terrier shivering at the side of the road.

'Wait! Stop.' Lindsey had the passenger door open before they'd come to a complete stop and she was out.

She approached the dog slowly and carefully, but he seemed too miserable to question her motives. When she picked him up, he yapped a few times before pressing himself against her.

'You know him?' Street asked with a shake of his head as she climbed back inside the cab, but Lindsey knew that he had the same soft spot for dogs as she did.

'It's for Reem. I want my dog back and I think this chap might be just the ticket.'

Street rolled his eyes, but couldn't hide his smile. He also had a soft spot for troubled kids. As she cleaned the dog as best she could using the sleeve of her hoodie, Levi shuffled a bit closer to Street, and away from Lindsey and her new companion, who quite frankly, could have smelled better.

*

They parked in the little car park and made their way on foot through the woods until they came to the make-shift camp, which was deserted.

'It's me.'

Lena's head appeared from behind a tree. 'We heard a lorry. We thought…'

'What are you doing back here? You said tomorrow?' Charlie asked, stepping into view.

'This is Adam, Damo, and Levi.' Lindsey indicated the three men with her.

The fourth man, who hadn't been introduced, remained with the truck.

'They're going to take you to a shelter in Cork where you'll be safe. And much warmer than here.' She smiled. 'Pack whatever you feel you need quickly. Everything else you can leave. Where's Reem?'

She directed her question to Lena, who responded by pointing to the tree that she'd stepped out from behind. Frank was sitting with him. He looked patient, but Lindsey knew that it was an act. He was dying to bolt towards her, but he wouldn't want to startle Reem by doing so. She could tell that it was killing him, and she smiled as she continued towards him while still talking to the group.

'The lads will help you pack, but just what you need, yeah?'

'Hey boy.' She spoke softly and got on her knees beside Frank, who whined and threw his front paws and his head dramatically onto her shoulders. She wrapped one arm around him, while the other still held the wriggly Jack Russell.

Beside them was a little ball of bony arms and knees.

'Look.' She held the small dog close enough that he could sniff Reem's hair, loudly enough for him to lift his head.

Reem stared wide eyed at the filthy Jack Russell and so did Frank. He was probably wondering how he'd missed him.

'You won't believe it,' Lindsey continued with a smile. 'I found this guy heading towards the woods. Clearly he's walked miles to get here. He had to be looking for someone.'

The dog sniffed Reem again, and as if he knew exactly what she needed him to do, he leapt from Lindsey's arms on top of Reem, yapping and pawing him frantically.

'I think he was looking for you, Reem. He's your magic dog.' She smiled brightly and it was a genuine smile.

Reem looked blown away as he tried to grab a hold of his new friend who was wriggling all over him like a live wire.

'Looking for me?' he asked, astonished.

'Why else would he be all the way up here? Dogs like him don't belong on mountains.'

'What's his name?'

'You need to give him one.'

Reem looked at him for a long minute and then he smiled for the first time since she'd met him. 'I'm going to call him Lindsey.'

Lindsey laughed quietly. She'd never had a dog called after her before; a male one at that. But she couldn't bring herself to be insulted.

'Come with me; there's someone I want you to meet.' She got to her feet and waited for him to haul himself up without once easing his grip on the dog, for fear that he might lose him.

'Adam? This is Reem.'

Street stepped away from the others to come and meet him. Adam Street knew exactly the right way to deal with a terrified child. Lindsey had no doubt in her mind that he'd make Reem feel safer than anyone else ever could. He held out his hand and waited the ten seconds that it took for Reem to respond and the two shook hands.

Street smiled his easy smile. 'And who's this?' He pointed to the dog.

'Lindsey,' Reem replied. It was barely audible, but the fact that he replied at all was something of a miracle.

Street stifled a smile as he glanced at Lindsey, the person. 'Lindsey, eh? That's a good name. Anyone with that name is a good friend to have.'

Reem looked up at him, smiled and nodded.

Lindsey, the person, was already amazed by the change in him. She had no idea whether it was Street's presence or Lindsey the dog, but whatever it was, it was a welcome addition.

'OK buddy, you and the others are going to come with me now. We'll get you a nice warm bed and you can get some sleep. We'll pick Lindsey up again in the morning, yeah?'

Street's tone was gentle; conversational. He never treated kids like kids. He always spoke to them as equals and they always responded well, and though Reem seemed to like him, he still looked nervously to Lindsey.

'It's OK. Lena and I are going to stay behind to mind all this stuff. We'll see you very soon.' She glanced at Lena as she said this.

Lena stopped packing and looked at Lindsey for a minute. She nodded, placing her stuff back inside the shelter.

'Why aren't you coming?' Charlie asked.

'There won't be room for all this stuff at the shelter. Plus, I kinda like it here. Lena is going to keep me company.'

Charlie hesitated for a minute but finally nodded. When everything was packed, they all walked together out of the woods.

Levi lifted the canvas cover and opened the tailgate. He lifted Reem and Lindsey the dog effortlessly up onto the truck. Charlie followed with Amir and when they were all seated, the third man climbed in with them.

'This is James,' Street finally introduced him, and James smiled.

It was quite a beautiful, friendly, and Hollywood-whitened smile that seemed to take everyone aback for a moment. It didn't suit his face somehow.

'He's going to take care of you all, and we'll be in Cork in just over half an hour.' Street locked the tailgate again and lowered the canvas.

'You sure there won't be a problem getting them all sorted for the night?' Lindsey asked quietly, so the others couldn't hear her.

'I'm sure.'

She nodded.

'You be careful, OK?'

'Aren't I always?'

'Is that a trick question?' He grinned, squeezed her shoulder and headed for the cab of the truck where Levi was waiting patiently. 'See you tomorrow.'

'Yip.'

She and Lena stood in the car park and watched them drive away. Only when the sound of the noisy engine was replaced with total silence did they make their way quietly back into the woods, their home for the night.

Chapter 21

'So, your family; did they leave Syria with you?' Lindsey asked as she got a small fire going. They couldn't get out of each other's way tonight, so really, they had no choice but to talk.

Lena shook her head. 'My uncle, Adnan, got to Germany almost six years ago.' She smiled fondly. 'From the moment he got settled, he pleaded with my father to send me to stay with him, to give me more opportunities to study. You can't imagine the bargaining he had to do with my father.' She glanced at Lindsey and gave a roll of the eyes. 'Adnan was my mother's brother you see. My father finally conceded. But only because he knew that it was just a matter of time before we'd all have to leave our home. At least this way, well… I'd be one less person to worry about when that happened.'

'And where's your uncle now?'

'Still in Germany I'd imagine. My father paid almost nine hundred dollars for my place on board a vessel that was once used to transport animals. We were packed in so tightly that we had to sit with our knees tight against our chests for almost two days. We saw no sunlight, no food and very little water.'

'What happened once you reached land?'

Lindsey had seen and heard enough about the migrant crisis and the dangerous crossings that they faced. But all that information came from news reports or from Navy lads returning from tours patrolling the Med, and they were horror stories for sure. They'd dived upturned vessels only to find hundreds of dead bodies that had been crammed into the hull; they'd fished dead men, women and children out of the sea; delivered babies on the deck of their own vessels. They resuscitated and failed to resuscitate countless others, but this was her first time hearing from a passenger on one of those vessels. While she was aware that it might be harrowing for Lena to talk about, she couldn't bring herself to change the subject.

'They were supposed to take us to Italy. Though I'm not sure if we ever got there. The engines stopped suddenly and there was commotion. Some men came pounding through, stepping on people as they went. I was pulled from the crowd along with a few others. We were taken onto another, smaller boat that smelled like fish. It was much more comfortable; still crowded, but we could breathe. We were a few more days on board, this time with scraps to eat. We reached land late at night and Hector was there to meet us.'

There was silence for a few minutes before Lena spoke again. They both stared into the small fire.

'Can you imagine reaching a point in your life where you would welcome your own death? Pray for it even?'

The memory of a time exactly like that came flooding back to Lindsey. It might as well have happened yesterday. She could see herself sitting on the quay wall in Cork, trying to decide whether to lose herself in the fast-flowing current of the River Lee or in all three of the eight balls that she clutched in her hand. But Lena was the one who needed to get stuff off her chest, not Lindsey, so she said nothing. Instead she continued to stare into the small flame and waited for the woman to continue. She was sure that she would.

'I was brought to Patrick. Once he'd inspected me, he just… he threw me to one of his men, like I was nothing. That man was followed by another and then another and this lasted until the sun came up. By that time, Lena Dweck was dead and this was all that remained.' She gestured to herself, as if she were an unrecognisable object. 'By morning, I was nothing.'

Lindsey's stomach turned at the thought of what had been done to her, but she had no words to offer. What could she possibly say?

'My mother made me promise that I would never return home. That I would make something of myself; live the life that she never had.'

'And your father?'

'Would wish me dead for the shame. My mother's life was filled with hardships that had nothing to do with the war.' She paused again before continuing.

'She was married to my father when she was ten years old, you know that?' She looked bitterly at Lindsey, but only for a second. 'Not as unusual as you might imagine. He beat her violently for reasons only he knew. That's not unusual either.' Another pause.

'When I was seven years old, my mother told me that I would soon have another brother or sister. She was happy and smiling when she told me. I immediately started working on making a blanket for my new brother. I'd already decided that it would be a boy; someone for me to take care of. But just a few weeks later I came to the kitchen one morning to find my mother curled up on the floor with blood flowing from between her legs. Of course I had no idea what was really happening. I thought she was dying.'

'She lost the baby?'

'She asked me to bring some warm water and rags. She warned me not to use the good towels and together we cleaned the blood off the floor. I could tell that she was in pain, but we worked in silence. After a while, my mother disappeared into her bedroom, while I continued to clean up as best I could. She stayed in there for hours, until it was almost time for my father to come home and only then did she return to the kitchen. Aside from her face, which was paler than usual, you'd never know that anything had happened and I was afraid to ask.

Maybe I'd imagined it all. As I helped her prepare dinner for my father, I became more convinced that had been the case; that everything was fine and I became happy again and when my father came home, I immediately began telling him about the blanket I was making for my new brother and how it would be the nicest blanket that any baby had ever been wrapped in. He listened and even smiled for five or ten seconds before losing interest and ignoring me. But I continued anyway. My stupid voice was the only sound in the house until finally my mother made me go to bed early. I protested, as a seven-year-old does, but she insisted, and the tone in her voice convinced me to cease my protestations and simply do as I was told.'

There was another pause, but Lindsey knew that there was more to this story. She also thought it might be the first time that Lena had told it, so she didn't dare interrupt her.

'Of course I couldn't sleep. It was hours before my bedtime. So I sat there on the floor working on my brother's blanket until I heard my mother's voice coming from the kitchen. She spoke so quietly that I couldn't make out what she'd said, but the long silence that followed… it wasn't unusual for my father not to respond. But this time something felt different. Something made me get up from the floor and start paying attention. Finally the silence was broken by a loud crash. Normally I didn't look when he beat her, but she'd been bleeding so much already. I couldn't help running to the door to see him kicking her as she lay on the floor, curled up with her arms wrapped around her belly. He kicked her and kicked her, and then he pulled her to her feet by the hair and threw her onto the kitchen table. I remember thinking that the food, which scattered off the edge of the table and onto the floor, was all we had. For a second I thought about running out there to rescue what I could for the following day, but before I could bring myself to move, my father's closed fist smashed into my mother's face once more. Then he pulled her abaya up over her head. Of course I couldn't understand what I was seeing; my father raping my mother on our kitchen table just hours after she'd lost his baby. But the sight of it was enough to glue me to the floor, unable to tear my eyes away; unable to scream. Unable to help her in any way. I became helpless. Useless.'

Both of Lindsey's hands were covering her mouth and nose now. She'd seen horrors in her life; more than her fair share probably. She'd seen and heard some of the worst of what humankind had to offer. But this made her wonder; with everything else she'd been through, how this woman hadn't killed anyone yet. Or maybe she had, in which case, no one could blame her. Certainly not Lindsey.

'Through it all, my mother never made a sound. She never screamed. She never so much as grunted in pain. She was silent. Why? Because she was strong. She is the strongest woman I know.' She stood up abruptly, suddenly as angry as hell. 'I will never go back there. I could never let her see what I've become.'

'Lena, this was all outside of your control. You didn't…'

Lena waved her hand and Lindsey stopped talking. She knew when to shut her mouth and she also knew first hand that there was nothing worse than someone issuing consolations where there were none.

'My uncle Adnan wanted me to have an education and it was he who made sure I got to go to university. He had a way with my father. He could make him believe that Adnan's ideas were his own sometimes. Even though Adnan is a traditional man in his daily life, he wanted more for me. More than what my mother, his sister, had.' She smiled almost imperceptibly then; 'He would approve of me being here with you.'

'He sounds like a good man.'

'He is.'

'Lena, I…'

She held up her hand again to stop Lindsey, as she sat down beside her again. 'Don't pity me, Lindsey. I don't need or deserve it. There's not a person in this world who hasn't endured hardship of some sort. What matters is that we survive, yes?'

Lindsey smiled as her admiration for this woman notched up a little further. 'And you will survive this, Lena. We all will.'

They sat in companionable silence for another few minutes. A picture of Lena's father had been painted in Lindsey's mind and she despised him. And others like him. She imagined hurting him in as many ways as it was possible to do.

'One way or another, we'll get you to Germany.' She finally broke the silence. 'You'll finish your degree and it'll be the biggest Fuck you that you can give to all the men in your life. Except for Adnan of course.'

Lena laughed quietly. 'Then one way or another, I must make it happen. All I need is a passport. Simple, eh?'

Not so simple, Lindsey acknowledged silently. She rummaged in the backpack beside her and pulled out two tins of beans, the makings of some tea and a pouch of beef in gravy for Frank, who was curled up, dozing happily beside the fire.

'What are you thinking about?'

Lindsey smiled. 'Malala Yousafzai.'

'Will she be joining us? Because you know, right now I wouldn't be surprised.'

'What was it she said? Extremists have shown what frightens them most; a girl with a book.'

'Then we must buy a thousand books,' she exclaimed. 'Perhaps then we can begin to educate the boys who will one day become men.'

'Now there's an idea.'

*

The hour after their humble meal was spent silently doing their own thing. Lena prayed for a while and then sat quietly under their shelter, while Lindsey emptied both backpacks and reshuffled their contents. She wanted to ensure that one pack held nothing but some absolute essentials; groundsheets for shelter, a torch, a waterproofed map of the area – not that she needed it – a compass, cooking equipment, some food and warm clothing, and night vision goggles. Essentially, that one was a go bag. She was fairly sure that they were in the safest possible place, but she still wanted to be prepared to leave at a moment's notice should the need arise. The last thing anyone wanted was to be stuck out on a mountain in Ireland without the proper gear.

'Always preparing for something,' Lena mumbled. 'Were you always like this?'

Lindsey smiled and shrugged.

'This man, Adam… he looks at you with such admiration.'

Lindsey didn't answer as she checked her pack for a third time before closing it up.

'You would not see a look like that from a man in my country. You should marry him, no?'

Lindsey laughed quietly.

'You find that funny?'

'You might too if you knew us.'

'There's always so much to learn about other people's cultures.' Lena smiled.

'Mmm. If only everyone wanted to learn. The world might have fewer problems, don't you think?'

'I do. I find it all so interesting. Men and women being friends; women beating the men who try to beat them; having the freedom to live in your own home, by yourself if you wish; getting a job outside of the home, and having children at forty. It's all so fascinating, no?'

Lindsey smiled as she shuffled in under their shelter alongside Lena. Those were just some of the things that Lindsey took for granted in life. But she could imagine how it must seem for a woman coming from where Lena had. She'd been there. She'd seen how they lived. 'Well, I think we did pretty well building this particular home for ourselves. What do you think?'

Lena looked up at the army green groundsheet, stretched out between the surrounding trees. It was doing its job perfectly in keeping the light drizzle off their heads. 'I like it,' she said with a smile.

'You've met some of the world's shittiest men, Lena.'

'That I have, my friend.'

'There are good ones out there too.'

'Yes. I believe there are. But if Allah is listening, then eventually my life will be one of independence. If a good man finds me, then so be it. But no one will decide my fate ever again. If Allah is listening.'

Lindsey looked to the sky and hoped that whoever was up there, was listening. She lay back, using their go bag as a pillow and closed her eyes. Darkness had fallen over the mountain and the temperature had dropped significantly, but with layers of warm clothing, Lindsey was more comfortable than she'd been in weeks and so sleep came in a matter of minutes. For however long it lasted, she was finally home.

*

Something woke her, but as she lay there listening to the gentle rain tapping on their overhead cover, she couldn't discern what. There was no other sound; just the rain. She breathed in the smell of damp pine and she would have smiled in delight if it weren't for Frank. He was on full alert, facing in the direction of the car park. He emitted a long, low growl. Then she heard it; a car door closing in the distance.

Lena was sleeping fitfully beside her. Slowly, Lindsey reached across and placed her hand across Lena's mouth. When her eyes shot open, Lindsey put a finger to her lips. Lena nodded her understanding, and Lindsey removed her hand. She got very slowly and quietly to her feet, reached down and pulled Lena up. Quickly, she dismantled their camp and strapped the groundsheets to the pack. She picked up the pack and strapped it to her back.

'Not a sound,' she whispered, and gestured for Lena to follow her, as she took off as quickly and as silently as she could in the opposite direction to the car park.

Lena literally followed in her footsteps while Frank ran alongside her. A hiker's path ran right around the wooded area and off up the mountain. But Lindsey chose to get off that as soon as they exited the tree line and crossed it. She climbed the small fence and helped Frank over, Lena close behind them. They moved down into a gully where they were suddenly knee deep in cold water. Once they climbed out of there, there'd be over a hundred yards of open ground between them and the next hedge line, so Lindsey chose to stay in the gully for now, low beneath the fence while she got her bearings and decided their next move.

'We need to get to that hedge line,' her voice was so low that the words barely came out.

Lena looked to where Lindsey was pointing and nodded her understanding.

'We're going to quietly get out of this water and then we need to run, OK? Once we get there, we can assess.'

Lena nodded again, so Lindsey led the way. The pack was heavy on her back, but she'd managed to keep it dry, which helped. Once she was out of the water, she stayed low and waited for Lena, and when they were both ready, Lindsey took off running. In less than thirty seconds they were over the hedgerow and lying flat on the ground.

'Why are we running?' Lena was breathless, but her eyes were on the woods.

'Someone's there.'

'The man from the house maybe?'

'Maybe. But I didn't see his car when I called there earlier, or any time since then.

'Maybe it's Adam?'

Lindsey shook her head knowing that it wouldn't be Street. He wouldn't arrive unannounced in the middle of the night for this exact reason. Unless of course something went drastically wrong, but she doubted it.

'We'll know soon enough. We're gonna head up. There're some old ruins up there.'

'Up the mountain?' Lena sounded more hesitant now.

'Just a little bit. We'll be able to see more from up there. You ready?'

'I'm ready.'

'OK. Stay low and move as quickly and as quietly as you can.' Lindsey waited for her to nod her understanding, then she moved out, running.

They stayed hunched below the hedge line with Frank still by Lindsey's side. The terrain wasn't bad but was inclining steeply now as they headed upwards where they climbed another fence and re-joined the path. There were several ancient ruins around the base of the Galtees. Lindsey chose the first one to take cover in so they jogged behind what remained of the front wall of whatever this famine era building once was. Probably a farmer's cottage. Lena slumped to the ground, breathless, while Lindsey pulled off her pack. Within seconds, she found her night vision goggles and had them trained on the car park below them, to the left.

There was an old saloon type car parked there, one that she didn't recognise. Its occupants were no longer visible. Maybe the guy in the house had a wife or a girlfriend. But maybe he didn't. His family could be the Walton's of Ireland for all she knew, but she wasn't about to bet on it.

She scanned the tree line below and listened for any sound. The moon was bright over the mountain tonight so visibility was good, and sound had a way of carrying in a place like this. But so far she saw and heard nothing. Even Lena's heavy breathing seemed to have stopped and she appreciated the fact that the woman wasn't bombarding her with questions.

She glanced briefly at her companion. Lena was wearing one of Lindsey's waterproof jackets over her green hoodie, the sleeves of which were pulled down over her knuckles. On her feet she wore socks and sandals, both now soaked.

Without taking her eyes off the trees, Lindsey reached in the pack which she'd filled meticulously. She easily managed to find two long sleeved dry-fit tops and some proper socks. She threw the socks one at a time at Lena's feet.

'Put those on. Take the boots that are tied to the side of the bag and put the sandals inside the pack.'

Again, Lena did as instructed without question. But she was no stranger to survival.

Lindsey strained her ears and scanned the area again. Who the hell was down there and what, other than Lindsey, Lena, or the man in the house, could have brought them to a place like this in the middle of the night? More to the point, how long was too long to wait before she made a decision on whether or not to drag this woman up and over the mountain in the dark.

Chapter 22

'Lindsey?'

The voice echoed through the landscape and reached them as clear as day. It was Ben.

Lindsey dropped below the wall. 'Fuck.'

Lena was frozen to the spot.

'Finish getting dressed now, Lena.'

Lindsey raised the goggles again to look in the direction the voice had come from. She still couldn't see him, not that that mattered.

'We're here to help you.' The voice, loud and appeasing, rose up towards them again.

'Hurry up, we have to move.'

As soon as Ben and whoever we were exactly, had finished scouring the woods, this ruin would be the first place he, or anyone with half a brain, would look. She gathered soggy socks and sandals off the muddy ground and stuffed them into the side pockets of her pack. She replaced her night vision goggles in the main pack and closed it up.

'We have to go.' She got to her feet, but stayed low behind the stone walls. 'Listen to me, Lena; Ben will expect us to follow this path around the base of the mountain. That's why we have to go up. We need to be as quick as we can, but more importantly, we have to be quiet. And we can't allow ourselves to be silhouetted, do you understand?'

'I understand,' she replied, as she looked worriedly up the looming mountain. 'But I'm not much of a mountain climber.'

Lindsey wanted to head for the col between Galtybeg and Galtymore, knowing that it would offer them some modicum of shelter and a chance to decide their next move. If they veered left and traversed around it, rather than going straight up, it was doable for Lena. She didn't like taking the easier option, but she didn't feel she had a choice. The Galtees had its fair share of dangerous ridges and sheer drops. She couldn't risk it in the dark with someone as inexperienced as her current climbing partner. Plus, there was Frank to consider. True, he knew this mountain as well as Lindsey did. But it was dark and whether he liked it or not, he wasn't as young as he used to be.

'Stay close to me, and if there's a problem, get my attention quietly if you can. Are you ready?'

'For this? No. But let's go.'

'Frank?' She took the dog's head in her hands, 'Sshhh.'

He nudged her and once again she was convinced that he was at least part human.

'Be careful,' she begged him, just loud enough for him to hear and she kissed his head.

They moved quickly from the ruin and stayed just right of the path. They followed it for a few minutes until they came to another, larger ruin of what was once a castle of sorts. This took them around and out of sight of the woods and car park below and only then did they start heading upwards.

'I know you're here, Lindsey!' His voice still carried to meet them and sounded far less friendly now. He was losing patience.

'Patrick knows where we are,' Lena barely got the words out. 'He must.'

They'd only been ascending for ten minutes. At this rate, she wouldn't be able to keep going for as long as Lindsey needed her to, so she forced herself to slow down. She needed Lena to keep moving, but still she stopped for a second and turned to face her. She reached back and pulled her upwards. They were surrounded by gorse now, so when they were side by side, Lindsey pulled Lena down onto her back. Frank lay down beside them. The woman needed a rest and here, hidden in the wild gorse, was the best place to give it to her.

'They won't find us. This is a big place and they don't know it as well as I do.' She hoped she sounded convincing. She pulled out her goggles again and scanned the area below. That was when she heard Charlie's voice and her stomach dropped.

'They're not here!'

It sounded like he was at the castle below. They were checking the ruins.

'Charlie,' Lindsey whispered. He was supposed to be at the second shelter in Cork. So how, or why, was he back with Ben?

She shook her head. If Ben had found them all, then Street, or at least some of his guys, would be involved by now. Either they'd be here as well, or Ben wouldn't. That meant that they couldn't know that Charlie was missing. But the hows and the whys weren't what she needed to think about just now.

'Charlie is better than Hector, no?'

Hector was no doubt in pursuit of the more valuable assets, Reem and Amir, and given the fact that they'd found Charlie… One problem at a time, Ryan.

'Can you continue?'

'Yes.'

Lena was breathless and now terrified as well. But Lindsey admired her for not vocalising any of it.

'OK. See that col up there.'

'Col?'

'The dip between the two peaks?' She made the shape with her hands and then pointed directly at it.

Lena looked up and nodded slowly.

'That's where we're headed. We can rest there.'

She didn't mention the fact that it would take them another hour at least to reach the col between Galtybeg and Galtymore, depending on their pace.

'We're going to head around that way.' She pointed in the direction that she wanted to travel, which would add yet more time onto their estimated arrival at the col, but would be slightly safer in the dark.

Lena nodded again as Lindsey moved out. As they trekked across the mountain, the only thing she could think about was Charlie. The right words from Ben would be enough to get a vulnerable lad like him to spill his guts. She didn't blame him for that. She worried about him though. Regardless of whether Ben got him here by telling him everything he wanted to hear, or whether he got him here using threats or violence, it was only a matter of time before Charlie got thrown under the bus. Aside from that, she was pretty sure that he'd be a liability on a mountain in the dark, so she sincerely hoped that he didn't attempt to follow them. Ben on the other hand, could drop right off the edge as far as she was concerned.

As they continued to move at pace going around and up, Lena stopped only twice to quietly throw up, before forcing herself to continue again. By the time they reached the col, it was freezing, but both women were sweating.

Lindsey took a moment despite herself to look around. On a clear day you could see for miles. Everything from the perfect, teardrop-shaped lake below, Aherlow, Slievenamuck, and the Silvermine Mountains away to the north. Tonight, they were surrounded by silhouettes and even under the circumstances, it was beautiful. The summit of Galtymore was even more impressive, with spectacular views, from the Wicklow Mountains in the East all the way to Ireland's highest peak of Carrauntoohil in the West. But they wouldn't be heading up there tonight. Even on the best of days, the Galtymore summit was eye wateringly windy and cold. Plus, it was too dangerous a climb in the dark. Instead, they found some level of shelter between the two peaks where Lindsey dropped her pack, pulled out a groundsheet and they both sat down.

Lena was exhausted and staring nervously now towards the summit of Galtymore. Frank was panting hard too.

'Don't worry; this is as far up as we're going.'

Lena mumbled something to Allah.

Lindsey reached into the pack and pulled out two more long sleeved fleece lined tops. 'Here, put these on.'

'I'm very warm.'

'Trust me; you won't be in a minute.' She pulled out another and wrapped it around Frank and then a second groundsheet, which she set down on the ground between them.

While Lena dressed, Lindsey assessed her options. They could descend the mountain in another direction, but this would see them ending up in another county. Assuming they made it down without injury. That wouldn't work. They needed to be at the King's Yard when Street showed up. He was Lena's ticket out of harm's way, not to mention the other passengers that he'd hopefully be carrying. Their other option was to stay put and wait it out until morning, which wasn't more than a few hours off. But Lindsey dismissed that option as quickly as the first.

'OK,' she mumbled, more to herself than to Lena, but Lena perked up nervously anyway.

'We move again?'

'Not you. I need you to stay here. Take whatever you need from the pack to stay warm and use this.' She draped the second groundsheet over her, as shelter from the biting wind.

'Where are you going?'

'I'm going back down.'

'No, Lindsey.' Lena grabbed her arm.

'I need to make sure Charlie's alright, Lena.'

'Lindsey...'

'Don't worry, OK? Stay warm and stay alert. I'll come back for you.'

'And if you don't?' She sounded stern now.

'Then wait until morning and head back down the way we came. If something happens, Ben won't hang around, and Street will come for you no matter what.'

'Can I talk you out of this?'

Lindsey forced herself to smile at her terrified companion. 'I won't be too long.'

Before leaving, she tied Frank to a rock beside Lena. There was a good chance that Lindsey would injure herself going down in the dark, but with Frank in tow, it was a surety. Then they'd be truly fucked.

'Frank, I promise this is the last time I'll leave you behind,' she whispered, as she rested her forehead against him, meaning every word. He whined quietly. 'I just can't have you breaking a leg on me, OK?'

She hugged him tightly. Then she pulled away and quickly got ready. She took out her compass, a torch, not that she planned to use it, her goggles and most importantly, her knife from the pack. She fitted them all into her various pockets. She also brought the blade from her Danny Chambers belt with her, which she handed to Lena.

'If you need to use it… use it.'

Lena took the blade and stared at it, perhaps thinking about where she'd like to put it.

'But if you have to move, untie Frank, OK?' She looked pointedly at Lena to make sure she understood that last bit. 'I'll see you in a while.'

Before Lena could protest anymore, Lindsey was on her feet and headed back down the mountain. She took the same route down that they'd taken to get up there, and the going was very slow. Going down was often more hazardous than going up and the last thing she needed was a careless injury. She also wanted to be able to hear anything that sounded out of place on her mountain. But regardless of what she found, or what found her, she'd still have to trek back up for Lena and then back down again before Street arrived, so energy conservation was also a factor in her decision to take her time. But she had another problem that was even more imminent. Her stomach had been making its way slowly towards her throat for a while and now the hairs were pricking the back of her neck. Her imagination was about to start doing what it did best these days. She began seeing shadows everywhere and she had no idea if they were real or not. Every now and then she came to a sudden stop and dropped to the ground, certain that she'd heard something. Each time she eventually discounted it, and that too was risky. She was sweating, despite the cold wind trying its best to bite her face off and waves of panic came and went. She was breathing heavily enough to be heard in Mitchelstown.

She heard her own voice clearly, either aloud or in her head issuing orders and asking questions. She crouched low as the castle came into view and as she focused intently on a phantom to her right, the blow, when it finally came, was from her left.

She was lifted into the air and slammed onto the rocky ground. A sharp pain tore through her rib cage as unbearable weight came forcefully to rest on top of her. She started to fight immediately, but before she had a chance to make any impact, her hands were pinned to the ground on either side of her head. Her legs were trapped under the weight of Ben, as he straddled her. He punched her hard in the face before speaking.

'Calm down, it's me.'

If the punch was his attempt at calming her, he'd failed in the worst possible way. Now all she could think about was getting to her knife, which was in the pocket half way down the leg of her pants. A whole new bunch of pains introduced themselves to her already damaged face and she wondered if he could hear the same loud throbbing that she could.

She bucked and struggled under his weight but her strength had waned. He wouldn't budge.

'Are you going to calm down, or are you going to make me hit you again?'

She stopped struggling. Not because she was afraid of being hit and certainly not because she'd calmed down. But because it wasn't doing her any good. She needed to use her head if she was going to get out of this, because physically, Ben had the upper hand.

'Are you really dumb enough to think you could fuck me over?'

A part of her was still somewhere other than the Galtee Mountains and she needed to get that under control before her brain would engage with her current situation. She breathed deeply for a few seconds, each breath causing her physical pain which she welcomed like a dear old friend.

'Well?'

'Get off me.' She spoke calmly, like this was nothing more than a lovers' tiff.

'Oh, so now you want me to get off you?'

'Is that what this is about?'

He pressed her wrists harder into the rough ground and straightened his legs, so that his full weight was on her now, his breath warm on her face. 'I think you're a teasing little bitch who doesn't know what's good for her, Corporal Ryan.'

She didn't answer, nor did she release the tsunami of rage building inside her.

'You thought I bought that story about the car crash, huh?'

Again, she didn't respond.

'You think I didn't do my homework on you? Or did you think you're such hot shit that I wouldn't see past you?' He pressed himself harder against her. 'I know all about you. How many, other than the Cork man, died while you were fixing your lipstick?'

He pulled her hands over her head so that he could secure them both with one hand. His other grabbed her between the legs and while she desperately wanted to kill him, instead she gave him the last thing he expected. She lifted her head and kissed him roughly on the mouth.

'Do it,' she whispered and bit down on his lip. She raised her hips, pressing herself against him.

For a second he didn't seem to know how to react. He didn't want her consent. He wanted power over her. Finally he let out a humourless laugh.

'You're a dirty little bitch, aren't you? You like it rough? I can do rough.'

Using his free hand, he pulled open the zip of her jacket before finally letting go of her wrists so that he could grab both of her breasts and squeeze them until he was certain she was in pain. It seemed to be a signature move for these apes, but instead of crying out, she smiled and writhed against him.

He wasn't happy with that, so he punched her in the face again. Then he lifted himself up, pulled her legs apart and dropped his full weight between them. She was blinded by the punch, but her hands were free now and while he pulled open her pants, she was able to reach into her right leg pocket and pull out her knife. It made contact with his throat just as his hand made its way inside her underwear and he froze.

'Lindsey…'

'Take your hand out of my knickers, Ben.' Blood poured from her mouth and her words slurred slightly, but her grip was tight on the blade.

He did as she asked and raised both hands slowly, bringing even more of his weight down on her hips. She didn't let on that she was bothered by that, even though her ribs and pelvis begged to be put out of their misery.

'Look, I'm sorry. I got a bit carried away. I've never hit a woman before…'

Keeping the knife pressed to his neck, she gripped his jacket and pushed him up enough that she could roll over, putting herself on top. She was in agony now and guessed that he'd cracked at least one of her ribs when he blindsided her. She was somewhere else entirely when that happened and not for the first time, she contemplated putting an end to it all when this was over. But first she had to see it through and she was damned if this crooked bastard was going to have any satisfaction in that regard.

'You're awfully good at something you've never done before.' She made herself smile just to annoy him, but the blood dripping from her mouth onto his seemed to bother him more.

'You're a freak, Lindsey. You know that, don't you?'

She'd stopped listening. Instead she was trying to figure out how she was going to get away from him without actually cutting his throat, because she knew that as soon as she moved the blade by any fraction, he'd be back in control. Lindsey was in a world of pain and had zero hope of fighting him off again.

'Tell me where she is, then we'll be on our way. And you and me… well, we can go back to being friends.'

'Why are you so interested in her?'

'I couldn't give a fuck about that washed up old slag. She'll be giving five euro blow jobs on the quay wall this time next week. She's done.'

'So why are you here?' Her words slurred a bit more as the mountain started to spin slowly around her.

'You don't get to say when she walks away and neither does she. It's as simple as that really. And you didn't stop with her either did you?'

She didn't answer. She couldn't.

'Who the fuck do you think you are?' he laughed, even as she pressed the blade harder against his rough skin.

Neither of them moved or spoke for another few seconds until Ben broke the expectant silence.

'It's time. Shit or get off the pot, Lindsey but either way, you'd better make it count because you don't look so good, girl.'

She moved slowly down along his body, keeping the knife exactly where it was, with enough pressure to let him know that she was willing to use it. Once her hips were below his and his groin was exposed, she balled her free hand into a fist and punched him three times in quick succession between the legs. The first blow was enough to make him double up in pain, which brought a trickle of blood from his neck as it pressed against her blade. By the third punch, the wind had been knocked from his body and Lindsey fell to the ground beside him.

'Lindsey?'

This time it was Street's voice that travelled towards her from somewhere on the mountain and her shoulders sagged with relief. Her options at that point were poor; she could have run down the mountain away from Ben, but A) she wasn't sure she could stand up and B) he'd follow her as soon as he was able to and from the woods, she had nowhere else to go. She was stranded here. It would have been a matter of time before he found her, regained control and eventually, he would have gotten Lena too.

'Up here,' she called. She rolled on top of Ben again and placed the knife back at his throat. Just a few more minutes, she told herself.

Lindsey directed Street for the next ten minutes, until he and Levi were by her side. By then, Ben was recovering and getting much stronger under her. She wouldn't have been able to hold him there much longer without actually using the knife and even then, only a kill would be enough to stop him.

Street pulled her off him, while Levi flipped Ben onto his stomach. In a nanosecond, he had cable ties wrapped around Ben's wrists and he was bound up like a Christmas turkey.

Lindsey meanwhile curled up on the ground, hugging her ribs.

'You OK?'

She nodded. She was too sore to talk now that she didn't have to.

The mountain was still spinning, but it was slowing down.

Street glanced at her open pants and dishevelled tops and pounced on Ben. He punched him in the kidneys, over and over again until Levi finally decided to stop him where Lindsey didn't have the energy or the inclination to. Ben needed a few punches in the kidneys.

'Did you find Charlie? Is he OK?' she finally asked. Her voice sounded almost unfamiliar as it fought its way out.

Street didn't answer as he dropped down beside her, breathing heavily.

'We found him,' Levi replied.

'And is he OK?' she asked, growing more impatient as she struggled to her feet.

'He is until I ask him how the fuck this happened. It'll very much depend on his answer after that.'

'You might be better off asking him that question.' She nodded towards Ben.

'He can't talk right now.' Levi grinned as he sat down heavily on Ben's back, right where Street had been punching him.

'Sit down a minute.' Street reached up and pulled her gently towards him.

'I need to see Charlie and then I have to go back and get Lena.'

'Charlie's fine, he's down at the truck with Damo. Now please woman, sit down. I haven't run up a fucking mountain in years. I might just die. And you look like shit by the way.'

'Thanks. Rest here for a while and then wait at the truck for me.' She struggled for a second to get going up the steep incline again. The pain was spreading from her rib cage, right up and down her body and for the first time in her life, the idea of going back up the mountain held no appeal for her. But the longer she put it off, the harder it would get. So she started walking.

'Oh for the love of Christ,' Street got to his feet. 'Where is she?'

'Up at the col,' she replied, without turning around. But she knew that he'd be coming up behind her.

'You're dead, bitch. You know that, don't you?' Ben sounded pathetic, so she didn't bother answering him.

'Levi, you OK to get that sack of shit back to the truck?' Street asked.

'Looking forward to it.'

Lindsey could hear the smile in Levi's voice, and for a minute she imagined him rolling and kicking Ben down the rest of the way and she too smiled, despite herself.

'Just like the good old days.' Street grinned, as he arrived by her side seconds later. He was still limping, but he didn't let on how tired he was.

'How's the leg?'

'A hundred per cent. How's the…' he looked her up and down.

'Ninety per cent.'

'Super. We're all good then.'

They climbed in silence for the next while, both concentrating on their footing and breathing. They stopped for a minute when they were just over half way there.

'Is this shit ever going to end?' Lindsey asked.

'That's something though, isn't it?'

She turned to look at her closest friend, who was staring out over Ireland's Golden Vale, as the sun rose and basked everything in an orange glow. She sat down heavily, facing the sunrise. He was right. It absolutely was something. She wondered if there was anywhere more beautiful in the world.

Street sat down beside her. He handed her some water which she used to rinse the blood out of her mouth. Then she lay back on the soft, boggy ground and stared up at the sky. He lay down next to her with a smile on his face.

'You still love this shit,' she grinned.

'Nah, no one loves this shit.' They lay in silence, looking up for a few more minutes. 'OK, maybe just a bit.' He rolled onto his side to face her and rested his head in his hand. 'So… none of your macho bullshit now; are you OK? How badly did he hurt you?'

'He wouldn't have hurt me at all if I'd been switched on. My damn head won't straighten out, Street.'

'You're always switched on. That's your problem.'

'Oh, is that what it is?'

'And another thing; why does it always take a massive shit storm to strike before we get to see each other?'

'Because we don't need to.'

That was true. They picked up exactly where they left off every time. But she suspected the real reason was that they reminded each other too much of Lenny. Lindsey would always carry the guilt of his death and the death of the little girl with her. They died because Lindsey reacted roughly three seconds too slowly. She should never be allowed to forget that.

Street was in charge of their patrol, so in his mind, it was all his fault. Each time he saw Lindsey, his eyes would eventually drift to where her scars were, despite the fact that they were rarely on show.

'Well whatever the bullshit reason, I'm calling a halt to it.'

'Are you?' She half smiled. It might hurt to see him sometimes, but she loved the man dearly.

'As soon as this shit calms down, we're coming up here and doing it properly. Like the old days. I forgot how much this place has going for it.'

'Yeah, OK. Now get up, you old dog, and let's go.'

They both smiled and before she had a chance to pull herself to her feet, Street reached around the back of her neck and pulled her to him. He rested his forehead against hers for a few seconds, while their smiles slowly faded.

'You have to stop scaring the shit out of me though.' He spoke much more softly now.

They stayed in their semi-embrace for a few more seconds. By the time they set off again, Lindsey felt completely at ease. She'd been pretending to be someone else for so long, surrounded by people who would never know her. Finally, she was herself again and she embraced the pain as her penance. The man beside her was the closest thing to family she was ever likely to have and right now, she could ask for nothing more.

Chapter 23

Back at King's Yard, Damo and Charlie were sitting with their legs dangling off the back of a flatbed truck that looked like it once belonged to a construction company. Levi was sitting awkwardly in the middle of the truck bed and as they got closer, she could see that he was still sitting on Ben's back. His face was pressed into the cement splattered floor. He looked like he'd been given a bit of a going over. Either that, or Levi actually had rolled and kicked him down the side of the Galtees. Either one was fine by her.

'Lindsey, I'm sorry.' Charlie hopped down from the truck and hurried towards her. By the time he reached her he had tears in his eyes.

'Not your fault.' She nudged him on the shoulder.

'He said he'd get my mam if I didn't tell him.'

Lindsey's face grew darker and she walked past Charlie towards the truck. When she got there, she pulled herself painfully up onto the rear wheel arch and reached into the truck bed. She grabbed Ben by the hair, picking his face up from the dirty floor.

'You're a big man, aren't you?' She spoke through gritted teeth.

Before he had a chance to say anything, she slammed his face against the floor, bringing an immediate flow of blood from his nose. No one else flinched. Levi lit a cigarette while Damo grinned and asked, 'So… did ye have a nice stroll up there?'

'Feeling a bit nostalgic now actually,' Street replied with a broad smile, as he tussled with Frank who'd bolted for Street as soon as he saw him up at the col.

Lindsey felt like her body was made of jelly and almost envied her dog, as he was carried down parts of the mountain by Adam.

'So what now?' asked Charlie, hesitantly.

'We're gonna hit the road.' Street looked from Lindsey to Damo to Levi. It was difficult to take him seriously while he was rolling around the ground with the furry, four-legged nutter who was becoming more emotional by the second.

'What're you thinking, buddy?' Damo asked.

'I'm thinking…' he struggled to his feet, 'you two take that piece of shit back to the city. Find him somewhere nice and comfy where he can reflect upon his decisions until the real coppers come pick him up. Then go get the others and come back for us.'

Damo jumped off the truck bed and headed for the driver's door. 'Consider it done. You comin' or what?' He directed his question to Levi.

'I'm kinda comfy right here.'

Levi looked anything but comfy. But Lindsey suspected that he'd quite happily stick it out for the whole ride back to Cork city, just to bother Ben.

She grinned. 'I like you, Levi.'

'I like you too, Ryan.'

'OK, see you soon.' Damo climbed into the truck and started the engine.

'What about me?' Charlie asked.

'You stay with us,' Street answered.

'But my mam…'

'No one will bother your mother.'

Charlie looked at Street for a few seconds, as he tried to make up his mind about him.

'You can trust him, Charlie.' Lindsey winked at him, as she turned and headed back towards the woods, where they'd left the majority of her belongings. 'They'll be at least a couple of hours if not more, and I for one am starving.' She threw an arm around Charlie's shoulder and led him away from the truck and away from Ben.

It was true, she could certainly eat something. But more than anything, Lindsey needed a rest. Her pain levels were almost intolerable. The muscles in her legs burned and mentally she was drained. She just wanted to sit down, switch off and shut up for a while. Lena looked like she could sleep for a month, while Charlie looked like he had a million unanswered questions and worries floating around inside his head. Street on the other hand, looked as happy as Larry now, so she was confident that he'd take care of Charlie's concerns as soon as he was ready to voice them. He'd give Lindsey the break that she desperately needed.

'Are you sure my mam will be OK?' Charlie finally asked, as they sat around a small fire, waiting for a pot of beans with pork sausage chunks to heat up.

'Ben won't be in a position to bother anyone for some time, bud. She'll be fine.'

'If Ben can't do Patrick's jobs for him, then he'll just get someone else to do it.'

'Your mother was on Ben's radar. Patrick has no interest in her, but I'll tell you what; when we get to Limerick, you tell us where to find her and we'll check in, make sure she's OK.'

'Limerick? I'm not going to Limerick,' Charlie replied, horrified.

Street glanced at Lindsey for a second. 'OK. What's your plan then?'

'I thought I could come work for you guys.'

Street thought for a minute then nodded, 'I suppose I could use someone around the gym.'

'The gym? I thought you were like, mercenaries or something.'

'Ah, see you don't know this guy,' Lindsey replied with a smile. 'He's an All-Army boxing champion. He's created Olympians in his gym.'

'Mmm...' Street nodded with a hint of a grin. He hated praise, even when he deserved it. 'Not as exciting as being a mercenary I know. But it's not half bad either.'

'What would I do?'

'Keep the place clean, make sure everything's in its place and in return, I'll train you up.'

'Me?'

'Why not?' Street gripped the boy's biceps and gave him an impressed nod. 'Job's yours if you want it. It's up to you.'

No one else spoke as Lindsey handed around spoons and the pot of pork and beans. Charlie needed to feel like a man, making decisions for himself, so she wasn't about to try convincing him either way. No one asked what awaited them in Limerick.

After a few mouthfuls it was Lena who spoke as she looked up at the Galtees again. 'I've never climbed a mountain before.' Then for the first time since they'd met, she smiled, like she'd achieved something. And really, she had. 'I'd imagine it would be very nice when no one is chasing you.'

*

They spent over four hours in the woods, around their small fire. They talked, they dozed, they wandered around the woods and it was actually relaxing. Exactly what they all needed after the past few weeks and by the time the construction truck came rumbling towards the car park, they were all packed up and ready to move.

This time a tarp was tightly pulled over the bed of the truck and as Damo emerged from the driver's side, Street opened the tailgate and they pulled it back to reveal Amir and Reem and his Jack Russell, all lying flat on a mattress wearing layers of warm clothes. No one looked particularly happy or comfortable, except for the dog. Wrapped up in Reem's coat, he actually looked quite pleased with himself. Reem on the other hand, looked a picture of misery. He was shrouded in a man's duffle coat, one that she'd never seen before but had more than likely come from one of Street's guys. Or maybe the lost and found at the shelter where they'd spent the night. She guessed he had a few more layers on under that because he looked like a Christmas pudding. At least the skinny little boy was warm, but he looked pale and had yet to raise his eyes from the floor of the truck.

'Hey Reem, how's Lindsey?'

He didn't answer. He seemed not to hear her.

'Sorry for the bumpy ride folks.' Damo smiled his broken toothed smile, which did nothing to brighten their spirits. Then he turned to Lindsey and Street and with his voice lowered he said, 'Patrick's on the move. He's pissed that Ben hasn't checked in and I think he somehow figured out where these guys were stashed.' He glanced in Charlie's direction.

Lindsey meanwhile was still looking at Reem, waiting for him to acknowledge their presence. The kid was in a world of his own, even more than usual. As for the news about Patrick; she wasn't at all surprised by that. She was just glad that they were finally on the move.

'Not the most comfy transport in the world.' Street looked apologetically at Lena. 'It's the last thing they'd expect you to be travelling in though.'

'Why don't we all jump out for a bit; stretch the legs eh?' Damo helped them out and then indicated that they should walk away towards the woods and Lindsey knew that, for whatever reason, he wanted them out of the way for a bit.

'What's up?' she asked, once they'd all wandered off.

'So you know Patrick What-his-face has a silent partner, Yousef Something-or-other?' His voice was low, so as not to be overheard.

'No,' Lindsey replied.

'He's a pretty hardcore fucker out of The Stan. From what I heard, he was pretty tight with the Taliban back home.'

'And now he pedals in women and children.'

'Probably always did. You know those fuckers; they're all, Do as I say, not as I do. Anyway, Yousef has a younger brother named Aazar who's trying to make a name for himself. We spotted that fucker not too far from the shelter when we went to pick up our passengers.'

'Charlie?' Lindsey asked.

Damo shrugged. 'Charlie isn't who I'm worried about. These boys were planning on making a shit load of money from those two young fellas, yeah? For them to get away… well that's risky shit for them, isn't it?'

'They won't take it lying down, that's for sure,' Street added. 'Time to go, yeah?'

After five minutes of stretching the legs, all four of them climbed into the bed of the truck again, including Charlie. They decided not to tell him that he'd inadvertently led Patrick right to his travelling companions, and could possibly have gotten them all caught. He was feeling badly enough as it was. Besides, Ben was out of the picture now and could no longer get to him, so they didn't worry so much about him possibly blowing their next location.

But Lindsey did worry about Amir and Reem and suddenly she wasn't convinced that Limerick would be far enough away for them. But it was definitely time to hit the road. With Damo at the wheel, Street, Lindsey, and Levi would be uncomfortably crammed into a cab that was designed for three, not four.

'Not much room for the luggage, Ryan.' Damo glanced at the backpacks and Frank.

'Give us a hand then.' She picked up one pack and indicated that Damo should grab the other. Lindsey had no mass in material possessions, but her camping and outdoor gear were what allowed her to escape whenever she needed to. She prized it above all else and had no intentions of simply abandoning it.

'Where we going.' Damo picked up the pack like it weighed nothing and gently removed Lindsey's from her sagging shoulder. He followed her towards the farm house. When they got there, Lindsey knocked on the door.

No answer.

She knocked again and a few minutes passed before it was answered.

'John?' She asked, as the door opened just a fraction.

Once he heard her voice, John opened the door fully.

'Yes, are you alright?' He asked, eyeing Damo nervously.

Lindsey looked back at her companion and could see why someone who didn't know him might be frightened of him. Even in his happy moments, he looked like he might eat a person without salt. And of course, Lindsey wasn't looking too hot either.

'This is my friend, Damien. I've had a bit of an accident.' She looked suitably embarrassed. 'Turns out even seasoned visitors can get complacent. Damien is taking me to hospital and I don't want my gear getting lost in the chaos. Would you mind if I leave it with you for a day or two? I'm really sorry to ask, but …'

John looked nervously at the packs.

Lindsey opened them and pulled back the drawstrings so that he could see inside. She didn't blame him in the slightest for being wary. The man lived in the middle of nowhere. He could be murdered on his doorstep and chances are, no one would find him until the summer rolled around and the first hikers rocked up looking for directions.

'There was a lot of commotion here last night.'

This was more of a question than a statement, and the man wanted an answer before agreeing to anything.

'Yeah, sorry about that.' It was Damo who replied, with another of his not-so-reassuring smiles. 'We got a call from this one in the early hours telling us she was in a heap up there. Our decorum went out the window in our rush to find her. Apologies if we worried you.'

Finally John nodded. 'Of course. I understand.' He opened the door a little wider and Lindsey pulled the packs inside. She lined them neatly against the wall in the narrow hallway.

'I'll be stiff, sore and embarrassed for a bit, but I'll live. Thanks, John. I should be back for these in a few days. Other than that, we won't be bothering you again.'

He finally smiled. 'It's no bother at all.'

As they turned to leave, Damo spoke one more time to the man. 'You helped my sister and her friends out once when they decided to tackle this bad boy.' He gestured towards the mountain with a smile. 'Thanks for that, buddy.'

'My pleasure. It's nice to see people getting the chance to enjoy it.'

Lindsey nodded and thanked him again as they left.

'Your sister?'

Damo shrugged with a grin. 'The guy was ready to shit a brick. I thought it'd make me sound more normal.'

Lindsey laughed quietly. 'It'd take more than an imaginary sister, my friend.'

Minutes later they were crammed into the truck and were on the road to Limerick. Though she was quite capable of looking after herself, ever since she'd taken on these people, Lindsey had been second guessing herself at every turn. It felt good to be back with her team; or at least, some of them. She was finally looking forward to getting these people to the accommodation that Street had lined up for them in Limerick.

What would become of them after that was anyone's guess. But apparently Street's Limerick contact had some good contacts of their own and if they had his trust, then they had hers too.

*

The road from Cork to Limerick wasn't a very good one, but the back roads were even worse. It was slow going in the lumbering old truck, whose clutch was on its very last legs. Lindsey doubted whether they'd make it there at all. Plus, the diesel fumes in the cab were overpowering, but however uncomfortable it was for those sitting up front, that discomfort was tenfold for those in the back, even though they'd been on the road for less than an hour.

'Why are we in this thing?' Lindsey looked at Street, but it was Damo who answered.

'What's wrong with it?'

Street grinned, as Damo continued, indignant. 'Why does everyone have a problem with my ride? It goes, doesn't it?'

'It's lovely, Damo. Really.' She shook her head with half a smile. 'What you reckon though, should we pull over for a minute to give them a bit of air?'

'I suppose. I'm bursting for a piss anyway. We'll stop at the next town.'

'Not for long, OK? No offence to these fine people, but I wouldn't mind seeing the back of them at this stage,' Street replied. He naturally took the lead in all situations and no one ever questioned it. Why would they? 'And stay on your guard. We're not out of the woods until we're out of the woods.'

Lindsey found herself feeling for the knife in her pocket. Like Street, she wouldn't relax until the people in their charge were safely ensconced in their new accommodation. Even though she was already thinking about how to get them even further away. But for now they needed to get out of this truck if only for five minutes, before they were overcome by fumes.

The sign post as they entered the next village said, Welcome to Hospital.

'That sounds ominous,' Damo grinned.

Hospital, County Limerick, was larger than the other villages they'd passed through. There was a small monument as you entered town and the row of houses and shops all looked fresh and clean. It was clearly a village whose inhabitants took pride in their surroundings.

'Ten minutes. You tell them if anyone's not back here, then they can consider Hospital their new home.' Street pointed at his watch as Damo pulled the truck over on the side of the road and jumped out.

Without waiting for anyone else to move, he opened his fly and pissed against the gable end of someone's house.

'You need to work on your social graces, Damo.' Lindsey shook her head as she got out and walked past him. She headed for the back to let the others out. As she pulled back the tarp, Frank immediately went to join Damo, and Lindsey noticed once again that everyone had some vomit on them. By the look on his face, most, if not all of it, came from Reem.

'Everyone alright?' she asked, offering her hand, but Amir and Lena were on the road, wiping themselves down before she'd finished her sentence. Reem shuffled out, still clinging to his dog for dear life.

'We have ten minutes, OK? And then we're back on the road. After that, we only have about another forty minutes or so until our final destination.' Assuming the truck would survive the rest of the journey.

As Reem attempted to wipe himself clean, he lost his grip on Lindsey and before they could stop him, the Jack Russell bolted across the road away from them.

'No!' Reem shouted and took off running awkwardly after him.

'Reem!' Lindsey called. 'Ten minutes.'

He didn't acknowledge her and Lindsey continued to watch him. Reem was struggling more than usual. He looked to be in pain. She watched as the dog bolted into a Londis shop on the other side of the road with Reem hurrying in behind him. Before anyone had a chance to go after him, the blast from an explosion shook the ground beneath them and showered them all with debris and large chunks of masonry. Lindsey was knocked to the ground, dazed. It took her a full three minutes to realise what had happened.

Frank was on her, pawing and nudging until she pulled herself into a sitting position. 'Lenny?' She asked, almost in a whisper as she looked around.

But Amir was the first person she saw and he was wandering up the street away from them. He was covered in dust and looked like he wasn't sure where he was or where he was going. Charlie had a similar look about him as he pulled himself into a sitting position where he landed, under the tailgate of the truck. Levi was just coming to on his back in the middle of the road, while Damo was the only one who looked like he knew what he was doing. He was running towards Londis, while Street was stumbling towards Lindsey.

'Frank?' Lindsey's throat felt full, the word barely got out as she desperately hugged her dog, her actual location slowly beginning to register.

'Are you alright?' Street asked.

Her head felt like pea soup and nothing made sense. She kept one arm around Frank and then she looked towards Damo again. She finally realised that he wasn't running towards Londis. He was running towards where Londis used to be. Now there was a gaping hole where the face of the building once stood.

'Reem...' she finally whispered, clambering to her feet. She tried to run towards the shop, but her legs had turned to lead. She stumbled for a bit with Street behind her. 'Reem!' She called as she came closer and managed to find her voice again.

By the time she got there, Damo was already using his hands to dig through the rubble. He was frantic. Lindsey and Street joined him immediately and all three of them pulled at chunks of masonry, desperately hoping for any sign of life. But Lindsey's body had never felt weaker.

'Reem?' she called, as loudly as she could now. She saw the glance between Damo and Street, but she kept calling. Lindsey wasn't much of a prayer person, but she found herself silently begging for the boy's life as a beautiful numbness spread throughout her almost broken body.

'I have someone!' Damo's voice cracked slightly, as he pulled a hand free from the rubble and then all three of them concentrated their efforts on that spot.

Several local residents suddenly joined them in digging. They followed the hand, freeing an arm and continuing until a face, covered in grey dust and blood emerged from the pile.

'Elaine.' A man's distraught voice called out, as he scrambled along the pile towards them. He frantically started pulling debris away from the woman.

When she was finally free, Street, Damo, and three local men pulled Elaine from the pile and out onto the road. She didn't look like she was breathing and as a local woman started chest compressions, Lindsey couldn't help thinking that she was wasting her time. Her body was mangled enough for Lindsey to know that Elaine was dead. What was left of her Londis uniform was in scorched shreds. Lindsey, Street, and Damo left Elaine with those who knew her, while they hurried back and started digging again, alongside Levi who worked like a machine. He ignored everything around him, focusing only on what was in front of him. By now there were twenty more people digging with them. All looked equally dazed.

'How many people work here?' Street called out, but no one answered. At least not for a couple of minutes, before a teenage girl, on her hands and knees pulling at the rubble farthest away from the rest of them, finally spoke.

'My mother worked here. Right here. This is where the deli-counter should be.'

The girl wasn't frantic or crying. Her words were informative and matter of fact. It was shock, Lindsey knew. This would hit her before long and when it did, it would hit hard. She crawled along the pile to join the girl in looking for her mother, but her mind was on Reem. That skinny little boy with the huge brown eyes was buried somewhere under here and judging by the intensity of the blast, chances of finding anyone alive were slim. But she wasn't ready to admit that yet.

Sirens wailed in the distance and were getting closer, but they weren't coming fast enough. They needed specialist equipment. They needed to get through this rubble before anyone who might be alive under there suffocated or bled to death.

*

Hours crawled past as they dug and dug. Fire crews arrived and moved the larger chunks and as the sun started to set, they pulled the seventh body from the pile. So far, they'd all been women. Four of them worked in the shop, including the girl's mother whose arms had been blown off in the blast. The girl and now her father too, were only able to identify her by a butterfly tattoo on her ankle. Three other women were in there shopping or gossiping or whatever else the women of the village of Hospital did with their mornings.

The sounds of anguish echoed through the small town and it was torture to Lindsey's ears. But she couldn't blame them. Their lives had been shattered in an instant and it still didn't occur to her to think about the hows and the whys of what happened. She'd been living with violence every day, most of which was in her head but was no less real than this. Violence was so normal to her that she still hadn't considered the fact that the people of Hospital could have gone their whole lives never knowing what real violence was. Right up until the time of their arrival. But for now, the part of her mind that was still capable of anything was set on finding Reem and as the natural light faded and was replaced with floodlights, she could tell that hope was also fading fast around her.

Chapter 24

As the sun rose again over Hospital, the town was filled with people and machinery. They'd come from all over Counties Limerick and Cork to help and all were working on the pile, which was getting smaller finally. But it yielded no signs of hope. Lindsey was exhausted, as was everyone around her. People kept arriving with trays of food and flasks filled with hot soup and tea, but Lindsey, Street, Levi, and Damo had yet to take a break. Charlie and Amir dug too, both resting when they needed to, while Lena worked tirelessly throughout the night. She'd formed a bond with Reem over their time together and it was clear from her face that she wasn't ready to give up on finding the boy alive.

Lindsey's arms burned, as did her throat and lungs, while her damaged ribs tried to eat their way out of her body. So when Damo grabbed her by the arm and pulled her away from the pile, she had little strength left to fight him. He pulled her across the road to where Street and Levi were sitting on the kerbside. Lena, Charlie, and Amir all sat together nearby, eating whatever they'd been given. There was a tray on the ground beside Street too, with a small pile of sandwiches and some tea in plastic cups. She all but fell onto the kerb beside him with Damo dropping down next to her. They'd been digging for over eight hours straight. Street physically shoved a sandwich into her mouth as she stared across at the rescue efforts. Over the next thirty seconds, she devoured two ham sandwiches and washed them down with lukewarm tea that contained more sugar than caffeine. Even the thought of food was enough to make her gag, but she knew that her body desperately needed it.

Finally the gears in her brain began grinding again. 'How the fuck did this happen?'

'Seriously?' Damo replied, without taking his eyes off the pile.

She shook her head. She knew what he was thinking and the thought had just occurred to her as well.

Rather than shove it in her face, he explained the facts. 'Yousef's brother and possibly his friends were outside the shelter yesterday morning. Chances are, they were inside before they were outside.'

'Reem.' She covered her face with her hands. 'Why didn't I look under his coat?'

'Don't start that shit,' Street ordered. 'This is fucking Cork, not the Middle East. You see a kid in a big coat here, you think, He looks warm. You don't think suicide vest. Shut that train of thought down now, Lindsey.'

She rested her forehead on her knees. Warm? He was weighed down with enough explosives to take out an entire building and everyone in it. Why the hell didn't she look?

'However the fuck they managed to get in, they knew they couldn't get him out of the hostel unnoticed.' Damo was thinking out loud. 'That made him a loose end; Amir too. It was meant for both of them.'

'It was meant for all of us. If we hadn't pulled over...'

Street filled all three plastic cups again from a flask and then he physically lifted Lindsey's head out of her lap. He grabbed her hand and placed it around the cup. 'Drink it, and then let's get back to work.'

She took the cup without looking at him. She didn't want to see the pain on his face any more than she wanted him to see the guilt on hers. She'd wiled away the last few months playing make believe. The one important job that she'd been given was to protect that boy and she'd failed catastrophically. Reem was wrapped in explosives and was placed right in front of them… in front of her. And now this.

*

As the day rolled on, the pile of rubble was almost completely cleared and it became obvious that they were never going to find Reem; because there was nothing left of him to find. The crater that remained was filled with army bomb techs, scouring for evidence of the device that was used. Street, Lindsey, Levi, and Damo were interviewed by detective Eddie Power. Eddie used to be an MP with the twelfth battalion in Limerick and all three of them knew him well. To those who didn't know him, Eddie was quiet, to the point that in a group, you'd almost forget he was there. But that was because he spent more time listening and watching than he did talking, and that was what made him so good at his job. He noticed things that no one else noticed and had one of the sharpest minds she knew. But his grey man persona ensured that he would never be credited as such. He was also a really nice guy and a good friend to Street in particular. They'd joined up around the same time. Eddie was now a member of An Garda Siochána. One of the good ones, she had no doubt.

Lindsey told him everything about what she'd been doing. About Patrick, Hector and Ben. She told him about Lena, Amir, and Reem because she trusted Eddie. Damo explained about Yousef and his brother Aazar but Eddie seemed to know plenty about them already. Still, he asked anyway,

'So, this Aazar character; any ideas where we might find him?'

'Corner building, behind the bus station, second floor. He'll show his face there at some stage. That place is one of their biggest earners and it's managed by his brother, Yousef.' Damo answered, homework well and truly done as always.

Eddie nodded and closed his notebook without ever writing anything in it. He didn't need to.

'And Patrick Adebayo?' Street asked.

'We're closing in on him. But he has a lot of friends in high places.'

'And they say money can't buy friends,' Damo mumbled.

'Turns out, it can.'

'I wouldn't mind a chat with little Aazar when you catch up with him.'

Eddie smiled. 'Don't worry, Street; I'll pass on your regards.'

Lindsey just wanted them all dead and she wanted to be the one to do it. They'd destroyed countless lives and now they'd blown an innocent boy to pieces, taking the lives of seven women with him. Seven women who'd died in place of Lindsey, Street, Damo, Lena, Amir, Charlie, and Levi.

'OK, well I'll have to take this lot off your hands. Can't really let you just drive off either; you're all witnesses. Trouble is, they'll probably end up back where they started in the end. It'd be great if they were just outta the picture.' He sighed loudly. 'Anyway, wait here. I'm gonna be over there keeping an eye on shit. There's so much going on, it'll be hard to watch everything.' He turned and walked away.

Street nodded, got to his feet and hustled them all towards the truck.

'I'm gonna hang around here and then head back to Cork with Eddie,' Levi announced, getting to his feet.

Levi was a man of few words, but his focus was clearly gone from their current objective, which was to get these people to Limerick. Levi's objective now was to find Yousef and Aazar, and Lindsey couldn't blame him for that. If anything, she was glad that he'd be on it. From what she'd come to know about Levi, he was a man who got things done by whatever means necessary and that's exactly what these so-called men deserved.

'Hey Eddie?' Lindsey asked, as they all got to their feet.

Eddie turned to face her. 'You're killing me, Ryan. I'm not supposed to be seeing you lot fucking off, remember.' Then he grinned. 'I remember you used to pass yourself off as an air hostess or a waitress whenever someone was brave enough to chat you up on army nights out. I can't believe you actually were one this time.'

'A bit of a shitty one as it turns out.' Lindsey forced herself to smile at the man. 'Hey listen; let's not forget the part that Ben Halpin played in this. He's one of your lot based in Cobh and he's balls deep in this too.'

'Oh I know all about that fucker. Leave it with me. We'll catch up over the next day or so.' He nodded and walked away, back towards the crater.

Lindsey and the others slowly made their way towards the truck and away from what was now Ground Zero. None of them really wanted to leave. It felt like they were walking away from Reem; giving up on the child. But the fact of the matter was that Reem was dead. Vaporised more like. Still; it didn't make it any easier to get back in the truck and drive away from the town of Hospital, and as she pulled the tarp back over the truck bed, Lena finally broke down.

*

No one in the cab of the truck spoke a word the rest of the way to Limerick and as they drove through the city, it was like it had always been driving through Limerick. Once upon a time, it was referred to as stab city. But it was in fact a vibrant city where people were going about their day as if nothing out of the ordinary had happened in their county. They were shopping, laughing, doing what people do. There was a group of teenagers outside Supermac's which had always been a good spot for a fight in Limerick. But usually not until after two am, when the pubs and clubs closed and someone skipped the queue, or made off with someone else's curry chips order. Every city had a spot like that. This was Limerick's.

'It's completely normal here,' Lindsey mumbled.

'As normal as Limerick gets,' Damo replied.

'It probably hasn't hit the news yet. But just wait til the words suicide and vest hit the headlines. Then you'll see all the crazies coming of the woodwork.'

They continued through the city in silence until they came to Dooradoyle and took a right turn onto the Fr Russell Road. At the top of the road, they took a left into a large housing estate. The houses were like those in every other modern estate in Ireland; a mix of townhouses, three- and four-bed semis, with the odd detached house thrown in, which would have been sold at a premium during the property boom. None of the houses looked very well kept at this point, but nor did they look too shabby; just lived in.

They took several twists and turns within the estate until they came to the end of a cul-de-sac and a four-bed semi-detached house at the end of a long row.

'This is it,' said Damo, sounding suddenly quite depressed. 'Street, why don't you take the lead on this one for a change eh? Let me wait here.'

'Not on your life, man. This one is all you.'

They all looked at the house for a minute until Damo got out. He mumbled something to himself and went to knock on the door. A minute later it was answered by a woman who looked like a professional street fighter. Her bleached blonde hair was gelled into tight curls and her skin looked leathery and not very well cared for. But she had a smile for Damo and it looked like the two were friends at the very least, despite his reluctance to leave the truck.

'Do we know her?' Lindsey spoke quietly to Street, even though there was no way the woman could hear her.

Street nodded. 'She's one of us.' Meaning that she was ex-army. 'Don't stare at the eye. She'll take the head clean off your shoulders if you piss her off.'

'The eye?'

But Street was out of the truck before answering her.

'Alright Jess?' He smiled at the woman as he approached the front door.

Lindsey hung back, near the tailgate of the truck.

'I'm alright, mucker. I heard ye had a bit of a rough trip though? I'm always telling ye to stay away from fucking Cork people. Stone mad the lot of them.' She knocked on the side of her head.

Lindsey didn't like her already. She was looking directly at Lindsey when she made her jibe about Cork people and the woman's eyes were scanning her from head to toe. Lindsey stared back at her, stone-faced.

'I'm joking, girl!' The woman bellowed. 'Christ, did she leave her sense of humour down South, or what?' She looked to Damo now before running her hand down along his chest.

Damo the ladies' man; who knew?

'It's been a rough couple of days, Jess. Go easy, eh?' Damo replied.

Jess laughed, sounding like she had razor blades in her throat. 'Why don't you and I step inside and catch up for a bit, while these two boring fuckers unload whatever trouble you're hiding in that truck?'

Damo looked back at Lindsey and she could have sworn he gave a half roll of his eyes, before he patted Street on the chest and said, 'You heard the woman. See you in a bit.'

With that Damo and Jess disappeared inside the house. Street came back to the truck and started peeling back the tarp.

'What was that?' Lindsey finally asked.

'That's Jess.'

'And Damo?'

'Believe it or not, someone has to do it and it sure as shit ain't gonna be me. It gets lonely running a women's shelter apparently.'

'Damo taking one for the team again, eh?' She turned her attention back to the faces that were staring blankly up at them from the mattress. 'Everyone alright?'

Reem's absence left a hole among them that may never be filled. Even Frank barely looked up from where he was lying between Charlie and Lena.

Charlie and Amir were first out again, while Lena seemed to struggle more this time. The past few days and weeks had caught up with her and were taking their toll now.

Inside, the house was spacious enough for a semi-detached. The hall led to a good-sized kitchen/dining room straight ahead, while a door to the right brought them into a nicely decorated and spotlessly clean sitting room. Street encouraged them all to take a seat on the three-piece furniture suite. Double doors led from the sitting room to what was possibly meant to be a formal dining room, but was now a bedroom. As Lindsey looked inside, she was once again impressed by its simple design and cleanliness.

She could hear a bed creaking overhead and immediately stepped back out of the bedroom and closed the doors behind her. 'Can we trust her with this, Street?'

He nodded. 'She'll huff and she'll puff and she'll go out of her way to wind you up, but she's very, very good at what she does. This is what she does. She's been running the house for about six years and a lot of people have passed through it. She has contacts everywhere. Trust me, this lot will be out of the country in no time. She was an MP once upon a time and she's never lost track of anyone yet. Oh, and by the way… pound for pound she's number three in the Irish women's MMA rankings.'

'Thought as much,' Lindsey replied, begrudgingly admiring the woman a little more. 'I still don't like her though.'

Street shook his head and rolled his eyes with a slight grin.

*

By the time Damo and Jess arrived back downstairs, Street had made tea for everyone, lacing each cup with sugar to help with the numb shock that they were all feeling.

'I'm Jess.' She spoke without a hint of a smile at the row of pale faces sitting on her couch.

As Jess scanned the room, Lindsey finally saw what Street meant when he said, don't stare at the eye. Her left one was glass; she was sure of it. An MMA fighter with a glass eye.

'You're my responsibility from here on and there's a list of rules on the back of each bedroom door. I suggest the first thing you do, after you've all showered, is acquaint yourselves with those rules. I don't repeat myself and I don't give second chances. You don't wanna be here? Fine, you're out. You can fuck off to wherever you want to fuck off to, but piss about with me, my house or my rules and we won't be friends anymore. Is that clear?'

No one answered her.

'I don't think there's any need…' Lindsey started, but was stopped abruptly by the palm of Jess's hand, which came to rest three inches from Lindsey's face.

'I know exactly what there's a need for in my house and if you have a problem, little Miss-Fucking-Sunshine, then you can fuck off too and take them all with you.'

Lindsey raised her eyebrows and bit her tongue, but only because they needed Jess and her house. The alternative was to take them all back to Cork with them and that wasn't an option.

'Ease up, babe.' Damo smiled what he thought might be a charming smile and who knows, maybe for Jess it was.

Lindsey threw her hands in the air and walked out of the room. She needed to calm down a bit. She didn't know this woman; certainly not well enough to dislike her as much as she did. Street trusted her and that would have to be enough to keep Lindsey from throttling her. Or at least starting to throttle her, before Jess went all MMA and kicked her ass.

'Like I was saying,' Jess continued in the sitting room. 'This isn't a prison. Unlike your last host, I won't be hiding anyone under the floor boards.'

Lindsey rolled her eyes and sat down on the bottom step of the stairs.

'You can come and go as you please, but we have a curfew of nine pm. You're not back, you'd better be dead somewhere. You'll all be given mobile phones. My number will be programmed in and they each have GPS tracking. You need to check in with me every two hours while you're not here and I must know where you are at all times for as long as you're living with me. Does anyone have a problem with any of that?'

She hated to admit it, but Lindsey liked Jess's rules. She liked the idea that she would be keeping tabs on each of them. That they could go about a relatively normal life, but stay protected until such time as they were actually safe.

'You will have no problems with us,' Lena finally spoke and Lindsey re-entered the room.

'Hello princess,' Jess beamed at her.

The list of insults that she could hurl back at the woman were piling up on the tip of her tongue. But Lindsey chose to smile at her instead, which she suspected would annoy her more. She was right.

'Do I have to stay here?' Charlie asked, looking from Lindsey to Jess and back again, seeming almost afraid of the situation between the two women.

'Yeah, Charlie, you do.' Lindsey replied, without taking her eyes away from Jess. The pair were now embroiled in a bit of a stare down.

'For how long?'

'Shouldn't be too long,' Street piped up, sounding forcibly chipper. 'Just til we can get Ben and whatever buddies he might have squared away. Then you can come back and help me get that gym sorted out, yeah? Couple of weeks, max.'

'On that note...' Damo added, also forcing some cheer into his voice, 'we should probably hit the road, eh?'

'Probably.' Street headed eagerly for the door, catching Lindsey by the arm as he passed.

Jess sneered, but was first to look away. Now Lindsey was happy to leave. More than happy in fact, but before she did, she asked if anyone had a pen.

Damo obliged by picking one up off the mantelpiece.

'Lindsey took it and wrote three mobile phone numbers on Lena's hand. One was hers, which she vowed to activate again as soon as she could. The other two belonged to Street and Damo. 'Put these in your phones too. You need anything, you call.'

'Trust is great, isn't it?' Jess's sarcasm sounded like it came naturally.

Lena stood up and pulled Lindsey into a tight hug. 'I don't know how I'll ever repay you for what you've done.'

'Get your degree,' Lindsey whispered in her ear, hugged her a little tighter and then pulled back.

Amir stood up and offered her his hand, which she shook firmly. He then shook hands with Street and Damo too. No one mentioned Reem. Not even Jess, who was expecting another person, and Lindsey was grateful for that much at least. His face was now added to the other faces that haunted her dreams and would remain there for the rest of her life. The last thing she needed was to be around people who insisted on talking about him. Though given the fact that the child came here as a nameless refugee and lost whatever family he once had, she was pretty sure that after today, no one would mention the name Reem ever again.

Chapter 24

As they left the house on the Fr Russell Road and headed back the way they came, Lindsey couldn't help thinking about the past few weeks. From that first night when Lena fell into her yard, to Grace McParland forcing Lindsey's attention onto a nameless little boy, who would lead to another boy, hidden in a trunk. She knew even back then that she'd probably get someone killed and she'd been right.

Street was driving now and Lindsey sat between him and Damo, while Frank stuck his head out the passenger side window and went to his happy place. Otherwise the mood in the truck was subdued; all three lost in their own thoughts until Damo finally broke the silence.

'I can feel my balls starting to itch already.' He pulled awkwardly at the crotch of his pants. 'Another week of bleach baths for me now. Why don't you ever take her on?' He looked across Lindsey at Street.

'I have too much respect for my main brain, man. Besides, she likes you.'

'Jess doesn't like anyone.' He readjusted himself again. 'She nearly put me through the fucking headboard. And I'm pretty sure the left cheek of my arse is no longer attached. It'll be found under her fingernails at her autopsy and I'll be blamed for doing her in.'

Lindsey finally smiled.

'Hey eh… let's not mention this to Eileen, yeah? I'm just starting to make a bit of progress there.'

'I like Eileen, Damo.'

'I do too. That's the problem. That back there,' he thumbed over his shoulder, 'that was penance and I don't plan on going back there for a very long time. And when I do, I'll be faking an STD. I'm gonna get a written doctor's note in case she doesn't believe me. Either way, that's not happening again. I feel like a blow-up doll whenever I go there. I'm fucking done.'

Street was laughing quietly as he drove, and Lindsey couldn't help it; she laughed too. The tension was easing in the truck, the way it always did when soldiers started to piss-take their troubles away. Until they reached Hospital that is. There were people everywhere. The area around Londis was cordoned off, the police were there in force and people from all over the vicinity were milling around, all looking equally helpless and lost. They stopped only for a while to talk to the techs, who hadn't found any more human remains. At least none large enough to collect, but they confirmed that Eddie was down in Cork. With that and not a moment too soon, they left Hospital in renewed silence.

*

It was after seven in the evening when they reached Street's place and she was stopped in her tracks when she saw Ben sitting awkwardly on the floor of the gym. His hands were cable tied to a pipe. His face was bruised and swollen, his lip split in two places and his eyes barely able to open and it made her feel slightly better to know that his current circumstances went some way towards what he deserved.

Levi was also there. 'Took a while to get a hold of the right cops. They'll be here to pick him up shortly.'

'Hello, Ben.' Lindsey did her best to keep all emotion out of her voice and she managed it well. What she wanted to do was choke the life from his body, but instead she stood over him.

He lifted his head to look at her, but didn't make a move to get up.

'Feeling at home?' she asked.

No answer.

'Did they tell you what you did?'

Nothing.

'You killed seven women and a child yesterday. Does that make you feel like a man?' her tone was still level. She would never give this man the opportunity to see her upset. She stepped closer. 'You're the biggest coward I ever met. Shielding yourself behind children…'

'I shielded myself behind no one.' Finally he looked up, indignant. 'You don't know the first thing about what I did; when I wasn't giving you exactly what you wanted, you sad, lonely bitch. So desperate for some male attention that you'd come to my door, begging for it.' A trickle of blood dripped from his bottom lip as he sneered. 'You'll pretend you didn't, but we both know you wanted another go on the mountain too, you fucking freak.'

Lindsey laughed, just to piss him off. 'You couldn't manage it though, could you? That's alright; you were shite the first time too.' She angled her head so that he was looking at her, whether he wanted to or not. 'That's all you're good for. You're a brainless, gutless piece of meat to me. That's all you've ever been.' She stood up again. 'Anyway, enjoy life on the other side. I hear they like cops and fellas who sell kids in the joint. You'll be a very popular boy.'

She tuned out his protests as she turned away from him with her stomach in her throat. As she headed for the stairs, Levi placed his hand on her shoulder and she turned to look at him.

'You know, I heard so much about Lindsey Ryan before I ever laid eyes on you?' He said with a smile.

She shook her head. 'Believe half of what you hear.'

'Yip; that's my motto too. But as it turns out, you're not bad, Ryan. Not bad at all.'

'Take good care of him for me, yeah?' She thumbed in Ben's direction.

'Will do.' He gave a lazy salute as she went upstairs.

*

'Well, that was fun,' Street groaned, dropping down on his couch and opening one of the three beers he'd placed on the coffee table.

'If I never see anyone's face ever again, it'll be fine with me. Where's Damo?' She asked, when she noticed that he hadn't come up the stairs behind her.

'He gone to wash his balls in carbolic soap and then he's heading for Cobh.'

'Eileen?'

'I've never seen him like this over a woman.'

Lindsey smiled, feeling herself relax slightly as she swallowed a mouthful of ice-cold beer. She didn't worry about Eileen; she could handle herself and Damo was a good guy, all things considered. Plus, he'd have Danny Chambers to contend with. If nothing else, that should be enough to keep him honest.

'You called for Lenny.'

'Can we not?'

'OK. So what now? You heading back to the caf?'

Lindsey shrugged. 'Eventually, maybe.'

'Eventually… right. And until then, you'll be staying here, helping me out with this place?'

She smiled and shook her head.

'Come on, Linds. Stay this time?'

'Is there more where these came from?' She held up her half empty bottle.

Street shook his head and got to his feet, returning seconds later with two six packs. He placed them on the small coffee table in front of them and stared at them in silence for a few minutes. Then he changed the subject, knowing that was why she asked for more beer in the first place, and as night fell over Cork City, two old friends talked, laughed and drank into the early hours, like they had on so many other nights. They rehashed old stories, adding arms and legs in all the right places. They brought tears of laughter to each other's eyes like no one else could and when Street woke the next morning, fully dressed on his bed where he'd fallen asleep beside her; Lindsey was gone.

*

The following night Lindsey sat under the shelter that she'd expertly made, back in the woods at the King's Yard. She was tucking into a mess tin of hot curry with Frank beside her, licking the last of the beef in gravy out of his bowl. They'd climbed to the Galtee cross that day, at the peak of Galtymore, and despite the tiredness and pain racking her entire body, Lindsey felt alive. She felt happy, as she only did in the most remote parts of the country with the only company she ever needed. She planned to spend another few days around the Galtees, but that was as far as her plan went. She had enough equipment to last them a few weeks at least, but if she could avoid the civilised world until it was civilised once more, then that would be fine too.

Deep down though, she knew she wouldn't stay away too long this time. She'd handed her business over to Eileen. Not that she cared much about the business, but she did care about the girl, and Patrick was not yet out of the picture. He might never be. It seemed the man was coated in Teflon. But he was being watched and not just by the cops this time. Still, Eileen didn't deserve to be left alone to deal with him.

For now though, she wasn't alone. Until such time as she gave Damo his marching orders, he'd be there. He'd be there after his marching orders too, just not as obviously. That was the thing with Damo; there really was no getting rid of him. She smiled, thinking about her old friend. They'd been through so much together; her, Damo, and Street, and the vast majority of it was good. But still, the bad always overshadowed everything else. That was why Lindsey could never agree to Street's requests for her to stick around.

Who knows; maybe someday Lindsey Ryan might be capable of forming some normal relationships with normal people. Maybe then she could bear to be around the people she loved more. But for now she was happy as she was; with Frank, on a mountain, and as she slipped into her bivy bag and close her eyes, a contented smiled played on her lips. The world around her was far from perfect and she was pretty sure that trouble was waiting for her when she chose to return to it. But who knows; maybe this place on this night was as close to perfect as a woman like her could ever hope to get. For now at least, that would be enough.

The End

About the Author

Michelle was one of those sporty types growing up, all bony elbows and knees, and as she lived on an island, it stood to reason she'd spend her first couple of decades taking in the salty, seaweedy air at the local rowing club. (Not the serene looking, posh rowing, but the other kind, undertaken by hardy fishermen.)

Here she learned just about everything she ever needed to know about anything. They brought home the County's, All-Ireland's were won, but the banter on the bus was always the real prize. From there it made sense she'd leave town and join another club/asylum and found herself wearing a blue helmet somewhere in South Lebanon.

She'd become attached to the UN, but more importantly, to B-Company, the boldest, brightest, bravest, the Irish army had to offer. She called them lots of other names too, but only to their faces. As tracer rounds lit up the sky above her and artillery rained down, she learned the words of every patriotic Irish song ever written and how to smile, laugh, and joke about things that would otherwise have you curled in a ball, rocking back and forth in the corner of the room.

Once her eyes had been opened and she returned to Irish soil, Michelle was promoted and following a spell back at college, is now a part of a company providing physiotherapy and staff training in nursing homes and hospitals all over Munster. A slower pace, but still an unruly bunch when they want to be. She's back living on the island of Cobh with her husband Dominic and their daughter Emily and the hundreds of colourful characters waiting to make their way onto a piece of paper.

The Invisible is Michelle's fourth book, and a sequel to *While Nobody is Watching*, drawing on her military experiences and the relationships that form within its ranks.

CPSIA information can be obtained
at www.ICGtesting.com
Printed in the USA
JSHW031221310722
28651JS00001B/1

9 781951 709822